THE
DEMON TRAPPER'S
DAUGHTER

THE
DEMON TRAPPER'S
DAUGHTER

A Demon Trapper Novel

JANA OLIVER

St. Martin's Griffin
New York

This is a work of fiction. All of the characters, organizations, and events portrayed in this novel are either products of the author's imagination or are used fictitiously.

To

Gwen Gades,

who opened the door

Hell is empty and all the devils are here.

—WILLIAM SHAKESPEARE

Acknowledgments

All the hard work comes down to this moment. Trust me, this is the fun part!

First a big hug and a heartfelt thank-you to my dear friend P. C. Cast, who kept murmuring "young adult" in my ear when I was first thinking about this book. Her daughter, Kristin, offered sage advice and made my teens sound their age, rather than like, well, old. All of this effort would have been for naught if my savvy literary agent, Meredith Bernstein, hadn't believed in my stories and found them a home. Jennifer Weis, my editor, and her assistant, Anne Bensson, along with editor Hilary Teeman and production editor Lauren Hougen, deftly herded this author through her New York debut experience and made this the best story possible.

Thanks also go to Ilona Andrews, who shared writing tips, and Gordon Andrews, who helped me establish Denver Beck's military background. William McLeod made Master Angus Stewart sound like a Scotsman and Oakland Cemetery provided the perfect backdrop for my series. A round of applause (and a stiff drink) is needed for my long-suffering beta readers and critique partners Nanette Littlestone, Aarti Nayar, Dwain Herndon, and Jeri Smith-Ready, along with Jean Marie Ward and Michelle Roper, who supplied me with manuscript advice and all those "no, your book doesn't suck" pep talks. And finally a moment of sincere gratitude that the great city of Atlanta hasn't suggested I move to another state. At least not yet.

Since the beginning I've had one man in my corner and that's my husband, Harold. I wouldn't be here without him. Dreams are always richer when they're shared.

ONE

2018
Atlanta, Georgia

Riley Blackthorne rolled her eyes.

"Libraries and demons," she muttered. "What *is* the attraction?"

At the sound of her voice the fiend hissed from its perch on top of the book stack. Then it flipped Riley off.

The librarian chuckled at its antics. "It's been doing that ever since we found it."

They were on the second floor of the university law library, surrounded by weighty books and industrious students. Well, they'd been industrious until Riley showed up, and now most of them were watching her every move. *Trapping with an audience* is what her dad called it. It made her painfully aware that her work clothes—denim jacket, jeans, and pale blue T-shirt—looked totally Third World compared to the librarian's somber navy pantsuit.

The woman brandished a laminated sheet; librarians were into cataloging things, even Hellspawn. She scrutinized the demon and then consulted the sheet. "About three inches tall, burnt-mocha skin and peaked ears. Definitely a Biblio-Fiend. Sometimes I get them confused with the Klepto-Fiends. We've had both in here before."

Riley nodded her understanding. "Biblios are into books. Rather than stealing stuff they like to pee on things. That's the big difference."

As if on cue, the Offending Minion of Hell promptly sent an arc of phosphorescent green urine in their direction. Luckily, demons of this size had equally small equipment, which meant limited range, but they both took a cautious step backward.

The stench of old gym shoes bloomed around them.

"Supposed to do wonders for acne," Riley joked as she waved a hand to clear the smell.

The librarian grinned. "That's why your face is so clear."

Usually the clients bitched about how young Riley was and whether she was really qualified to do the job, even after she showed them her Apprentice Demon Trapper license. She'd hoped some of that would stop when she'd turned seventeen, but no such luck. At least the librarian was taking her seriously.

"How long has it been here?" Riley asked.

"Not long. I called right away, so it hasn't done any real damage," the librarian reported. "Your dad has removed them for us in the past. I'm glad to see you're following in his footsteps."

Yeah, right. As if anyone could fill Paul Blackthorne's shoes.

Riley shoved a stray lock of dark brown hair behind an ear. It swung free immediately. Undoing her hair clip, she rewound her long hair and secured it so the little demon wouldn't tie it in knots. Besides, she needed time to think.

It wasn't as if she was a complete noob. She'd trapped Biblio-Fiends before, just not in a *university* law library full of professors and students, including a couple of seriously cute guys. One of them looked up at her, and she regretted being dressed for the job rather than for the scrutiny. She nervously twisted the strap of her denim messenger bag. Her eyes flicked toward a closed door a short distance away. "Rare Book Room." A demon could do a lot of damage in there.

"You see our concern," the librarian whispered.

"Sure do." Biblio-Fiends hated books. They found immense joy rampaging through the stacks, peeing, ripping, and shredding. To be able to reduce a room full of priceless books and manuscripts to compost would be a demon's wildest dream. Probably even get the fiend a promotion, if Hell had such a thing.

Confidence is everything. At least that's what her dad always said. It worked a lot better when he was standing next to her.

"I can get it out of here, no problem," she said. Another torrent of swear words came her way. The demon's high-pitched voice mimicked a mouse being slowly squashed by an anvil. It always made her ears ache.

Ignoring the fiend, Riley cleared her suddenly dry throat and launched into a list of potential consequences of her actions. It was the standard demon trapper boilerplate. She began with the usual disclaimers required before extracting a Minion of Hell from a public location, including the clauses about unanticipated structural damage and the threat of demonic possession.

The librarian actually paid attention, unlike most clients.

"Does that demonic possession thing really happen?" she asked, her eyes widening.

"Oh, no, not with the little ones. Bigger demons, yeah." It was one of the reasons Riley liked trapping the small dudes. They could scratch and bite and pee on you, but they couldn't suck out your soul and use it as a hockey puck for eternity.

If all the demons were like these guys, no big deal. But they weren't. The Demon Trappers Guild graded Hellfiends according to cunning and lethality. This demon was a Grade One: nasty, but not truly dangerous. There were Grade Threes, carnivorous eating machines with wicked claws and teeth. And at the top end was a Grade Five—a Geo-Fiend, which could create freak windstorms in the middle of shopping malls and cause earthquakes with a flick of a wrist. And that didn't include the Archdemons, which made your worst nightmares look tame.

Riley turned her mind to the job at hand. The best way to render a Biblio-Fiend incapable of harm was to read to it. The older and more dense the prose, the better. Romance novels just stirred them up, so it was best to pick something really boring. She dug in her messenger bag and extracted her ultimate weapon: *Moby-Dick*. The book fell open to a green-stained page.

The librarian peered at the text. "Melville?"

"Yeah. Dad prefers Dickens or Chaucer. For me it's Herman Melville. He bored the . . . crap out of me in lit class. Put me to sleep every time." She pointed upward at the demon. "It'll do the same to this one."

"Grant thee boon, Blackthorne's daughter!" the demon wheedled as it cast its eyes around, looking for a place to hide.

Riley knew how this worked: If she accepted a favor she'd be obligated to set the demon free. Accepting favors from fiends was *so* against the rules. Like potato chips, you couldn't stop at just one, then you'd find yourself at Hell's front door trying to explain why your soul had a big brand on it that said "Property of Lucifer."

"No way," Riley muttered. After clearing her throat, she began reading. " 'Call me Ishmael.' " An audible groan came from the stack above her. " 'Some years ago—never mind how long precisely—having little or no money in my purse, and nothing particular to interest me on shore, I thought I would sail about a little and see the watery part of the world.' "

She continued the torture, trying hard not to snicker. There was another moan, then a cry of anguish. By now the demon would be pulling out its hair, if it had any. " 'It is a way I have of driving off the spleen, of regulating the circulation. Whenever I find myself growing grim about the mouth; whenever it is a damp, drizzly November in my soul . . .' "

There was a pronounced thump as the fiend keeled over in a dead faint on the metal shelf.

"Trapper scores!" Riley crowed. After a quick glance toward a cute guy at a nearby table, Riley dropped the book and pulled a cup out of her bag. It had the picture of a dancing bear on the side of it.

"Is that a sippy cup?" the librarian asked.

"Yup. They're great for this kind of thing. There're holes in the top so the demons can breathe and it's very hard for them to unscrew the lids." She grinned. "Most of all, they really hate them."

Riley popped up on her tiptoes and picked the demon up by a clawed foot, watching it carefully. Sometimes they just pretended to be asleep in order to escape.

This one was out cold.

"Well done. I'll go sign the requisition for you," the librarian said and headed toward her desk.

Riley allowed herself a self-satisfied grin. This had gone just fine. Her dad would be really proud of her. As she positioned the demon over the top of the cup, she heard a laugh, low and creepy. A second later a puff of air hit her face, making her blink. Papers ruffled on tables. Remembering her father's advice, Riley kept her attention on the demon. It would revive quickly, and when it did the Biblio would go into a frenzy. As she lowered it inside the container, the demon began to twitch.

"Oh, no, you don't," she said.

The breeze grew stronger. Papers no longer rustled but were caught up and spun around the room like rectangular white leaves.

"Hey, what's going on?" a student demanded.

There was a curious shifting sound. Riley gave a quick look upward and watched as books began to dislodge themselves from the shelves one by one. They hung in the air like helicopters, then veered off at sharp tangents. One whizzed right over the head of a student, and he banged his chin on the table to avoid being hit.

The breeze grew, swirling through the stacks like the night wind in a forest. There were shouts and the muffled sound of running feet on carpet as students scurried for the exits.

The Biblio stirred, spewing obscenities, flailing its arms in all directions. Just as Riley began to recite the one Melville passage she'd memorized, the fire alarm blared to life, drowning her out. A heavy book glanced off her shoulder, ramming her into the stack. Dazed, she shook her head to clear it. The cup and the cap were on the floor at her feet. The demon was gone.

"No! Don't do this!"

Panic stricken, she searched for it. In a maelstrom of books, papers, and flying notebooks, she finally spied the fiend navigating its way toward a closed door, the one that led to the Rare Book Room. Ducking to avoid a flight of reference books swooping down on her like a flock of enraged seagulls, Riley grabbed the plastic cup and stashed it in her jacket pocket.

She had to get that fiend into the container.

To her horror, the Rare Book Room door swung open and a confused student peered outward into the melee. As if realizing nothing stood in its way, the demon took on additional speed. It leapt onto a chair recently vacated by a terrified occupant and then onto the top of the reference desk. Small feet pounding, it dove off the desk, executed a roll, and lined itself up for the final dash to the open door, a tiny football player headed for a touchdown.

Riley barreled through everyone in her way, her eyes riveted on the small figure scurrying across the floor. As she vaulted over the reference desk something slammed into her back, knocking her off balance. She went down in a sea of pencils, paper, and wire trays. There was a ripping sound: Her jeans had taken one for the team.

Scrambling on all fours, she lunged forward, stretching as far as her arms could possibly reach. The fingers of her right hand caught the fiend by the waist, and she dragged it toward her. It screamed and twisted and peed, but she didn't loosen her grip. Riley pulled the cup from her pocket and jammed the demon inside. Ramming her palm over the top of the cup, she lay on her back staring up at the ceiling. Around her lights flashed and the alarm brayed. Her breath came in gasps and her head ached. Both knees burned where she'd skinned them.

The alarm cut out abruptly and she sighed with relief. There was another chilling laugh. She hunted for the source but couldn't find it. A low groaning came from the massive bookshelves to her right. On instinct, Riley rolled in the opposite direction, and kept rolling until she rammed into a table leg. With a strained cry of metal the entire bookshelf fell in a perfect arc and hit the carpeted floor where she'd been seconds before, sending books, pages, and broken spines outward in a wave. Suddenly all the debris in the room began to settle, like someone had shut off a giant wind machine.

A sharp pain in her palm caused her to shoot bolt upright, connecting her head with the side of the table.

"Dammit!" she swore, grimacing. The demon had bitten her. She shook the cup, disorienting the thing, then gingerly got to her feet. The world spun as she leaned against the table, trying to get her bearings. Faces began to appear around her from under desks and behind stacks of books. A few of the girls were crying, and one of the hunky boys held his head and moaned. Every eye was on her.

Then she realized why they were staring: her hands were spotted with green pee, and her favorite T-shirt was splashed as well. There was blood on her blue jeans and she'd lost one of her tennis shoes. Her hair hung in a knotted mass over one shoulder.

Heat bloomed in Riley's cheeks. *Trapper fails.*

When the demon tried to bite her again, she angrily shook the cup, taking her frustration out on the fiend.

It just laughed at her.

The librarian cleared her throat. "You dropped this," she said, offering the lid. The woman's hair looked like it had been styled by a wind tunnel, and she had a yellow sticky note plastered to her cheek that said "Dentist, 10:00 AM Monday."

Riley took the lid in a shaking hand and sealed the demon inside the cup.

It shouted obscenities and used both hands to flip her off.

Same to you, jerk.

The librarian surveyed the chaos and sighed. "And to think we used to worry about silverfish."

⁘

Riley grimly watched the paramedics haul two students out on stretchers: One had a neck brace and the other babbled incoherently about the end of the world. Cell phones periodically erupted in a confused chorus of ringtones as parents got wind of the disaster. Some kids were jazzed, telling Mom or Dad just how cool it had been and that they were posting videos on the Internet. Others were frightened out of their minds.

Like me.

It wasn't fair. She'd done everything right. Well, not everything, but Biblios weren't supposed to be psychokinetic. No Grade One demon would have the power to cause a windstorm, but somehow it had. There could have been another demon in the library, but they never work as a team.

So who laughed at me? Her eyes slowly tracked over the remaining students. No clue. One of the cute guys was stuffing books in his backpack. When she caught his eye, he just shook his head in disapproval as if she were a naughty five-year-old.

Rich creep. He had to be if he was still in college.

Digging in her messenger bag, she pulled out a warm soda and took several long gulps. It didn't cut the taste of old paper in the back of her throat. As she jammed the bottle into her bag the demon bite flared in pain. It was starting to swell and made her arm throb all the way to the elbow. She knew she should treat it with Holy Water, but the cops had told her not to move and she didn't think the library would appreciate her getting their carpet wet.

At least the cops weren't asking her questions anymore. One of them had tried to bully her into making a statement, but that had only made her mad. To shut him up she'd called her father. She'd told him that something had gone wrong and handed the phone to the cop.

"Mr. Blackthorne? We got a situation here," he huffed.

Riley shut her eyes. She tried not to listen to the conversation, but that proved impossible. When the cop started with the attitude, her father responded with his you-don't-want-to-go-there voice. He'd perfected it as a high school teacher when facing down mouthy teens.

Apparently campus cops were also susceptible to *the voice*: The officer murmured an apology and handed her the phone.

"Dad? I'm so sorry. . . ." Tears began to build. No way she'd cry in front of the cop, so Riley turned her back to him. "I don't know what happened."

There was total silence on the other end of the phone. *Why isn't he saying anything? God, he must be furious. I'm so dead.*

"Riley . . ." Her father took in a long breath. "You sure you're not hurt?"

"Yeah." No point in telling him about the bite; he'd see that soon enough.

"As long as you're okay, that's all that matters."

Somehow Riley didn't think the university would be so forgiving.

"I can't get free here so I'll send someone for you. I don't want you taking the bus, not after this."

"Okay."

More silence as the moments ticked by. She felt her heart tighten.

"Riley, no matter what happens, I love you. Remember that."

Blinking her eyes to keep the tears in check, Riley stowed the phone in her messenger bag. She knew what her father was thinking: Her apprentice license was history.

But I didn't do anything wrong.

The librarian knelt next to her chair. Her hair was brushed back in place and her clothes tidied. Riley envied her. The world could end and she'd always look neat. Maybe it was a librarian thing, something they taught them in school.

"Sign this, will you?" the woman said.

Riley expected a lengthy list of damages and how she'd be responsible for paying for them. Instead, it was the requisition for payment of demon removal. The one a trapper signed when the job was done.

"But—" Riley began.

"You caught him," the librarian said, pointing toward the cup resting on the table. "Besides, I looked at the demon chart. This wasn't just one of the little guys, was it?"

Riley shook her head and signed the form, though her fingers were numb.

"Good." The librarian pushed back a strand of Riley's tangled hair and gave her a tentative smile. "Don't worry; it'll be okay." Then she was gone.

Riley's mom had said that right before she died. So had her dad after their condo burned to the ground. Adults always acted like they could fix everything.

But they can't. And they know it.

TWO

Forced to wait outside the library, Denver Beck gave a lengthy sigh as he ran a hand through his short blond hair. His mentor's kid had just topped the list for Biggest Apprentice Screwup. That upset him not only for the ten kinds of grief she'd get from the Trappers Guild but the fact that that had always been *his* honor. Who'd have thought she could outdo his nightmare capture of a Pyro-Fiend in a rush hour MARTA station? A disaster that had required not only the fire department but a hazmat team.

"But somehow ya did it, girl," Beck mumbled in his smooth Georgia drawl. He shook his head in dismay. "Damn, there's gonna be hell to pay for this."

He rolled his shoulders in a futile effort to relax. He'd been wired ever since Paul phoned him to say that Riley was in trouble. Beck was on the way to the library even before the conversation ended. He owed Paul Blackthorne nothing less.

Barred from entering the library by the cops, he'd cooled his heels and talked to some of the students who'd been inside during the trapping. It'd been easy to get information—he was about the same age as most of them. A few reported they'd seen Riley capture a small demon, but none of them had been clear as to what had happened next.

"Somethin's not right," Beck muttered to himself. A Biblio-Fiend could make a damned mess, but that usually didn't involve emergency personnel.

A pair of college girls walked by, eyeing him. Apparently they liked what they saw. He ran a hand over the stubble on his chin and smiled back, though now was not the time to make plans along that line. At least not until he knew Riley was okay.

"Lookin' fine," he called out, which earned him smiles. One of them even winked at him.

Oh, yeah, mighty fine.

A campus cop came within range, the one who'd told him he wasn't to move. They'd traded words, but Beck had decided not to push the issue. He couldn't collect Paul's daughter if he was handcuffed in the back of a patrol car.

"Can I go in now?" Beck called out.

"Not yet," the cop replied gruffly.

"What about the demon trapper? She okay?"

"Yeah. She'll be out pretty soon. I can't imagine why you guys would send a girl after those things."

The cop wasn't the only one thinking along those lines.

"It's not legal if she's bein' questioned without a senior trapper there," Beck warned.

"Yeah, yeah. Your rules, not ours," the man replied. "Nothing we care about."

"Not until ya get a demon up yer ass, then yer all over us."

The cop snorted, hands on his hips. "I just don't understand why you don't cap their asses, like those demon hunters do. You guys just look like a bunch of sissies with all your little spheres and plastic cups."

Beck bridled at the insult. How many times had he tried to explain the difference between a trapper and a hunter? Trapping a demon took skill. The Vatican's boys didn't bother; they went for firepower. To the hunters, the only good demon was a dead demon. No talent needed. There were other differences, but pretty much that was the dividing line. The average Joe just didn't get it.

Beck summed it up. "We got skills. They got weapons. We need talent. They don't."

"I don't know. They look pretty damned good on that television show."

Beck knew which one the cop was talking about. It was called *Demonland* and was supposedly all about the hunters.

"The show's got it all wrong. Hunters don't have any girls on their team. They live like monks and have about as much sense of humor as a junkyard dog."

"Jealous?" the cop chided.

Was he? "No way. When I get done with my day's work, I can go have a beer and pick up a babe. Those guys can't."

"You kidding me?"

Beck shook his head. "Nothin' like that TV show."

"Damn," the cop muttered. "Here I thought it was all chicks and flashy cars."

"Nope. Now ya know why I'm a trapper."

Beck's jacket pocket erupted into song: "Georgia on My Mind" floated across the parking lot. That earned him a few stares.

"Paul," Beck said, not bothering to look at the display. It had to be the girl's dad.

"What happened?" the man asked, his voice on edge.

Beck gave him a rundown of the situation.

"Let me know the moment's she out," Paul insisted.

"Will do. Did ya trap the Pyro?"

"Yeah. I wish I could get away, but I have to finish up here."

"No sweat. I'll keep an eye on things for ya."

"Thanks, Den."

Beck flipped the phone shut and jammed it in his jacket pocket. He'd heard the worry in his friend's voice. Paul was fanatic about keeping his apprentices safe, and even more so when it came to his daughter. It's why he'd slowed her training to a snail's pace, hoping she'd change her mind and pick a safer profession. Like walking the high wire for a living.

Not gonna work. He'd told Paul that countless times, but he wouldn't listen. Riley would be a trapper whether her father approved or not. She had that same stubborn streak as her mother.

Beck's attention moved to the news crew positioned near the building's entrance. He knew the lead reporter, George something or other. He'd covered Beck's catastrophe. The media loved anything to do with demon trapping as long as it went wrong. A quiet catch in an alley would never land on tape. A Hellfiend going berserk in a train station or a law library and they were all over it.

A lone figure appeared out of the milling crowd. It took Beck a moment to recognize her. Riley clutched her messenger bag to her side with whitened knuckles like it held the Crown Jewels. Her chestnut brown hair was a mass of tangles, and she walked with a slight limp. Even covered by her jean jacket he could see she'd filled out in places that would make boys dream of her at night. She seemed taller now, maybe five inches or so shorter than his six feet. Not so much a kid anymore. More like a young woman.

Damn girl, yer gonna break hearts.

When the newshound headed for her Beck went on alert, wondering if he would need to run interference. Riley shook her head at the reporter, pushed the microphone out of her face, and kept walking.

Smart girl.

He could tell the moment she spied him: Her expression went stony. No surprise there. When she was fifteen she'd gotten a huge crush on him even though he was five years older than her. He'd just begun his apprenticeship with her dad, so he'd done the smart thing: He'd avoided the kid, hoping she'd latch on to someone else. She had, but that story didn't have a happy ending. Riley got over her puppy love but not the hurt feelings. It didn't help that he spent more time with her father than she did.

He flipped open his phone and called Paul. "She's okay."

"Thank God. They've called an emergency Guild meeting. Warn her what she's in for."

"Will do." Beck stashed the phone in his jacket pocket.

Riley halted a few feet away, her eyes narrowing when she saw him. There was a rip in the leg of her jeans, a bright red mark on a cheek, and streaks of green on her face, clothes, and hands where the demon had marked her. One earring was missing.

Beck could play this two ways—sympathy or sarcasm. She wouldn't believe the first, not from him, so that left the other.

He cracked a mock grin. "I'm in awe, kid. If ya can do that kind of damage goin' after a One, I can't wait to see what ya got in mind for a Five."

Her deep brown eyes flared. "I'm not a kid."

"Ya are by my calendar," he said, gesturing toward his old Ford pickup. "Get in."

"I don't hang with geezers," she snapped back.

It took Beck a second to decipher the insult. "I'm not old."

"Then stop acting like it."

Seeing she wasn't going to give an inch, he explained, "There's an emergency Guild meetin'."

"So why aren't you there?"

"We both will be, just as soon as ya get in the damn truck."

Realization dawned in her eyes. "The meeting's about me?"

"Duh? Who else?"

"Oh . . ."

When she reached for the door handle, she hesitated. Beck realized the problem by the way she held her hand. "Demon bite ya?" A reluctant nod. "Did ya treat it?"

"No. And don't bitch at me. I don't need it right now."

Grumbling to himself, Beck dug in his trapping bag on the front seat. Pulling out a pint bottle of Holy Water and a bandage, he headed around the truck.

Riley leaned against the door, weary, eyes not really focusing on much. She was shivering now, more from the experience than the cold.

"This is gonna hurt." He angled his head toward the news van. "It would be best if ya not make too much noise. We don't want them over here."

She nodded and closed her eyes, preparing herself. He gently turned her hand over, studying the wound. Deep, but it didn't need stitches. The demon's teeth didn't rip as much as slice. The Holy Water would do the trick, and it would heal just fine.

Riley winced and clenched her jaw as the sanctified liquid touched the wound. It bubbled and vaporized like some supernatural hydrogen peroxide, removing the demonic taint. When the liquid had entirely evaporated, he shot a quick look at her face. Her eyes were open now, watering, but she'd not uttered a peep.

Tough, just like her daddy.

A few quick wraps of a bandage, a little tape and it was done.

"That'll do," he said. "In ya go."

He thought he heard a reluctant "Thanks" as she climbed inside the truck, still clutching the messenger bag. Beck hopped in, elbowed the door lock, and then started the engine. He pushed the heater control to its highest mark. He'd broil, but the girl needed warmth.

"Do you really use that thing?" she asked, pointing a green-tipped finger at the steel pipe that poked out of the top of the duffel bag on the seat between them.

"Sure do. Handy for Threes when they get rowdy. Really good if they sink a claw in ya."

"How?" she asked, frowning.

"Gives ya leverage to push the fiend away. Of course, that rips the claw out, but that's for the best. Worst case, the claw breaks off inside ya and yer body starts to rot." He paused for effect. "It's this really gross brown stuff."

He'd been graphic on purpose, testing her. If she was squeamish she might as well give it up now. He waited for her reaction, but there was none.

"So what happened back there?" he asked.

Riley turned toward the window, cradling her injured hand.

"Okay, don't tell me. I just thought we could talk it out, figure out where it went wrong. I've had my ass chewed enough by the Guild, so I thought I could give ya some pointers."

Her shoulders convulsed, and for a moment he thought she would cry.

"I did everything like I was supposed to," she whispered hoarsely.

"So tell me what happened."

He listened intently as she told him how she'd trapped the Biblio-Fiend. The girl really had done almost everything right.

"Yer sayin' the books were flyin' all over the place?" he quizzed.

"Yeah, and the bookshelf tore itself out of the wall. I thought it was going to crush me."

Beck's gut knotted. None of this was right. To calm his worries, he tried to remember how Paul had handled him after the MARTA incident when he was sure his career was over. "What would ya do different next time?"

Riley's misty eyes swung toward him. "Next time? Get real. They're going to throw me out of the Guild and laugh about this for years. Dad is so disappointed. I totally blew it. We won't be able to pay the—" She looked away, but not before he caught sight of a tear rolling down an abraded cheek.

Medical bills. The ones left behind after Riley's mom died. From what Paul had told him they were barely getting by. It was why they lived in a dinky-ass apartment that used to be a hotel room and why Riley pushed herself so hard to learn the business. Why Paul had to take any trapping job he could find to make money, though it cost him time with his only child.

Troubled silence fell between them as Beck concentrated on the traffic and what the evening might bring. The trappers weren't easy about change, and having a girl as one of their own made a lot of them just downright pissy. Riley needed to talk it out, get over the guilt before the meeting, or they'd eat her alive.

After honking at a rusty MINI Cooper that cut him off, he took the turn toward downtown. The intersection ahead of them was a tangle of bikes and motor scooters. One guy was pushing a shopping cart filled with old tires, another on Rollerblades, his hair streaming behind him, gliding through the traffic like a speed skater. Nowadays people used whatever it took to get around the city. With the ridiculous cost of gas even horses made sense now.

The biggest problem was the empty air above the intersection: the traffic lights were gone.

"They keep this up and there won't be one damned light left in the city," Beck complained.

Most of them had been stolen and sold for scrap by metal thieves. It took some guts to climb up on those things in the middle of the night and dismantle them. Every now and then a thief slipped and ended up a grease spot on the road, buried in a tangle of metal.

Like so many things, the city turned a blind eye to the thievery, saying they couldn't afford to replace every missing light. Too many other things to worry about in this bankrupt capital of five million souls.

Beck nearly clipped some idiot on a moped and then made it through the intersection; his hands clutched the wheel tighter than was needed.

Talk to me, kid. Ya can't do this alone.

Riley flipped down the visor and stared into the cracked mirror.

"Omigod," she said. He watched out of the corner of his eye as she gingerly touched the green areas where the demon pee had dyed her skin.

"It'll be gone in a couple days," Beck said, trying to sound helpful.

"It has to be gone by tomorrow night. I've got school."

"Just tell 'em yer a trapper. That should impress 'em."

"Wrong! The trick is to blend in, Beck, not glow like a radioactive frog."

He shrugged. He'd never blended in and didn't see why it mattered that much. But maybe to a girl it did.

Turning to the mirror, Riley began to dislodge the tangles. Tears formed as she pulled a comb through her long hair. It took time to get presentable. She put on some lip gloss but apparently decided it didn't work with the splotchy green and wiped it off with a tissue.

It was only then she looked over at him and took a deep breath.

"I should have . . . treated the doorway into the Rare Book Room with Holy Water. That way if the demon got loose, he wouldn't have been able to get in there."

"Dead right. Not protectin' that room was the only mistake I see. Bein' a good trapper is just a matter of learnin' from yer mistakes."

"But *you* never learn," she snapped.

"Maybe so, but I'm not the one who's gonna get reamed by the Guild tonight."

"Thanks, I'd *so* forgotten that," she said. "Why were the books flying all over the place?"

"I'd say the Biblio had backup."

She shook her head. "Dad says demons don't work together, that the higher-level fiends think the little ones are nuisances, like cockroaches."

"They do, but I'll bet there was another demon in that library somewheres. Did ya smell sulfur?" Riley shrugged. "See anyone watchin' ya?"

She gave a bark of bitter laughter. "All of them, Beck. Every single one of them. I looked like a total moron."

He'd been there often enough to know how that felt, but right now that wasn't the issue. Why would a senior demon play games with an apprentice trapper? What was the point? She wasn't a threat to Hell in any real sense.

At least not yet.

Riley shut down after that, staring out the passenger-side window and fidgeting with the strap on her bag. Beck had a lot of things he wanted to say—like how he was proud of her for holding up as well as she did. Paul always said the mark of a good trapper is how he handled the bad stuff, but telling Riley that wouldn't work. She'd only believe it if she heard it from her father, not someone she considered the enemy.

They passed a long line of ragged folks waiting their turn to get a meal at the soup kitchen on the grounds of the Jimmy Carter Library. The line's length hadn't shortened from last month, which meant the economy wasn't any better. Some blamed the demons and their devious master for the city's financial problems. Beck blamed the politicians for being too busy taking kickbacks and not paying attention to their job. In most ways, Atlanta was slowly going to Hell. Somehow he didn't figure Lucifer would object.

A few minutes later he parked in a junk-strewn lot across from the Tabernacle and turned off the engine. He was used to ass chewing, but the girl wasn't. If there were any way he could take her place tonight, he'd do it without thinking twice. But that wasn't the way things worked when you were a trapper.

"Leave the demon here," he advised. "Put him under the seat."

"Why? I don't want to lose him," she said, frowning.

"They'll have the meetin' warded with Holy Water. He'll tear himself apart if ya try to cross that line with him in yer bag."

"Oh." Before every Guild meeting an apprentice would create a large circle of Holy Water, the ward as it was called, which would serve as a sacred barrier against all things demonic. The trappers held their meeting inside that circle. Beck was right, the Biblio wouldn't cross the ward. She pulled out the cup, tightened the lid, and did as he asked.

"One piece of advice: Don't piss 'em off."

Riley glared at him. "You always do."

"The rules are different for me."

"Because I'm a girl, is that it?" When he didn't answer, she demanded, "Is. That. It?"

"Yeah," he admitted. "As long ya know that goin' in."

She hopped out of the car, hammered down the lock with her uninjured fist, then slammed the door hard enough to make his teeth rattle.

A green finger jabbed in his direction the moment he stepped out.

"I'm not backing down. I'm Paul Blackthorne's daughter. Even the demons know who I am. Someday I'm going to be as good as my dad, and the trappers will just have to deal. That includes you, buddy."

"The fiends know yer name?" Beck asked, taken aback.

"Hello! That's what I said." She squared her shoulders. "Now let's get this over with. I've got homework to do."

THREE

Riley paused on the sidewalk, shaking inside. Her outburst had cost her what little energy she had left. She needed food and a long nap, but first there was the Guild to deal with. She could already imagine their smirks, hear the good ol' boy laughter. Then there'd be the crude jokes. They were really good at those.

I don't deserve this. The other apprentices made mistakes but they'd never rated an emergency Guild meeting.

The sun was setting, and for a moment she could believe there was no disappointed father waiting for her inside that old building. Her nose caught the tantalizing scent of roasted meat. Smoke rose in thin, trailing columns from multiple wood fires across the street at Centennial Park. The grounds were dotted with multicolored tents, like some modern-day Renaissance Faire. A tangle of people wandered the grounds as vendors called to them from tables piled high with goods. She could hear a baritone voice announcing that he had fresh bread for sale.

They called it the Terminus Market, after the city's original name. At first it'd just been open on the weekends, but now it was a permanent thing. As the economy got worse the market blossomed, filling the missing holes as regular businesses went under. You could buy or barter almost anything, from live chickens to magical supplies like the spheres the trappers used. If the vendor didn't have what you wanted, by the next night he would, no questions asked.

"Sign of the times," Beck said under his breath. "Not that it's right."

Caught by the deep frown on his face, her gaze followed his. On the sidewalk was a dead guy, loaded down with packages from the market. He wore clean clothes and his hair was combed, but you could tell he was dead. The pasty gray complexion and the zoned-out expression gave it away every time. He stood a few steps behind his "owner," a thirty-something woman with strawberry blond hair and designer jeans with the words "Smart Bitch" in sequins on the butt. Everything about her shouted money, including the car. No solar panel on the top, so she wasn't concerned how much a gallon of gas might cost. No dents, no rust, just clean and new.

Probably has the dead guy wash it.

From what Riley had heard, a Deader wasn't like a zombie in the movies, just a sad reminder of a past life. For people with money they were the perfect servants. They never asked for vacation and they weren't entitled to wages. Once a necromancer pulled a corpse from the grave it was good for nearly a year, the downside of better embalming techniques. When it ceased being useful it was buried again, if the owner was compassionate. If not, the Deader would be found abandoned in a dumpster.

"They're just slaves," she said. "Once you're dead you should be left alone."

"Amen to that." Beck cleared his throat. "Well, ya won't have to worry. If a trapper gets chewed up by a demon, the necros don't want 'em."

Now that's great news.

Riley watched as the Deader piled the packages into the trunk of a car. When he was finished he climbed into the backseat. They were good for simple tasks, but driving wasn't one of them.

Riley turned back toward their destination. Built of red brick, the Tabernacle had clocked over a century of use. It'd been a Baptist church, then a concert hall. She'd come here for an Alter Bridge concert to celebrate her dad's thirty-fifth birthday when they'd lived in Buckhead and her mom was still alive. Back when her parents were teachers at a real school and everything was good.

Beck paused at the entrance, leaning against a rope that served as a handrail. The metal ones were long gone. Still holding his duffel bag in one hand, he turned toward her, his face unusually solemn.

"It's not just because yer a girl," he said in a lowered voice, his mind still on their earlier conversation. "A lot of these guys are gettin' older, and they're not happy competin' with younger trappers."

"Like you?"

He nodded. "Don't expect a good time, okay? But don't let 'em push ya around. It was a good trappin' gone wrong. That's happened to every one of us. Don't let them claim anythin' different."

Then he left her on the street, putting distance between them like he didn't want to be seen with her.

Creep.

Her dad was waiting inside that building. What would he say? Would he tell the Guild he'd made a mistake, that she wasn't trapper material? Or would he try to defend her?

If he does, they'll roast him.

That thought pushed her forward. Her father wasn't going to face this alone. This was *her* mistake, not his.

Riley limped up the steps and entered the building, closing the street door behind her. Nothing much had changed since the last Guild meeting: Cobwebs still hung from the ceiling, and the floors were laced with dust and discarded foam cups. A sneeze overtook her. Then another. Pulling a tissue out of a pocket, she blew her nose as she wandered into the huge auditorium. It was a vast space with uncomfortable wooden benches in three sections that rose to the rear of the building, most of it in the dark now. There used to be a pipe organ but it was long gone. Metal was too valuable.

On the floor in front of her was a wet line in the dust that encircled the area where the meeting was being held. Why the trappers bothered to have a Holy Water ward never made sense to Riley. No demon would wander into a roomful of trappers. It'd be a way-dumb move. Still, it was tradition, and it fell to an apprentice to ensure the ward was properly applied. One day it would be her turn.

This was only the second time she'd been in front of the Guild. The first hadn't been a blast, with lots of argument over whether to issue her an apprentice license. Most of the trappers hadn't cared either way, but a few clearly resented her. Not because of her dad, but because she wasn't male. They'd be her foes tonight.

And I gave them all the ammunition they need.

Only the ground-floor General Admission Section was illuminated. Above her, dust hovered in the bright streams of light pouring down from the floods. The lights doubled as a heat source, which left the rest of the building uncomfortably chilly.

The meeting had already started, and her dad was at one of the round banquet tables, arms crossed. It was his you're-standing-on-my-last-nerve pose. He was wearing his Georgia Tech jacket and sweatshirt and faded blue jeans. His brown hair really needed a trim. Just like an average dad—except he trapped demons for a living.

"How'd this simple job go so far off the rails, Blackthorne?" an older man asked. He was gray at the temples and had a deep crescent-shaped scar that ran down one side of his face. His nose had been broken and hadn't healed right. It made him look like a cross between a pirate and a convict.

Harper. The most senior of the three master trappers in the Atlanta Guild.

"That's what we're here to find out," her dad replied, his voice clipped. "Riley should be here soon; then we can hear the full story."

"Don't care if she's here or not. She's done as far as I'm concerned," Harper replied. The sneer on his face pulled the scar out of alignment.

"We've all made mistakes." Her dad pointed toward a beefy black man at a nearby table. "Morton destroyed a courtroom trying to trap a Four right after he became a journeyman. Things happen."

"What did I know?" Morton said, spreading his hands. One of the few African Americans in the Guild, he looked like he should be selling houses rather than trapping fiends. "The defense lawyer acted just like a demon. I'm still getting sued over that one."

There was muted laughter.

Her dad nodded. "My point is that Riley is smart and she listens to instructions. She'll learn from this, and the next trapping will be picture perfect."

"That's better than your last apprentice," someone joked. "He never did listen."

Beck stepped into the circle of light. "Evenin' all," he said.

"Speak of the devil," the same trapper called out. "What do you say about this, Mile High?"

From the way Beck tensed, Riley could tell he didn't like the nickname. He just shrugged and parked himself at her father's table, then pulled two beer bottles out of his duffel bag and set them in front of him. Twisting the top off one, he took a long swig and settled back like he was there to watch a stage show.

You selfish jerk. He wasn't going to stand up for her. How many times had her father saved his butt? *So much for gratitude.*

Gnawing on the inside of her bottom lip until she drew blood, Riley stepped into the light, blinking to clear her vision. When they spied her, some of the trappers snickered. She held her ground, hands knotted at her side.

"There's Little Miss Fuckup now," Harper said.

Riley's father glared. "Keep it clean, Harper."

"If she can't take it, she shouldn't be here."

"There's no need to be crude," another trapper insisted. It was Jackson, the Guild treasurer. He was a tall, thin man with a goatee and ponytail. He'd worked for the city before the first round of layoffs a few years back. In lieu of a response, Harper spat on the floor then dug out another wad of chew.

Though Riley really wanted to run into her father's arms, she took her time crossing to him. She refused to act like a scared little girl in front of these jerks, though deep inside she was freaking out.

Her dad stood and put his hands on her shoulders, looking deeply in her eyes. When he saw the damage to her face, he winced.

"You okay?" She nodded. He squeezed her shoulders for support. "Then tell them what happened."

He'd treated her like an adult, not a frightened kid. That simple gesture gave her the courage to face this.

She scanned the circle of men around her. There were about thirty of them. Most were middle-aged, like her dad. They'd become trappers when their other careers had ended, destroyed by an economy that had never found anything but the bottom. Bitterness hung on them like a heavy winter coat.

Riley cleared her throat, preparing herself. Harper snapped his fingers impatiently. "Come on, spill it. We don't have all damned night."

"Don't let him goad you," her father murmured.

Hoping her voice wouldn't quaver, she gave her report. Her words sounded so insignificant inside the cavernous building, a mouse squeaking to a pack of lions.

When she finished Harper huffed and crossed his arms over his chest, revealing a blood-red tattoo on his forearm. It was a skull with a writhing fiend in its mouth.

"Demons don't work together," he said. "Every apprentice knows that. 'Cept maybe you."

He made it sound like she was lying.

"How else would you explain all the damage?" Morton asked.

"Don't know, don't care," Harper said. "All that matters is that we're the laughingstock of the city, and we know who's to blame."

Murmuring broke out among the men.

"It's not as easy as that," her dad began. "If the demons are banding together, we need to know why they've changed tactics."

"You're just trying to save your brat's ass, Blackthorne. She would never have been given a license in the first place if she wasn't your daughter."

Beck stirred and set his beer bottle down on the table with a clunk. "Why not? She met all the requirements."

Harper swung his dark gaze toward him. "Why do you give a shit? Looking to get a piece of that, are you?"

Riley's dad shifted in his chair, his face growing red with anger. Beck, on the other hand, was icy calm. It wasn't what she'd expected of him.

He popped open the top of the second bottle, took a long swig, then smacked his lips. "Nah, she's too young. She can't buy me beer."

"Damned straight," someone called out. "Nothin' more than jailbait."

Her father's frown deepened.

"I say we eyeball the library's security tapes," Beck said in a thick drawl, heavier than usual. "That'll tell us if there was another demon there."

"Take too long to get them. We need to vote on this," Harper argued.

"We don't need the tapes, Master." That was Simon Adler, Harper's apprentice. He was tall and blue-eyed with bright blond hair that swirled in waves. When Riley was small, her mom bought an angel for the top of the Christmas tree; Simon's hair was the same color. A couple of years older than her, he wore jeans and a Blessid Union of Souls T-shirt. A wooden cross hung from a thick leather cord around his neck.

"There's already a video of it on the Internet," he said, gesturing toward a laptop on the table in front of him. She was surprised he'd bring it into this dustbowl.

Harper threw him a furious look. "Who the hell asked you?"

"Sorry," Simon replied, "but I thought we'd want to know the truth."

"You keep your goddamned mouth shut unless I say otherwise, got it?"

The apprentice winced at the blasphemy.

Beck cut in. "Come on now, Simon's doin' what any *good* trapper would do—keepin' tabs on the demons. That's what yer teachin' him, isn't it?"

Harper's face turned dark with anger, making the scar stand out.

"Let's see it," Jackson called out. "Maybe it'll make our report to the Church easier."

The Church. The trappers only captured the demons; the Church was responsible for dealing with them after that. It was a complex arrangement, but it had held together for centuries. The Guild always went out of its way not to piss off the Church.

Simon tapped away on the keyboard as men crowded around. There were too many trappers, so it looked like they'd have to take turns watching the screen. A running commentary began at the same time as the video.

"Damn, look at that flying tackle," Morton said. "That had to hurt."

It had.

"She got him!" one of them called out.

"Oh, my God, look at the—"

Bookshelves. A tremendous crash came from the computer speakers. Exhausted and shaking, Riley sank into the closest chair. Her dad pushed a bottle of water her way. She twisted off the plastic cap and sucked the cool liquid down, gulp after gulp. Her stomach rumbled, a reminder she'd not eaten since breakfast.

Her dad hadn't hurried over to watch the video. There was only one reason for that. *He thinks I screwed up.*

That hurt more than the burning demon bite.

Finally, Simon set the computer in front of her father. "Just press this key and it'll play," he said. He gave Riley a quick smile and retreated.

Trappers moved in behind her, talking among themselves. One of them was Beck. She gritted her teeth at what was to come.

"You ready?" her dad asked.

She nodded.

It was worse the second time around. Like watching one of the *Demonland* episodes on television, only this time she was the star and there was no stunt double. Whoever captured the video did a pretty good job, though the picture would swing wildly every now then.

This is all over the Internet. People in foreign countries would watch it and laugh at her. Mock her. There would be no hiding from this.

"Look at all that stuff blowing around," someone exclaimed.

Beck sucked in a sharp breath as the bookshelves committed suicide. The final portion of the video showed Riley limping out of the library, bloody and battered.

"My God," her father whispered, pulling her into an embrace so tight she couldn't breathe. He wasn't mad at her or disappointed. He only hugged that hard when he was scared. When they broke apart, she saw it on his face, though he tried to cover it. Then he smiled, soft crinkles appearing at the corners of his brown eyes. "You did very well, Riley. I'm so proud of you."

Her mouth fell open as the threat of tears returned.

"Ditto," Beck said as he returned to his beer.

When she looked up, all eyes were on her. A couple of trappers gave her a nod of respect. Jackson looked over at Harper, then back at her.

"That sure as hell wasn't just a Grade One," he said.

"I agree. That's a Geo-Fiend for sure," another said.

Harper straightened up. "Doesn't matter. We can't give this one a pass. Makes us look bad."

"Oh, go screw yourself, Harper," Jackson growled. "You've hated every apprentice we've had. Those you train you treat like dirt. I should know."

"If you weren't such a jerk-off, Jackson," the master began.

Her dad tugged on her sleeve. "Why don't you go outside? It's going to get nasty, and I'd rather not have you hear it."

"But what about my license?" she asked.

"That's why it's going to get nasty."

Oh.

Beck tossed his keys on the table in front of her. "Keep the demon company, will ya? He's probably missin' ya by now."

She glowered at him.

Her father intervened. "Wait in the truck and lock the doors. I'll be out soon. Go on. It'll be okay."

It'll be okay.

It sounded like a curse.

FOUR

The moment Riley reached the truck she kicked the closest tire, imagining it to be Beck's head. It was a stupid thing to do because now her foot ached like the rest of her. Her anger wouldn't make a bit of difference. If Harper bullied the others long enough they'd revoke her apprentice license. Once they voted her out, she was done. There was no going back.

Then what? She'd have to get a job waiting tables or something. *That's so not me.*

A chittering sound brought her eyes upward as a whirl of bats exploded from under one of the Tabernacle's eaves. She watched them skitter away into the dusk, envying their freedom. In the distance a thin chorus of howls echoed in the streets. Coyotes. They hunted every night, slinking around in packs looking for a stray meal to wander their way. The city slowly reverted to nature's laws.

She eyed Beck's ride. It was so him. Who else would drive around in a battered rust-red Ford F-250 with a Georgia state flag decal in the rear window? Next to that was the official Trappers Guild emblem and underneath, the unofficial slogan—"Kicking Hell's Ass One Demon at a Time." A mass of beer bottles in the truck bed rolled around like bowling pins every time Beck took a corner. He'd be adding more to the pile soon enough.

She unlocked the door and climbed in, eager to get out of the cold. The interior smelled like the owner's leather jacket. Digging under the seat, she retrieved her demon and stuck it in her bag. She ignored its offer of a favor to free it and then the upturned middle finger. Sometimes the sippy cup's transparent sides weren't a blessing.

How long will this take? "Just vote me off the island and move on," she groused. If it took too long she'd have to start the truck to get some heat, but that would be wasting gas.

To try to keep her mind off all the drama, Riley raided the glove compartment. It was a lot like snooping in someone's medicine cabinets: You learned a lot about a person that way. The first thing she found was the gun. That didn't surprise her. Trappers went into rough neighborhoods. She cautiously pushed it out of the way. Next up was a flashlight. She flicked it on and spied the condoms. There were three of them and they were marked "extra large."

Riley snorted. "In your dreams." Then she hit pay dirt—the horndog's Trappers Manual.

Apprentices received their manuals in sections as they progressed through their training to prevent them from going after bigger demons before they were ready. All she had was the section about Grade Ones, like the Biblio-Fiends. Denver Beck was a journeyman trapper, one step below a master. This manual had almost all of the good stuff, except the parts on the higher-ranking fiends and Archdemons.

Riley hesitated. They were going to kick her out, so why bother? *But if they don't . . .* She'd never get an opportunity like this again.

She did a mental coin flip and curiosity won. It always did with her.

Riley made sure the doors were locked, then she angled her body so the flashlight hit the pages and began to read, lured like the time she'd found her mom's stash of smutty romance novels.

"Grade Three demons are territorial and are best known for their ability to completely gut and eat a human in as little as fifteen minutes."

Maybe this isn't such a good idea.

She'd just started on the section on how to trap Threes when a knock came at the window. Riley jumped. After frantically jamming the book and the flashlight into the glove compartment, she looked up. It was Simon, Harper's apprentice. Embarrassed at being caught, she sheepishly climbed out of the truck.

"Sorry I scared you," he said, stepping back a few paces, seeming to understand she needed her space. Not all guys did that. "I thought I'd check and see how you're doing."

Here I am with a seriously hunky guy and I'm covered in demon pee. Why does the universe hate me?

She tried to run a hand through her hair, but the bandage pretty much ended that effort. Feeling she should say something, Riley stammered, "I was . . . was reading . . ."

A slow grin crawled onto Simon's face as he adjusted the computer bag on his shoulder. ". . . The manual. I saw that. But it wasn't yours. Too thick."

Busted. She slumped against the truck. "It's Beck's. You won't say anything, will you?"

Simon shook his head. "I pulled the same stunt with Harper's manual, except he was the one that caught me." His face darkened at the memory.

"Dad doesn't tell me anything. I hate it." A moment after she vented, she wondered if that was a good thing. Could she trust Simon?

"Harper's the same way, and then he yells at me when I don't know something he thinks I should." Simon frowned. "I'll make journeyman yet, just to prove him wrong."

"I won't. They're going to throw me out."

"You never know," he said. "Some of them were pretty impressed." He paused and then added, "I think you were awesome."

That caught her off guard. *He thinks I'm awesome?* "Ah . . . thanks!"

Simon smiled, and suddenly she didn't feel so cold anymore.

They heard voices: Beck and her dad were headed in their direction, talking animatedly. Neither of them looked happy. Beck was gesturing, and she thought she heard a curse word or two.

Simon began to edge away. "Better go. Nice to meet you, Riley," he said.

"You too, Simon." Right before he crossed the street, he looked back at her. She waved. That made his smile widen.

He's really cute.

Riley hopped into the truck to get the Biblio that had caused all the problems. The flashlight was still on inside the glove compartment, issuing a glow around the edges of the door. She hurriedly fixed that problem, then grabbed her messenger bag.

"I see Simon was keeping you company," her father said as he walked up. "I'm glad he checked on you."

That made her feel even better. If her dad liked the apprentice, then he was probably okay.

"So? What's the verdict?" she asked, clenching her hands into fists to prepare for the bad news. The one with the demon bite promptly throbbed in response. "They tossed me out, didn't they?"

"You're still an apprentice, for the time being," her dad announced. "The video convinced them there was another demon present, one that you weren't qualified to trap. The next time there's a problem, you're out."

They weren't telling her everything. "And?" she pressed.

Her dad and Beck traded looks.

"There're also sanctions against me," her dad replied. "If you lose your license I won't be able to take on another apprentice for another year."

"That was Harper's little roadside bomb," Beck grumbled. "Miserable bastard."

Riley was stunned. Her dad was a born teacher, whether it was history classes in high school or bringing a new trapper up through the ranks. Not only would he lose his one joy in life but the stipend they paid to train new members. That money bought their groceries. No apprentice, no food. It was that simple.

"Bottom line, you're still in the Guild. We'll worry about the rest later." Her dad put his arm around her. "Come on, let's get you home."

"Yeah, I hear she's got homework to do," Beck chided.

She threw him a glare but didn't bother to reply. He was the least of her hassles.

⬩

As they pulled out of the Grounds Zero drive-thru, Riley's hot chocolate steamed up the side window and made her feel good for the first time all day. She had to admit it wasn't only the hot beverage. She was with her dad, and that always made her feel better. The feeling wasn't going to last. Once they got home he'd take off with Beck for another night of trapping. They'd been trying to capture a Grade Three demon down in Five Points and it kept getting away. Now it was a matter of pride for both of them.

Riley knew it was selfish to be upset that he was gone all the time. She knew they needed the money, but sometimes she craved spending more time together, even if it was trapping demons. But that wasn't going to happen until she learned to trap a Three. Then she and her dad could work as a team and Beck would have to find someone else to trap with. She wondered if Backwoods Boy had figured that out yet.

Riley poked absentmindedly at the rip in her jeans. She wouldn't bother to mend it; ripped jeans were okay, but the green demon pee was another matter. It bleached out the denim. There was no way she could afford a new pair.

When she set her hot chocolate in the center console, she spied a computer disk next to a pile of crumpled gum wrappers. Probably some of her dad's Civil War research. When he had free time, which wasn't very often, he'd go to the library and use one of their computers. Faster than the one they had at home, that was for sure.

"So what is it this time?" she asked, pointing at the disk. "Antietam or Battle of Kennesaw?"

He seemed startled at the question and quickly tucked the disk into his pocket. "How's this for a deal? After I make the rent money I'll take a night off. We'll get some pizza, maybe watch a movie."

She nodded enthusiastically. "Sounds good! I'd love that." *Every night.* Then a thought came to her. "Just us. No Beck."

"You really don't like him, do you?"

"No, I don't. On the way to the meeting he said he wanted to help me, but he didn't do a thing. He's a creeper."

Her dad shook his head. "You're not seeing the bigger picture."

"Really? He sat there drinking his beer, acting like it was some picnic. You said his mom's a drunk, and the way he's going, he's going to end up the same. I don't know why you bother with him."

Her dad didn't answer, his brow furrowed in thought. Riley cursed to herself. Why did they always argue about *him*?

Feeling guilty, she blurted, "What do you think of Simon?"

Her father appeared pleased at the change of topic. "Quiet kid. A lot going on in that brain. He's a methodical trapper. He'll do well in the business if Harper ever signs his journeyman's card."

"I like him."

"And I think he likes you. Just be careful of Harper. He's really hard on the boy."

Riley's phone emitted a chorus of cricket chirps. She studied the display and smiled. It was her best friend. "Hey, Peter. How's it going?"

"Hey, Riley. I saw your video. You rock! The stats are off the chart. You're going viral!"

Riley groaned. Just what she always wanted—thousands, millions of people laughing at her.

She could hear the sound of a keyboard. Peter was into multitasking, so he was probably IM-ing with a couple of his buds while talking to her on the phone.

"It wasn't that much fun in person," she admitted.

"Yeah, but you nailed that little guy. All that stuff flying through the air looked like something out of Harry Potter!"

Peter would love that kind of thing. He'd collected all the books and the movies.

"Hold on," he said. She heard a voice in the background. That would be Peter's mom finding out who he was talking to. "Okay, I'm back," he said. "It was the warden making sure I hadn't escaped."

Riley looked over at her father and then sighed. She liked talking to Peter, but her dad wasn't going to be around all evening.

"Ah, Pete, can I call you later? I'm with Dad right now, and he's going to have to leave pretty soon and . . ."

"Understood. Call me when you get a chance, okay?" her friend said. "You still rock, by the way." Then he was gone.

Her father halted at a stop sign as an old man puttered across the intersection. Tied to his shopping cart was a scruffy dog toting something in its mouth.

"You see that?" her dad asked.

"You mean the old guy?"

"You don't see the white outline around him?"

All she saw was an old guy with a dog.

"He's an angel," her father explained.

"No way!"

Riley stared at the man. He looked like any one of the other homeless dudes in the city. "I always thought angels would have wings and wear robes or something."

"They do. The ministering kind can look like us, unless they want to reveal their true form."

The man/angel reached the sidewalk, petted the dog, and set off again.

"There are more of them in Atlanta now," her dad observed.

Something in his tone caught Riley's notice. "Keeping an eye on the demons. That's good, right?"

Her father shrugged. "Not sure."

"Do they really do angel sorta things, like miracles and such?"

"So it's said." He was silent for a while, concentrating on his driving. Then out of the blue he asked, "You and Peter ever going to date?"

She blinked in surprise at the question. *Where did that come from?*

"Ah . . . no."

"Why not? He's a nice kid."

"He's . . . Peter. I mean . . ." She struggled to come up with the best explanation for what seemed obvious to her. "He's just a friend."

Her dad smiled knowingly. "Got it. I knew a girl like you when I was in high school. Never once thought I might have a thing for her."

Dad rarely talked about his past. She couldn't resist. "Who was she?"

"Your mom." He waggled his eyebrows at her groan.

"He just calls me because he's lonely," she explained.

"Or because he really likes you."

"Yeah, yeah. Nice try. He'd got his eye on Simi."

"The punk barista at the coffee shop?" her dad quizzed. "The one with neon hair?"

Riley nodded. "You should have seen her last month. She had black and white stripes with purple tips. Seriously breathtaking."

"Don't even think it," her dad replied, lifting a warning eyebrow.

"As if." She had enough problems as an apprentice without looking like a Halloween costume gone wrong.

"How's school going? They still have you juniors sit near the dairy case?" he quizzed.

Riley wrinkled her nose. "It's okay. The store smells like moldy cheese and has all the old signs hanging from the ceiling. It's yucky in there. There are mice creeping around and dead roaches." She wiggled her fingers in disgust.

Before her father lost his job and started trapping demons, she and Peter had attended a real school. Now, because of budget cuts, they went to night school three times a week in an abandoned grocery store. Most of the teachers had other jobs hauling garbage or selling hot dogs at convenience stores.

"Some of my teacher buddies are saying there are plans to reorganize the classes again," her dad warned. "You might be moving locations."

That wasn't good news. "Just as long as Peter goes with me, I don't care where they stick us."

"At least you got a grocery store this time. It could have been an old Mexican joint, and you'd come home smelling like stale bean burritos."

"Euuuu . . ." she said.

"I always figured I'd have a teaching job for life," her dad admitted. "I even thought it was a good deal when the city sold the schools to Bartwell, figured it would get us more money for education." He shook his head. "I was so wrong."

Riley knew this story well. Bartwell Industries had leased the school buildings to the city and kept raising the rent. In the midst of a budget crisis and unable to handle the increased expense, Atlanta farmed out their classrooms to uninhabited businesses, hoping to pressure their landlord to lower their rates. Bartwell promptly went bankrupt. The result was dilapidated school buildings, classes held in defunct grocery stores, and a lot of unemployed teachers.

"At least I can trap," he said ruefully.

"We both can."

He nodded, but she could see he wasn't eager to agree.

Her father was usually in a hurry to leave, keen for the hunt, but they took their time walking from the parking lot to the apartment complex.

"I don't expect you to become a trapper just because I am," he said, his tone pensive.

Riley thought about that as they wove their way through the rusty bikes and the scooters. "I want to do this, Dad." She caught his hand and squeezed it. "I don't want to work behind a counter somewhere. That's just not me."

A resigned expression settled on his face. "I'd hoped you'd change your mind, but tonight I knew it wasn't going to happen. You stood up to Harper, and that takes guts."

"Why is he such a dick?" she asked. "He acts like he hates everyone."

"He's had a lot of losses. Everyone has a breaking point, Riley. He hit his a long time ago."

"But you didn't."

He smiled and squeezed her hand. "Because of you."

Weaving his arm around her waist, they walked up the stairs in tandem.

Someday he'll be home all the time. Then it'll be good again.

FIVE

Once her dad had departed, Riley spent a long time in the shower. To her relief it took most of the green off of her skin. With some creative makeup application she might pass for human by tomorrow night. She hoped none of her classmates had seen the video. Besides Peter, that is.

Right. Dream on.

Every evening she tidied the apartment. Tonight wasn't any different, despite the fact that she felt she'd been body-slammed by a sumo wrestler. Cleaning never took very long as the place was Barbie-sized, two hotel rooms joined together, the walls an industrial beige. The extra bathroom had been divided in half and converted into a closet. There were three rooms total—a twelve-by-fifteen-foot living room and kitchenette, a bathroom, and a tiny bedroom. A decrepit wall unit offered minimal heat and air-conditioning. They didn't run it very often because it was too noisy.

When I'm a journeyman, Riley mused, *we'll move into a nice apartment.* She knew what it would look like—she'd found a picture in a magazine—all wood floors and big windows and gleaming stainless steel appliances. The picture was stuck to the ancient refrigerator. Her dad kidded her about it, but he hadn't taken it down. He had dreams, too.

Riley plopped onto the couch and dialed her friend. Peter answered on the first ring.

"Hey, Riley," he said. There was the sound of rustling paper. "Our term papers are due tomorrow."

"Yeah, I'll work on it tonight."

"Mine's done," he boasted. She heard a slurping sound like he'd taken a drink through a long straw. "I tore apart the South's assertion that slavery was necessary for their survival."

Peter wasn't really a nerd, but he acted like one. He'd been that way since they'd met in fourth grade. With his round face, mouse-brown hair, and glasses he looked like an accountant or a computer programmer.

"Sounds deep," she said. "You think Mr. Houston's going to like it?"

"It's solid. He'll accept it."

No way. Houston had a Dixie accent as thick as Atlanta's smog and was always talking about the "War of Northern Aggression." Peter's paper would not be met with applause, or an A.

"What's yours about?" her friend asked, followed by more slurping. It made her thirsty, so she chugged down the last of the hot chocolate before answering.

"General Sherman and why he was actually a terrorist."

There was a sharp intake of breath across the line. "Wow! I would never have made that connection."

"Thought I'd try it on for size. Can I use your printer tomorrow?" she quizzed.

"Sure. I'm getting drilled and filled in the morning, so make it after four. Maybe the ghouls will be out." The ghouls were the twins, Peter's younger brothers. He'd called them that ever since they'd started to walk. Something to do with the fact that they followed him everywhere, even into the bathroom.

"Dentist in the morning. Got it," she said, grinning.

"Better yet, send the file over tonight and I'll have it all ready for you."

"Cool! Okay, see you tomorrow night, Peter."

"Later, Riley."

She settled at the card table that served as a makeshift desk and pulled up the computer file entitled "General Sherman—War Hero or Domestic Terrorist?" Typing proved harder than she'd expected—the bite on her right palm wasn't cooperating. Then the *N* key popped off the keyboard and flew toward the stained carpet.

"Ah, come on!" she groused. "Why does everything fight me?"

Digging under the card table yielded the key, which she carefully reattached, leaving a trail of *n*'s across the screen. At least the gold star she'd stuck on it made it easier to find when the thing went AWOL.

It was times like this she longed for the computer system she'd owned before the condo fire—a Mac with speakers and everything. Now all she had was leftovers because the insurance company only paid enough for the condo mortgage and to buy some secondhand furniture but not a new computer.

Her dad had found this one at a secondhand store, and they'd scavenged the keyboard from the trash bin behind a sub shop. It'd taken a lot of time to clean it up, and it still smelled like rubbing alcohol and onions.

A scratching sound came at the door. She ignored it, studying Sherman's bio. He'd warmed up with the Seminoles and then moved on to scorching large parts of the South, including Atlanta in 1864.

"Pyromaniac. I'm just saying."

An e-mail from Peter popped up. *Check this out!* the subject line read.

It was a hyperlink to another one of her videos. There were over a hundred thousand hits on it already.

"I'm so viral," she said, groaning. No way she was going to watch it. She clicked the page closed and went back to Sherman.

More scratching. That had to be Max, Mrs. Litinsky's Maine Coon. He was a giant of a cat with a patchwork of thick white, brown, gray, and black fur. His sensitive feline nose would be telling him there were demons inside the apartment.

Opening the door, she found the cat digging at the threshold. Riley knelt, petted him, and she got a throaty purr in response. Some nights she let him in and he'd keep her company. But not tonight.

"Sorry. You'll tear the kitchen apart trying to get to our stash," she said. Not that the three Biblios currently housed inside the cupboard with the canned green beans actually constituted a stash. Tomorrow her dad would make a run to one of the local demon traffickers, who would relieve him of the fiends in exchange for cold hard cash. Then Max would be welcome in the apartment once more.

Riley gave the cat a few more cuddles, shooed him out, and shut the door, making sure to lock it. Sinking into the creaky office chair, she yawned and cautiously stretched. Something popped in her back and the ache diminished. Considering how hard she'd landed on the library floor it was amazing she wasn't one solid bruise.

When she put her hands on the keyboard the *N* was missing again. She made a quick check of the floor. Not there.

"Now that's weird."

Another check of the floor turned up a rusty paperclip and an expired roach, but nothing else. Riley leaned back in the chair, trying to work out what was going on. The missing key's gold star gave her a clue.

Can't be. To test her theory, she checked the top of the battered dresser in the bedroom. The silver seashell earring she'd found in Centennial Park last summer was missing, too.

Riley grinned. No other explanation—there was a demon in their apartment. Maybe she could redeem herself by catching it. Besides, the fiend was worth seventy-five bucks, and that would take them one step closer to their pizza and movie night.

She returned to the front room, retrieved her Trappers Manual from the bookshelf and thumbed to the second section, the one that dealt with types of Hellspawn. Running a greenish finger down the list she found:

Klepto-Fiend (Magpie, Hell's Cat Burglar): Three inches tall, light brown skin, pointed ears. Often seen in ninja garb toting a small bag of loot. Cannot resist jewelry, coins, or shiny objects.

Should be easy to trap. Or not. At least these fiends didn't curse or pee on you. Their demonic activity was confined to stealing bright and shiny stuff.

But why is it in our apartment? That would seem to be the last place a demon would want to be discovered.

Riley slumped on the worn burgundy couch and conducted a visual search around the tiny room. The demon could be anywhere, though most likely it would be hunting something shiny. Nothing near the makeshift bookshelf they'd constructed from salvaged two-by-fours. Nothing near the family pictures on the top shelf of the bookshelf. One of those frames had sparkles on it, but it was probably too big for the tiny fiend to cart off.

"Where are you?" she called out in a singsong voice. Nothing moved. Well, she was a trapper, after all. Flipping farther into the manual she found the section that told her how to trap a Magpie. She scanned the text to refresh her memory. She really had to find him; it'd be hard to finish the paper without the full keyboard, especially since the name of the term paper's subject ended in an *n.*

A sharp hiss came from the hallway. Then a growl. Had the demon slipped out of the apartment? Riley grabbed a sippy cup from the cupboard, one her father had specially prepared with a layer of glitter on the bottom. When she slowly edged open the door, she found Max a few feet down the hallway, his fur on end and his back humped. Every whisker bristled at attention.

The reason crouched near the floor register. It was one of Hell's cat burglars. Similar in stature to a Biblio-Fiend, the Magpie was the same size with humanlike hands and a forked tail. Its eyes were red, but not that Hellfire bright that bothered her. Just like the manual said, this one was clad in ninja black, and even wore boots. It was furiously trying to jam its canvas bag through the fins of the floor register. Even Riley could tell it wasn't going to fit. The demon wouldn't leave the bag behind; the "pretties" were everything to them.

Max took another step closer, his growl deepening now. If this had been a Biblio, the demon would have slammed a fist into the cat's nose or peed in his eyes then made a run for it. Magpies survived by stealth. Unfortunately, this one had nowhere to run.

"Max?" The cat's back rumpled in irritation at her voice, but he didn't break his vigil. "You can't eat it. It'll make you sick. All your hair will fall out, then you'll go into convulsions. Dead cat, get it?"

The feline growled in response. It was matched in volume by the demon's warning hiss.

"Come on, Max. Let it be," she coaxed.

In exaggerated slow motion, he took one more step toward the Magpie.

A door slammed on a floor below and Max jumped at the sound, momentarily losing eye contact. It gave Riley the diversion she needed. With a quick sweep of her foot she shoved the hunter down the hall. Flailing her arms in the air, she shouted nonsense at him. The feline took off.

When she turned back, the demon was still trying to cram its loot through the vent. She knelt, tipped open the cup, and dropped a few pieces of glitter on the floor. Magpies were wired for bling. All she needed to do was provide the bait.

The demon stopped its frantic attempts to escape. It stared at the glitter and began to pant, fingers twitching in anticipation. More twitching. Faster than she'd expected, it zoomed up to the sparkles, despite the danger. She snagged the fiend right before it picked up the last one, and dropped the Magpie into the cup. Instead of a flood of swear words or the offer of a favor, she heard a long, tortured sigh. Then it sat, sorting the glitter into piles *by color.*

Now she'd seen everything. She screwed on the lid, grabbed up its bag, and hurried into the apartment before Max had the courage to return.

Before getting back to work on her assignment, Riley sorted through the demon's horde, reclaiming the earring and the *N* key. It rapped on the side of the container and pointed at the bag with a concerned expression. She understood. It would be like someone making off with her favorite lip gloss.

"Okay, Flash, here you go." Unscrewing the top, she carefully dropped the bag inside, then tightly resealed the lid. The Magpie promptly pulled out a shiny penny and someone's tie tack. Those earned her a grateful demon smile. It curled around the treasure and fell asleep.

Pleased at how things turned out, she sent a text to her dad.

I caught a Magpie in our apartment! Score one for me!

Riley waited, but there was no response. Probably busy trapping that Three. When she finally shut down the computer a couple of hours later, there was still no reply.

"You go, Dad! Movie night, here we come."

SIX

Whistling "God Rest Ye Merry Gentlemen" louder than was necessary, Beck waited in the middle of Alabama Street as night settled in for keeps. The steel pipe stuck in the back of his jeans was uncomfortable, but he left it in place. If they were lucky it wouldn't be there much longer. To his right, Paul was hidden behind a dumpster, armed and waiting for their prey.

Beck had to admit that Five Points was one of his favorite trapping locations. "Demon Central," as the trappers called it, perfect for Grade Three fiends. Threes loved the tangled warren of gutted buildings, seemingly bottomless holes, busted concrete, and overflowing dumpsters. Those few buildings still intact had metal gates over every window and door to keep Hell's evil outside. It was the only part of the city that had much metal left. It was too dangerous to try to scavenge down here, though some folks tried. All of them regretted it.

Any exposed concrete sported long claw marks starting at four feet up, the way Threes marked their territory. That and stinking piles of demon crap acidic enough to melt asphalt. At least the cold weather had cut the stench a notch.

Beck was summoning their prey on a couple of levels. Threes detested Christmas music and couldn't resist rabbit entrails, especially if they were a bit ripe. They had one-track minds: If something moved, they ate it. If it didn't move, they ate it anyway just to be safe. While on the hunt, which was pretty much once it got dark, they ripped apart anything that got in their way. They'd grown so ferocious that most trappers had a buddy along as backup.

Beck caught movement near one of the countless holes that littered the street. It was a skulking rat, probably the only one within a square mile. That was a side benefit of a Three infestation: The rat and pigeon population dropped dramatically.

Even though he was growing impatient, Beck forced himself to hold his position. Pulling off his Braves cap, he smoothed his hair. It was getting shaggy by his standards, but he didn't have the time for a haircut. The last two girlfriends had liked the look. Not that they hung around long, but there was always another one giving him the eye.

As Beck waited he swore he could feel the ground settling all around him. Built on top of what used to be street-level Atlanta in the nineteenth century, this part of town had been sinking for the last decade. Holes developed over the old steam vaults. Then the holes got bigger. And bigger. The last cave-in had been near the Five Points MARTA Station. With the city bankrupt, the holes kept enlarging. Only the demons found that a blessing.

Beck shifted his eyes sideways toward the battle-scarred dumpster fifteen feet away. Even in the dim glow of a single streetlight he could see the serene expression Paul wore when on the hunt. How he managed that, Beck never understood. It was probably why his partner had outlived his encounter with an Archfiend.

I sure as hell won't.

There was a sound near one of the holes as a Three climbed out of whatever lay below.

"Demon at one o'clock," Beck murmured. Paul nodded, holding his silence.

The beast should have been solid black, but this one had big white splotches like a lethal Holstein cow. Repeated applications of Holy Water did that to a Three, like a bad bleach job. This one had seen a lot of it and was still going strong.

The slavering beast hunkered down next to the bunny bait and gobbled the offering in one gulp. Then it looked up, those laser-red eyes scanning the terrain for the real bait—Beck.

"Trappperrr," it hissed.

"Deemonn," Beck hissed back. He waited for it to charge. They always charged, howling and waving those scimitar claws. Instead the thing's paw closed around a beer bottle, arming itself. That was a new tactic. Usually they leapt on you and kept slicing until they had you on the ground.

"Incomin'!" Beck taunted. He ducked as the bottle flew by him. "Ha! Ya couldn't hit yer own fat-assed mama with a throw like that!"

"Chew yourrr bones!" the demon cried, waving its furry arms above its head like a demented orangutan.

Beck mirrored the gesture and then sneered. "Yeah, yeah. If yer the best Hell can do, no wonder yer boss got kicked outta Heaven."

"Name not He!" the demon shouted, cringing.

That was a sore point for those who were on Lucifer's leash: They didn't like to be reminded. Beck got an idea.

"Let's see now, what's his name?" He tapped his forehead in thought. "Yeah, that's it!" He grinned and then started chanting, "Give me an L. L! Give me a U. U! Give me a C . . ."

Enraged, the demon sent a volley of beer bottles his way. Only one came close. Beck executed an exaggerated yawn, which only infuriated the fiend further. He could sense Paul's disapproval from the direction of the dumpster. The master was never happy when his former student showboated, as he called it.

But damn, this is fun.

The telltale scrape of claws across the broken pavement brought Beck back to reality. He kept his eyes on the thing as it scrambled toward him. Twenty feet. Fifteen. Ten. Sweat broke out on his forehead. Beck remembered how those claws felt when they'd dug into him. The smell of rancid breath in his face. The click of incisors as they went for his neck.

"Now!" he shouted, brandishing the steel pipe.

A clear globe arced through the air and impacted directly on top of the creature's head. Glass shattered and Holy Water drenched the fiend's fur-covered face. The demon began to dance around like it was on fire, swiping at unseen enemies. Then it crumpled.

Paul stepped out from behind the dumpster, studying the monster from a respectful distance, another sphere already in hand.

"Damn, yer good," Beck said, edging closer. "I can never hit 'em when they're runnin' like that."

"Takes practice. You be careful," his mentor urged.

"No problem. I learnt my lesson about these things." Beck gingerly prodded the steel into the side of the demon. It wasn't breathing. Which meant it was getting ready to strike.

"Heads up!" he shouted. The fiend was on its feet in an instant, moving faster than he'd expected. One of its paws clamped onto the pipe. Beck knew better than to keep hold of it. He'd made that mistake before and been pulled into the other set of claws. He surrendered the pipe, but by that time the demon was already lunging for him, Hellfire eyes glowing. He kicked with his steel-toed boot and caught the thing on the shoulder. As it spun around, one of the claws ripped the hem of his jeans, pulling him off balance. If he hit the ground he was dead.

As it turned, another sphere smashed into the Three's back full on, causing it to shriek and bat wildly at the soaked fur. Before either trapper could react, it raced toward the closest hole, dove into the darkness, and disappeared.

"Ah, shit!" Beck spat.

Paul joined him, slipping the strap of the duffel bag onto his shoulder, his face radiating disapproval.

"Go on, say it."

"What's the point? You never listened when you were an apprentice; you're not going to now."

Beck waited him out. There was always more.

Paul shook his head. "You can't do it straight, can you? Always a hotdog. It's going to get you dead, Den."

Beck was used to this lecture. He'd heard it often enough.

"It's just . . . never mind." Skating on the edge made him feel alive, kept things interesting. But he knew better than to try to explain. "The Holy Water hardly touched the thing. It shoulda been out for at least a couple minutes."

"It's happening more often now."

Beck arched an eyebrow. "Any idea why?"

His companion shook his head. "No, but I'm working on that." Paul studied the alley. "We need to rethink our strategy, at least for this demon."

Beck reclaimed his pipe. It had four new claw marks on it. "Yeah, big-time."

They turned and began to walk to the truck, both of them on edge. It reminded Beck of when he was in the Army, out on patrol. Waiting for that first burst of gunfire or a thundering explosion along the road-side. Here it was teeth and claws, but the effect was the same. If a trap-per didn't pay attention, he got injured or he got dead.

"That Five at the library today," Paul said out of nowhere.

Beck had wondered when that subject would come up.

"Why did it come after *my* daughter?"

"No clue. Anyway ya can keep her from trappin' for a while?"

"Probably not, but I can restrict her to being with one of us. That'll keep her safe until we get this sorted out."

"Better not send her out with me. She'll feed me to the first Three she sees," Beck said, trying to lighten the moment.

"She's not got a crush on you anymore, Den, if that's what you're worried about."

"Oh, I know that. Now she just hates me. I don't know which is worse." A grunt of agreement came from his partner. "Ya think the Five made itself look like one of the students?"

"That's my guess. They don't change forms very often, but it's pos-sible. As long as it kept its feet from touching the ground, it could work its evil."

A breeze stirred, kicking up puffs of concrete dust. The hair on Beck's neck ruffled. He shot a concerned look at his companion.

"Just the wind," Paul said. "A Five's not going to mess with two of us."

"Tell him that," Beck said, pointing down the alley.

A Grade Five Geo-Fiend materialized thirty feet in front of them, hovering a foot or so above the road. Beck estimated it was at least seven feet tall; its coal-black face was dominated by curved canines and twin horns that sprouted from the side of its head, curving upward like a bull. It had a massive chest, like an Olympic weightlifter who'd overdone the steroids. Brilliant red eyes glared at them, flickering in the dim light.

This was one of the big boys. Unless they were very careful, it'd turn them into sushi.

"That's one damned ugly demon," Beck muttered.

Paul palmed a Holy Water sphere.

"Hey, dumbass," Beck shouted. "Trash any books today?"

The resulting laugh cut like razor blades. "Blackthorne's daughter nearly mine."

Paul's legendary composure fled. His voice went low, urgent. "Circle around to the truck, Den. I'll handle this."

"Kiss my ass, Blackthorne." It was exactly what he'd said the first time they'd met in history class.

After a worried frown, Paul called out, "Demon, this is your only warning."

Warning? Trappers never warned demons. *What's he doing?*

In response, the Geo-Fiend made slight hand movements like it was flicking lint off its clothes. Blue-black clouds began to form, the warm-up to a full meteorological assault. The fiend laughed again, its eyes glowing bright in anticipation.

"So what's the plan?" Beck asked, his throat turning dry.

"Back up slowly."

A snarl came from behind them. Beck looked over a shoulder. The Three had returned, drooling and clicking its claws together.

"Not happenin'."

Paul shook his head. "This is so wrong."

"Like they care," Beck said, slowly rotating until his back was against Paul's, his eyes on the furry omnivore bringing up the rear. "Got another plan?" he asked, testing the weight of the steel pipe in his hand.

"No," Paul replied. He hurled the sphere, but a full blast of wind hit them a second later, like a summer squall, causing the orb to disintegrate in midair. Stinging rain and hail pelted them as a thunderclap shook the air, making their ears pop. Beck yelped and dropped the steel pipe, cursing as lightning sparked off it. Slowly they were pushed toward the slobbering demon. It held its position, its meal being catered.

Paul dug in his duffel bag and handed a blue grounding sphere to Beck. Then he pulled one out for himself. "You go left," he ordered. "Count it down."

Beck took a deep breath, his gut twisting in fear. "Three ... two ... one!"

He hurled the sphere to his left as Paul slung his in the opposite direction. Glass smashed and the spheres' contents erupted in a blaze of brilliant blue light. The grounding magic began its run across anything metal, making it look molten. It shot along a section of rusty fence, leapt to the battered dumpster, then to a mangled bicycle. If the two portions met and formed a circle it would ground the Geo-Fiend into the earth. Once grounded the fiend lost its ability to use the forces of nature against them.

The Five hesitated, seeing their plan, and then moved higher into the air. It swept its hands upward creating two new whirlwinds. Pieces of debris sucked into the vortex, like iron filings to a powerful magnet. Nails, shards of glass, slivers of wood, and pieces of brick all whirled in a huge circle.

Beck picked up a broken two-by-four, gritting his teeth as the slivers drove themselves into his scorched palm.

"Eyes!" Paul shouted, smashing a shield sphere to the ground.

Even though his were closed, Beck could see the sheet of white light as it bloomed around them. Once he felt the brightness subside, he pried them open. A white veil hung in the air around him and his friend, a defense against the storm. It wouldn't last long.

The twin whirlwinds struck hard against the magical wall, debris attacking from every quarter. It sounded like a hail storm against the magical shield. As the storm intensified, ripples of magic, like long blue tentacles, stretched upward to the Geo-Fiend. It fought the grounding, hurling wind, snow, and lightning like a vengeful god.

The white protective shield evaporated. A second later Paul cried out and slammed into Beck, causing the younger trapper to tumble to the ground. Rolling to the side, Beck came to his feet, crouched and ready for battle. Adrenaline pumped through him with every staccato heartbeat. It made his vision clear, each breath deeper. It made him feel alive.

There was a final wail as the weather demon sank into the earth behind them. The grounding spheres had saved their asses. As the wind died there was the patter of urban debris hitting the ground.

"Sweet Jesus," Beck murmured, his breath coming in sharp gasps. Edging sideways, he picked up the pipe in his sweaty hand, dropping the two-by-four. Keeping a wary eye on the Three, he moved backward, step by step, until he was even with his friend. His fellow trapper was on his knees, bent over like he was in prayer.

"Paul?" No reply. "Ya okay?"

His mentor slowly raised his head, his face a bluish gray. In the fading glow of the grounding sphere's magic Beck saw a quarter-sized dot of blood over his friend's left breast.

Paul took a tortured, sucking breath, one that made his whole body shake. "Lies . . ." Terror filled his eyes. "Riley . . . Oh, God, Riley . . ."

As his mentor crumpled into Beck's arms, the remaining demon charged.

SEVEN

Beck began his slow ascent. Right leg. Left leg. Right. Left. He concentrated on the movement up the two flights of stairs, sixteen steps total to the second floor and the apartment where Riley Blackthorne slept. There was one step for each year of his life before it'd been forever altered by the girl's father.

Beck didn't remember much about his first two years—probably for the best. From age three on he remembered too much. Nights alone in a cold room, his mom gone. When she did come home she was too drunk to know who he was. No food, not even a hug. Night after night he curled on the floor in a makeshift bed of dirty clothes, thinking he'd done something to make her hate him. On his fifth birthday, he remembered, his mom had been passed out on the worn plaid couch in their living room, the man who'd come home with her zipping up his pants. When Beck had told him it was his birthday, the guy had laughed, tousled his hair, and gave him a dollar bill. Beck had cried himself to sleep that night, wondering why he hadn't gotten real presents like the other kids.

At ten he knew his father was a phantom, someone who had picked up Sadie's bar tab the night he'd been conceived. Probably on that damned plaid couch. He also knew what his mother was—an alcoholic whore. No, that wasn't right. Whores sold themselves to make ends meet. His mother just got drunk and didn't care who fucked her.

By the time he turned eleven, Beck knew she wanted him to run away. He refused. That would have been too easy for her. As he reached the thirteenth step he recalled the beatings. One of the men who'd moved in had taught him fists were a great weapon. Beck learned that lesson well and used it on other kids. On anyone who challenged him. He'd spent his next two birthdays in juvenile detention.

In his sixteenth year he'd met Paul Blackthorne. The history teacher hadn't treated him like some of the others at school. Hadn't told him he was a loser headed for prison or an early grave. Instead, Blackthorne talked about the future. In his own way Paul had seeded Beck's desire for revenge—the ultimate revenge—turning out better than his alcohol-soaked bitch of a mother.

When Beck reached the seventeenth step he moved onto the landing, like his own life at the same age. He'd bailed out of high school early, barely getting his diploma. For three years in the Army he took on an enemy he never understood, watching friends die while they cried out to God and to their mothers. Beck didn't believe in either. At twenty he was back in Atlanta. Back with Paul—the only person in the world who ever gave a damn about Denver Beck.

In the end he'd proved his teacher wrong. The smart-mouthed kid with no future wasn't any better than his mother or the bastard who'd knocked her up.

He halted in front of the apartment door feeling the blood cracking on his face, the pulsing burn on his right hand, the prick of glass in his left knee. Raising his fist, he let it hang in the air, not wanting to take that final step. Finally he hammered on the door. A decade passed. Riley's sleepy voice asked who it was. He told her.

"Dad?" she called out. "Are you there?" When he didn't answer, she began to frantically undo the locks. "Dad?"

As she wrenched the door open, their eyes met.

Beck's heart turned to ashes.

✢

"What do you want?" Riley asked. When he didn't reply, she shoved past him, not caring that she was in her nightclothes. "Dad?" she called out.

There was no one else in the hallway.

She whirled around. "Where's is he? Is he hurt?"

A shudder coursed through Beck's body. "Gone," he murmured, then looked down at the floor.

"What do you mean gone?"

"I'm so sorry, girl."

Confusion gave way to anger. "Is this some sick game?" she asked, jamming a finger at him. "Why are you doing this to me?"

"I tried, but there were two of them and . . . He's gone, Riley."

Her hand was in motion before she realized. He made no effort to block the blow, and the slap landed soundly on his cheek. Before she could strike him again, Beck snagged her arm and pulled her up against him. Though she struggled and swore, she couldn't break free.

"Goddammit," she heard him whisper.

He hugged her so tightly she couldn't breathe, then broke his embrace.

Unable to think of what this meant, she shoved him away. Her hands came away sticky, imprinted with blood.

It was only then she saw the gouges on Beck's face and hands, the long strips of leather missing from his jacket that revealed a shredded T-shirt underneath. Both legs of his jeans were ripped and stiff with dried blood.

The rational part of her examined those injuries, cataloged them and told her that if Beck was that badly hurt, her dad wasn't coming home.

Her heart refused to accept it.

No. He's alive. He'll be here in the morning and . . .

With each passing second the pressure built inside her. It coiled around Riley's chest, forcing itself up into her throat. She wrenched herself away and fled into the apartment, stumbling into the bedroom. Only then did she let the scream loose into the depths of her pillow, let it rend her throat until she had no more breath. Then the tears came, streaming hot, salty. She tried not to let them overwhelm her, but it was no use. She choked on her sobs, hammering the bed with her fists.

Images of her father came to mind—teaching her how to ride her first bicycle, comforting her after she took a headlong tumble down a flight of stairs when she was five, holding her hand at her mother's funeral.

Not this. Please, not him.

How long she cried she couldn't tell; her sense of time stripped away. When Riley could finally catch her breath, she wiped her eyes and blew her nose with a wad of tissues from the box on the nightstand. There was the sound of running water in the bathroom. When it shut off she heard thick sobs through the thin wall.

Beck.

Her father was really gone.

Later, when she rolled over in the bed she found Beck sitting on the chair near the door. His eyes were swollen, dark red, and he stared at nothing, unaware that the wounds on his face were still oozing. He only roused when she pulled herself up against the headboard.

Beck hoarsely cleared his throat. "We tried to catch . . . that Three. It got away. We were walkin' . . . to the truck when—" He broke off and looked down at the floor again, his elbows on his knees. His jacket was off and there were claw marks on his chest. "A Five popped out of nowhere. Then the Three came back. They were workin' together."

That wasn't what she wanted to know. "How did he . . . ?"

"A piece of glass got through the shield. Doc said it hit his heart."

Now she knew. It didn't help.

"Where is he?"

He looked up at her. "Oakland Cemetery. None of the mortuaries will have anythin' to do with a trapper."

"I want to see him," she said, shifting her feet to the edge of the bed.
"Not 'til mornin'."

"I don't want him alone." She bent over to try to find her socks.

"He won't be. Simon's with him."

She ignored him.

"Riley, please. Simon will watch over him. Ya need to stay here."

Beck was right, but it robbed her of something to do when every minute promised unbelievable heartbreak.

Riley sank onto the bed. "I have no one left now," she said. "No one."

"Ya have me."

She glared him. How could he possibly think he was interchangeable with her father? "I don't want you!" she snarled. "If you really cared for him, he'd be alive and you'd be the one who—"

Beck took a sharp intake of breath like she'd broken something inside of him. She turned her back on him and let the tears fall. A door closed, and then there was silence.

A few minutes later something touched Riley's knee and she jumped. It was Max. He settled next to her, leaning into her body, purring as loud as she'd ever heard him. At first she resented his presence, but he kept rubbing up against her. Finally she gave in and hugged him tight. His thick fur soaked up her tears.

"Riley? I have tea for you, child," Mrs. Litinsky offered. Riley pried her face out of the cat's fur. Her elderly neighbor stood in the doorway, a cup in hand.

"No . . . thanks."

"It is chamomile. It will help you rest. That is what you need right now."

Knowing Mrs. Litinsky wasn't easily put off, Riley sat up and took the cup. The herbs smelled fresh and they helped unstuff her nose.

The old woman settled on the side of the bed in a robe, her pure white hair in a braid that nearly reached her waist. She seemed almost ethereal, like a fairy. "Mr. Beck has left. I urged him to get his wounds treated. They look bad."

Then what does Dad look like?

Riley nearly choked at the thought. She forced herself to take a sip. It was hot and tasted sweet, like there was honey in it. She took another long drink, accompanied by the old woman's approving nod.

"Mr. Beck said to tell you he took the demons with him. They were making considerable noise."

"What?"

"The small ones in the cupboard," the woman explained.

"Oh." Which was why Max was lounging on the bed rather than trying to tear the kitchen apart. She reached out and stroked his thick fur.

"He will stay with you tonight, keep you safe," Mrs. Litinsky said.

That seemed silly. What could a cat do?

The yawn caught Riley unawares. She finished the drink and handed the empty cup to her neighbor, her hands quaking.

"I'll be out on the couch," the woman announced. "Call if you need me."

Before Riley could protest, there was the soft shuffle of slippers and then the door closed. She fumbled for a photo on the nightstand. It was one of her and Dad from last summer mounted in a picture frame they'd bought at a dollar store. It had orange kittens running around the edge. Dorky, but cheap.

They'd gone on a picnic that day, just the two of them. She'd made sandwiches and cupcakes and lemonade. She could almost smell the fresh lemons and see the blue sky draped like a canopy above them. The picture had been taken by a young man who was there with his new wife. They'd been all over each other. Her dad was embarrassed, but she'd thought it was cute.

Her father looked younger in the picture, content, like all the bills and worries didn't exist. She hugged the frame close to her body, wishing time had stopped that day in the park. Then she and her dad would be together again.

Max moved closer to her, wedging himself up against her stomach, his rich purr reverberating throughout her body. She curled around him, clutching the photo to her chest. The last thing she could remember was him licking her hand and her father's reassuring voice saying that everything would be okay.

EIGHT

Riley woke to household noises, the sound of clanking pans and water running in the sink. Her dad was making her breakfast. He often did that, even though he was exhausted from being up all night.

She rubbed the sleep out of her eyes, puzzled why she was so tired. There was a thump as something tumbled to the floor. Bending over, she saw the framed picture. She stared at it, her heart tightening.

"Dad?" she called out. "Dad?!"

The noises ceased in the kitchen, followed by heavy footsteps in the hall, the same solid *clomp, clomp* her father's work boots made on the wood.

"It was a nightmare," she whispered. And an ugly one at that. *But how could it have felt so real?*

When Beck's unshaven and scored face appeared in the bedroom doorway, Riley shoved herself up in bed, biting back a sob. Without saying a word he returned to the kitchen. She jammed a hand over her mouth, feeling the tears prickling on her cheeks. It hadn't been a nightmare or Beck wouldn't be here. Her dad was dead.

The tears burst free, scorching her throat raw, making her nose drip and her neck wet. When she finally hauled herself to the bathroom, the face in the mirror seemed alien. Hollow, puffy, red-rimmed eyes stared back at her. She doused her cheeks with cold water, blew her nose again, and then jammed her hair in a clip, not caring that it stuck out like a porcupine. Tugging on fresh underwear and her last pair of clean jeans, she dug in the clean clothes basket until she found a T-shirt. It had a tombstone on the front.

With a sharp cry, she slung it away in revulsion. More digging unearthed a plain one. It had been her dad's. She slipped it on, the thin cotton brushing against her skin like a whisper.

Now came *the firsts*. The first morning without her father. The first breakfast, the first day, week, month. She'd gone through this painful accounting after her mom died. After a few months she'd ceased the mental math, but this morning there was no way to shut it off.

Her visitor had his back to her. He was being domestic, cooking something on the gas stove despite his bandaged hand. For a moment she wanted to believe it was her father, though he wasn't the same height and his hair was the wrong color.

Beck looked over his shoulder, ruining her delusion. "I've got some breakfast for ya."

"You're not my dad," she said defiantly.

"I can't be if I tried." He pointed toward the table. When she didn't move, he put the oatmeal in a bowl and set it down, along with a plate of scrambled eggs and some sausage. Mismatched silverware followed. "Come on, girl, ya gotta eat."

She stared at the food, wishing it would disappear with the guy who'd made it. When Beck pulled out her dad's chair to join her, she snapped, "Don't sit there!"

He looked puzzled for a second, then nodded like he understood it meant more than just a place at the table.

"Keep the doors locked. If ya need me, call," he advised. "I'll be back at four. The service is at four-thirty. Pack a bag for the cemetery. You'll be stayin' there tonight."

"Why would I stay—"

But he was already out the door. Riley waited until she heard his footsteps on the stairs before she turned the locks. Then she kicked the door for good measure, making her toes ache.

He'd planned the funeral without her. How could he do that? Muttering under her breath she retreated to the kitchen. Her dad's empty chair mocked her. She pushed it all the way under the table so no one would ever sit there again.

Yesterday her father had been so tired after the night's trapping, but he'd sat and talked to her over a cup of coffee as she'd eaten her breakfast. His hair had been wet from his shower and he'd smelled of cheap shampoo.

She'd wasted their last morning together. She'd chirped on about Peter's latest run-in with his dictatorial mom and the dumb *Demonland* television show. He'd listened so patiently, like everything she said was really important.

When his eyes began to droop, he'd given her a kiss on the forehead and gone to bed. "Sleeping in shifts" as he called it. He was a sound sleeper, so yesterday she'd tried to find where he'd concealed his manual. He always hid it too well. Now she wondered if she'd ever find it.

Their last morning together. And neither of them had known it.

When Riley looked down the food was cold. Grease congealed on the plate. Something beeped and the noise dragged her eyes to her father's cell phone tucked up next to the salt and pepper shakers. Beck must have left it for her. The low battery light was blinking along with an occasional warning sound. Flipping it open she studied the messages. The text she'd sent him about the Magpie sat at the top of the list.

He'd never had a chance to read it.

⁜

It *was close* to two in the afternoon when her other visitor arrived. The woman was a tall brunette, toting a backpack with the Guild logo. Her hair was pulled into a tight braid, and her brown eyes were rimmed with red. She was wearing black slacks and a turtleneck and one of those thick red insulated vests.

"Riley, I'm Carmela Wilson," the woman said. "I'm the Guild's doctor. I was a . . . friend of your dad."

When Riley didn't respond, she added, "Den asked me to check in on you."

It took Riley a moment to realize she meant Beck.

"I'm okay," Riley said reflexively. It was easier to say that so everyone didn't freak. She started to close the door, but Carmela wedged a booted foot so it wouldn't shut.

"Other people might buy the 'I'm okay' line, but I'd say that's bullshit. I'm not okay with Paul's death, so I figure you're pretty much torn to hell. Am I right?"

Riley nodded before she could stop herself.

"Just as I thought."

Riley stepped back and the woman strode into the apartment, did a visual inventory of the crowded space, and then headed for the kitchen where she dumped her medical bag on the table. She sank in the closest chair; it was Riley's.

"First off, I want to see that demon bite you got yesterday," she said, her voice not allowing for argument.

I don't need this. Not now. Riley began to back away toward the bedroom.

"I lost my dad when I was ten," Carmela explained, her eyes meeting Riley's. "I've been there, so I'm not playing head games with you."

Riley froze, caught between the need to fill the vacuum inside her and the overwhelming urge to bury herself in the pillow again.

Her visitor shifted uneasily. "Come on, let me look at the wound. I promise it won't hurt that much."

Riley reluctantly sank into her dad's chair. The doc immediately went to work, pulling out a fresh bandage, a bottle of Holy Water, and some medical tape. After removing the old bandage, she poked, prodded, and pinched the area around the bite. Riley ground her teeth against the discomfort.

"Looks good," she said. "Den was sure your hand would be rotting off by now."

"He could have asked me," Riley retorted.

"Would you have told him the truth?"

"Probably not."

Carmela nodded her understanding. "Besides, we can talk girl to girl. Guys don't get half of what we say even when we say it reaallllly slow."

Riley scrutinized the woman more closely now. "You don't let him run over you, do you?"

"No way. You're going to be the same. He'll bitch and moan, but he'll respect you for it."

"Right. Don't see that happening." *Not in this lifetime.*

Carmela broke the seal on the pint bottle of Holy Water and handed it over. "This'll sting. The stuff's only a day old."

Riley took herself and the bottle to the sink and cleaned the wound. The doc was right, the stuff was strong and it made her wince. The trickle of the water down the drain brought back memories. How many times had she treated her dad's wounds? None of them had been that bad, except when he'd first started trapping and her mom had taken care of those. He'd always joke that no demon would ever best him.

But one did.

When the plastic bottle was empty, Riley returned to the table. There was more poking until the doc was satisfied with the condition of the wound. From what she could tell, it was already closed, only a thin red circle left where the demon's teeth had met flesh.

But what does Dad look like?

"You saw him after . . ." she began, than faltered.

Carmela's expression flattened. "Den called me so I could certify Paul's death." She let loose a long sigh and blinked her eyes rapidly like she was trying to hold back tears. "A glass shard embedded in his heart, that's what killed him. It would have been very quick." The woman's hands fumbled with the bandage. "Paul looks asleep, not . . ."

Dead. "What about the demons? Did Beck catch them?" *Kill them?*

Carmela tidied up the table before she answered, buying time. "No. They only grounded the Five. The Three ripped the hell out of Den, but he wouldn't let it get near your dad's body. Which means you have a decision to make."

"What decision?" Riley asked, puzzled.

When the woman looked up, there was pity in her eyes. "Your dad's body is in good shape. In such good shape that he's prime fodder for the necromancers."

Riley's stomach heaved. She barely made it the bathroom before the soup from lunch vaulted into the toilet. She kept retching until there was nothing more to off-load.

A cool hand touched her forehead, causing her to jump. "Ah, damn. I'm sorry. I should have said that better," Carmela murmured.

Riley flushed the toilet, dropped the lid, and then flopped down. Her throat burned from the acidic taste of vomit. Carmela handed her a wet cloth, and she mopped her face.

"Why didn't Beck tell me this?" Riley demanded. "He was Dad's partner."

"He couldn't. This is hurting him as much as it is you."

Like hell. "What's this decision I have to make?"

The doc sat on the side of the tub, rubbing her arms like she was cold. Her eyes were pointedly fixed on her boots.

"If your dad's body remains the way it is," she said, her voice barely audible, "the necros will try to steal it. That is, unless you decide to sell him to them."

"Sell him? No way!" Riley growled. "Not happening." Her stomach tumbled and she swallowed hard.

Carmela's eyes met hers. "In that case, you'll have to sit vigil every night until the next full moon to keep him safe."

"What do you mean?"

"You cast a magical circle, and it keeps the necromancers from summoning your father. After the full moon, they can't touch him." Carmela paused. "Or there's another way."

Riley waited her out.

"You have one of the trappers . . ." The woman took a deep breath, "make your father's body less whole. If he's no longer in one piece, the necros won't come after him."

Riley stared, horrified. "You mean have Beck slice up my dad?"

"It won't be Den," Carmela replied, her voice taut.

"Doesn't matter who it is!" Riley frowned. "Can't we cremate him or something?"

"State law doesn't allow trappers that option if they've been killed by a demon. Some nonsense about contamination or something."

This was a nightmare.

"So either I sit vigil or have my father . . . dismembered?" Riley asked. "That's *so* medieval."

"No argument there," Carmela said. "It's your call. There are consequences no matter what you do."

There was only one answer. "He goes in the ground like he died. I swear to God if anyone touches him—"

There was a low sigh of relief from her visitor. "That'd be my call. Just realize it's going to be a bitch for the next few weeks."

"Can't be any worse than now."

The doc gently smoothed away a strand of hair from Riley's face.

"You might be surprised, hon."

NINE

Riley dug out the black dress and held it to her body. She hadn't touched it since her mother's funeral. It reached just above her knees now. She remembered her father bringing it home for her, thinking at the time how plain it was. He hadn't had a clue about her size and bought it too big. Now it would probably fit perfectly, as if he'd foreseen she'd have to wear it again.

A shiver launched up her spine and wedged at the base of her skull.

No way. He couldn't have known this would happen.

Though she really wanted to curl up on the couch and bury herself inside the heavy comforter to forget what this evening would bring, Riley forced herself to get ready. Black tights. Black dress. Black boots. She creaked open the lid of the tiny ballerina jewelry box and found the heart locket her dad had given her on her sixteenth birthday. It had a picture of her parents inside. She kissed the cold metal.

"Thanks, Daddy," she murmured, her tears wicking into the dress, unseen. Maybe that was why people wore black when someone died.

A knock came at the door.

It was Beck. They gravely studied each for a few moments like they were afraid of what the other might say. She'd never seen him in a suit before. He'd been on leave when her mother died, and he'd worn his dress blues to the funeral. His face was shaved; it must have been tough to work around the cuts. The dark circles under his eyes told her he hadn't slept any better than she had. There was the hint of aftershave, something like pine trees, she thought.

"It's time," he said, voice low and raspy.

She picked up her mother's wool dress coat, and Beck helped her put it on, though she could tell his shoulder hurt him. He took possession of the bag she'd packed for the graveyard. As she shut the apartment door, she swore she could hear her father's voice calling out his good-bye.

✛

Beck's truck didn't look the same as the night before: It had been washed, and all the beer bottles in the bed were gone, the inside swept, and the console cleaned. It smelled like the new peach air freshener hanging from the rearview mirror.

Why did he do all this? It wasn't like her dad would care.

She solemnly buckled herself in and then stared out the side window.

"Riley . . ." he began.

She shook her head. There was nothing he could say that would make it better. If anything, he'd only make it worse. Beck took the hint and fell silent. As he drove, the only sounds were the tires on the pavement and the occasional *click-click-click* of the turn signal. Not much different than when they'd driven her to the cemetery for her mom's funeral. On that trip Beck sat in the backseat of the car, his hair so short it made him look bald. Every time he'd moved, she'd heard the stiff fabric of his uniform.

They parked outside Oakland Cemetery's main gate, joining other cars and trucks in the parking lot. Most of the vehicles sported the Guild emblem in their rear windows. Riley got out of the truck and tugged her dress into place. She knew the area fairly well. Situated east of the state capitol building, the graveyard was bordered on the south by

Memorial Drive and on the north by the MARTA tracks. Every few minutes a train would roll in or out of the station with a peculiar whirring sound.

They crossed underneath the brick archway and onto the asphalt road that led along the oldest section of the graveyard. It'd been here since the 1850s. Some of Atlanta's most famous people were buried here, like the lady who wrote *Gone with the Wind*.

And now my dad.

Beck cleared his throat. "There'll be a short service and then the burial," he explained. "After that, ya change clothes and we'll set the circle."

"We?"

"Simon and me. He offered to stay with ya tonight, keep ya safe."

That she hadn't expected. Rather than dwell on that, she asked, "How does this circle thing work?"

"Don't really know," he said, shaking his head. "The magic keeps the necros from summonin' yer daddy, that's all that matters."

As they walked past the redbrick Watch House, she asked, "Why didn't you tell me about the necros?"

He stopped in the middle of the road. "I couldn't," he said. "That's why I asked Carmela to do it. If ya'd wanted him cut up—"

"You know I wouldn't," she said, stunned that he'd think she'd have her own father mutilated to save a few uncomfortable nights in a cemetery.

"I didn't know," he admitted. "If ya'd asked me to do it . . ." Beck shook his head. "Not possible."

"For either of us."

They started walking again, the tension between them draining away like they'd crossed some unseen barrier. Around them, birds settled into the trees, and dried leaves rustled as a squirrel bounced its way past a row of graves.

"Yer daddy had a life insurance policy," Beck said as they followed the road to the left. "It'll take a while for the money to come through.

It's not much, but it'll bury him and give ya some to live on." He paused and then added, "Oh, and the others took up a collection, bought some flowers for the funeral."

Riley's throat tightened. "Thanks. I didn't think of that."

He gave her a sad smile. "Me neither."

The Bell Tower, a two-story building that held the cemetery office, was stark white in its simplicity. As they approached, she saw Simon waiting for them. Like Beck, he was in a suit.

After a quick look at the other trapper, almost like he was seeking permission, Simon stepped forward. "Riley," he said quietly. Without hesitation, he embraced her. It felt good.

"Thanks for watching over my dad," she murmured. She felt a nod against her cheek.

"He's down here," Beck said, gesturing to a set of stairs that led to a lower level. After a deep breath, Riley followed him, her hands knotted around a bunch of tissues she'd pulled from her coat pocket.

The stench of the Easter lilies hit her nose the moment she reached the door. There was a big vase of them just inside the room. She hated them. To some they spoke of resurrection. To her they meant nothing but death and loss.

At the far end of the room sat a plain pine coffin on a raised stand. The lid was closed.

Dad.

Riley remained rooted in place. She could lie to herself until she saw him in the casket, then all those lies burned away.

Beck cleared his throat. "Riley?"

"Give me a minute," she said, though no amount of time was going to make this bearable.

"It never gets any easier."

She looked over at him, caught by the emotion in his voice.

"I still remember my granddaddy's funeral," he said. "I was ten and my uncle came down to Waycross to pick me up. Hauled me all the way to North Georgia so I could be there. I cried like a baby."

"What was your granddad like?" she asked, curious. Beck never talked about his family.

His face turned thoughtful. "Elmore was a cantankerous old cuss. Lived up in the hills and made moonshine." He looked over at her. "Taught me how to trap squirrels and roll cigarettes."

"Skills every ten-year-old should know."

He shrugged. "Some might not see it thatta way, but he was a good man. He'd tell me I could be anythin' I wanted." He looked over at the coffin. "Like yer daddy."

The throbbing ache in her heart grew. "Dad . . . really liked you."

Her companion's eyes misted. He swiped at the tears like they were a weakness. "I never wanted anythin' but to make him proud."

Without thinking, she took hold of his hand and carefully squeezed it, mindful of his wounds.

"Did he . . . say anything when he . . . ?"

"Your name."

Oh, God. Riley's shoulders hitched, and the sobs erupted before she could stop them. Tears followed. Beck let go of her hand and placed his arm around her shoulder, holding her close. Her tears soaked his suit coat.

When she finally pulled away, they took slow steps toward the coffin. The room closed in on her, choking her in the stench of those damned lilies. She pressed the tissue to her nose.

On the coffin lid was a brass plaque. The script was fancier than she'd expected, but it was easy to read.

PAUL A. BLACKTHORNE
MASTER TRAPPER, ATLANTA GUILD

He was more than that, but she knew there wasn't enough room on that piece of metal to tell the world everything he'd been.

"Ready?" Beck asked.

No. Never. But she nodded anyway, and he slowly opened the lid.

Now she knew why Beck had been rummaging through the closet

when she was in the bathroom. He'd picked out her father's burial clothes. Her dad was in his best suit and his favorite red tie, the one she'd bought him for Christmas a few years back. He looked like he was asleep, like Carmela said.

Riley bent over and kissed his pale cheek. It was so cold, like kissing stone. She smoothed back a lock of brown hair, the one that always fell into his eyes.

"He's with Mom now," she said, with stinging tears slipping down her cheeks. "Bugging her about her cooking and those dumb soap operas she used to watch." *The ones Dad liked, too, but he'd never admit it.*

Beck sucked in a jagged breath. His eyes were closed and his cheeks wet. His whole body shook with grief.

No matter what she thought of him, her dad had always cared for Denver Beck. It looked like that love went both ways.

※

Riley headed up the asphalt path toward her family's mausoleum. It was designed like a miniature cathedral with a tall spire at the top, and built of reddish stone. The two bronze doors had lion's head door pulls. The rear of the building was curved and held five stained-glass windows, each with a verse from the Bible.

Back in the late 1880s her family had money, and the mausoleum was ample proof of it. One of the Blackthornes had been a banker and made his fortune before the Civil War, and his wealth had left the structure for his descendants.

The mausoleum was full, so her father would be placed right next her mother on the west side of the building where they could watch the sunsets together. That'd been her mother's choice.

Riley turned at the sound of boots scuffing on asphalt. Six trappers carefully maneuvered the casket toward the grave. It was difficult work and they went slowly. Despite his wounds, Beck was at the head of the coffin, Simon on the other side. One of the men began to sing, and his tenor voice carried throughout the graveyard.

Swing low, sweet chariot,
Coming for to carry me home . . .

Her dad had always liked that song, especially the part about the band of angels. There were no angels here tonight, at least not that she could see, but he wasn't alone. Trappers stood in dignified rows, hands clasped in front of them; the two remaining masters were in the front row. Harper wouldn't meet her eyes, but Master Stewart did. He was in full Scottish regalia and cradled a bagpipe in his arms.

Another knot of men stood a short distance away, but none of them looked familiar. Carmela leaned close to her, apparently noticing her confusion. "Demon traffickers. Fireman Jack is the one in the dark blue suit. He and your dad were good friends."

Riley found her eyes drifting to the man Carmela had indicated. He nodded to her in response. Now that she knew who he was, she remembered her dad saying that Jack always wore barber-pole suspenders, like his trademark. She couldn't see them now, apparently hidden by his suit coat.

A hand touched her elbow—it was Mrs. Litinsky. She was in a royal blue coat, her hair braided and tucked up on her head in a thick bun. Riley gave her a wan smile. At best there were thirty or forty people here. She'd trade them all to hear her father's voice one more time.

Once the coffin was situated, Beck stood next to her. He awkwardly offered his hand and she took it. His emotions were shuttered again. Riley didn't know how he could do that so easily.

The Guild's priest, Father Harrison, took his place in front of the coffin. He was young, almost boyish in his looks, with dark brown hair and eyes. It was tradition for a priest to handle the services, even if the trapper wasn't Catholic.

He began by talking about her father, how he was always eager to teach the newer trappers and how he possessed that quiet sense of destiny.

"To lose such a man might make us question God's mercy. I believe that Paul was called home because his work was done. He had fought the amy of darkness and fallen in battle but will always remain in our hearts. O Lord, in your mercy, grant him eternal rest."

"Amen," Riley murmured along with the others.

Father Harrison looked over at Beck. "We also give thanks, O Lord, that we are not mourning the loss of another this night."

Beck lowered his eyes as if embarrassed he was still breathing.

What if he had died, too?

Riley shivered at the thought. In response, Beck put his arm around her shoulder, thinking she was cold. It was deeper than that.

Harrison turned toward her. "O Lord, father of us all, please watch over Riley, as she takes up the fight against all that is evil in this world."

"Amen."

As the priest spoke of resurrection and heaven, they lowered her father into the ground. During the final prayer she didn't look down into the grave, but up at the sky. Dad was up there somewhere, watching over her. No demon could ever hurt him now. Once the full moon came, no necro could either. He'd kept her safe all these years, she'd do the same for him.

I promise.

Beck and Simon stripped off their suit coats and handed them to another trapper. Then they began to shovel the dirt into the grave.

"It's tradition," Carmela explained. "Trappers have a lot of them. Some of them even make sense."

Beck didn't go for very long, his face radiating pain. Jackson took over as Simon handed his shovel to Morton. And so it went, trapper after trapper, until the entire coffin was covered in red Georgia clay.

Then the gravediggers took over. As they completed the job, the trappers departed in reverse order of seniority. Another tradition, apparently. Stewart's bagpipe stirred to life, and the strains of "Amazing Grace" filled the air. Riley bowed her head. When the final note faded, the remaining mourners drifted toward her.

One by one they introduced themselves: Some were teachers who'd known her father from years before; others were former clients. They each had a story to tell. Her dad had removed a demon from their basement, saved their beloved Doberman from a ravenous Three, captured an incubus that had terrorized a private girls' school.

Her father had done so much, and yet his daughter felt she knew so little about him.

"Riley?"

She turned to find Peter watching her with the saddest expression. His eyes were red, and he was wearing a suit that seemed a size too big.

"Peter?" They hugged awkwardly and he stammered how sorry he was.

"Son . . ." a woman standing behind him nudged.

"Sorry. Riley, this is my mother," he said, looking embarrassed.

So this is the warden. Riley had never actually met the woman, which she'd counted as a good thing. Keen to make a favorable impression, at least for her friend's sake, Riley politely shook hands.

"You have my condolences," Mrs. King said. "Who will you be staying with now?"

What? That was a very direct question. "Haven't worked that out yet."

"You can't stay on your own," the woman cautioned. "Do you have any other family?" Peter shifted, clearly not pleased by his mother's inquisition.

Her tone rubbed against Riley's raw nerves, though Mrs. King probably thought she was being helpful. "I have an aunt in Fargo." *Who hates me.*

"Then I suspect you'll be moving, won't you?"

"No!" Peter exclaimed. "You can't leave Atlanta."

Riley took her friend's hand and gave it a squeeze. "Don't know yet. Too much to think about right now."

That seemed to settle him down. When Mrs. King announced they had to leave, he protested, but it got him nowhere. He gave Riley another hug and then was gone.

Beck joined her. "His momma doesn't like ya."

"Never has. Thinks I'm a wild child or something."

Beck snorted. "Not even close." He looked over at the mounded grave. "Yer daddy got a good send-off. I think he'd be pleased." When she didn't reply, he handed her the bag she'd packed for the vigil. "Best get changed. We need to get the circle in place before sundown."

And then it begins.

TEN

As Riley peered through the grill on one of the bronze doors, her fingers traced the cold metal of a lion's head. Those had always fascinated her, unlike the gargoyles high on the mausoleum's roof. They had the same lion faces, but she'd always thought the gargoyles were creepy. Her dad said they guarded the dead.

Now they'll watch over you.

When she was younger her family would often come to the mausoleum and visit the dead relatives. Her mom would clean the stained-glass windows then sweep the floor. Her father would tell her stories about some of the people buried there. Then they'd have a picnic on the grass, just like the Victorians who built the cemetery.

Now as she peered inside the structure, the sun's final rays poured through a couple of the stained-glass windows, projecting a mosaic of primary colors onto the stone floor. Riley unlocked the doors and pulled them open with a noisy scrape. As she walked inside she ran a hand along one of the vaults.

JOHN HARVEY BLACKTHORNE
BORN 17 AUGUST 1823
DIED 4 JANUARY 1888

I will not cease from mental flight,
Nor shall my sword sleep in my hand . . .

Her mom had said the verse came from an old poem. It seemed an odd thing to put on the tomb of a banker. In the rear of the building was a raised platform covered in a thin stone veneer which cleverly concealed a storage bin. She levered open the lid with considerable effort. A tiny spider crawled out and vanished over the side, its rest disturbed.

The interior looked like her father had left it a few weeks before. She took the sleeping bags out of their cases and shook them out one by one. She'd need them tonight.

"Good choice for a bolt hole," Beck observed from the doorway.

Trappers called them different names—bolt hole, sanctuary, bunker. Most had one in case of a demon uprising. They were always located on hallowed ground and included stores of dried food, spare clothing, water, and medical supplies. Some had a weapons stash. Her father had instructed Riley and her mom what to do if the demons ever waged war. Now it would be up to her to keep it stocked and ready.

"Mine's in a church basement," Beck added. When she didn't reply, he struggled on. "It's quiet here. I like that. Mine isn't. It's next door to the furnace room."

It was clear he was going to keep talking no matter what. Maybe it was nervous energy. Whatever the reason, it was bugging her.

"It's too bad yer daddy's not in here," Beck said. "It'd be easier to sit vigil."

She shoved the sleeping bags and extra blankets in his arms. "I'm changing now, so you need to go."

"Oh, sorry."

Riley swung the bronze doors closed behind him and stripped out of her dress and boots. The bare stones felt chilly beneath her feet. She pulled on the blue jeans, leaving the tights underneath for warmth, then added a heavy sweater. Then the boots, hopping from one foot to the other as she zipped them. Finally a heavy coat, because her mom's wasn't going to be warm enough.

As she stepped outside, the sun backlit the capitol's golden dome.

"It's time," Simon called out. He'd changed too, in jeans and sweatshirt now. He stood inside a large circle of candles that ringed both her dad and mom's graves. Each candle was about twelve inches from its neighbor.

When Riley drew close, both of the trappers looked over at her. Beck's face was set in a determined expression. Simon's was full of compassion.

"You really think they'll come for him?" she asked.

"They read the papers just like everyone else," Beck replied.

She hadn't even thought about that. How big of an article would her dad have rated? Front page? *No way*. Inside the paper somewhere, probably buried underneath notices for lost pets. Trappers only made the front page if they trashed law libraries.

Belatedly, Riley began to think of what this long night might be like. She wasn't that good with being cold and sitting still. Never could stand camping. Then there was Simon. She really didn't know him. What if he was creepy or something? She shoved that thought aside instantly. Her dad had thought he was okay. Then another worry caught up with her.

"What if I . . ." She sighed. "What if I need to go to the bathroom?"

Beck didn't smirk like she figured he would. "There's a toilet in the basement of the cemetery office. The door's locked. The code's in there," he said, pointing at a booklet in Simon's hand.

Oh.

Beck took a deep breath. "Whatever ya do, don't break the circle. If ya kick over a candle or walk through the circle without doin' it proper, it's history. Ya understand?"

She nodded.

"Do ya really understand?" he pressed.

She glowered. "I'm not slow."

Simon's grin quickly vanished when the other trapper noticed it.

"It's not that easy. The necros play all sorts of head games." Beck looked over at Simon. "You're in charge."

Riley ground her teeth.

"I'll keep them both safe, I promise," Simon said diplomatically.

"Be sure ya do." Beck turned on his heels and marched off toward the truck, fueled by some emotion Riley couldn't fathom.

"Jerk," she muttered.

"He's okay," Simon replied. "He's just worried about you and your dad."

The young trapper lit a kerosene lantern and set it on a flat piece of ground. "He says you've never done this before. Is that right?"

She nodded. "Mom died of cancer. It wasn't pretty."

His eyes softened. "I'm sorry." She shrugged like it wasn't a big deal, but she was lying.

"Everything you need is in here," he said, gesturing at the booklet. "There are sample invocations, or you can use one that has special meaning to you."

"Like?"

"Some people call the circle into existence by invoking the names of the Archangels, others use football teams. It's the intention that counts."

Intention. "Ohhkay."

"A necro's power is strongest at night, so you have to reset the circle each sundown. Doesn't matter if it's raining or whatever."

"What happens during the day?" she asked.

"The cemetery has volunteers who sit vigil during the daylight hours."

"Ah, does that cost anything?" she asked. Money was more of an issue than ever before.

"The Guild pays for it. They don't have enough funds to cover twenty-four/seven. They figure the family will be here at night."

"Got it." She puzzled for moment. "Why didn't a necro come for Dad before he was buried?"

"From what I understand, if a necromancer summons the deceased before the first sundown, the spell doesn't work right."

"Oh. So, how does this all work?" she asked, growing more nervous by the minute. What if she screwed something up?

Simon looked down at the booklet and then pointed at a gallon plastic jug. "Run a line of Holy Water just inside the candles."

Riley broke the seal, twisted off the cap, and dribbled the water as instructed. Hunched over like a gnome wasn't a comfortable position, so by the time she'd made the entire circle her back was beginning to cramp.

"Now you do it again in the other direction."

Riley groaned and did as he asked.

"These aren't ordinary candles," she said, studying one. The wick looked more like a coiled metal rope than twisted fiber. The candle was short, like a votive.

"No, they're special. The cemetery has more of them if you want to expand the circle. They don't charge for them, but they would appreciate a donation."

He went back to the instructions. "Move the candles onto the circle of Holy Water. Make sure they're the same distance apart."

More bending. When she stopped to rest, Simon urged her on. The sun was almost gone.

"Perfect!" he said. "Now light every other candle, *clockwise*, while I recite the invocation. Once you're done, light the remaining candles in the opposite direction. Don't pause in between. And whatever you do, don't say a word until I've completed the invocation."

Riley sort of freaked, trying to remember all the instructions.

He gave her a reassuring smile. "Don't worry, you'll do okay."

"What are you going to say?"

"The Lord's Prayer."

She took a deep breath and began to light every other candle. Her hand kept shaking, the demon bite causing her fingers to cramp. The wicks flamed in a sudden burst, then settled into a clear white light. Behind her, Simon's strong voice filled the night air, slowly intoning The Lord's Prayer in English and Latin.

Pater noster, qui es in caelis,
Our Father, which art in heaven,
Santificetur nomen tuum . . .
Hallowed be Thy name . . .

He didn't stumble over the Latin, but sounded like he was born to it. After she'd lit all the candles Riley went still, afraid of doing something stupid and ruining everything.

Simon raised his arms to the heavens. "By the blessing of God, His Only Son, and His holy angels, let all inside this sanctified circle be safe from harm. Amen."

"Amen," she whispered and then grimaced. She wasn't supposed to talk. Had she messed it up?

To her relief, a brilliant flash of light leapt from candle to candle until the entire circle was blazing. The flames shot high in the air like torches, then sent fiery tendrils above her, creating a glowing sphere around them. She felt a strange tightness, and her ears popped. The sphere shimmered for a few seconds, then the flames sank to ground level, dimming to a soft ethereal glow.

"Wow! It's like magic!" she exclaimed.

Simon shook his head. "It's God's love. That's stronger than any magic. As long as it flashes like that you know you've set the circle. If it doesn't, you redo the invocation."

"How do I get outside the circle without breaking it?"

"Ah, good question," Simon replied. "You walk up to the candles, clear your mind, and visualize yourself walking through the barrier without disturbing it."

Huh? "But what if I kick over a candle?" she said.

"That would be bad. Here, I'll show you."

Simon rose, walked to the circle's boundary, murmured something under his breath, and stepped over the candles.

"Okay. So how do you get back in?"

"You have to give me permission to enter." Before she could ask how, he pointed at the booklet. "Page five, last paragraph."

Riley found the passage and read, "If you mean no harm, then pass within."

Simon stepped across the candles and returned to his place on the sleeping bag.

"And if you were a bad guy . . ."

"The circle would not let me in."

"How does it know who's a bad guy?"

He shrugged. "It's a lot like a Holy Water ward. Evil things stay away."

Sounds really iffy to me. But if Simon and Beck believe in this circle thing, there must be something to it.

"What if I accidentally break it?"

"Then you start all over, right after you set the candles. Oh, and every night you have to move the candles away from the original circle of Holy Water. Most folks make it a bit smaller."

So many things to remember. "What if it rains?" she quizzed.

"Rain won't break the circle, neither will wind, for that matter, though you will feel it. What's important is that the circle remains intact and that you state its purpose clearly." He sat on the sleeping bag, popping his knuckles one by one, clearly pleased with himself. "Now we wait until sunrise."

"That was a lot more work than I realized," she said, plopping down next to him. This would have been way hard if he hadn't been here.

"Once you've done it a few times it's no big deal. It's harder when you're on your own."

She looked over at him. "How did you learn all this?"

"I come from a big family. Someone's always dying, so my uncle taught me how to do the invocation. He's a priest."

A big family. What would that be like? There'd only been her. Her mom had always joked that after you achieved perfection, why try again? Riley had always figured there was something more to it.

"I'm an only," she said, then grimaced. He knew that.

Simon didn't act like she'd said something stupid. "I wanted to be sometimes. I have four sisters and three brothers."

"What's it like with that many bodies in one house?"

"Like living in a beehive. We had a schedule posted on the two bathrooms. My sisters were the worst."

Riley chuckled, wondering if that was true. His hair looked too good for a quick shampoo and blow-dry. She rearranged her coat so it would cover her legs. Luckily there was no wind. Or rain. Wouldn't hurt the candles but it would be way ugly for the person stuck in the circle. In the distance a pale haze hung over the city. She could see the skyscrapers in downtown Atlanta, at least the few still lit at night. The high-pitched whine of the MARTA train heading east echoed around them.

She waited for Simon to say something. He just stared out into nothingness. It was going to be long night if he wasn't going to talk.

"How old are you?" she asked, desperate to avoid the silence.

"Just turned twenty. You?"

"Seventeen."

"You're a little younger than my sister Amy. She got married last summer." He paused and gave her a quizzical look. "So what are you going to do now that you're on your own?"

On my own. "Don't know. There's only my mom's sister left. She lives in Fargo."

"You could continue your apprenticeship there."

"She wouldn't go for that. She blames my dad for Mom's death, like he personally planted the cancer in her or something. Nasty woman. I can't live with her. No way."

"Then who will you stay with?" Simon prodded.

"I don't know. There is no one else."

"Well, I'm sure Beck will help as best he can."

THE DEMON TRAPPER'S DAUGHTER   89

There was the sound of footsteps. The man approaching them was as short as he was wide. His trench coat almost reached the ground, and he wore a fedora.

"Is he a necro?" Riley whispered.

"I'd say it's a good bet," Simon replied. "Be on your guard. They can be tricky."

The man stopped just outside the circle of candles and tipped his hat.

"Good evening to you," he said.

"Good evening," Simon replied. He was polite to everyone, even someone who sold corpses for a living.

"My name is Mortimer Alexander and I am a licensed summoner," the newcomer announced proudly.

"Darn. I'd hoped you were the pizza delivery guy," Riley quipped.

A skiff of a smile crossed the man's face. "No such luck." He sobered instantly. "First, I wish to offer my sincere condolences for your recent loss."

"Ah, thanks."

"However, now is the time to be practical. Your loved one resides in a better place," the necromancer continued, vaguely waving toward the sky. "His earthly shell, however, can be put to use for a better society." He dug in his pocket and consulted a piece of paper. "I see that Mr. Blackthorne would occasionally donate to charity. Perhaps we can reach an arrangement where I will contribute a sum in his name and in trade he will act as a paid domestic for a specified period of time."

"Ah, well," Riley began. Why had she been warned against these guys? This one sounded so reasonable. Her dad was always for the underdog. Wouldn't he want to help out even now?

"Riley?" When she didn't respond, Simon joggled her elbow. Then he shook it. "Riley!"

"What?" she snapped.

"He's using persuasion magic. They'll do anything to get to your father."

"Got it," she said. Simon relaxed and his hand retreated. She wished he'd left it there.

The necro shuffled papers. "I understand your sacrifice and am prepared to make monthly payments into an account to cover the . . . inconvenience of having your loved one exhumed. At the end of a year, we agree to inhume him in a dignified ceremony and pay all expenses required to do so."

Riley remembered the Deader on the street toting packages for the rich lady. What if that had been her dad? She shuddered.

"No way," she said, crossing her hands over her chest in defiance.

"Ah, I see that you have some reservations," the necromancer continued. "That is expected. It is a big step and—"

"Not happening. Now go away."

"Please," Simon added. She wondered if he was that nice to the demons when he trapped them.

Mortimer looked crestfallen. "I understand. You should be aware that I'm the most ethical of the summoners you'll meet before the full moon. It earns me no end of grief from the others, but I feel honesty is important." He placed a business card at the edge of the burning circle. "In case you wish to contact me."

"Not likely," Riley replied.

"I understand. Thank you for your time. Again, my sincere condolences."

Then he was gone, walking slowly up the path while consulting his pile of papers. When he passed the cemetery office, he cut west toward the parking lot.

Riley sighed in relief. "Well, that's over."

Simon shook his head. "Like he said, he's the first of many."

"Why?" she asked, surprised.

"Rich folks like to collect unique things. In this case, it'd be a famous master trapper as their servant. No one else would have one, so that would make him very special."

Damn. "No wonder people have the corpses cut up."

Simon shot her a horrified look. "No! What you did was right. Mutilation is unholy," he retorted, then appeared chagrined at his outburst. "Sorry, it's a hot button for me."

"Really?" she jested.

"Yeah," he admitted. "At least you've only got twelve more nights of this."

Riley rolled her eyes at the thought. Twelve loooong nights filled with lying necromancers, a cold butt, and no sleep.

Thanks a bunch, Dad.

ELEVEN

"Whatcha want?" the bartender asked, his tattooed bicep announcing to the world he was "One of The Few. The Proud."

A Marine. Beck had never really liked the *Semper Fi* crowd, but at least he knew how they'd act.

"Shiner Bock," he replied. "Start a tab."

"Need to see some ID."

Beck frowned. "I'm legal."

"Don't doubt it, but it's the law now," the man replied. "Gotta card everyone, even if they come in here using a goddamn walker."

Beck fished out his driver's license and tossed it to the bartender. The guy gave it a quick look and handed it back. "You look older. I'd have figured you for thirty."

"Ya can blame the Army for that."

"Where'd you serve?"

"Afghanistan."

"Shit," the man replied, grinning now. "No charge for the first beer. I was over there, too."

The bartender placed a bottle of Shiner Bock on the bar. He reached for a glass, then changed his mind.

"Good call," Beck muttered. He raised the beer in the air. "To those who didn't make it home." He took a swig and then raised the bottle again. "And to Paul Blackthorne. Rest in peace." Then he downed half of it in one long gulp to ease the ache.

"That the guy who died down in Five Points?" the bartender asked.

"Yeah. He was good people." *Good people always die sooner than the assholes.*

"You a trapper?" the man asked, eyeing him.

No reason to deny it. "Yeah."

"I don't hold much with trappers."

"I'm not fond of jarheads, so we're even," Beck replied.

The bartender snorted. He picked up a glass of Scotch from the back bar and raised it high. "To those who made it home."

"Amen," Beck said, raising the bottle again, then downed the rest.

"No trouble, you hear?"

"None planned. Just wanna get drunk, maybe get laid. In that order."

"Sounds good," the bartender replied. "You want another?"

"Hell, yes."

This was his second bar. Beck had started the evening at the Six Feet Under Pub & Fish House, the trappers' favorite watering hole. He'd stayed there for a couple of drinks to honor Paul, as was custom, then decided he didn't want be there anymore. Didn't want to be around if anyone accused him of not doing right by his friend. Not that any of them had. They all knew better, but that didn't mean they weren't thinking it. He was, so why wouldn't they be doing the same?

This bar wasn't one of his usual haunts but they had his favorite beer. By the time he was on his sixth bottle, there were two voices competing for his attention: Paul's was nagging about how he should be working, not drinking. How he had responsibilities now, at least when it came to Riley.

Responsibility wasn't as strong a message as the anorexic redhead sitting next him, talking dirty. Real dirty. It was firing him up, and that he didn't mind. It kept him from thinking about anything that hurt deep down.

"Come on, let's get out of here. Take me to your place," she urged, moving her hand a bit closer to where it counted. Her hair was a mix of brassy colors, and her eyes glassy from too much booze. Not that he cared.

Beck's Rule Number One: he didn't take any girl to his place. At least not one like this. If she was real fussy, they'd get a room at one of the cheap hotels. If not, his truck did just fine.

"So what's yer name?" he asked, feeling he should know something about her before he screwed her.

"Does it matter?" she said, laughing.

"Yeah." *Sorta.*

"Jamie."

"Whatcha do for a livin'?"

"Nothing much." She grinned as if that wasn't a big deal. "I meet nice guys who buy me drinks."

"And . . ."

"Then we go somewhere and fuck."

Beck's hackles rose. "Ya put out for drinks," he said flatly.

She giggled. "Don't we all?"

It was the wrong answer. This could have been Sadie a couple of decades earlier, working some guy for drinks and a night in the sack. Beck had been the product of one of those nights. No way he could go with this one now, not without conjuring up a lot of really bad shit.

He lurched off the bar stool, eager to be away from her. Too many memories were floating through his head, the kind that made him want to hit something or someone.

"What's wrong?" she asked, tugging on his arm. It was the injured one, and the pain cleared his mind.

"The damned whole thing," he growled. He threw money on the bar to cover their tab and headed for the door. The girl called out to him but he ignored her. As he reached the exit, he turned, hoping she wasn't following him.

It wasn't a problem. She was already pawing another guy, one who didn't look like he was going to say no.

✥

On a scale of one to ten Beck knew he was about a seven when it came to being drunk. Decent buzz, but not too loaded. He'd learned how to handle the booze in the Army. You wanted to be intoxicated enough to feel good, but not too trashed to show up for roll call.

Except right now the feel-good thing wasn't working out so well, not with that flashback to the bitch everyone else called his mother. He slammed the truck door and turned the key. The radio blared. He turned it off. A moment before he put the truck in gear he spied an Atlanta cop sitting at the corner in his patrol car, scoping the street.

"Shit." He didn't dare drive, not in his condition. The pigs came down hard on drunk driving: It was a lucrative bust, what with that new law. Not only did they toss you in jail but they took your vehicle and sold it to pay the towing and court costs. A thousand-dollar fine and a five-thousand-dollar truck? Somehow the bankrupt city never bothered to pay you the difference.

A few years ago he would have risked it, wouldn't have given a damn, but now he had Riley to worry about.

Beck groaned. "Dammit, how'd I get into this mess?"

By not saving Paul. It all came down to that. Now Riley was his responsibility, at least until she was eighteen or one of her family stepped up and took charge of her. Like he knew anything about playing big brother to some girl.

Beck pulled himself out of the truck, locked the door, and headed for the nearest Stop 'n' Rob on foot. Once there he scoured the aisles, steering clear of the old guys buying cigarettes. He didn't know how they afforded them, not at a hundred a carton. That had made it easy for him to kick the habit.

He needed to get back in the game tonight, but trapping while buzzed was a sure ticket to joining Paul in the dirt. He grabbed a six-pack of energy drinks and a large bag of peanuts—salty ones. The peanuts would make him thirsty, and all the fluid he'd have to chug would dilute the booze.

"Pack of rubbers," he said to the clerk. "Extra large." Why they kept them behind the counter he had no idea.

The clerk, a young black woman, gave him the once-over. He smiled in return. Though some thought it sacrilegious, the condoms were for Holy Water. He used them in places where the glass spheres weren't welcome. Like swimming pools and shopping malls. Of course, he wasn't going to tell the clerk that and ruin her daydream.

Once he was in his truck he started in on the food, alternating energy drinks and peanuts. He could remember when the drinks came in aluminum cans. Now they used thin plastic that cracked too easily, just one of the reasons he usually put the stuff in an empty whiskey bottle.

As he drank, the ache under his breastbone kicked in again. He'd like to believe it was sore muscles, but it wasn't. It was the same feeling he had when his granddaddy died. Every time he lost someone he cared for a bit more of him went with them. In time, there wouldn't be much of him left.

Now that Paul was dead he'd have to trap every night to keep both him and Riley in good shape, at least until her aunt came for her. From what Paul had said, the woman was like a buzz saw. Still, she was a relation and that was important.

"No more playin' pool," he said, shaking his head. No more doing what other guys his age liked to do. He'd lost his childhood to Sadie's drinking, and now he was going to lose even more of his life to taking care of Paul's kid. He twisted off the top of another bottle and took a long swig, followed by a handful of nuts. His stomach rumbled, complaining about the abuse.

By the time the first three bottles of energy drink were gone, he'd thought out a plan. It was a simple one: Find the fucking demon who'd killed his friend and waste the thing. It was an insane plan, but Beck didn't care.

"I'm gonna carve ya up, ya bastard. Send a message to Hell."

To do that he'd have to work the lower ranks of demons until one of them squealed on the Five, gave him an idea where to find it. He knew

Paul wouldn't want him jonesing for revenge, but he didn't care. Beck wanted payback.

And not just for the kid.

⁜

In a few short hours Riley knew one thing for sure—she needed earplugs. From what she could tell each necro had a different sales pitch, like infomercials. As predicted, Mortimer was the nicest. The next four had grown increasingly malicious. All but Mortimer tried to breach the circle and went away with scorched shoes and a bad attitude.

By the final visitor she was so bitchy, so sleep deprived, she'd told him off even before he'd opened his mouth. That had earned her a profanity-laced rant that would have impressed a rapper. Simon surged to his feet and told the guy to blow off, without using curse words. To her surprise, the necro had done just that.

After his rare flash of anger, her companion went to sleep, curled up in a sleeping bag, his hand thrown over his face like a cat. Every now and then he murmured to himself, though she couldn't make out the words.

Much to Riley's annoyance, she had to wake him a few hours later. It was either that or she'd wet herself.

"I'll stay awake until you return," he said, still half asleep. "Be careful."

She took a deep breath and did exactly as he'd said, wincing as she stepped over the glowing line. Nothing happened but a brief flicker and that strange popping sound in her ears, like she'd crossed some unseen barrier. Riley trudged off to the cemetery office. It was spooky. The Victorians were big into symbols, like weeping angels and obelisks to represent resurrection and eternal life. That only added to the creep factor. It was really dark with no moon. The faint rustle of leaves made her turn around more than once. All that was needed was a thick fog and a baying wolf and it'd be the stuff of slasher films.

After she returned and Simon allowed her entrance, he slipped around the rear of the mausoleum for a quick pee.

Guys have it so easy.

When he returned he began to talk again. "Be careful when you're here on your own. Necromancers can pretend to be cemetery employees, cops, you name it. They try to con you into breaking the circle or inviting them inside. Not everyone in the cemetery is after your dad's body. But I've heard tales, you know?"

She stifled the shiver. His warnings delivered, Simon curled up and fell asleep. She wished she could. Instead, Riley snuggled in the sleeping bag and stared up at the night sky. A hunting owl winged by a few times, then perched in a nearby tree to announce his territory. She watched him for a long time. He seemed to be doing the same of her.

When a mouse skittered across the path, he was all business. With an expert glide and lethal talons, he collected his startled meal.

Her back began to cramp, so she rose and walked to her mom's grave. The flowers they'd left a couple of weeks ago were withered now, victims of the night frosts. Riley knelt and brushed away the dried leaves that covered the plain granite headstone. It was nearly three years since Miriam Henley Blackthorne had left them. There wasn't a day she'd not been missed. Riley moved to her dad's grave, the smell of fresh earth filling the air around her. The flowers on top of the mounded earth were tipped with a thin layer of frost.

Mom was probably waiting for him on the other side. Riley crinkled up her face. That won't be a good meeting. As her mother lay dying, she'd made her dad promise to keep Riley safe. Now their daughter was on her own.

Yeah, Mom is going to be severely pissed.

She touched the cold dirt, thinking of her father lying underneath it.

They're together now. It didn't help. They were together and she was all alone. No one left to laugh at her jokes, hold her. Love her.

A bottomless pit opened in front of her, and a choked sob escaped her throat, then another as warm tears coursed down her cheeks. She bent almost double, crying for herself more than her parents.

Someone touched her and she jumped. It was Simon. He didn't say a word, but opened his arms to her. She fell into them and continued to weep. He murmured comforting words, but she didn't understand them. What mattered most was that he was holding her. When she could no longer offer up any tears, she pulled away from him and blew her nose, embarrassed she'd lost it in front of him.

"Sorry . . . I . . ."

"They know you love them and that you miss them. That's what's important."

"I don't know what I'm going to do," she admitted.

"You'll find your way. I know you will."

Simon took her hand and led her to the sleeping bags. He tucked her in. He climbed into his own bag and wiggle-wormed over until their sides touched. Pulling his arm out, he had her rest her head on his shoulder. She snuggled in, grateful for his kindness.

"Your arm is going to freeze off," she said in between sniffles.

"You're right." He took one of the blankets, covered himself, and settled back in place. She snuggled close, feeling warm and secure for the first time since her father's death. That she could feel that way said a lot about Simon.

"Thanks. You're . . . really sweet."

"It's easy with someone like you. Now get some sleep. Dawn is in a few hours," he whispered.

Knowing he was there to watch over her, Riley drifted into an uneasy dream filled with leering necros, thieving Magpies, and dark laughter.

Simon's wristwatch beeped and he sat up and stretched.

"Good morning," he said.

Riley blinked her eyes open, then wiped the sleep out of them. When she sat up, her hair moved weird. She ran a hand through it. To her relief there were no icicles.

Sleeping outside sucks.

"It'll get easier each night," Simon said. "Just be sure you don't sleepwalk."

He made another trip around the back of the mausoleum to water the grass.

So unfair.

When he returned he sat Indian style, fingered his rosary beads, and began to pray. Definitely an NCB—a Nice Catholic Boy, as her mom called them. Polite and so not a sleaze. No wonder her dad liked him.

After a few minutes of prayer he tucked the rosary away.

"Good morning," he said again, more cheerfully this time.

"Yeah, right . . . morning," she said, struggling into a sitting position.

"You usually this grouchy?" he asked, as if taking notes for future reference.

"I've earned the right. My butt hurts, I'm tired, I'm cold, and I want to go home. This has been one of the worst nights of my life."

"Oh." There was hurt in his voice.

Riley slapped her forehead. "Sorry! That was dumb. Thanks for staying with me tonight. I would have been freaked on my own."

Simon recovered instantly, smiling at her like she hadn't been a completely ungrateful dork. "Glad I could help."

Can this guy be for real? If he was, he had to have a girlfriend with six more waiting in line.

"Did you get any sleep?" he asked.

"A little. I had weird dreams about demons who acted like angels. Confusing." She thought for a moment. "Have you ever seen them . . . angels I mean?"

"One or two. They only reveal themselves when they want to." He sounded disappointed.

"Dad said there's this glowy sort of light around them, but to me they look like everyday people."

"Maybe someday we'll see them clearly," Simon replied wistfully. "I'd like that."

A voice called out. It was right before dawn, so it should be the cemetery guy. At least she hoped it was.

A man walked up to the line of candles and gave a toothy smile.

"Good morning. My name's Rod. I'm here for the day shift. You Miss Blackthorne?"

"Uh-huh."

"Glad to meet you. Don't worry, I've been doing this for years. No body's been stolen on my watch."

"That's good to hear." *Really good to hear.*

The volunteer waited until Simon issued the invitation, then he stepped over the candles. They flickered and returned to normal.

Riley let out a sigh of relief.

The newcomer chucked off his coat, revealing a heavy sweatshirt. He set up a camp chair and dropped a bag marked "Vigil Supplies" next to it.

"Those are for tonight when you reset the circle."

"Thanks," she said. She hadn't even thought that far.

Out of his backpack came a newspaper opened to the sudoku page, followed by a pencil and a big green thermos.

Thermos equals hot chocolate. She made a note to bring one.

While he was settling in, Riley rolled up the sleeping bags as her companion folded the blanket. By the time she was ready to leave the volunteer was already in his chair, paper on his lap.

"So who showed up last night?" he asked cheerfully.

"One guy named Mortimer and some others who didn't say who they were. They swore at me a lot."

The volunteer broke out in a smile. "Figured Mort would stop by. Best of a bad lot."

"So I noticed."

"Just make sure you're here before sundown. If there's an emergency, call the office and let them know."

"Got it."

Riley gingerly crossed the circle, ears popping once again. She doubted she'd ever get used to that. After she'd stashed the sleeping bags and blanket in the mausoleum, she locked the door. Out of habit she gave them a firm rattle to make sure they were secure.

Simon fell in step with her as she headed for the parking lot.

"Congratulations. You've survived your first night." He sounded genuinely proud of her.

"Yeah, I did." Then it dawned on her. "Do you have wheels?"

A nod. "Beck asked me to drop you at home. Said he'd be too tired this morning to do it."

Tired? No way. He'll be hung over. You can bet on that.

In a few short minutes she was headed toward her apartment in a car with a St. Christopher's medal hanging from the rearview mirror and a statue of St. Jude on the dash. After she gave him directions, he went quiet. She was getting accustomed to her escort's lengthy silences, so it didn't trouble her.

It was only when he pulled into a parking lot near the front of the apartment building that he spoke up. "Looks like an old hotel."

"It was. They converted it to apartments a few years back. It's nothing fancy."

"At least it's a home," he said. "If you need help tonight, call Beck."

That sounded like he was happy to be rid of her. "Tired of me already?" she asked, hurt.

"Oh, no, I'm sorry," he said, embarrassed. "That came out wrong. I have to trap with Master Harper tonight, so Beck said he'd be able to help you."

Backwoods Boy? No way. "I'll be okay on my own. Thanks for showing me what to do."

She pulled herself out of the car. It took a lot of effort. Sleeping on the ground was for little kids.

Simon rolled down the window. "Just don't listen to the necros. They're as bad as the demons."

She put her hand on his arm. "Thanks for everything. I mean it."

"No problem."

Right before he turned onto the street, he gave a wave. She returned it.

What a cool guy.

Riley forced herself across the parking lot and up the stairs. She could still remember when they'd moved into the apartment. It'd been a blazing hot Atlanta day. After they'd finished, they'd gone for ice cream. Her dad had bought her a sundae and laughed when some of it had ended up on her nose.

By the time Riley reached her floor, her hand was shaking, making the keys rattle. For one last time she could believe that everything was alright. Her dad would be sitting on the couch, organizing his paperwork, a cup of coffee in his hand. He'd look up and smile at her when she came in. He'd make room on the couch and ask how her day went. He always did that. Always made time for her. Always loved her.

The door swung open on rusty hinges. The couch was empty. She could hear the soft *plink, plink* of water dripping into the oatmeal pan from yesterday's breakfast, the faint hum of the refrigerator. A fluff of Max fur sat underneath the kitchen table. The light on the phone answering machine was blinking frantically. Probably necromancers too lazy to make the trek to the graveyard.

Her dad had said he was lucky that he had her to come home to, how some folks had no one.

Like me.

Riley swung the door closed and methodically engaged all the locks, shutting out the world that had made her an orphan.

"It's not fair!" she hissed, slamming her fist into the wood. "Why both of them? You took Mom. Wasn't that enough?"

No answer. No cosmic "Sorry about that." Just emptiness. The tears came again and she let them fall.

When she'd cried herself out and blown her nose, Riley took a marker and found the date of the full moon on the calendar. She circled it and marked it with a big *D*. That would be the day her dad was truly free.

I won't let them get you. I swear it.

TWELVE

Beck peeled open his eyes and did a slow scan of the terrain. The parking lot was deserted, unless you counted a pair of rusty shopping carts and a pile of old tires. Quiet, open space. That was the way he liked it. Not that a trapper could park anywhere else since the pair of demons in the truck bed limited his choices.

Morning wasn't his favorite time, especially when Beck's head felt like it was being torn apart by rabid weasels. Energy drinks and booze were a toxic combination, at least for him. Once he'd sobered up enough to trap he'd gone after the first Three he could find. It hadn't been hard, as the thing was snuffling around the dumpster behind a butcher shop. Too busy scoring cast-off bits of fat and rancid beef to realize it had a trapper closing in, the thing was bagged by Beck without a hitch. But it wouldn't squeal on the Five that had killed Paul. Pissed, Beck kept hunting until he found another Three. Same deal—lots of swearing, lots of threats to tear him apart, but no information.

"Honor among demons," he grumbled. "That's so wrong." At least the Threes didn't offer boons for their freedom. That would have been hard to pass up if the boon was how to find Paul's killer.

Groaning at his thumping head he flipped the radio off, poured three more aspirin into his palm, and gulped them down with some water. The previous dose hadn't done a thing and he figured these wouldn't either.

Sleep. That's what he needed, but that was going to be tough with all the caffeine skulking in his body. If he was lucky he'd flame out sometime this afternoon. If not, it could easily be tomorrow.

His phone rang and he dug it out of his jacket pocket.

"Beck."

"Simon. She's home safe."

He sighed in relief. "Thanks, man, I owe ya."

"I didn't mind it a bit."

Beck flipped the phone closed and frowned. "Bet ya didn't."

He wasn't quite sure what he thought of Simon Adler. Just because he was religious didn't mean he might not hit on Riley. Any guy would. She was real pretty. No ignoring that fact.

"If things were different, I might have asked her out myself."

But not now.

Beck settled back against the seat and closed his eyes, if nothing more than to keep the increasing sunlight out of them. In the distance he heard a garbage truck pick up one of those big dumpsters and bang the hell out it. After a long yawn, he did the perimeter scan again. This time the lot wasn't empty.

"Dudes at ten o'clock," he said, shifting his position. He moved his steel pipe closer to him on the seat and then did the same with his SIG 9mm. The pipe was the first resort, the gun the very last.

He was in a part of town where people came in two kinds—predator and prey. He knew where he stood, but some of the locals might not have gotten the memo. Like the three gangbangers who were sauntering toward the truck. "Urban youth," as Paul called them. They could be poster kids for multiethnic Atlanta—one white, one black, and one brown.

All stupid. He could guess that much from their swaggers. They were wearing the latest fashion, their jeans pulled down over their high-tops with long red laces woven up the leg and tied below the knee. The color of the laces was supposed to tell you what gang they belonged to. Beck didn't care. They were all losers to him.

They started laughing among themselves and pointing in his direction. Probably figured he was a drunk, snoozing off the buzz. They could score some cash, a truck, and give him a good ass kicking just for fun.

"Got no sense," he said, shaking his head.

When they were within twenty feet, he hopped out of the truck, leaving the steel pipe on the seat just behind him. If he was lucky he wouldn't have to go all medieval on these guys.

"Mornin'!" he called.

One of them flipped him off. Beck's fingers curved around the pipe. He adjusted his grip, keeping it hidden behind the door.

"Now that's not polite. Didn't yer momma teach ya manners?"

"What you doin' here, asshole?" the kid demanded. He pulled a knife and the others followed his lead.

"Waitin' for breakfast. Ya got some?"

The kid sneered. "We ain't no fuckin' McDonald's." They began to fan out, getting into position, watching for a chance to jump him.

"Breakfast isn't for me, dumbass. It's for them." Beck hammered on the side of the truck with his fist. "Chow time, guys!"

The demons erupted into snarls as they thrashed around in their steel bags. The noise was impressive in the still morning air. One reared up just high enough for the losers to see him, claws and all.

"Oh, shit, man, those are—"

"Demons," Beck said. "And boy, are they hungry. Can y'all step a little closer, make it nice 'n' easy for 'em?" he asked, all serious.

The trio took off in a panicked retreat. One fell, rolled, and was back up on his feet without taking a breath. If it had been an Olympic event, Beck would have given him a 9.8 or a 9.9, but the kid lost points for dropping his weapon.

He peered down at the demons. "Sorry, guys. Looks like yer breakfast made a run for it."

More snarling. The fiends were cursing again.

Beck strolled up to where the switchblade rested on the concrete. He picked it up.

"Sweeeet," he said, grinning. "And it's all mine."

⬍

Close to nine in the morning Beck wearily climbed the stairs to Fireman Jack's office in the old fire station. The demon trafficker was behind his desk, a steaming mug of coffee in front of him. His barber-pole suspenders made a nice contrast to the black chamois shirt and blue jeans. A thick stack of papers sat in front him. When he wasn't buying demons, he wore his lawyer hat and handled the Guild's legal work.

"Beck!" he called out. "How you doing?"

"Jack." He slumped in the closest chair and rubbed his eyes in exhaustion.

"You look like crap," his host observed.

"Feel like it. Been up too long, I think."

"Coffee?"

"God, no more caffeine." He leaned back in the chair and it creaked in protest.

Jack reached into the mini fridge near his desk, then offered Beck a cold bottle of water.

"Thanks. Maybe that'll help." Beck drained half of it without pausing for breath.

"What have you got for me this fine morning?"

"Two Gastros."

"Two? You've been a busy boy," Jack said, smiling. "Who are you trapping with now?"

"No one."

"You took those down on your own?" Jack asked, surprised.

"Yeah. I know, it wasn't smart. Don't wanna split the money with another trapper. Until Paul's life insurance comes in, his kid's gonna need cash to live on."

Jack rose, opened his safe, and counted out the money. He placed it in front of Beck, who stashed it away in his jeans pocket. After signing the paperwork, he pushed it across to Jack to finalize the deal.

"Who'll be her new master?" Jack asked, settling back into his chair.

"I'm hopin' it's Stewart," Beck said, tucking away his copy of the paperwork. "He'd be good for her. He doesn't yell at everythin' that moves, not like Harper."

"I'd love to find out what idiot put a burr up Harper's ass all those years ago. I'd personally feed the fool to the first demon I saw."

"Ya'd have to stand in line," Beck said.

"How's Riley doing?"

Beck shook his head. "Lost. Ya can see it in her eyes. She's tryin' to be tough, but it's killin' her."

"Can't imagine what it's like losing both your parents."

"Sucks, that's what it's like."

Before Jack could reply, Beck's phone erupted in music. He flipped it open without looking at the Caller ID. "Yeah?"

"Oh, my God, they're going to dig him up!"

"Huh? Riley?" he asked. "What's wrong?"

"One of the debt guys was here and he said they're going to take Dad and sell him."

It took a moment for Beck to realize what she was saying. "What debt guy?"

"The one for Mom's medical bills. Consolidated Debt Collectors. He was really mean."

Beck's anger ignited. The kid had just buried her only surviving parent, and some parasite was harassing her about money.

"Did ya sign anythin'?" he demanded.

"Of course not!" she retorted. "I'm not stupid."

"Okay, calm down. I'll ask Jack what we should do."

"Fireman Jack?"

"Yeah, he's the Guild's lawyer. Just hold on." He muted the phone and laid out the situation. Jack listened without interruption, penciling notes on a legal pad, his brow furrowed. Once Beck was finished he leaned forward and tented his fingers.

"First thing, she's a minor, so she's not responsible for any of her parents' debts. Don't let them guilt her into paying a cent."

"That's good, but what about diggin' him up? Can they do that?" Beck pressed.

"If Paul's loan agreement had that option, they can. They just need to present the proper paperwork to the cemetery and he's theirs."

Beck shook his head. "I can't imagine he'd go for somethin' like that."

"Probably figured he was going to be in too many pieces for a necromancer to mess with. Unfortunately, that's not the case."

"So what do we do?" Beck asked.

"I'll request a copy of the contract from the debt company and see if they left us any wiggle room. If not, Paul could be out of the ground in short order and his daughter won't see a penny of that money."

"That's the best ya can do?" He got a curt nod in response. "No wonder everybody hates lawyers."

"Tell me about it."

Beck relayed the news to Riley. He could imagine her pacing around the dinky apartment, scared she'd lose her dad. Again.

"Sorry, I kinda freaked," she admitted. "I just got to sleep and he scared me."

Beck knew how much it took her to admit that, at least to him.

That bastard's lucky I wasn't there.

"Don't worry, yer daddy stays in the ground no matter what." Brave words that he might not be able to back up, but she needed some hope right now.

He heard a weak "Thanks" and then she hung up.

"Just keeps gettin' worse," he grumbled, and dropped his phone into a pocket.

"If they have the legal right to reanimate him, what are you going to do?" Jack asked.

"Too god-awful to think about."

Their eyes met. "If you really want to keep Paul from being sold, it may come to that. They won't touch him if he's not whole."

Beck swallowed, his stomach executing a warning lurch. "Just do what ya can. Send me the bill. I don't care what it costs."

"It's Guild business, so I'll bill them."

Beck heaved a long sigh of relief. "Thanks."

"Let's get those demons unloaded. Then you go get some sleep. I do not want to attend another friend's funeral anytime soon, you got that?"

"Yeah, I hear ya."

THIRTEEN

Peter's voice rose in indignation. "You're, like, kidding me, right? They want to *sell* your father's corpse?"

"Yeah, that's the plan," Riley said, cradling her phone against her shoulder as she waited for her computer to boot up. "The guy said Dad was a fung . . . a something asset."

"Fungible," Peter corrected. "It means interchangeable. In this case he'll act as payment against the money you owe them."

"Whatever. Beck talked to the Guild's lawyer. He's going to try to stop them."

"God, Riley, that sucks."

"Welcome to my new life. One long moment of suckage."

There was an awkward pause. "What's it like now?"

Riley thought a moment before answering. "Too quiet. I always knew Dad would be home every morning, so the quiet didn't bother me. Now it's . . . forever."

"Not forever," Peter said. "Maybe you could get a roommate or something."

"How many people want to live with someone who stores demons in their kitchen cupboard?"

"Good point." More silence. "So what are you working on?" he asked, sounding eager to change the subject.

"My computer is getting weird again, so I thought I better do a backup."

"Weird how?"

"It locks up all the time and I lose stuff."

"Yeah, definite backup time. I'll see if I can get over there this weekend and work on it for you."

You'll come here? Peter had never been to the apartment. *What would he think of it?*

"Will the warden let you loose?" she asked.

A tortured sigh came through the phone. "I don't know. She's just not that into you, Riley."

"I noticed. Why doesn't your mom like me?"

"Because I do."

Riley blinked a couple of times. "Wow, that's radical."

"Just the truth. All of us are on short leashes after what happened to Matt."

Peter's oldest brother—the one who'd mixed a fatal combo of alcohol and automobile. His girlfriend had supplied the brew and walked away from the crash with a few cuts. Pete's mom never forgave her.

"But we're just friends, not like Matt and Sarah."

"She doesn't see the difference. In her mind any girl is a threat to her sons. It's how she copes."

"Sorry, Peter. That has to be brutal."

"It is. But don't worry, I'll find a way to get over to see you."

"Cool." *Something to look forward to.* Maybe she'd make pizza.

Riley spied the yellow computer disk near the keyboard. Apparently her dad had dropped it off before he went trapping. *Before he . . .*

She shoved that thought away, pushing it behind that opaque curtain. It was that or she'd be blubbing tears onto the keyboard. She pushed the disk into the slot, and its contents appeared on her monitor. There was only one file, and it was labeled "Research."

"Password? What's this?" she mumbled.

"Riley?" Peter asked. "Talk to me. What's going on?"

"This is weird. Dad never locked any of his files. I mean, who would want to read about the Battle of Shiloh?"

"So what's his password?" Peter prompted.

Riley tried a couple—her name, her mom's. Nothing happened.

"No clue. Damn, now he's got me wondering what's on this thing."

"Bring it to school. I'll hack it for you. I'll need your birthdates, common stuff like that. People use those rather than something harder."

"Will do." She popped out the yellow disk, dug in a shoebox next to the computer, and inserted a blue one. That one wasn't password locked. The computer whirled and the backup commenced.

Riley noted the time on the monitor. "Gotta go. It's going to take a while to pack for the cemetery. I need *much* warmer clothes." Tonight there would be no Nice Catholic Boy to snuggle up next to. *Drat.*

"Watch out for the big, bad necromancers," Peter said, jokingly.

"I will." *I'll ignore them and they'll all go away.*

Rather than drive the car up to the mausoleum, Riley parked in the lot and proceeded to load herself up like a burro. As she hiked her breath puffed out in the chilly air. The exercise felt good, but it reminded her that she was still sore from playing tag with library demons.

The cemetery guy from this morning was gone, replaced by a woman sitting in a chaise longue. She was wearing a heavy black dress that came to her ankles and pair of orthopedic shoes with really thick soles. On top was a thick black coat. Her bright silver hair pegged her at about seventy, maybe older.

"Hello!" the volunteer called out brightly.

What is it with these people? Do they, like, give them happy pills or something?

"I'm Martha, by the way," the woman explained. Before Riley could reply, the lady rattled on. "It might rain. Did you bring an umbrella?"

Riley waved at the pile at her side. "It's in there somewhere, I think."

"Good. You should get some plastic tarps. They work great for keeping you dry, and you won't have to sit on the wet ground."

"Thanks," Riley said, meaning it.

The old woman's eyes twinkled. "You learn a few tricks over the years. If the weather really gets bad, just make the circle bigger and sit vigil inside the mausoleum."

Riley made a note of that one. "Do you really enjoy doing this?"

"Yes, I do! I'm in the fresh air and I help people," Martha replied. "I love this old cemetery. No better place in this world."

Riley decided not to argue that point.

Martha drew herself up. "If you mean no harm, then pass within."

Riley cautiously lifted her gear over the candles and walked inside.

"You need help setting up the new circle?" the volunteer asked.

Riley almost said yes but changed her mind. She'd have to do this on her own eventually. "I'll be okay."

"Then have a safe night, dear." The woman marched up the path like she was half her age, with a folded chair in one hand and a paisley knitting bag in the other.

"Okay," Riley muttered. Now it was up to her. "This is doable," she said, although it felt like there were a swarm of monarch butterflies in her stomach trying to migrate in all directions at once. "How hard can it be? I lay out the circle, do the invocation, and I'm good."

It sounded too easy.

Riley dug through the canvas bag marked "Vigil Supplies."

"How many candles do I need?" She did a quick count of the ones currently in place and added a few more just in case. After a nervous glance at the booklet she began the ritual. Holy Water in one direction, then the other. She carefully set a new line of candles on top of the moistened ground, just inside the existing circle, trying hard to keep the exact distance between them. Carrying the pamphlet and the fireplace lighter she'd borrowed from Mrs. Litinsky, she began igniting the candles while saying the Lord's Prayer in English. She added, "Keep us safe, please," and waited. All the candles went out at once, including the ones in the old circle.

"Omigod! No, don't do that!"

Her dad was totally unprotected.

Riley panicked. It was too close to sunset for mistakes.

I'll call Simon. No, he's trapping. Beck? No way I'm calling him. He'll think I can't do anything on my own.

She took two deep breaths to steady herself and opened the book.

"Oh, jeez!" Serious Simon hadn't told her one vital bit of information. If there was only one person setting the circle you lit the candles first then did the invocation and the intention. From what she could tell, the invocation wasn't mandatory, but ensuring that the circle knew whom to repel was the most important part.

She relit the candles and then paused. The Lord's Prayer was okay, but it didn't feel right for her. But what to use? She heard a car door slam and jumped. Maybe now was not the time to be picky.

"Ah, God, sorry to bother you, but this is Riley . . . Blackthorne. Could you keep my dad safe inside this circle? I mean, don't let the necromancers take him away. I'd really appreciate it if you could."

The candles didn't flare like they were supposed to. Maybe she hadn't been specific enough. Or put enough force of will behind the words.

Taking a deep breath, she called out, "If someone wants to harm us, do not let them inside this circle!"

The candles flamed high in a deep whooshing sound, then died down, making her ears snap from the pressure.

"Cool."

It was only then she realized she was sweating despite the chilly night air.

Riley giggled nervously. "See, Dad? I did it on my own. Yay me!"

The self-satisfied glow was still bubbling around inside her when Mortimer appeared. He politely tipped his hat and began his sales spiel in the same monotone he'd used the night before. Riley listened, taking time to study him. He was probably in his mid-thirties and the kind of guy who still lived at home with his widowed mom and collected stamps for fun.

When he'd finished his spiel, she shook her head.

Mortimer took the rejection graciously. "Well, thank you for your time," he said, placing his business card in front of the circle like the night before.

"So do you work for debt collectors?" she asked, her eyes narrowing.

"No," he said, shaking his head in disgust. "I won't reanimate for anyone but the deceased's family."

A necro with conscience. Now that was refreshing.

"I think I'm starting to like you, Mortimer," she said.

He looked embarrassed. "Be careful, will you? Don't trust any of us."

"Not even you?"

"I have scruples," he replied proudly. "As I see it, I am treading far enough off the path by summoning the dead."

"Then why do you . . . summon the dead?"

"It's pretty much the only thing I'm good at." Another tip of the hat and he left her alone inside the ring of candles.

"If all the summoners were like you this would be easy."

Riley knew better. This was the second time Mortimer had warned her about the others.

Maybe it wasn't so smart being out here on her own.

FOURTEEN

A sharp, sparking noise caused Riley to sit bolt upright in the sleeping bag, her heart hammering. For a second she thought it'd been a dream, but the candles told her otherwise. The flames were higher now, some twenty feet off the ground, like a force field that had repelled something nasty. Slowly the light dimmed to its usual level.

Probably a leaf. But there was no wind. Riley dug for her cell phone, then shook her head. Even if she called someone it would take too long for them to get here. This was her vigil and she had to brave it out.

As her eyes adjusted to the darkness she saw the figure. It was just outside the circle, clad in a long black cloak like you'd expect a wizard to wear.

He's just trying to scare me.

"Cool cloak," she said, pumping confidence into her voice though there was none. "Is there like a Necromancers'R'Us shop or something?"

A weird laugh came from behind the hood. It reminded her of one of those wraiths in *The Lord of the Rings.* She couldn't see the figure's face, but the ice that ran down her spine told her this one wasn't anything like Mortimer.

"Paul Blackthorne's daughter," the voice said. "Break the circle. Do it now."

"No."

"Break the circle," he repeated, this time with more intensity.

Her mind began to whisper that she should do it. What would be the harm? After all, her dad was dead. He wouldn't care. She would be able to sleep in her own bed every night. No one would fault her for wanting that.

"That's right," the dry voice soothed. "You keep the money for yourself."

"How much?" she asked before she could stop herself.

"Five thousand dollars. That will be a comfort to you, wouldn't it?"

Five . . . thousand. That was a lot of cash. She could live on that for a long time.

"Your father would want this. Drop the circle and everything will be good again. You know you want to."

Without realizing what she was doing, she opened the locket her father had given her. Inside was a picture of her mom and dad in Lincoln Park. It was summer, and sitting between them was Riley, still a baby.

Their loving faces cleared her mind instantly.

"Not happening," she said. "Back off."

"You will break the circle," the necromancer commanded.

"You're wasting your time. Dad stays put." She snapped the locket closed, clutching it tightly in the hope her parents' memories were stronger than the summoner's persuasive magic.

"You are not listening to me," the voice said, deeper now. "That's a mistake."

"Not my first."

If that circle doesn't hold, he's going to toast me.

The figure cocked its head, like he was weighing a number of extremely unpleasant options. "Perhaps blood magic will do the trick." He reached inside his cloak and pulled out something small. Something that hissed and wriggled.

It was a kitten, all cute and cream colored with black splotches.

"Get real. I'm not into bribes," she replied. "Just go away so I can get some sleep."

There was a glint of a blade, though there was no moon. It seemed to generate it own light. It wasn't like one of those you find in a kitchen drawer. This was a ritual knife, the kind in horror movies. The kind of blade used for serious magic.

He wouldn't. . . .

The necromancer poised the blade an inch from the kitten's neck.

Riley leapt to her feet. "What the hell are you doing?"

"Break the circle or I cut its little throat. Your choice. Your father is too valuable to leave in the ground, child."

"You can't do that!"

"Of course I can."

The kitten cried piteously, twisting in vain to sink a claw in its captor's hand.

Dad for a cat? He didn't even like them that much.

She couldn't let him hurt it. Could she? If he killed the poor creature, what would he do next? Kill her?

When Riley didn't move, the knife shifted closer.

"Last chance. Break the circle or it dies. You wouldn't want its blood on your hands, would you?"

"You bastard!" she shouted. He responded with that creepy laugh, like it was a compliment.

Riley's toe scraped across the ground, then stopped the moment before it reached the circle. She looked over her shoulder at her father's grave and then back again. Clenching her fists, she teetered on the edge. The kitten looked up at her, helpless. Only she could save it.

There was a flash of green fire in its eyes.

"No." Then she jammed her own eyes closed, feeling like a monster. There was a hissing snarl followed by a shrill screech of pain.

"Heartless bitch," the necro called out. It sounded like praise. "I'm impressed."

Riley pried open her eyes in time to see him toss the kitten on the ground in front of the circle. It was still alive.

She heaved a thick sigh of relief.

"Your dad's corpse is mine, child. It's only a matter of time." With a swirl of the cloak worthy of any movie villain, he strode away. Partway up the path he disappeared into a whirl of dried leaves.

Oh, now that's just creepy.

The kitten trembled at the edge of the circle and began to keen.

"Ah, you poor thing," she said, stepping closer. Maybe she'd been wrong about its eyes. A trick of the light, not that there was much tonight. "It's okay. He's gone. He can't hurt you anymore." All it needed was cuddling. She could do that at least. It'd be nice to have the company so she wouldn't feel so alone.

Simon's voice filled her mind. *They'll do anything to get to your father.*

Something felt wrong. The kitten should have taken off the moment it was dropped, found somewhere to hide. Instead it was outside the circle, like it was waiting.

Waiting for me. Those eyes again. Now they were fiery blue, glowing in the night. Riley took slow steps backward. "I don't think so."

The beast hissed at a volume ten times its size and shot a claw at the nearest candle. The circle responded instantly, leaping dozens of feet into the air, glowing brilliant white. The kitten yelped and disappeared in a resounding snap of energy. The wind grew, slinging branches and leaves against the barrier. Then it grew deathly still. The candles returned to the usual height.

"Nice try, jerk!" she shouted, retreating to her sleeping bag. The shakes caught up with her almost immediately, and she hugged herself to try to stop them. That hadn't been some foul-mouthed dude trying to talk her into some stupid deal for her dad's corpse. That had been dark magic.

And I almost fell for it.

✢

By four in the morning she'd had the same number of visitations as Scrooge on Christmas Eve, if you counted Beck in the total. He moved slowly, deliberately, like he'd exceeded tired and moved right on to totally wiped. As usual, he was toting his duffel bag.

Probably sleeps with the thing.

Wary of necro games she watched him approach, fearing this was yet another trick.

"Riley," he said. When she didn't answer, he added, "How bad has it been?"

"Just fabulous. The demonic kitten really made my night."

He didn't act surprised. She intoned the invitation and he marched through the circle without effort. His timing was excellent. A pee break was seriously needed.

"I'll be back," she said, heading toward the candles.

"Ya got something with ya? A weapon?"

"No. Just going to the bathroom."

He dug into his duffel bag and handed her the steel pipe. "Take this."

Riley rolled her eyes but took it nonetheless. As she hurried off into the darkness, she heard him flop down on the sleeping bag and yawn. Now he'd spooked her about taking a pee.

Thanks a lot for that.

Clicking on the light in the bathroom, she checked both stalls before finding relief. When she stepped outside, a moth streaked by her face causing her to execute a squeak of panic. Then she felt dumb. Luckily Beck couldn't see her or she'd never hear the end of it.

Beck wasn't alone now. A heavyset man stood a respectful distance from the circle. He was dressed rather flashy for a graveyard—blue suit, pink shirt, and a glittering phalanx of rings. More like a pimp than a necro.

Riley scooted to the other side of the circle and waited until Beck invited her in. The moment she crossed the line of candles she felt it flash behind her, shoving her inside.

"Lenny," Beck scolded. Apparently the necro had tried to cross over the circle at the same time, but had failed the "no harm" test.

The necro shrugged. "Had to try."

"Yeah, right." Beck retrieved his pipe and dropped it near his pack.

"You two know each other?" she asked, surprised.

"Sure," Beck responded, like she was being silly. "We play pool together at the Armageddon Lounge. Lenny's pretty good."

The necromancer beamed. "Thanks. That's a compliment coming from you." He turned toward her, polishing the glittering rings on his right hand against a coat sleeve. "I was explaining to Beck that your father needs to earn his keep. Best way to do that is aboveground. So how about it?"

"Nope."

"Pity. A few more nights in the cold and you'll see things in a different light." He looked over at her companion. "Later, guy."

"See ya, Lenny."

Riley settled on the sleeping bag as far away from Beck as she could. He may have been her dad's favorite trapping partner, but something about him made her uncomfortable. Not creepy uncomfortable, like he'd jump her or anything. More like she never knew where his mind was at any given moment.

"You hang with necros?" she asked. "They're like . . . pond scum."

"Some folks think the same of trappers." He lowered himself onto the blanket. "So what happened tonight?"

She ignored him, digging out a bottle of water and taking a long swig.

"Come on, I'm not the enemy. I know ya have a problem with me, but I owe it to yer daddy to look after ya."

"Don't need you helping me," she shot back. "I'm fine."

"Right, kid," he said.

She glared at him. "Why do you always call me that?"

"What?"

"Kid. I'm not twelve."

"I know. It's just easier," he mumbled.

"Huh?" That didn't make much sense.

A frown flitted across his face. "Ya remember when I first got back from over there, how goofy ya got?"

Goofy? Riley's temper stirred. "I wasn't like that."

"Well, ya had yer eyes on me, that's for sure."

She gave him stony silence, because he was right. His time in the Army had left him tanned, muscled, and way cuter than when he'd left. A total hunk, and she'd fallen hard.

Then you shot me down like I was nothing.

"So why the kid thing?" she asked, still savoring the anger.

He glowered at her. "Ya know I couldn't go there, not with yer daddy and me workin' together and ya only bein' fifteen and lookin' so fine and . . ." He faded out, his eyes riveted on the ground.

Riley hid the grin. She'd managed to push one of his buttons, or that explanation wouldn't have been so long.

"Okay, I got it," she said. If he acted like she was a kid he didn't have to work through all the emotional stuff, which suited her just fine. The idea he thought she was *fine* wasn't something she could handle right now. "Just don't call me kid anymore, okay?"

"Or?" he challenged, back in control in a heartbeat.

"I'll go all *goofy* on you again, whatever that means."

Beck seemed to weigh the option and then muttered, "Deal."

He dug a bottle out of his duffel bag. The label said Johnnie Walker. After a long swig, he smacked his lips.

"What're you doing?" she demanded. "You keep it up and you'll be a drunk like your mom."

He snarled at her and her blood ran cold. The flames were taller now, maybe a foot off the ground, registering his anger. Was that even possible?

Suddenly it didn't seem so safe with him *inside*.

"Ya leave that . . . *her* out of it," he spouted, jamming the bottle into his bag. "That's none of yer damned business."

Riley curled up in the sleeping bag, feeling sick to her stomach. She shouldn't have said that to him. He couldn't help what his mom was like.

Just apologize. "Beck . . ."

"What?" he said, his voice muffled. Even in the dark she could see the lines etched into his face. They made him look so much older, like he'd experienced everything bad the world could throw at him.

"I'm sorry," she admitted. "It wasn't right for me to say that."

His shoulders twitched for a second. "Go to sleep."

"I can't." Riley tugged the blanket around her.

"Just because she's a drunk doesn't mean I am," he growled.

"Got it. Won't make that mistake again."

He turned toward her. "It's an energy drink," he explained. A long yawn followed. "Supposed to keep me goin' when I don't have time to sleep. It's not workin'."

Now she really felt like a dork. "Why put it in a whiskey bottle?"

"Just do."

It wasn't that simple and they both knew it.

"What's it taste like?" she asked. He handed it over and Riley took a tentative gulp . . . and nearly gagged. The stuff was a blend of super strong coffee laced with raw kerosene. "Yuck."

"Ya get used to it."

"Not me. When was the last time you slept?"

"Doesn't matter," he said.

"Tired trapper equals demon bait. Dad told me that."

Beck looked over at her. "Told me the same."

"Then get some sleep, will you?" she urged.

"Ya need it more than I do." He took another swig. "I sold yer demons, the ones in the cupboard. The money's under the microwave. Just forgot to tell ya."

"Thanks," she said grudgingly. She'd miss the Magpie, but the money was vital. "Who's going to take over my training now?"

"Don't know yet." He yawned again. "I'll try to help ya when I can, but I have to trap or I can't pay my own bills. We need to figure out where ya can live."

"What?" she said, caught off guard.

"Ya can't stay on yer own, and ya sure as hell can't move in with me."

Got that right. She could imagine what his house was like—probably ankle deep in grubby old pizza boxes and empty beer bottles.

Then the first part of his statement caught up with her.

"I'm not moving. That's my home," she protested. It wasn't much, but she couldn't lose the last connection with her dad.

"It'll take time for the Guild to pay the life insurance, and I can't afford to cover both places. Call yer aunt, see if she'll take ya in for a while."

Crap. He'd overheard her talking to Peter. "I'm not moving," she repeated, stronger this time.

Beck kept rambling, caught in his own personal minefield about how she'd need clothes and food and how she had to keep going to school.

You're not listening, Backwoods Boy. I belong here.

The power struggle had begun.

FIFTEEN

Morning brought Max to Riley's door and more bills in the mailbox. She welcomed the cat but not the stack of windowed envelopes. At least none of them was marked "Overdue."

Not yet.

Max promptly sprawled on the couch, licked a paw, and then tucked himself into a massive ball like a furry armadillo. He acted like sleep was the answer to all the world's problems.

Only if you don't dream.

Riley grimly studied the pile of envelopes on the kitchen table.

"Welcome to your new life." From what she could see it was way worse than the old one. At least her old life had a parent in it. Now there was no dad, no dad income. The first hurt really bad. The second just amped up the heartache.

Max made a snorking noise in his sleep and twitched. At least one of them was happy. In the background the television droned on. It was one of those local talk shows discussing the rise in teen suicides, how the economy was causing kids to hit the wall. Most didn't survive the impact.

Riley had hit the wall and bounced so many times she didn't know any other way. Her mother's death, then the condo fire. Now her dad.

With a tortured sigh, she started with the first bill—the rent. That wasn't optional unless she wanted to move into a drafty refrigerator box under one of the city's leaky bridges. It went into the life-really-sucks-if-this-isn't-paid pile. Electric, gas, and water. Ditto.

She continued on through the rest of them—monthly dues to the Guild Fund, both national and local; cable and cell phone bills. The final one was the biggest—her mom's medical care.

"$54,344.75?" she said, boggling at the amount. She knew it was outrageous, but not the exact amount. Over the last three years her father painstakingly whittled it down from a high of $65,000. The interest was taking a massive bite out of the payment, and there was still another seven years on the loan.

She'd be twenty-four by the time this was paid off. By then she'd be a master trapper. It seemed so far off.

Riley stuck the bill in the when-everything-else-is-paid pile. "Sorry, Dad, but that's the way it has to be."

Using her cell phone to do the math she realized that even if she ignored the medical bill, she was going to be in real trouble in five days when the rent was due. Maybe the life insurance payment would come in really quickly and . . .

Life doesn't work that way. Riley had learned that much from watching her dad strain to balance the finances month after month. The urge to binge on chocolate reared its head. After a quick hunt through the apartment she didn't locate any. She ate a banana instead. No comparison.

While she was rummaging, she found the demon money right where Beck said it would be, another $225, along with paperwork that said he'd sold the demons to a trafficker named Roscoe Clement. Riley had heard of the guy. Her dad had described him in two words and those were "total sleaze."

Bet Beck shoots pool with him, too.

Slumping into the chair, she counted the pile of cash she'd dug out of their makeshift "bank" inside one of the throw pillows. Her dad had always joked that they looked like drug dealers with the stacks of fives, tens, and twenties on the kitchen table. Keeping money inside a pillow wasn't really a smart idea, but they'd had little choice. If they put anything in the bank the medical bill dickheads would siphon it right out as part of the claim. They'd learned that the hard way and lived on ramen noodles for a month because of it.

Riley repeated the math.

"Better, but I still need three hundred dollars," she said. If she could find that somehow, she could pay the rent, the utilities, and leave a bit for food. She'd worry about the rest of the bills when their time came.

Her dad had faced this every day, every week, month after month. He'd remained cheerful, at least around her, but she knew it'd dragged him down. She gazed at the chair. Empty. No smile, no laugh. That emptiness spread throughout the entire apartment, an invisible choking fog.

Riley sprawled on the couch next to Max. The packing box coffee table received a sound kick, startling the cat.

"Where am I going to get three hundred bucks?" she groaned. Max's answer was to yawn, exposing a long pinkish tongue. He curled up again.

"Borrow it from Beck?" she pondered. Riley shook her head even before she finished the question. He was already trying to take control of her life, and owing him money would only give him more power.

She had to find a way to live on her own or Beck would drive her crazy.

Riley's eyes lit on her father's trapping bag near the door. Beck had brought it home for her. She retrieved it and returned to the couch. The sides of it had small tears, and there was dried blood on it. Zipping the bag open, she studied the interior. Her dad always repacked it every night, replacing any supplies he'd used. Since he wasn't here, the job fell to her.

A plan slowly formed. It was pretty bold, crazy even, but if she could pull it off . . .

Paul Blackthorne couldn't trap anymore.

"But his daughter can."

⊹

Riley parked underneath one of the few working security lights near the old grocery store. The light was on life support, blinking on and off at random intervals. Farther away from the building were other cars with windows steamed opaque because the occupants were busy making out.

Tonight was going to be a bitch. By now her classmates would have heard what happened at the library, maybe even about her dad. She didn't think she could handle false pity right now. Or insults. Somebody would get hurt.

Riley sat in the car for a few minutes, leaving the motor running. It would be so easy to ditch class. Beck would never know. She could be in Five Points hunting demons rather than hanging around here.

She spied Peter by the front door. He was watching for her, like he did every night they had class. He was holding something—her report. She couldn't blow him off when he'd gone to all that work. And then there was the computer disk mystery. The longer she'd thought about it, the more it had bugged her. Like trying to guess what was inside a Christmas present, except rattling a disk didn't tell you much.

As she stepped out of the car Peter saw her and waved. Shouldering her messenger bag, she headed toward him.

He'll help me get through this.

"Hey, Riley," Peter said as soon as she drew near. She noticed he kept his voice muted so it didn't carry across the parking lot. "Glad you're here."

"No choice," she said, then felt bad. "How're you?"

His smile thinned. "Worried about you."

She didn't even think twice when he gave her a hug.

Peter stepped back and opened his mouth. Then he shook his head like he knew nothing he could say would help her heal.

"Here you go," he said, and handed over the neat stack of paper. "Your report."

"You're a great guy, you know that?" she said, all serious.

"Sure am. Destined for fame and fortune," he joked. "I still think my paper's better."

"You would."

"Hey, Blackthorne," one of the other students called out. "Trashed any libraries today?"

Before she could respond, a classmate elbowed the ass, then whispered in his ear. The guy's eyes grew large.

"Sorry, I didn't know about your dad," he mumbled. Around them, other kids watched nervously, wondering if she was going to lose it.

Riley turned her back on him. No tears. Not here. She felt Peter's hand on her elbow, then a gentle squeeze of reassurance.

"Ah, did you bring that computer disk?" he asked. He was trying to distract her, and she loved him for it.

Riley unearthed the disk from the bottom of her messenger bag and delivered it into his eager hands, along with a list of birthdays and other personal information.

"Cool. Now I can hack your bank account," he said, winking.

"Hack away. We . . . I don't have any money."

Peter cocked his head. "How bad is it? Do you, like, have enough for food?"

"I'm three hundred short for the rent," she admitted. "I could ask Beck, but he's . . ." She shook her head. "Not going there."

"I've got almost a hundred I could loan you."

She studied Peter anew. He was serious. She knew he'd been laying aside cash for a new hard drive, but he was willing to help her without even thinking about it.

"No," she said, shaking her head. *I have to do this on my own. I can't sponge off my friends.* "Thanks, but I'll work it out."

The worried expression on Peter's face didn't budge. "What do you have in mind?"

A field trip to Demon Central. Instead she said, "I'm thinking of getting a part-time job." That wasn't really lying, was, it? Peter would never agree to her trapping on her own. Neither would Beck.

So I won't tell them. At least until she caught her very first Three.

When Riley dropped the report on Mr. Houston's desk, the older man looked up, his pale blue eyes barely focusing on her. He murmured his sympathies then returned to his paperwork. That angered her. She didn't want sympathy, but her dad was more important than a few words that didn't mean anything.

Riley took her chair and fell into tortured silence despite Peter's attempts to cheer her up. The new curriculum required teachers to teach multiple subjects, even if they didn't really understand them. Mr. Houston was a good example. He was great with English, but not so hot with the other classwork.

Like math.

As he droned on about the finer points of calculating the volume of a cylinder, she was light-years away from the here and now. Almost everything triggered memories of her dad; like being in class. She'd sat in on some of his history classes when she was a kid. He was a great teacher, not like Houston, who could put stones to sleep. She'd met Beck in one of those classes. He'd checked her out, then laughed, making fun of her braids and knobby knees, not realizing she was the teacher's daughter.

"You're kidding!" Peter exclaimed.

Riley pulled herself back to the present. "What?" she asked, wondering what she'd missed. Peter was never that emphatic about math.

"They're closing this school," he said, angling his head toward the teacher.

Houston had a pile of envelopes in his arthritic hands. "These are your assignments. Your next class will meet in the new locations."

"Why are they closing this one?" one of the kids asked.

"Just are," Houston said. He looked around at the dead bugs and the maze of multicolored wires protruding from the dairy case. "Any place will be better than this, guys."

"Got that right," Peter whispered.

An envelope landed on her desk. Official news always came in white envelopes with neatly typed labels. This one was no different.

BLACKTHORNE, RILEY A. (Junior)

She looked over at Peter, and they ripped open their envelopes simultaneously.

"I've got an afternoon class now," she said. *How had that happened?* It'd always been at night.

"Where?" Peter asked, leaning over to look at her paper.

"Fourteenth Street. An old Starbucks."

Silence.

"Peter?"

His face fell. "Damn," he muttered and handed over his letter. The day got worse. Peter wasn't in her class anymore. Instead, he was going to be somewhere on Ponce de Leon Avenue at a place named Kids Galore!

Riley returned the letter, trying not to let this news body-slam her. She failed.

"We've always been together, ever since elementary school," she said.

"Maybe if I ask them to change it . . ." he began. Then he shook his head. "I bet Mom's behind this."

If so, Mrs. King had discovered a truly cruel way to separate them.

Peter adopted his game face. "We'll talk every night after class," he said, trying hard to put some positive spin on this disaster. "We'll have twice the stories, you'll see."

"Yeah." He was doing the happy-talk thing, but it wasn't working.

"Riley?" he said. She looked over at him. "No matter what, I've got your back."

Not if you're on the other side of the city.

SIXTEEN

Serious nerves kept Riley rooted to the car seat. She sat just inside Demon Central, near Underground Atlanta. Her dad said it was a rundown area, but he'd been too kind. It hadn't always been that way.
When her mom was alive, they'd come down for the New Year's Peach
Drop. It'd been cool back then. Now it was a dump. If she was going to
find a demon, it would be here.

Riley had everything she needed—her dad's trapping gear and the
special steel mesh bag to hold the Three after she'd caught it. She'd spent
nearly forty-eight dollars for a pint of Holy Water and three spheres
from a gun shop on Trinity Avenue. Only one thing was missing—guts.

I can do this. She'd been saying the same thing to herself for the last
ten minutes, ever since she'd called Beck and lied to him.

Not a lie. I am tired.

But she had lied, at least about class running late and that she
needed to get some sleep and could he watch her father's grave until
midnight?

He'd agreed without giving her any hassle. It would have been easier
on her conscience if he'd been a jerk. Instead, he'd sounded really concerned, and that made the lie turn to rock in her stomach. Would bor-
rowing money from him be the end of the world?

Yes.

Time was passing.

Riley tapped her fingers on the steering wheel. If she was truly Paul Blackthorne's daughter she'd be out there hunting a Three rather than worrying herself sick in the car. She'd be taking care of herself rather than waiting for someone else to do it for her.

Her hand shook as she reached for the door handle.

"I'll just see what it looks like, then decide," Riley said, trying to find some middle ground that didn't allow the stone in her stomach to grow any heavier.

After the trunk lid popped open, she slipped the straps of her father's trapping bag on her shoulder. It seemed heavier than when she'd hauled it out of the apartment.

"No wonder he lifted weights," she grumbled, dropping it to the ground. There was the sound of breaking glass.

"Ah, crap!" She'd broken one of the spheres. They were designed to crack easily, and she only had three. Squatting down, she rummaged in the bag. One of them had split open and a sea of Holy Water flooded the interior.

She gingerly fished out the broken glass, trying not to slice her fingers, and tossed the shards into the gutter. After removing the bag's other contents, she drained the water onto the ground. It splashed on her tennis shoes and her feet began to tingle. Now she'd have cold and holy feet all night.

Her ham sandwich was soaked. That was okay. When she caught a demon she'd haul it over to Fireman Jack and collect her money. Then there'd be a celebratory trip to McDonald's for supper on the way to the graveyard. She might even supersize the fries.

An odd, shuffling noise caught her notice. She leaned around the truck lid. An old black man made his way up the broken sidewalk, dwarfed by layers of clothes like he was wearing everything he owned. He hunched against the cold, shooting glances over his shoulder every few steps as if he expected trouble.

Once he was gone, Riley repacked only what she needed into her messenger bag and slipped the strap onto her shoulder. *Better.* After slamming the door and pocketing the keys, she set off into the heart of Demon Central, her heart thudding in her ears.

Fifty feet down the abandoned street she came to a stop.

"There just had to be holes," Riley muttered. She hated them. Things lived down in those holes. Things that would love to eat her.

She paused and studied the closest abyss. It was jagged and deep, with pieces of metal sticking out from the edges like porcupine quills. She thought she heard water running somewhere underground.

This place was a Three's dream home—loads of trash strewn around and hardly any light. What light there was seemed to be timid, barely illuminating the center of the street and avoiding the corners entirely. She strained to see into one corner, but it was impossible. Anything could be watching her, waiting, choosing the moment to bring her down.

A few streets over a coyote howled, high and throaty. The howl was picked up and amplified into a wild and energetic chorus. Riley began to shiver.

Was Beck this afraid when he trapped his first Three?

She wasn't sure. He didn't seem to be scared of anything, but then her dad had been with him, and that would have made all the difference.

As Riley edged forward her shoes crunched on something. Broken glass and white powder spread in a wide arc on the rippled asphalt. Debris had swirled around that circle, like a hurricane does its eye. Edging closer, she found tracks through the powder. She knelt. The powder came from a shield sphere, and the tracks were from work boots. Like the kind trappers wore. Dry, rust-brown stains were splattered like someone had shaken out a paintbrush. She picked up a strip of ripped brown leather crusted with dried blood and examined it.

It was from Beck's coat, the one he'd been wearing the night her father died. She could remember what it had looked like in the hallway, slashed and shredded, coated with his blood.

Riley lurched to her feet, stumbling backward. She barely stifled a cry of anguish.

This is where her dad had died.

What am I doing here?

Her dad and Beck trapped as a team. That wasn't to keep each other company. Apprentices didn't start trapping Grade Threes until almost six months in, and then only with a master at their side. Even then, they still died.

Get the hell out of here!

It was her father's voice, echoing deep inside her head.

Riley executed the turn as slowly as possible, eyes darting from hole to hole, expecting a furry body to be crawling out of every one. She wanted to run, but she kept her movements steady. Demons chased their victims. If she acted as if she were in control, maybe nothing would come after her.

Four steps later she heard the sound.

"Just a rat," she whispered. Not that she'd seen any, but they had to be down here, right?

The sound grew louder. A sort of sloppy snarl. Muscles tensing and heart jittering, Riley looked over her shoulder. Crouched in front of one of the holes was a Grade Three demon. The thing looked like some monster out of a science fiction movie—four feet tall, a patchwork of black-and-white spiked fur with scimitar claws and horrifically sharp teeth that protruded beyond the lower jaw. The creature rose, stretching like it was limbering up for gym class. It examined her with menacing red eyes.

"Oh ... my ... God."

"Blackthorne's daughter," it bayed. It slicked its thick tongue across its lips. Drool rolled down its chin.

"Niiice demon ... That's it. Just stay there." Riley fumbled in the bag and pulled out the cow entrails she'd retrieved from the freezer. Slinging the package as hard as she could, it landed with a plop on the asphalt. Louder snarls came from the beast. In a move that seemed impossible for its bulk, it leapt on the food and swallowed the entrails and the plastic wrapper in one big gulp.

"Ah, God," she said, stumbling backward. That had been her only diversion and it was long gone. Her hand closed on one of the spheres. "I'm leaving now. No need to get upset, Mr. Demon."

"Chew yourrr bones!" it cried, waving its arms in the air.

A second later, all Riley could see was a whir of black and white, all teeth and claws, moving toward her at frightening speed. She stumbled, nearly falling. Cursing, she tossed one of the spheres at the oncoming fiend. It missed and smashed to bits on the uneven ground close to where her father had breathed his last.

Riley ran, the messenger bag banging into her side. Once she got to the car the thing wouldn't follow her, would it?

The beast had other ideas, growing closer, calling out her name. It snarled and clawed the back of her jacket, spinning her around like a top. Falling hard, the wind knocked out of her, Riley rolled to protect her final sphere. She shrieked as the demon dove at her, claws raking across the asphalt in a trail of sparks just inches from her face. It yowled in frustration when it missed. Riley regained her feet only a second before it dodged sideways, sending its glistening ebony spikes at her belly. She forced the bag forward, trying to block its lethal reach. It gnawed on the canvas, snarling and growling as she fumbled for the last sphere.

A thick paw arced around the bag and dug into her left thigh, burying the claws deep into her flesh. Riley screamed in agony and slammed the sphere into the fiend's open maw, imbedding the glass into the beast and deep into her palm. In slow motion, the Three ripped its claws out of her leg and sank to the ground, bloody and unmoving.

Riley fell to her knees and began to retch, the adrenaline making her heart thud so fast she thought she'd faint. Prickles of light danced at the corner of her eyes. She forced herself to slow her breathing, studying the still form. The demon was taking quick puffs of air through its mouth, its laser red eyes staring up at nothing. Black blood dripped from its tongue onto its neck. Riley forced herself to her feet and, with fumbling hands, broke open the seal on the steel bag.

How do I get this thing inside?

In the end, she kept jamming the fiend's legs, body, and arms into the bag, like stuffing a pillowcase with foul-smelling fur. The thing stank like sulfur and rotten meat, making her stomach roil and acid singe her throat. She worked left-handed as the right was bleeding, waves of pain telegraphing up her arm.

With incredible effort, she locked down the two clamps that secured the demon inside the bag. She'd actually done it—caught her first Grade Three Hellspawn.

Rising to her feet, Riley wobbled for a few seconds. The adrenaline was gone, leaving a sour stomach and a sick, pounding headache. It was only then she dared look at her thigh. Thick red blood bubbled out from the six holes in her slashed jeans, one for each claw. The leg felt numb, which was weird. It should be hurting like hell.

"Trapper . . . scores," she said weakly. *Sorta.* Folding out the steel bag's handle, she dragged the dead weight up the street one-handed. It was slow going; the fiend was much heavier than she'd expected.

How am I going to get this thing in the trunk? It certainly wasn't riding up front with her.

"One problem at a time," she said, refusing to admit this was more than she could handle. Riley looked down at her catch. She couldn't wait to see Beck's face.

Hey, Backwoods Boy! Guess what I did tonight?

It was going to be *sooo* sweet.

She heard laughter. For a moment it didn't register as a threat.

"Hey, girlie!" someone called out.

Riley whirled around to find two guys following her. One of them was chunky, like a Beck gone to seed with a roll of flab around his middle. He was wearing a faded ball cap, and his long hair needed washing.

"She looks tasty for a trapper," the second said. He was short and wiry, with an unlit cigarette dangling out of his mouth.

Just a couple of jerks from the Guild trying to psyche me.

Riley fired up the attitude. "I'm with Beck," she fibbed. "He's not going to be happy you're messing with me."

"So where's this guy?" the first one asked. He had a load of chew in his mouth and he kept working it.

"Down there," she lied, pointing toward the end of the street.

The big man spit. "Ain't no one down there. You're on your own."

"Just the way we like 'em," the second added.

This was bad. These guys weren't trappers. They were too shabby, and neither of them had any trapping equipment with them.

"What do you want?" Riley asked, tightening her grip on the steel bag.

The sick leer that formed on the big man's face sent a frigid shiver to her toes. "The demon . . . to start with."

Riley shook her head. "No way. Go catch your own."

"Seems we just did. That thing's worth a lot of money."

"You can't sell a demon," she protested. "You have to be a trapper."

"Hear that, Dodger? She says we can't sell it." He chuffed. "Never stopped us before. It'll get us five hundred, no sweat."

Five hundred? Who's paying that much for a Three?

The wiry guy began to circle around her. "How's about we share, girlie?"

"Yeah," the big man agreed. "Get some booze, some blow, and have a party, just the three of us."

Oh, God.

"I get first crack," the man added. "I like breakin' 'em in."

Rage-laced panic exploded inside her. She couldn't escape with the demon. It was too heavy to move quickly. Even if she dialed 911 it'd take the cops too long to get here, even if they could be convinced to come to Demon Central. By then . . .

The demon or these sick perverts?

Slinging a torrent of hellish curse words at them, Riley dropped the bag and limped off as fast as her injured thigh would let her. The wounds fired to life, sending jolts of pain into her leg. If she only had a steel pipe, anything that would keep them away from her. Keep them from touching her and . . .

"Run, girlie!" Dodger taunted as he started after her. His heavy boots crunched across the pavement, moving closer with each step. He was just playing with her. There was no way she could outrun either of them.

A strange sound filled the street, a combination of a throaty howl and a deep, raspy snarl.

"Oh, shit," the big man shouted. "The thing's awake. Help me with it!"

Riley risked a glance over her shoulder. The small guy was still gaining on her. Behind him, the demon clawed and bit at its steel prison like a rabid dog, thrashing so the metal bag rolled around the pavement.

The smaller man was catching up. She scooped up a charred piece wood, holding it like a club, and turned to face him. A hundred words came to the tip of her tongue, but she was too scared to say any of them.

The big man was losing his battle. "Dammit, Dodger, forget her! She's not worth the five hundred."

With a snarl that would have impressed any fiend, Dodger whirled and ran at top speed to help his partner.

Riley limped away, pushing as fast as she dared. As she turned the corner she saw the two men wrestling with the bag as the Three tried to tear it apart.

"Go, demon," she urged, blinking away tears of anger. Maybe it'd get free and rip those losers apart. Eat them both. "That'd be so righteous."

By the time Riley reached the car, she shook like a dog in a thunderstorm. Her thigh felt as if it were boiling from within, shooting pain into her groin and all the way down to her toes. Popping open the trunk, she grabbed the pint bottle of Holy Water, broke open the seal, and soaked her thigh, jeans and all, making it look like she'd wet herself. Instead of the burning pain she'd expected, it only stung a little then eased off.

Maybe the wounds aren't that bad.

Riley swallowed, twice, and took some deep breaths. Her heart still drummed in her ears and her stomach felt seconds away from erupting. At least the claw marks wouldn't infect, though she'd still feel like crap for a couple of a days. Like a bad case of the flu is how her dad described it.

"I have nothing to show for it," she growled. Tossing the empty bottle in the trunk with more force than was necessary, she slammed the lid. There'd been no choice. If she tried to fight them, they would have jumped her and . . .

"You asshats!" she shouted, thumping her uninjured fist on the trunk lid. She'd bagged her very first Three and they'd taken it away from her like a bully steals a kid's lunch money.

If Dad had been here . . .

Tears welled in her eyes again. If her dad had been here, they'd have that demon in the trunk and those two losers would have learned what it meant to tangle with a master trapper. Instead they'd tangled with her, and won.

Epic fail.

"Beck is so going to kill me." The Three had been her best defense against his anger. He'd have bitched at her, but in the end he would have respected her.

Not now. He's never going to trust me again. He'll just tighten up his leash.

Instead of heading for the graveyard, she drove home one-handed, tears coursing down her face. They felt icy against her skin as a full body shiver cramped her muscles and her teeth began to chatter. She turned off the heater. Sweat bloomed on her forehead despite the chilly night air.

Once she got home, she'd call Beck, tell him what happened. Then it would get really bad.

"Someday," she muttered in between intense shivering sessions. Someday she'd catch up with those guys and make them pay. Someday they'd know what a mistake it was to mess with Riley Blackthorne.

But not today.

SEVENTEEN

The dial on Beck's watch glowed blue in the growing light. It was a half hour until dawn. With each passing hour he'd talked himself out of dialing Riley's cell phone and rousting her out of her bed. The kid had to be worn out, the shock of her dad's death hitting home about now. He knew how that felt.

There'd always be sadness whenever he thought of Paul. The man could have easily blown him off, treated him like everyone else, but Paul told him he'd seen that spark in Beck's eyes, that drive to be something better. Beck had never thought to argue the subject. His teacher had such a reasoned way of explaining things, it sounded like gospel.

Beck sighed, feeling that dull ache deep in his chest again. He still expected to see his phone light up and it would be Paul, checking in on him, just wanting to talk. That would never happen again. He was truly on his own now. *Just like Riley.*

It was a still night and the swirl of dead leaves immediately caught his attention. Mortimer had already visited, polite as ever. Lenny had dropped by a little after two, and another necro named Christian at three. It was as if they had assigned times. The leaves coalesced into a form outside the circle, causing the candles to flare. It reminded Beck more of a high-level demon than a summoner of the dead.

"Wastin' your time," he called out.

The form wavered for a moment and then took a more defined shape. Black cloak, carved oak staff, all the theatrical props.

"I can give you what you most want in life," the voice within the hood said in a sibilant whisper.

"The hell ya say," Beck replied, too tired to be polite. "Ya can give me a night in Carrie Underwood's bed? Damn, that woman's fine, and she can sing too. Or maybe a new truck. That'd be nice."

"Nothing so mundane." A dramatic pause. "I can deliver the demon who killed Paul Blackthorne."

Beck's heart double-beat, his humor gone. "Yer kind only messes with dead folks, not Hellspawn."

"I am prepared to make an exception in this case."

"Why is Blackthorne so important to ya?"

The figure leaned on the staff in a pensive pose. "Just accept that he is. It's not like Mr. Blackthorne will be in service forever."

The necro did have a point. Paul would be returned to his grave in a year at the latest, and the demon would be dead. There were ways to hide the truth from Riley, especially if she went to live with her aunt. With the grave so fresh, once the body was exhumed and reanimated, Beck could smooth over the dirt and she'd never know.

"Certainly you want to see justice done," the figure soothed, "and prevent the chance the fiend will come after the one remaining Blackthorne."

He played to Beck's greatest fear. The only way to keep Riley safe was to kill that Five and send a message to Lucifer to back off. Beck wanted that more than anything else in the world, even sleeping with his favorite country music singer.

He rose, taking a few tentative steps toward the glowing circle.

The figure fell silent, drawing him closer. Beck slowly turned to look at the mound of dirt. What would Paul think of him if he disturbed his rest? What would Riley say if she knew he'd betrayed her?

"All for a good cause," the necromancer insisted. "You must keep her safe. She has a will of her own, and it has put her in danger tonight."

Beck whipped around. "Whadda ya mean?"

"She went hunting in Five Points. Alone. I hear it went very badly."

"Yer lyin'," Beck retorted.

"And if I'm not?" the necromancer replied, his tone too sure for Beck's comfort. "What if she's dying right now? Would it make sense to guard this grave when she's heading toward one of her own?"

"No way she'd go to Five Points alone." The moment Beck uttered the words, he knew he was wrong.

Damn, girl, ya wouldn't. He frowned, the truth hitting as hard as a slug to the gut. *Yeah, ya would, just to spite me.*

First the necro had said the demon might hurt her. Now he claimed she was already hurt, maybe dying.

Lies.

Beck forced himself back to the blanket. "I'm not buyin' it."

The cloak shifted in what passed as a shrug. "Then it's on your head," the summoner replied, no hint of disappointment in his voice. "By the full moon this man's body will be mine. Do not doubt it."

The form reverted to leaves and scattered in a light wind.

Riley's cell phone went unanswered, rolling over to voice mail again and again. When the cemetery's volunteer arrived a few minutes later, Beck bolted for his truck.

✦

Riley pried open her eyes to find sunlight on the bedroom ceiling whirling like a kaleidoscope. All sorts of colors. It was really pretty. With considerable effort, she pulled herself upright on the bed, wondering what time it was. She hiccuped, and the shivering began again as her fever rose.

The left thigh was the problem. It was swollen, the denim soaked with something brown. The entire leg pulsated with each heartbeat.

The Holy Water was supposed to neutralize the poison.

"Not so much," she said, falling back onto the pillow. Time slowed.

Riley knew what was happening. She'd heard her dad talking to her mom about this when he thought she wasn't listening. Her leg would go septic in a few hours and the poison would spread throughout her body. It would kill her.

Maybe that's best. She could be with her parents. Do whatever angels did all day. No worries about money or school or demons.

An annoying noise pulled her out of her fevered imaginings. It was her cell phone. She faded out until it started making noise again. With sweaty hands Riley flipped it open. Someone called out to her in a frantic voice. "Riley? Are you okay?"

"Sick . . ."

"What happened?" the voice asked.

"They . . . stole it."

"Stole what?"

"Demon got me. . . . Sorry. You were . . . right."

She flipped it closed and let the phone fall next to her on the bed, knowing that Beck would find her body and bury her next to her parents.

No vigil needed.

✛

Violating scores of traffic laws on the way to the apartment, Beck worked his cell, calling in favors. He started with Carmela, rousing the doc out of bed and earning him an earful until he explained the situation. Then he called the Guild's priest. Father Harrison had just stepped out of the shower but promised to come over as quickly as possible.

After making a parking place where there wasn't one, Beck leapt out of the truck and took the stairs, two at a time. Hammering on Riley's door got no response. He called out. Nothing. He tried Mrs. Litinsky's, then he remembered something about her going to visit her family in Charleston.

For half a second he thought of kicking in the door but discarded the idea. Paul had spent a lot of time reinforcing it, worried about Riley staying home alone at night. He had to find a key.

Swearing under his breath, he ran down two floors to the door marked "Superintendent." He banged on it. Time crawled by until a scrawny, unshaven face appeared at the door. Beck physically bullied the guy up the stairs, then glowered menacingly while the super fumbled with the keys.

To his relief Riley hadn't engaged the chain lock. The instant the door opened he shoved past the super calling out her name. She wasn't in the living room or the kitchen. He found her in the bedroom, a tangled mass of sweat and delirium.

It was worse than he'd feared.

She was fully clothed, her hair matted on the pillow and her face deep crimson. The brown sludge oozing out of her thigh was the reason. The necro had been right: She'd tangled with a Three. They loved to hook their prey, drag them in so they could gnaw on them. Their claws were lethal.

Huge sweat rings soaked her T-shirt. Her eyes were closed and she moaned with each breath. The sweet, cloying smell of infection clouded the room. But it was her leg that made Beck nauseous, swollen twice its usual size. He knew all about that. His first Three had clawed him. He'd gotten sick, but not this bad. Paul had made sure of that.

The super took one look at the feverish body and fled.

Beck threw his jacket in the corner and flung open the rusty window to gain some fresh air. He gulped it in to keep from throwing up. He knew what the sweet smell meant. She was rotting from the inside out.

He heard someone call his name. "Back here!" he said.

Carmela paused in the doorway. "Den?" Her eyes went from him to Riley. "Holy shit."

"Yeah, big-time," Beck said.

Carmela paused to hit the light switch by the door, then hefted an orange suitcase onto the end of the bed. Flipping it open, she tossed out medical supplies like a squirrel unearthing acorns. Bandages, scissors, empty trash bags, IV solution, and tubing all fell in a disorganized heap on the covers.

"The Holy Water I have is a few days old. We need fresher than that," she said.

"Harrison's on his way," Beck replied. He grabbed a pair of surgical scissors and applied the business end to the left blue jean leg, trying to keep his cool. He'd treated soldiers on the battlefield. You worked on what would kill them first. In this case, it was the poison in Riley's system. But this wasn't some young private from Ohio. This was Paul's daughter, the little girl who used to follow him around like a heartsick puppy.

"Hey, don't be stupid," Carmela said. She tossed him a pair of latex gloves. "You don't want that crap in your system. All it takes is a paper cut."

"Thanks." Why had he forgotten that? His hands shook as he tugged on the gloves, making the job twice as hard.

Get your head in the game! It was Paul's voice and it had the desired effect. He bent down and began to work on the denim. The pants leg came free, leaving only an inch or so for modesty at the top. He examined the thigh—six individual claw marks, all of them swollen and draining brown pus.

"Now that's seriously gross," the doc said. She gently placed an electronic thermometer in Riley's ear and then whistled the moment the numbers appeared on the digital readout. "104.3. I'd expect 103, tops. Something else is going on."

Carmela took hold of Riley's ankle, carefully lifting the leg. The girl moaned in response. "Lay down a plastic barrier, then a bunch of those disposable towels. By the time we get done this place is going to look like an oil slick."

Beck did as he was told, trying not to wince every time Riley moaned.

"What happened?" the doc asked.

"She went trappin' on her own."

"Why the hell didn't she treat it?"

He had no answer.

"Beck?" They turned to find Father Harrison in the doorway. He was in his usual black suit and clerical collar, a large backpack in hand.

"Father," Beck said. "Thanks for comin' so quickly."

He could tell the moment the priest saw Riley: Harrison's face sobered and he made the sign of the cross. "How much do you need?" the priest asked.

"At least a half gallon to start with," Carmela replied, her back to him.

It took three attempts before the doctor found a decent vein in Riley's right arm. Once the IV was secured, she flipped it wide open, then applied a snug bandage. "Maybe that'll keep her from tearing the thing out. This is going to get rough."

"Yeah." The fresher the Holy Water, the more it hurt when it came in contact with anything demonic. The treatment was going to rip the girl apart.

Carmela studied him. "I know what you're thinking. Trust me, it beats being dead."

"Maybe that's what she wanted," he replied.

"Ugly way to go."

Beck caught her tone of voice. "Ya don't think she'll make it, do ya?"

"Not sure. The one thing she's got going for her is her age."

"And God," Father Harrison added from his position near the door. He offered up two quart jugs of Holy Water.

"Him, too," Carmela replied. She took the jugs from Harrison and then handed him a pair of gloves. At the priest's quizzical look, she explained, "Hold down her legs. You try to keep her on the bed, Den. I'll do the honors."

As he bent over to pin Riley's shoulders down, Beck whispered in her ear, "Sorry, girl. This is gonna to hurt like a sonovabitch."

Father Harrison closed his eyes and began to pray, his steady voice filling the room with verbal hope. Beck wondered if it would be enough.

Beck heard the doctor mumble something as she spread wide the first claw mark. The priest changed tone, speaking louder now.

"In the name of the Father, the Son, and the Holy Ghost, we humbly implore you to heal your servant who has valiantly fought the legions of darkness. Drive out the poison that afflicts her body and purify her soul. . . ."

Beck swallowed hard as the sacred liquid sank inside the wound.

The reaction was immediate. Riley's shriek nearly deafened him as she shot straight up off the mattress. He forced her down as she screamed and cried, her fingernails digging into the flesh on both his arms. He winced at the rush of pain as she found his healing wounds. No matter how bad it hurt, it was nothing compared to what she was feeling.

Come on girl, pass out, will ya?

But she didn't and continued to tear at him. Carmela moved to the next wound, then the next. The Holy Water bubbled and hissed, sending up a thick vapor that hovered in the air for a moment then evaporated.

Father Harrison continued to pray, his face as white as his collar.

"No! No!" Riley screamed. As she twisted and cried, Beck knew how it felt—like someone was burning her bones from the inside out.

"There's the problem," Carmela said, sounding relieved. "A broken claw. No wonder she's like this." The doc plucked a set of forceps from the bag and turned her attention to the wound.

As the doc removed the hooked claw, Riley painted the room with an earsplitting scream. Then the darkness pulled her under.

⁂

His muscles aching from the effort, Beck slumped against the wall, his stomach tumbling. He swallowed repeatedly to keep from heaving. Riley had looked right at him, cursing him. She would never forgive him.

"Sweet Jesus," he whispered.

"Yeah," Carmela muttered.

Father Harrison slowly made the sign of the cross and finished his prayer.

"Hands of God and all that?" Carmela asked, regrouping with that particular resilience that doctors seemed to possess.

"It always is," the priest replied. His forehead remained furrowed. "Do you need more Holy Water?"

"I think we've got enough. At least the next time it won't burn so bad."

Stripping off his gloves and throwing them on the bed, Beck crossed to the window and sucked in deep gulps of air to clear his head. When he turned around, Carmela was sitting on the wooden chair near the bed, her mouth a grim line.

"Tell me that was worth it," Beck said.

She arched an eyebrow. "Too soon to tell."

Someone pounded on the apartment door and the priest headed in that direction. Words were exchanged and then the priest reappeared.

"Tenants from downstairs. They were upset that we woke them up. I reassured them that we'd be quiet from now on."

Beck snorted. He turned and stared out the window for a long time, listening to the whimpers coming from the bed behind him.

What if she dies? The very thought felt like ice in his veins.

"Den?"

"Huh?" He found Carmela packing her bag. The bed was clean and she had a trash bag on the floor by the door. "Yer leavin'?" he asked, feeling an uncharacteristic panic.

"Only for a few hours. I've got some other folks to check on."

When he didn't reply, Carmela cocked her head. "You okay?"

He waved her off. No way he could admit what he was feeling at this moment.

"You know how to change the IV, so I can skip that lecture," Carmela said. "I bandaged her hand. Looks like she sliced it on something. It should heal just fine."

"I didn't even see that," he admitted.

"Easy to miss with the thigh being as bad as it is. I've put one liter of fluid through her and I've set the rate at one-fifty an hour. If she starts to pee, turn it down, though I doubt you'll have that problem to contend with." She scratched her chin. "I'll file the tax paperwork for the Holy Water."

"Yeah, can't have the city not get their tax money," Beck replied bitterly.

"I'll be here at noon and we'll do it all over again."

"Noon. Okay." He could make it until them. "Harrison still here?"

"Gone. He's got mass this morning, so he had to scoot."

Carmela zipped the suitcase closed, watching him more closely than he liked.

"Thanks. I owe ya," he said.

The doctor nodded. "You do." She glanced over at Riley. "If the Holy Water works, she'll live. If not . . ."

The words hung in the air, like a sword pulled from a sheath.

When Beck heard the apartment door thud closed, he collapsed into a chair near the bed. His eyes shut immediately, the stress and exhaustion pulling him down toward needed oblivion.

Riley called out for her dad. Then her mother. It tore his heart to hear her like that. He took her sweaty hand, holding it as gently as possible.

"Sorry, girl, they're gone."

All ya got is me.

EIGHTEEN

Riley awoke in semidarkness. She wasn't boiling hot now. That was good. Her mind felt hazy from the fever, and all her muscles ached like she'd run a marathon. It took a while to realize she was in her own bed. There was a creak of wood; someone was sitting in the chair, reading by the light of a dim lamp.

"Dad?"

"No honey, it's Carmela."

"Carmela?" The brain wasn't cooperating. It felt like it was full of week-old pudding.

When she didn't reply, the woman added, "The Guild's doctor?"

"Oh, yeah, sorry," Riley said, trying to sit up. "Where's my dad?"

The doctor didn't answer, but Riley's memory did, slitting through the fog with frightening clarity.

Dad's gone. The tears wouldn't come.

Why didn't I die? I'd have been okay with that.

More bad memories trooped in like an avenging army: She'd caught a demon and lost it, but not before it had ripped her to shreds. Riley tried shifting her left leg, but she couldn't feel it. Maybe they'd sliced it off. They'd probably give her one of those high-tech titanium legs, like some of the soldiers used.

I'll never find shoes to fit.

"My leg, is it—"

"It's still here. The Holy Water makes it numb. Trust me, it's for the best." A pause. "Why didn't you treat your wounds, Riley?"

"I did. It hardly hurt at all. When you guys did it . . ." She shuddered.

"You must have used older Holy Water. Father Harrison was here, so ours was really stout. He'd consecrated it that morning."

They called in a priest? That was sobering. Riley pulled herself up again. It was hard to move when her leg acted like it wasn't there.

"Here." Carmela handed her a glass of clear soda, and she took a lengthy sip. The cold fluid felt good going down and rinsed away the yucky film in her throat.

"So what happened?" the doc asked as she settled on the edge of the bed. Her hair was in a bun at the back of her head, and she was wearing a light orange shirt and blue jeans.

Riley didn't think a lecture was in the works, so she laid it all out. "I caught a Three all by myself and it, like, got me. Then they took it away from me."

"They?" Carmela asked, brows furrowed.

"A couple of guys. I thought they were trappers at first, but they weren't."

"They stole your demon?" There was shock in the woman's voice.

"Yeah. I told them I was with Beck, but they didn't believe me. They wanted to party." She bit her lip at the memory of the pair of them leering at her.

"Come on, tell me," Carmela urged. "Did they hurt you?"

Riley shook her head. "No." She straightened the sheet on her lap. "I had no choice. I had to leave the Three behind or they would have . . ."

The doctor lightly touched her arm. "Got it. What did they look like?"

Riley gave her the descriptions, including that one of them was named Dodger.

"I'll tell Den."

Riley frowned. *Why does everyone think Beck's my babysitter?*

"I don't need his help," she snapped. "I caught the demon, didn't I?"

Carmela frowned back. "Not asking for help bought you six claw marks in your leg. Den will handle it. He'll make sure they learn some respect."

"Why would he even care?" Riley asked. "He doesn't owe me anything."

Carmela's frown faded. She leaned closer, pensive.

"Den never had a father. The closest man to fill that role was your dad. I think he sees you as his little sis, and he's not going to let anyone jack with you."

"He acts like he knows everything."

Carmela chuckled. "Honey, that's what all guys are like. You should know that by now."

Riley managed a weak smile, causing her lips to crack. "How mad is he?"

"In-can-descent. Prepare to have your butt chewed. Major league. You scared the hell out of him. I've never seen him that worried."

"If you say so."

The doc wasn't reading him right. Beck believed the world should do whatever he said, just because he said it. He was only upset because Riley wasn't playing his game.

Carmela took the glass to the kitchen, refilled it, and returned. Riley sucked down half of it in one long gulp.

"So, you got a boyfriend?" the doctor asked, propping her feet on the bed. Then she grinned. "Inquiring minds want to know."

Peter came to mind. "Just a friend who's a boy." *But then there's Simon.* Riley couldn't hide the smile.

"I know that look. You have your eye on someone. Good for you."

Riley wasn't so sure. "I don't think it'll go anywhere. He's Harper's apprentice."

"Simon Adler?" the doc guessed. Riley nodded. "Cute. You've got good taste."

"He's way tightly wrapped," Riley admitted.

"Well, you won't have to worry he'll paw all over you, that's for sure. Some of those guys . . ." Carmela shook her head in disgust.

Riley's bladder kicked in, sending an urgent message to her brain.

"Ah, can I get up and pee and take a shower? I smell," she said, wrinkling her nose.

"Yes on the toilet, no on the shower." Carmela rose. "That leg's going to feel like dead wood, and I don't want your IV to get screwed up. You can wash at the sink if you want, sitting in a chair."

"How soon will it be out?" Riley quizzed, peering at the clear tubing in her arm.

"Since you're peeing, tomorrow morning. The wounds look tons better."

"Can I see it?"

Carmela reached over to uncover Riley's leg. "You ready?"

"Is it really gross?" she asked, scrunching her face.

"Sorta. Not as bad as two days ago."

"Two days?" Riley gasped. "I've been sick that long?"

Carmela nodded. She pulled off the gauze. "Ta da!"

Riley gasped. It looked like a moonscape. The claw marks were encircled by red, puffy skin, but at least there was no brown gunk now.

"No shorts in my future."

"Hey, I'd show off those scars. How many girls can say they caught a demon?"

"But I didn't get to keep him," Riley complained.

"That's not the point. You *caught* a Three. That takes chutzpah. Next time have Den waiting in the wings. He'll teach those thieves some manners."

That sounded like a plan, despite the fact that it involved Beck. She could only imagine what Backwoods Boy and his steel pipe could do to Dodger and his fat buddy.

"It's healing so fast," she said, peering down at the slices.

"The Holy Water does that. Doesn't do much for regular wounds, but get chewed up by a fiend and it's the treatment of choice." Carmela looked around the room as if searching for something. "There was a claw in one of them. I took it out. It's around here somewhere."

Euuuu . . .

Riley pondered that as she hopped her way into the bathroom, Carmela holding on to her arm. When she saw herself in the mirror she moaned.

"Medusa hair. That's so gross."

"But curable."

Riley pushed a greasy lock out of her face. Then a horrible thought hit her.

"Simon didn't see me like this, did he? I mean, he didn't come over and—"

Carmela's musical laugh filled the small room. "I wouldn't do that to you. Now hit the can and let's get you cleaned up. You're going to run out of steam really quickly."

Riley hated to tell her—she already had.

✢

By morning, the IV was out and Riley had experienced a long hot shower. Two, actually, though one had been plenty. The Holy Water treatments only stung now, and the wounds were knitting together. Carmela had found some clean sheets in a drawer, and when Riley flopped in bed after the second shower it felt like heaven.

It was late in the afternoon when she woke to find Beck parked in the chair, arms crossed over his broad chest as he glared at her like a malevolent gargoyle. He had three days' worth of beard and a powerful frown on his face.

He was clearly over being worried about her.

"Lookin' better," he said, his drawl thicker than usual. That wasn't a good sign.

"Thanks," she said weakly. She reluctantly sat up in bed, tucking the sheets around her waist. When he made no move to help, she knew she was in for it.

"So let me get this right," he began. "I blew off an entire night's trappin' because ya just had to get yer beauty sleep."

Riley remained mute. Experience had taught her that if you jumped in too quick, people only got madder.

"But instead of sleepin', ya decided to play trapper and take yer little ass down to Five Points. Demon Central, no less."

She bit the inside of her lip and tried not to fidget.

"And ya went down there . . . *alone*."

Riley studied the geometric pattern on the sheets, waiting for the shouting to begin. She hated when people shouted.

"Tell me what happened," he barked.

Riley blinked at the demand. "I caught a Three and—"

"No!" Beck retorted, surging to his feet. He would have paced if the room had been bigger. "I want it from the beginnin'. Why ya went down there, all of it."

She took a deep breath and told him the story, including the part about the two jerks who'd taken her prize. When she finished, she looked up at him. His frown was deeper now.

"They didn't touch ya. Is that right?" he asked, his voice cold steel.

"No. But they wanted to."

"Did that scare the hell outta ya?"

Riley nodded. It still scared her when she thought about it, how things might have fallen out if that demon hadn't woken when it did.

"Well, at least ya got some sense," he said, his voice thick with derision. "What about the Three?"

"It moved faster than I thought it would. It clawed me, so I rammed the sphere in its face."

"Yer supposed to throw 'em."

"I did. The first one missed."

He dropped into the chair. "Anythin' else?"

When she didn't answer, he repeated the question with more force.

She sucked in a deep breath. "It didn't look like I thought it would. They're supposed to be black. This one was all spotted."

"Did it have a big white patch on its neck?" he quizzed.

"Yeah. It was way heavy, and it smelled *really* bad."

"They do, because of what they eat."

She shuddered, realizing it could have been her instead of the cow guts.

"What did ya learn from this dumbass stunt?"

Here's where she was supposed to apologize, promise to be a good little girl and never do anything like this again.

Screw that.

Riley locked eyes with him. "I learned that the Holy Water better be fresh, that I need practice throwing the spheres, and that someone has to watch my back so asshats don't steal my demons."

Beck's expression alternated between anger and something she couldn't quite comprehend. Almost like . . . pride.

"Ya lied to me and put yerself in danger. If the Three hadn't ripped ya apart, those two bastards would have. Ya gotta listen to me, girl. I've been down this road myself."

Riley smirked. "Those guys wanted to party with you too?"

She knew the joke was a huge mistake the moment it left her mouth. Beck's face went dark crimson, the veins popping in his neck.

"Dammit, girl, cut the crap! I owe it to yer daddy to keep ya safe. I can't do that if yer jackin' with me all the time."

His anger ignited hers. "Guess what? You're off the hook, Beck. I'll take care of myself."

"Like ya did with the demon?"

"I did okay for my first Three," she protested. "I made some mistakes, but I caught the damned thing! *Without* backup."

He smirked. "Yeah, well, from now on ya won't be able to do diddle in this city without a master at yer side."

"I have to trap or I can't pay my rent!"

"I'll loan ya the money."

"No deal," she said, shaking her head. "You think you own me now. It'll only be worse if I take money from you."

The muscles in his jaw twitched. "I'm too damned tired to argue with ya, girl. I'll have somebody watch yer daddy's grave. Yer here until I say otherwise." He held up two key rings. One held her car keys, the other her father's. "I'll be keepin' these, in case ya think of joyridin' to Five Points again."

"You can't strand me here!" she argued.

"The hell I can't," he said, and stomped out of the room. A few seconds later the front door slammed, rattling the pictures on the living room wall.

"You arrogant son of . . ." She pounded the pillow, but it didn't help. Why was he so mad? Did he really think she was going to let him take care of her like she was some helpless girl?

Riley slid down under the covers, pulling them over her head.

My. Life. Totally. Sucks.

As long as Beck stood in her way, that wasn't going to change.

NINETEEN

Beck's anger began to fade about the time he wheeled his truck into Cabbagetown and made the turn toward his house. Not that he hadn't cursed Riley most of the way home.

She's just like me at that age—all badass attitude. Except with him it'd involved too much booze and the belief that if he didn't get laid at least a couple times a week, the world was going to end.

He'd not been able to tell her, but he was so damned proud that she'd trapped her first Three on her own. He hadn't even done that. Still, it scared the hell out of him. She wasn't thinking stuff through and that had almost gotten her killed.

If Harper finds out about your little adventure, there'll be hell to pay. The master had been jonesing to have her license revoked, and this time he might pull it off.

Might be for the best. But it wouldn't be right. The Three she'd caught was the one Paul and he had been hunting for the better part of a week. She'd brought the thing down on her own, newbie mistakes and all.

"Damn, Riley girl, ya got stones," he muttered, shaking his head in astonishment. Problem was, this job took smarts as well. You had to think out a situation, not bulldoze your way through.

"God, now I sound like Paul," he said. That was damned ironic.

After a shower and a quick run through McDonald's, a trip to Five

Points was on his radar. Riley had mentioned seeing an old black guy on the street with a strange sort of shuffle. That was probably Ike. The old veteran might know what really went down the other night.

�֒

Beck had always believed that the homeless guys living around Forsyth Street had more on the ball than the politicians at the state capitol. Ike was a good example. He was a transient, as the bigwigs liked to call them. As in, they hoped Ike and his kind would move on to Birmingham or Chattanooga, anywhere as long as it wasn't Atlanta. None of that bothered the old guy. His family had been here since the Civil War. Once he figured out how to work the system, leaving Atlanta wasn't in the cards.

That's not exactly how the city had imagined their social experiment would work. A few years ago they'd put yellow and blue "donation meters" around downtown so folks would feed the meters rather than whatever panhandler was pestering them. The cash was collected and was supposed to go to the shelters, but with the city short of money, who knows where it ended up. Though fewer people donated now, Ike had learned he could score cash for his booze and food if he collected his cut before the city. It just took a crowbar and a little leverage.

Beck wandered up to the guy, slow and easy. It was best not to spook him, because Ike had logged his time in hell during the First Gulf War and still suffered nightmares. They shared common ground in that department.

"Ike," he said politely, setting his duffel bag on the ground.

The old black man looked over, and his face broke out in a toothy smile. "Denver, good to see you."

Ike was whippet-thin underneath the layers of grimy clothing. The clothes were mismatched—whatever he could scrounge at the local shelter, including the Steelers stocking cap. His fingers were gnarled by arthritis, and he had a strange shuffle that made it seem as if he were trying to go forward and sideways at the same time.

Beck pulled the McDonald's sack from his bag. "Figured ya might like some food."

The smile grew toothier. "Never turn down chow. Give me a moment, will you? Need to do some banking."

After a look around to ensure they were alone, Ike placed a hand over the front of the donation meter. A little bit later he lowered it and waited. The hatch at the bottom of the meter sprung open and coins spilled out. He shoveled them into his pockets, tossed a few in for seed, and then fished something out of the meter, which he carefully placed in the opposite pocket. No crowbar needed.

Ike clicked the meter shut and grinned. "All done."

Beck frowned, trying to determine what had just happened.

"Figure it out?" the man teased.

Then it clicked. "It's a demon, isn't it?"

Ike nodded. "Found him outside the casino digging through the trash. We made a deal. He gives me the money out of the meters and I make sure he gets lots of pretty stuff for his stash."

He fished the fiend out of his pocket. The Magpie was wearing the trademark bandana and holding a little bag of treasure, like all Klepto-Fiends. "I call him Norton."

Beck studied the demon, who frowned back, recognizing a trapper when he saw one. "Hi, Norton."

The fiend squeaked in return, clutching his bag like Beck was going to snatch it away from him. Little Norton was a problem. Trappers were supposed to capture Hellspawn, even if they were keeping a buddy fed.

Ike scrutinized him, like he'd heard Beck's thoughts. "You're not going take my demon away, are you?" The fiend issued a worried squeak.

Beck raised his eyes from the infernal thief, knowing what he had to do.

"Demon?" he asked. "Where? I don't see one."

Ike chuckled and returned a relieved Norton to his pocket.

"Thanks, man. The priest tells me I'm going to Hell for doing this."

Beck gestured at the broken city. "And that would be different . . . how?"

Ike guffawed. "Let's go up the street. I like to be on holy ground as much as possible, even when I'm eating."

Smart. The homeless learned that lesson quickly—stay on sanctified soil or risk being taken down by a Three. That's why there were always scruffy men clustered on the steps of nearly every downtown church.

A block farther on they passed a mailbox. Ike dropped off the demon, and the fiend wasted no time scrambling up the side and then diving down the mail slot. Beck could only imagine what sort of fun it would have going through all the letters and packages.

They settled on the stairs that led to the Shrine of the Immaculate Conception on Central Avenue. Beck handed over the supersized cheeseburger, the fries, and the large vanilla shake. The more calories the better. Ike looked like an ebony toothpick.

"No onions. Got it right, man," Ike said, peering under the bun. "You always remember."

Beck pulled out his supper, which was pretty much the same, except he went for extra cheese on the burger to up his protein intake. They ate in silence, too hungry to be chatty. It wasn't until the burgers were gone and they were closing in on the last of the shakes that Beck posed his question.

"A few nights ago a trapper got rolled by pair of losers down here. One of them is called Dodger. Ya know these guys?"

"Yeah, I do. They hang around looking for someone on their own. Then they pick 'em off. Mostly it's the casino folks." He chuckled. "They're stupid, though. They hit 'em *after* they've been inside and lost all their money."

"Have ya heard anythin' about them traffickin' in demons?"

"Don't know about that, but I saw 'em with one the other night. It was in a steel bag like the kind you guys use. They were dragging it along the street, bitching and moaning how heavy it was. Man, was that thing howling up a storm."

"Was that Sunday night?" Beck asked. Ike nodded and took a long slurp of his shake. "Ya see a girl down here?"

"Sure did. Young thing. She was pulling a bag out of a car, acting like it was too heavy for her."

"That was Paul Blackthorne's daughter."

Ike's expression saddened. "Ah, man, I heard about him. Sorry. I know you were tight."

"Yeah, we were."

"Why'd you let her down here alone? You know what it's like," Ike scolded, shaking a bony finger at him. "You lost your mind?"

"I was watchin' her daddy's grave. I didn't know what she was up to."

"She okay?" Ike asked.

Beck shrugged. "Got clawed up, but she'll make it. Those two assholes took her demon. I wanna let them know that's not polite."

"I can imagine how that'll go," Ike said and smirked, issuing a wheezy chuckle. "Want me to keep an eye out for 'em?"

"Sure do." Beck rose, wadding the paper bag in his hands and giving it a twist like it was someone's neck. "Just be careful, okay?"

"I will," Ike said. "She's a good-looking girl. You sweet on her?"

Beck hesitated, not sure what to say. "She's real young."

"You looked in a mirror today? You're not much older than her."

"Way older up here," Beck said, tapping his temple.

"Yeah, well, that don't count until you been *over there*," Ike replied. "The rest of the world don't understand."

"God, that's the truth." Beck fished out a twenty and handed it over. "Thanks for yer help."

"No sweat," Ike said, palming the bill. "Could you drive me to the shelter? It's a long walk for my old bones."

"Sure. I'll go get the truck," Beck offered. As he walked down the street, Ike descended into a deep coughing fit, one that shook his thin frame like an earthquake.

That'll be me someday.

TWENTY

"You trapped a what?" Peter asked, confused. Riley had called him to complain about Beck, in particular, and about losing her demon, in specific.

"A Gastro-Fiend. Look them up on the Internet," Riley advised. She'd hopped her way out to the couch and was enjoying a leftover piece of pizza she'd found in the refrigerator. It was all vegetables, which made her think it wasn't Beck's. "Any luck cracking the password on the disk?"

"Not yet. I've tried all the obvious ones. I'll get it. Only be a matter of time." More keyboard noises. "Holy crap! These Three things are wicked!"

Before Riley could respond, there was a voice in the background—Peter's mom asking why he was shouting. It was like the woman lurked outside his bedroom door. He gave her some lame excuse and then came back on the line.

"Sorry, it was the warden."

"Did she see the demon on your computer?" Riley asked.

"No way. She doesn't like you as it is. If she thought you were hanging with things that look like abominable snowmen, she'd freak."

"Too short for an abominable. More like a really tall Tasmanian devil."

"Does it make all those weird noises?"

Riley laughed. "Pretty close." *Right before it eats you.*

"So was Beck impressed?"

"Ah, not so much." She gave him an overview of what had happened, without mentioning how close she'd come to joining her mom and dad.

There was a prolonged silence on the other end of the phone. She thought maybe he was IM'ing one of his buds, but there wasn't any keyboard clicking.

"Peter?"

"Are you, like, crazy?"

"I need the money."

More silence.

"Peter?"

"I always thought your dad would look out for you, and now that he's gone it's . . . more dangerous."

"Stop worrying. I'll apprentice with one of the master trappers and get my full license. Then I can go after that Geo-Fiend."

Peter's voice got all strange. "Ah, I need to go, Riley. Let me know what the new school is like. Anyway . . . later . . . bye."

Riley found herself listening to the dial tone. He'd never left her hanging on the phone like that, even when pestered by his mom.

"Thanks, dude. I knew I could count on you." She clicked off the phone and dropped it on the couch next to her. When it bounced off the cushion and hit the floor, she made a gun out of her fingers and riddled it with bullets. No one understood what it was like unless they were a trapper.

Which was how her life was going to play out from now on. She'd put in her time at school until she got her diploma, but her real life was the demons. And just like Peter, there would always be people who wouldn't understand that. Wouldn't know the thrill of trapping a Three and living to tell about it. She'd never be normal again.

If I ever was.

Leaning back on the couch, Riley stared at nothing, letting her thoughts ramble. At least until the nothing moved. Sitting up, she caught sight of something small and stealthy toting a little canvas bag as it crept along the edge of a bookshelf.

The Magpie had returned. At least it looked like the same one she'd caught that night in the hallway.

"How'd you get away?" The demon just grinned and parked itself on the edge of the shelf, legs swinging back and forth like a kid. It began to unpack its bag, laying out a variety of shiny objects with studied reverence. One of them was the *N* key from her keyboard. Riley bet if she checked her dresser the silver earring would be long gone.

She could catch it, and that would be seventy-five bucks, money she really needed. If it was that good at escaping it'd just come back and she could earn another seventy-five bucks. She could make her rent off this one demon.

Riley rose off the couch. In a flash the fiend was gone, along with the bag. It hadn't moved that fast the other day.

"Wow. You're supersonic." Clearly it'd decided it was going to stay. "Just don't let anyone see you," she advised. "And put my *N* back right now!"

There was a blur toward the keyboard and then to the shelf. The key was in place, and not one foul word had been uttered.

"*So* not a Biblio."

✦

Beck had barely walked inside the Tabernacle and settled at a table for the Guild meeting when Simon edged up to him.

"How is she?" the young apprentice asked, keeping his voice low. At Beck's quizzical expression, he added, "Doctor Wilson told me what happened."

"She's doin' better."

"Would Riley like me to visit her?" Simon asked.

Riley might, but I'm not so sure I do. He hadn't quite worked out what he thought of Simon, especially since the guy definitely had his eyes on Paul's little girl.

Ah, what the hell.

"Yeah, go see her," Beck replied. "She'd appreciate talkin' to someone who doesn't piss her off."

Simon brightened. "I'll call her later."

"Anyone else know about this?" Beck asked, letting his eyes trail across the other trappers in the room.

"Harper doesn't, if that's what you're asking." Simon retreated across the open space to take his place behind the master. Harper glared and snapped at him out of habit.

Beck took a chair and went still, like a sniper in a tree. Besides his usual bottles of beer, in his pocket was Exhibit A, the three-inch claw the doc had excavated from Riley's leg.

Just in case there's show-and-tell.

The first part of the meeting was the usual stuff—Guild housekeeping, as Paul had called it. Collins, the Guild's president, announced an increase in dues to cover the cost of meeting at the Tabernacle for the next year. That earned groans from the members. There were the usual complaints about trappers not filling out their paperwork properly.

"Anyone had any problems with the Holy Water?" Collins asked.

"I have," Beck replied. "It didn't take down a Three like it was supposed to."

"Was the Holy Water fresh?"

"Yeah. One day old."

"It helps if you actually hit the demon, Mile High," one of the other trappers jested.

Beck wasn't in the mood. "Paul hit it straight on, but it didn't matter." The mention of the dead master's name shut down the joking immediately.

"Speaking of which," Collins began, "why don't you tell us what happened the night Paul died."

Beck dreaded this moment. Out of respect for his mentor, he rose. The room fell silent.

"This is hard," he began, feeling the prickle of tears in his eyes. He blinked them away, took a long, deep breath, and delivered the report in measured tones as if he were in front of a superior officer. When it was over he remained standing in case there were questions.

"Ya say the beasties were workin' tagether?" Master Stewart quizzed.

"Timin' was too good to be coincidence."

"Bullshit," Harper said, glaring over at Beck. "He's just saying that because he fucked up and got his partner killed."

Beck's heart began to hammer in his ears. Fists clenched, he forced himself to stay put, not vault across the room and take Harper out.

"I didn't fuck up. I did every goddamn thing right and he still . . ."

Beck unclenched his fists and put his hands palm down on the table to keep from losing it.

Better tell them now.

When he looked up, all eyes were on him. "It was the same Five that went after Paul's daughter in the library."

Harper smirked. "How'd you know that?"

"I asked it. The damned thing laughed at us, like we were nothin'." He hesitated and then let loose the final secret. "It was the first time I ever saw Paul afraid of a demon."

Some of the trappers shifted nervously, whispering among each other. If a Geo-Fiend could take out someone as experienced as Blackthorne, then any one of them was at risk.

Even Harper. And the old master knew it.

"Any other questions?" Silence. "Thanks, Beck. Sorry about Paul." A pause. "Jackson, you're up."

The Guild's treasurer rose. "Got a report that someone is selling demons illegally. You guys heard anything?"

"Fireman Jack mentioned something about it the other day," Morton replied. He still hadn't made master because Harper refused to sign off on his application, which had made for bad blood between them.

"That fag?" Harper huffed. "Wouldn't trust a thing he'd say."

"As long he treats us fairly, I don't care what church he worships at," Jackson shot back.

"You wouldn't."

Beck shook his head. Harper never failed to amaze him. The man was a natural-born asshole.

Jackson cleared his throat, twice, his way of keeping his cool. "I checked with a few of the traffickers. One of them was complaining that someone paid five hundred for a Three earlier this week. He didn't know who bought the thing and wanted to know why the Guild was allowing that."

"We aren't," Harper said testily. "Any you guys trap a Three this week?"

One of the trappers raised his hand. "I did. I sold it to Jack for three hundred."

"Anyone else?" Seven more men raised their hands, and all of them had sold the fiends for the standard fee.

"I sold two," Beck added.

"So this story is bullshit then," Harper said. "Let's move on."

They don't know about Riley's demon. Beck weighed the situation. He might be able to bury her misadventure deep enough that they'd never find out, but it wouldn't change the fact that someone was stealing demons and selling them illegally. That would eventually come back to haunt them.

Pain now. Pain Later. Never a good call.

Sorry, girl, the shit's gonna hit the fan.

"There was another Three caught this week."

"Who trapped it?" Collins asked.

"Paul's daughter. She took it down in Demon Central Sunday night."

Harper broke out in a thick laugh. "Nice one, kid."

"I'm not jokin'. She was worried about payin' her rent, so she loaded up Paul's gear and went huntin'. She took down a Three . . . *on her own.*"

"No way," Jackson said. "For real?"

"For real."

"She tell you that?" Harper asked. Beck nodded. "Then she's lying."

Beck's muscles tensed. He moved his neck to loosen them, like a fighter does right before a bout. Harper caught the gesture and sneered at him.

"She's got six claw marks in her leg that say otherwise," Beck retorted. "And just in case you think *I'm* lying . . ." He raised the claw fragment in the air so the others could see it. The trapper closest to him winced.

"Doc Wilson dug this out of her thigh."

"Claws marks don't mean she trapped the thing," Harper protested.

"Once it hooks you, it only goes two ways: You trap it or it eats you. There's no other options," Morton replied. He gave Harper a hard stare. "I would expect a master to know that."

Harper spat on the floor in disgust.

"I did some checkin'," Beck replied. "Seems there's a couple of losers down there who like rollin' folks. Riley trapped the Three and then they showed up. They told her they could get five hundred for it."

"You sayin' they stole her demon?" Jackson asked, astonished.

Beck nodded. "It was easy. Young girl on her own. They figured they'd score some serious cash and have a party. She had to leave the demon behind if she didn't wanna get jumped."

"That ain't right!" someone called out from the back of the room. "Those two need some thumpin'."

"Amen to that," another voice said.

Collins looked over at Beck. "How's the kid?"

"Healin'. And seriously pissed."

There were nods around the room. Beck kept the smile to himself. These guys were hard-core, with a simple view of how the world should work. Trapper Rule No. 1: No one messed with your capture. Rule No. 2: No one messed with a fellow trapper. Violate either of those rules and serious pain was in your future.

Jackson frowned, his face deep in thought. "Who's buying these fiends for that kind of money? The legit traffickers know better. The world falls in on them if they deal under the table."

"What do they do with the demons after they buy them?" Morton asked. "They have to go to the Church. But if the buyer's illegal, they can't do that without the paperwork."

"We need to get a handle on this," Collins interceded. "Stewart, can you check in with the Archbishop and find out if anything's happening on that end?"

"Aye," the master replied.

"What about Blackthorne's brat?" Harper asked. "She was trapping illegally. We can't let that happen."

Stewart chuckled and rose, supported by a cane. "Nay, we canna. Paul was one of the best damned trappers I ever knew. If his lass can pull down a Three at this stage, I'd say it be in the blood."

"You willing to take that on?" Collins asked. "She sounds damned willful."

"Aye, I'd be pleased ta train the lass. All she needs is a firm hand."

Beck allowed himself to exhale. Stewart was a good man. A bit slower now that he'd gotten banged up tangling with an Archdemon, but still a lot kinder than the other choice. *And a lot less prejudiced.*

"No," Harper barked. "I'm senior trapper and I get my choice of apprentices. Blackthorne's brat is mine to train."

Stewart eyed his rival. "Ya gonna be fair with her?"

"Just as fair as she deserves," Harper retorted. The unholy smile on his face said it all.

Simon went pale. He gave Beck a desperate look, but there was nothing they could do. Harper had seniority.

Shit. His plan had failed.

Collins gave Harper a long look. "We'll want regular reports on her progress."

The smirk grew wider. "And you'll get them, trust me."

"Okay, let's move on. What's this about not telling mall security when you're trapping in a department store? You guys know the rules."

TWENTY-ONE

Riley heard the telltale clomp of boots in the hallway before the knocking started. It was close to eight at night. Simon wasn't due until nine, which meant this was probably Beck returning for another lecture.

"Hey, girl, ya awake?"

Riley muted the television and hopped to the door. With a groan, she flipped the locks and opened the door partway but not enough to allow her nemesis to barge in. "What's up?"

Beck waved a bag in front of her face. It sported the logo of the Grounds Zero. "Brought ya one of their brownies. Thought ya liked them."

"I do. Just don't like the delivery guy."

"Sucks, don't it?" he said. "So do ya let me in or do I toss this in the dumpster on the way out?"

Riley gasped at the thought of such cruelty and waved him in. Beck plopped on the couch, placing the bag on the packing box coffee table. He still looked tired, like sleep no longer held any value for him.

"New coat?" she asked. His old one had been dark brown. This one was a creamy brown, and it looked good on him.

Beck nodded. "Found it at the market. It's used, but I like 'em that way. Not as stiff, makes it easier to move." He stared at her for a few seconds. "Ya have any soda?"

Riley hobbled into the kitchen, retrieved the drink, and then began to fume. She was the one with the gored leg. Why wasn't he getting his own drink? When she returned to the living room she realized why. He'd set out the plastic wrapped brownie, and leaning up against it was a colored envelope adorned with a smiley face.

He bought me a card?

She handed over the drink and then eagerly thumbed open the envelope.

Oh.

The card wasn't from Beck but from the baristas at the coffee shop. They'd signed their names in different colors, along with more smiley faces. Simi's was in bright orange.

Riley made sure to smile anyway. "Cool."

"Thought ya'd like that." He placed something next to the brownie. It was a demon decal. She'd receive one for each Three she trapped. Most trappers put them on their vehicles like fighter pilots did during the wars. Beck's truck had a lot of them. He'd joked they were what held it together.

She grinned, studying the decal. "Way cool! Thanks!"

"Ya earned it." He took a long drink of the soda, gave a distinct burp but no apology. A white envelope landed next to the decal. "For your rent. Consider it a loan."

"How much?"

"Five hundred."

Five hundred more reasons you'll think you own me.

"Thanks," she muttered. She'd accept the cash or sleep in the streets. No coin flip needed.

Riley peeled off the plastic that entombed the brownie. As long as she had a fix of chocolate, she could handle anything. "Who is watching Dad tonight?"

"One of the journeymen. Don't worry, nothin' will happen."

He seemed so sure.

"How'd the meeting go?"

Beck frowned. "How'd ya know about that?"

"Carmela. She dropped by to make sure I hadn't gone all furry or anything."

"Ya won't. Not 'til the full moon," he said. "I can't wait to see that."

"I do, and you're the first one I maul."

He didn't look worried.

"Meeting?" she nudged. Simon had hedged when she'd asked him about it on the phone, which meant she might not like the news.

Beck took another sip of soda, this time minus the burp. Slouched against the couch, he had one booted foot up on the packing box like he was watching a football game.

"Did ya hear from Simon?" he asked, changing the subject. She nodded. "He comin' over?" She nodded again.

He fell silent, which made her wonder if he was happy with that bit of news.

"Let me help you here," she said, reluctantly placing the brownie on her lap. "I say, 'How'd the meeting go, Beck?' and you say 'Well, Riley, it was . . .'" She gestured for him to complete the sentence.

That got her a glower. "Not terrific. Harper was on his high horse, and the Guild knows ya were out trappin' on yer own."

"You ratted me out?" *You couldn't wait to tell them, could you?*

"Yeah," he said, but his face told her he didn't find any joy in that. "The Guild's not happy about yer stunt."

"Surprise." She'd be naive to assume they'd give her a round of applause.

The enticing scent of chocolate wafted into her nose. She closed her eyes and savored the moment as a tiny moan escaped her lips.

"What is it with girls and chocolate?" Beck grumbled after another swig of soda. "Tastes like burnt coffee to me."

Her eyes snapped open, annoyed he'd ruined the moment. "This from a guy who guzzles energy drinks out of recycled whiskey bottles?"

"Better than that stuff."

This wasn't getting her anywhere. "So what happened?"

He sighed, running a hand through his hair. It made it stick up in the front. "Yer not to trap again until yer workin' with a master. Period. The end."

Better than she'd expected. Riley took a bite of brownie in celebration. The chocolate hit her mouth like gooey bomb.

Heaven.

"So who's going to train me?" she asked around the confection.

Her visitor didn't answer, suddenly fascinated by the ingredients listed on the back of the soda bottle.

Stall alert. "Harper?"

A curt nod. "He's senior. He has the right."

"But he hates me! He'll make sure I fail. That's not fair."

Beck walked to the kitchen while guzzling the last of the soda. The glass bottle landed in the recycling bin with a rattle. When he returned, his right eyebrow crooked upward.

"Not fair? If ya want fair, Princess, don't be a trapper."

Princess?

Beck paused near the door. "If yer good, ya survive. If not?" He shrugged like it was no big deal.

So much for sympathy. "What about my car keys?"

"Take the damned bus. It's good for the environment."

Then he was gone, combat boots thumping on the stairs.

Riley sighed and scratched her thigh through the denim. The wounds were torturing her in a new way—near constant itching.

"Wait a minute," she said, a grin sprouting. There was *one* bright side to apprenticing with Badass Harper and that was his other apprentice. Simon would be training alongside her for a few months until he became a journeyman. "Maybe this isn't as horrible as I think."

If she could survive Harper's blistering bitchiness, she'd become the first fully licensed female trapper in Atlanta's history.

"Then I'm gonna kick your ass, Backwoods Boy."

⟊

Three outfits later, Riley finally decided what to wear. Simon had seen her post-library disaster in all her green-hued glory, but this was a chance to look good for a change. She glanced up at the clock on the nightstand. Twenty more minutes before he was scheduled to arrive at her door.

"Please don't be early," she muttered. Beck had taken up more time that she'd realized, though the brownie had given her extra energy.

Riley hopped into the bathroom and donned her makeup. At least Simon hadn't seen her in full rotting mode. There was no amount of foundation or lip gloss that would erase that image.

She scrutinized herself in the mirror. Her hair was back to normal—which meant it had a will of its own—and the pink on her cheeks had nothing to do with a fever. After another liberal dose of lotion to the demon scars in the vain hope they'd stop the itching, she dressed in black slacks, a red turtleneck, and black boots.

She fidgeted in front of the long mirror on the back of the bedroom door, adjusting the turtleneck's sleeves, her hair, everything. Nothing seemed right.

HER REFLECTION: You're freakin', girlfriend. Get a grip!

HER: Of course I am. This is Simon. He's totally cute.

HER REFLECTION: No argument. So what's the problem?

HER: Why's he coming to see me? He's got to have a girlfriend. He's too hot not to.

HER REFLECTION: Yeah, I can see Simon cheating on his lady. Not! Why don't you ask him if he's taken?

HER: Because I might not like the answer.

HER REFLECTION: Now that's honest.

HER: Shut up.

Only one way to solve this—find a way to ask the guy without sounding pathetic. Then he'd say he was dating and it'd be all over.

At least I'll get out of this cage for a while.

Simon was all smiles when he appeared at her door wearing a black jacket, navy blue shirt, and blue jeans. The navy went well with his white-gold hair and deep blue eyes. As usual, the wooden cross was in plain sight.

For half a second Riley eyed him, soaking in the view. *Yummy.*

"You look very nice," he said.

"Thanks. It's good not to be green anymore."

Dork! Why did I say that?

"Are you up for a hot chocolate run?"

"Yes. YES! Anything to get out of here," she exclaimed.

Riley grabbed her bag by the door. Something landed on the floor in a rattle of metal. The two key rings. Beck had returned them and not said a thing.

You are such a creeper.

The moment she locked the apartment door, Simon offered his arm. Way old-fashioned, but thoughtful, especially since her leg could go from fine to crampy in a matter of seconds.

"Too bad the elevator's broken," he said. "It'd be easier for you."

He was always thinking of other people.

"I could carry you down the stairs," he offered. "You don't weigh that much."

He isn't joking.

"Ah, no, that's okay. I have to get used to this. It's feeling better, honest," she fibbed.

When Riley faltered a few steps down, he moved his hand to around her waist. Not too tight, but enough to let her know he wasn't going to let her fall. She hoped he'd leave it there.

"So what have you been doing since Beck's grounded you?" he asked.

"I've tried to find Dad's manual." Each step made the thigh cramp, which shot a bolt of pain into her groin. "I've gone through every drawer, bookshelf, and box," she said, trying to keep her mind off the discomfort. "No go."

"You try his car? Like maybe under the spare tire?" Simon asked.

Riley gaped at him.

"I saw him put it in there after one of the meetings. He made me promise not to tell you. But now, well . . ."

Now it didn't matter. "Thanks! I'd never have thought of looking under the tire."

His grin widened. "Duh! Why else would he have put it there?"

She elbowed him. "What's happening with Harper?"

"I hear he's got a new apprentice," Simon replied. "A pretty one."

"How hard is he going to be on me?"

Simon's good humor withered. "Way hard. He'll tear you apart. He does that to all of his apprentices, and it'll be worse for you because of your dad."

"What happened between them?"

"No idea," he said, shrugging. "But whatever it was, Harper's never forgotten it."

"And now he has another Blackthorne to torment."

"He's expecting you at nine in the morning. I'll give you directions."

When they reached his car, Simon opened the door for her. She climbed in, but it proved harder than she'd expected. Finally she realized it was best to sit and then use the center console as an anchor so she could pivot herself inside.

"Ouch, ouch, ouch," she said, rubbing the leg to try to ease the cramp.

Simon knelt next to her, concerned. "Anything I can do?"

"Just get me high on hot chocolate, that's all."

His worried expression eased. "For you, anything."

              ✦

Her friend Simi changed her hair color more often than she did boyfriends, which was saying something. Tonight her locks were coal black with brilliant purple highlights. On anyone else it would have looked silly, but Simi's exotic face allowed her to do almost anything and look great. It came with her unique ancestry—a mashup of Lebanese, Chinese, Irish, and Native American.

"Hey, Blackthorne!" the barista called out. Heads turned and Riley inwardly groaned. The coffee shop wasn't that busy, but she much preferred to be anonymous right now. The family name had been in the papers too much recently.

"I escaped!" she replied, holding her hands up in triumph.

"You did. I'm impressed. You get the card?"

"Yes," Riley said. "Thanks!"

"It was the trapper's idea. He brought it in and had us sign it," Simi admitted.

Beck bought the card? Why didn't he say that?

"So is he, like, dating or anything? He's way hot," Simi remarked.

Beck hot? Well, maybe a little. His serious case of attitude got in the way of his hotness every time. In lieu of an answer, she gestured toward Simon.

"This guy has offered to buy me all the hot chocolate I can drink," she said, beaming up at her escort.

"Niiice," Simi said, raising a black eyebrow. She didn't mean the "all the hot chocolate" part either. "You want the same?" Her eyes remained on Simon.

"Yes, thank you," he replied.

"Real nice," she said, then went to work creating the drinks. "How's your leg doing?"

"Better," Riley replied. "Itches a lot. Feels like I've been bitten by a five-hundred-pound mosquito."

Simi gave a sympathetic nod. "The trapper said you'd gone after a demon on your own. Is that right?"

Riley nodded. "Wasn't the smartest thing I've done." She heard a grunt of agreement from Simon.

Simi's eyes lit up. Since they'd been talking about demons, Riley knew what was coming.

"No, I did not watch *Demonland* last night," Riley said, hoping to short-circuit the subject. It never worked, but she still tried.

"Oh, man, it was awesome," Simi proclaimed. "Blaze took out a Winnebago full of demons with a Walmart shopping cart."

Any television producer who would put Walmart, demons, and an RV in the same episode was just asking for trouble, but then Hollywood's idea of the Vatican's Demon Hunters was more flash than reality.

"Was Blaze wearing those screw-me heels again?" Riley grumbled, leaning against the counter for support.

"Yup. And that skintight leather outfit you hate, the one that barely covers her butt," Simi replied. "It was a totally kick-ass episode."

"But the demon hunters don't admit women," Simon said, perplexed.

Simi gave him a look like he'd just flattened her favorite puppy.

"You've never watched the show, have you?"

Simon shook his head. Riley's estimation of him grew tenfold.

"Then you can't judge it," the barista said, returning with the hot chocolate. "You have to admit last season's final episode was truly epic."

Simon gave Riley a raised eyebrow.

"One of the hunter guys destroyed a mega-demon on top of Saint Peter's Basilica," Riley explained.

"Saint Peter's is holy ground," Simon began, "so no demon can—"

"Are you, like, an authority or something?" Simi retorted.

Riley left them to it, limping her way to the closest booth. She slid in, happy to let her thigh rest. It was doing its dull burn thing now.

Her eyes tracked to *her* booth along the far wall, the one where she and her dad had always sat. A familiar shard of guilt drove itself in a little deeper. How could she be out with Simon when she should be watching over the grave? Not that Beck would let her until her leg healed, but it still felt selfish.

"No, Dad would want me here," she said resolutely. *He liked Simon.*

Her escort delivered the hot chocolate.

"Who won?" Riley asked, angling her head toward the barista.

"It was a draw. Either that or coffee stirrers at twenty paces."

For the next few minutes they drank in silence. Riley spent that time savoring the exquisite goodness of the drink and screwing up her courage to ask The Question.

"Ah, thanks," she said. "This is really good."

"There's more if you want some."

Simon didn't seem like he wanted to be somewhere else, and he wasn't checking his phone every few minutes as if he were expecting a call.

Just ask him.

"Are you dating someone?" she blurted. *Oh, that was smooth.*

His forehead crinkled in amusement. "Maybe."

"Oh." She sighed. *Of course he's dating, you idiot. He's way too cool to be on his own.*

"I've just started seeing someone," he said.

That made it even worse.

Simon touched her hand with his fingers. "There's this really nice girl. She's got the most amazing brown eyes and an incredibly sharp mind."

"Oh." *So not me.*

"And we've got something in common. We both trap demons."

It took her a second to realize he was talking about her.

"Me?" she asked. He nodded. *Me!* "Then it's all good." *Really good.* She gifted him with a smile

"But we can't let Harper know we're dating or he'll make it worse for you." He gnawed on his lip for a moment. "Will you promise me something?"

"What?" she asked, caught off guard by his serious expression.

"Promise you won't go hunting on your own again, at least not until you're a journeyman."

What? Where was this coming from?

She pulled her hand away. "I can't make that promise, Simon."

"Riley, you're really brave, but you're still a—"

"Girl?" she asked, her temper rising.

"Apprentice," he replied, an edge to his voice.

"Who happens to be a girl," she pushed back. That was always the bottom line with these guys. She wasn't one of them.

"No!" he said emphatically. "Not everything is about gender. This is about you being safe."

Riley's eyes bored holes into her cup. She really liked this guy, and yet here he was trying to box her in, just like Beck.

"Do you think I'm crazy wanting to be a trapper?" she demanded.

Simon frowned. "Yes." When she opened her mouth to protest, he raised his hand to cut her off. "I understand why you could want this so badly. I know I do, even if it makes no sense."

He's not playing power games. He really cares.

The realization left her breathless. Simon took her hand again and squeezed it, rubbing his thumb over her palm in a gentle motion. "Just be careful, will you? That's all I ask." His voice was so gentle.

"Only if you promise the same."

"Deal."

They held hands for another minute or so, and then he rose to fetch more hot chocolate. After he placed the order, he looked over at her and smiled. The rest of the room faded to gray. There was only him, his brilliant blue eyes, and that amazing hair.

Something had changed between them. Whatever it was, it felt right.

TWENTY-TWO

It took Riley a while to decipher the peeling sign on the concrete building. "Ming and Sons Auto Repair."

The sign boasted Ming could fix transmissions, radiators, and CV boots.

Not anymore. Now the building housed the most senior trapper in Atlanta, and the one with the shortest temper.

At least it's close to the cemetery. Real close, like down Memorial Drive. Now that she went to school in Midtown, she'd have to drive through Atlanta to class, put in her three hours, then drive all the way down here to spend the night watching over her dad.

She yawned at the thought. *Only five more nights.* Despite her tummy being full of luscious hot chocolate and the toasty inner glow Simon had kindled, Riley hadn't slept well. Too worried what today would bring.

Her cell phone began chirping. It was Peter.

At least he's talking to me again.

"Hey, dude," she said, making sure not to let the relief show in her voice.

"I cracked it!" he crowed.

It took her a moment to realize he was talking about the computer disk.

"So what was the password?"

"Eleven, nineteen, eighteen sixty-three."

"Huh?"

"The date of the Gettysburg Address," he replied proudly.

"Makes sense. Dad wrote his thesis about it."

She heard a groan. "You couldn't have told me that up front and saved me hours of hacking?"

"Don't give me that. You loved every minute of it."

She knew he was grinning. "Busted," he said. "I'm still digging through the files. From what I can tell, it's research about Holy Water. History, folklore, all of it. It'll take a while to get through all this."

"I wonder what he was up to," Riley admitted.

"We'll find out. So what's your day like?"

"I'm standing outside my new master's place. Not impressed."

"Well, have at it. Call me when you get a chance."

"Later, Peter."

She put away the phone and trudged across the gravel parking lot to the metal door located at the front of the building. The door was battered and scratched and definitely needed a paint job. She raised her hand to knock, but the door opened before she could do the honors.

It was Simon and he was frowning. "Riley."

"Hi. How are you?" she asked, remembering how pleasant last night had been.

"Good," he said, but it didn't sound that way. "Harper's inside. Be careful."

Riley nodded and mustered her game smile. "It helps that you're here."

He shook his head. "It'll only make it worse, for *both* of us." He pushed past her and headed toward his beat-up silver Dodge.

Ohhkay.

After he'd pulled away, she had no further reason to stall. The moment she stepped inside the smell hit her. Lube. Old tires. And something else. Raw sulfur.

Demon.

The building was laid out like any garage—twin double doors led to service bays. All the metal lifts were gone, and the exposed ceiling rafters sported wires and ropes that ran over the beams like spaghetti. In one corner was a huge pile of plastic jugs and bottles, the kind used for Holy Water. Apparently, Harper's place was some kind of recycling location.

One half of the building had been sectioned off. To her right along the wall were five heavy-duty steel cages, only one of which was occupied. Unlike the demon she'd tangled with, this Three was all black, like they were supposed be. It slavered and slobbered, reminding her of an overly hairy dog, except this one's long claws raked against the sides of the reinforced steel enclosure like it was sharpening them.

"Blackthorne's daughter," it growled.

Before she had a chance to reply, a voice bellowed, "Get the hell in here, girl!"

With a pleading look heavenward, Riley made the journey into what must have been the shop's office. It was small and crowded with furniture. On one side of the room was an old wooden desk with an equally ancient desk chair. On the other, Harper was sprawled in a tattered dark blue recliner that had been new before computers were invented. His eyes were red and his face unshaven, probably because of the half-empty bottle of Jack Daniel's at his elbow. His shirt was clean but wrinkled, and his jeans had black stains in them. Behind him was a wooden door that led into the rear of the building. Through it she could see an unmade bed and what looked like a kitchenette. Dirty dishes were piled in the sink.

He lives here? She'd expected he had apartment or a house, like the other trappers.

Riley had never really paid much attention to Master Harper, mostly because he was always hating on her dad. Now she'd be with him for the next nine months. *Less if he wants to get rid of me.*

"Mr. Harper," she said. No reason to piss him off right off the bat.

"Brat," he replied, daring her to challenge him. He flicked a lighter on the end of a cheap cigar.

"I'm Riley, sir."

"No, you're Brat." Smoke coursed out of his mouth, revealing surprisingly decent teeth. "Or maybe I'll call you Bitch."

She sighed. "Brat works for me."

Establishing the pecking order. Maybe that was as far as it'd go.

"All my apprentices need to know one thing: My word is law. You fuck up and you're gone, and no other master in this country will touch you. Got it?"

Annoy you and I'm gone. "Yes, sir."

"Just because you're Blackthorne's girl doesn't mean you're going to get any slack. I don't trust you as far as I can spit you, got it?"

"Yes, sir."

"It's clear to me Blackthorne was doing a piss-poor job of training you, so we're starting over from the beginning." He pointed to a battered metal bucket and a scrub brush in a corner. "The floor under the cages need cleaning. Get to it."

"Yes, sir." She looked at the implements, remembering the sizable piles of demon crap. "Do you have a shovel and some gloves?"

He took a pull on his bottle. "Yeah, I do."

She waited, but he didn't move, didn't tell her where to find them. Then it dawned on her. She wasn't going to be using them.

"You can shovel the shit like I did when I started . . . with your hands. Put it out back. It kills the roaches."

She opened her mouth to protest, then jammed it shut. He was waiting for her to refuse; she could see it in his bloodshot eyes.

"Out back. Got it."

⊹

As the morning progressed, Riley began to learn a lot about demon scat. It stank like brimstone and whatever the thing had eaten recently, which was about everything. The crap stained concrete, and it stung her skin like scalding water if it was fresh.

She'd started on the farthest cage from the occupied one, kicking at the mound of dried excrement with the toe of her tennis shoe. Mistake. The kicking had no effect on the mound.

Leverage. That's what I need.

Digging around the back of the building revealed a collection of junk and a fairly decent stockpile of discarded metal that included bent hubcaps and broken manhole covers. Since the yard was fenced and secured with a padlock, it made Riley wonder if her new overlord traded in the stuff.

More digging unearthed a tire iron and a hammer with a cracked handle.

Better than nothing.

After prying, pounding, and tugging until her arms ached, the mound of crap broke up chunk by chunk. The outside might have been like concrete. The inside wasn't.

"Oh, gross," she muttered, her stomach churning as the smell and heat reached her nose. Had her dad started out like this?

Another scrounge around the warehouse turned up a battered garbage can lid, but nothing to scoop with. That made her think Harper had hidden anything she might be able to use.

Hands or nothing. Before she got them any dirtier, she rolled up her sleeves. At least the wound on her palm had closed and she no longer needed a bandage.

Riley closed her eyes and started scooping the mess onto the lid, trying to imagine it was anything but what it was. Tears formed as liquid heat cooked her fingers, palms, even her nails. Her hands quickly turned an abnormal shade of purple-red, even though the demon crap was solid black. She kept shoveling until the mound was gone, then stood. Her thigh cramped no matter what she did.

This wasn't demon trapping. This was scut work, some form of hazing apprentices had to endure.

No way I'm wimping out.

Riley looked down the line of cages. There were four more, one of which held its own peril. The demon watched her with the intensity a snake does an injured bird.

It took most of the morning to make it to the occupied cage. Midway through, Harper stood at the door to his office, watching her, a bottle of JD in hand. From his glassy eyes she knew it was booze, not an energy drink.

"Not what you thought, huh?" he called out, his voice rough with liquor and cigars.

If she said no, he'd gloat. If she said yes, he'd dream up some other torment. Riley clamped her mouth shut. It was either that or she'd sling some of this stuff in his direction and she'd be an ex-apprentice in a heartbeat. Once she was out of the Guild, their lawyer would probably bill her for all those legal fees.

Shut up and scoop.

"Bet your dad never had to do that," Harper taunted. She heaved a sigh of relief when he returned to his office. The recliner creaked under his weight as the television began to drone sports scores.

Doesn't he ever go out and trap anything?

It was nearing noon when she reached the occupied cage. The fiend had eyed her all morning, making those slobbery noises and licking its ebony lips. Knowing its time had come, it called out her name again.

"Yeah, that's me. So who are you, fur bag?"

It seemed surprised, then it answered with some long name that made no sense unless you were one of Lucifer's own. Like Argabettafingle something or other.

"Sorry I asked." She eyed it, testing the weight of the tire iron in her hand. The only way to clean under the cage was to get within range of those claws.

"Don't even think about it."

It snarled and swiped a paw in her direction. A second later, it howled, that paw held up to its mouth, red eyes blazing.

She waved the tire iron at it. "You were warned."

Bending over, she began to scoop the dung out from under the cage. It was fresh and burned like acid, making her eyes and nose flood like a toddler with a head cold. A claw snicked through her hair and cut off a few strands, which floated to the ground, embedding themselves in the pile.

"Hey, stop that!" Pissed, she tossed a handful of the steaming manure at the thing. The stuff stuck in its fur and the demon howled again, batting at it like it hurt.

Maybe it does.

"Don't like that, do you? You keep messing with me," she said, shaking a mucky finger, "and I'll bury you in it. Got it?"

The demon hissed and backed into the corner of the steel cage.

"That's better."

Riley finished digging out the mound under the cage and added the crap to the heap behind the shop. Harper was right: There were dead roaches in a four-foot radius of the pile.

"If the pest control dudes could figure out how to use this stuff they'd make a fortune."

Riley swore she could feel the flesh melting off her bones, so she fled to the bathroom. Hitting the light switch with her elbow, she prepared herself for the worst a guy bathroom had to offer. There was an unwritten code that they had to be disgusting.

To her relief this one was better than most, even though the toilet seat was up. She stared at the pile of adult magazines on the floor, and then up at the bimbo poster on the wall. The blonde was only wearing a neon green G-string, and her melon boobs clearly weren't anything close to natural. A blue tattoo sat just below her navel. Riley leaned closer to read the words.

Welcome to Heaven. An arrow pointed downward.

"Right," Riley huffed. She wondered what Simon thought of that. Knowing him, he probably kept his eyes averted while he peed, in case he might be tempted into sin.

The sink was clean but didn't stay that way by the time she finished washing her hands and arms with the dishwashing soap she'd found on the top of the toilet tank. Now her hands smelled lemony fresh, but they still burned.

It took another few minutes to return the sink to its previous state. No way was she going to let the guys claim she'd messed up their bathroom.

That left hosing down the floor under the cages. As she worked, the demon jammed its face up against the bars trying to reach the spray. Did the things drink water? Did Hell even have water?

She turned down the pressure and aimed the stream so the fiend could reach it. It drank greedily. Then it issued a lengthy and profound burp.

Riley shook her head. "You and Beck. Separated at birth."

There was a chuckle, and she turned to find Simon watching from a respectful distance. For a half of a second, she thought of wetting him down just for the smirk on his face.

"Looks good," he said encouragingly.

"If you say so."

He angled his head toward the outside door. "Got something for you." She looked toward the office, on the alert for Harper. "Passed out," Simon mouthed.

Stepping into the sunlight, Riley gasped when she saw her arms. Blotches of bright red and dark purple covered her skin, making her resemble a plague victim. Her nails were black. Simi would love them.

"No blisters," Simon observed. "That's good news." He retrieved something off the car seat, broke the seal, and offered it to her.

It was a quart of whole milk.

Riley blinked at him. "Ah . . . thanks. I'm thirsty." Actually she was.

"It's for your arms. The fat in it'll cut the sting. Jackson told me about it when Harper pulled that stunt on me." He gestured for her to hold out her arms and then did the honors.

It looked stupid, all that white liquid splashing off her and coating the gravel. But it worked. The burning sensation damped down considerably.

"You still may end up with some blisters, but not as bad as if you hadn't treated it." He handed her the bottle. "Drink the rest. Maybe it will work from the inside out."

She gulped down the remainder of the moo juice. "Good!"

"Just like in the commercials." He executed a cautious look toward the warehouse. "Don't tell Harper I did this. He'll be pissed."

Pissed because you were nice to me? That sucks. "Why is he such a dick?"

"Don't know." He took the empty container and put it the car. "You'd best get in there before he wakes up."

As he turned away, she touched his arm. "Thanks, Simon."

"Watch yourself, okay?" he said, his brow furrowed in worry.

"You too."

When she returned to the office Harper was still asleep in his chair, his mouth open, snoring. The whiskey bottle was empty and lay discarded near the trash can. Riley placed the bucket and scrub brush in the corner, trying not to make any noise. When he didn't stir she hurried out into the office. As she saw it, the smelly demon was better company than her new master.

TWENTY-THREE

"Déjà vu," Riley grumbled, pulling into the parking lot near the defunct Starbucks. She'd been here a few years ago on a date when the coffee shop was still open for business. The guy behind the counter had been seriously adorable. Model-level cute. She'd mentioned that, and Allan, her then boyfriend, hadn't taken it well. That's when she'd learned that male egos and fruit had a lot in common: Both bruised easily.

The moment she stepped outside the car she saw the other kids. There were three distinct groups plus a few stragglers. She'd probably end up being one of those.

Wish Peter was here. He was the one constant in her life, the friend who'd helped her transition through the last four school changes. He viewed change as an opportunity. Riley only saw it as a hassle.

Why bother? In a few months the Powers That Be would move all the kids around to new locations, like throwing a deck of cards in the air. The educational types had fancy names for the reshuffling, but in the end it was the students who got the worst of it. Why become friends with someone who'd be gone in a couple of months' time? If Riley didn't play the game, the kids would think she was stuck up or weird or both. But did she really care?

"Nope. I'm sitting this one out," she announced. With all that had happened in her life, it wasn't worth the effort.

The closest group was all girls about her age. They dressed nicer than she did but couldn't be from rich families or they wouldn't be going to school in a defunct coffee shop. As she moved closer to the entrance, she studied the pack. The girl in the center, a tall, stick-thin brunette with large brown eyes and full lips, was surrounded by five others who gazed up at her like androids waiting for instructions. All of them were wearing the same color. Give the main girl a few years and a boob job and she could pose for pictures like the one in Harper's bathroom.

Tattoo and all.

Riley suspected they were not destined to be best buds.

The girl pointed at Riley's car. "Is that yours?"

Didn't I just get out of the thing? "No, I stole it on the way over here. Mine's a red convertible."

One of the other girls giggled but shut down immediately when The Self-Proclaimed Center of the Universe shot her a dirty look.

"So what's your name?" the girl asked.

"Riley. Yours?"

"Brandy."

Of course.

"You're new here," Brandy observed. "Where'd you go to school before?"

"A grocery store over on Moreland."

"Sounds gross."

"It was."

Before Brandy could throw more questions her way, the double doors swung open and an authority figure waved them inside. According to Riley's paperwork, that would be Mrs. Haggerty. It wouldn't be hard to guess what the kids called her behind her back.

Mrs. Haggerty looked fifty with silver streaks at her temples. Her hair was cut short at the collar and she dressed in layers. An angel pin decorated the lapel of her cloth coat.

Riley queued up, and the moment she crossed over the threshold, she took a deep breath. *Coffee.* The place would always smell like that, even though it had been some time since the last bean had been roasted.

Better than moldy cheese.

The students clustered toward the front of the store near the big windows, still in their groups. As they settled into their seats, Riley did a quick look around. The counter was gone, as were all of the displays. The benches along the rear wall were still there, and all the original tables were still in place, though they looked way worse than she remembered. More tables had been added and lined up in rows facing the front windows. Riley picked one of the smaller ones. The way the thing wobbled told her why no one wanted to sit there. Riley bent over and jammed the strap of her bag under one of the legs, and the table became pretty stable. The top wasn't something she could fix. It was covered in graffiti, most involving the *F* word. In one case it was spelled wrong.

When Mrs. Haggerty finally paused behind the card table that posed as her desk, Riley rose and made her way to the front. She knew this drill: Hand transfer papers to authority figure, receive acknowledgment of her existence, then return to her seat. Mrs. Haggerty eyed the forms, looked up, frowned at Riley, then looked down at the name and sighed.

"You were supposed to be here last Monday."

"I couldn't make it," Riley said. "I was ill." *Like dying from demon cooties.* It was a good bet every single student was listening to this conversation, trying to scope out the new kid. Maybe the teacher would let it drop.

"Attendance is very important," the woman replied. "You have to think of your future."

That's a laugh. Riley nodded obediently. Teachers were less hassle if they thought you agreed with them.

"I'll need a parent's signature for your excuse," Mrs. Haggerty added.

"Sure." *I'll just dig him up.* Luckily she was pretty good at forging her dad's signature.

"Students? This is Riley. Please welcome her to our class."

Cool. She didn't use my last name. Maybe this was going to work out after all.

Then Mrs. Haggarty pulled the pin. "You can sit down, Miss Black-thorne."

Crap.

As she headed for her seat, Riley could see her last name rattling around in the students' heads. Their eyes widened when it hit home. If one of them was clueless, another would lean over and whisper in an ear. A couple pulled out their cell phones, no doubt hunting up one of those online videos.

Now that her secret was out, Riley wasn't surprised when the kid sitting next to her, the bony one with the dull brown hair, watched her out of the corner of his eye like she was going to conjure up a fiend in the middle of class.

Sometimes I wish it worked that way.

Mrs. Haggarty immediately dug into the classwork. It was the same as at the other school, following the state-mandated curriculum, so they started with a half hour of math, which really wasn't a stretch for Riley. Then a half hour each of English, science, and literature. The final hour was history, in particular the Civil War. Riley had that down cold, courtesy of her dad. During Mrs. Haggarty's snore-inducing account of the Battle of Lookout Mountain, she thought she could hear whispering behind her.

The three hours moved quickly, despite the smirks and the chatter behind her. Five o'clock came and went. Then it was 5:10. Riley began to fidget because class was supposed to be over by now and she had to get to the cemetery. If she wanted something to eat, that would chew up even more time. The cemetery volunteer would stay put, but they'd charge her extra if she wasn't there by sunset.

Money I don't have.

Mrs. Haggarty kept talking. And talking. Riley glanced at her watch again 5:15. She began to pack her stuff. That immediately caught the teacher's notice.

"Miss Blackthorne? We're running late tonight. That happens from time to time."

Riley stood. "I'm sorry, I have to go. I have ... something I have to do."

"Which is?" Mrs. Haggerty asked, giving her the teacher stare.

Damn. "I have to sit vigil over my dad's grave," Riley replied.

The teacher blinked. "You're *that* Blackthorne?"

Apparently the teacher was the only one in the classroom who hadn't connected the dots.

"Okay class, we'll call it an evening. Read the chapter on Sherman's destruction of Atlanta for Sunday."

Riley shouldered her messenger bag and hurried toward the door, but it took some time to get outside, as everyone seemed to be in her way. The reason for the delay became obvious when she reached her car. A message was scrawled on her windshield.

"Demon whore!"

The color of the lipstick looked familiar.

Riley shot a venomous look at the pack of girls. Brandy grinned at her, waving a lipstick tube like a mini light saber.

Bitch.

Riley hopped in the car, flipped the lever to clean the windshield. Bad plan. The lipstick spread itself across the glass in long, greasy smears. She kept working the lever until there was a clean patch, then drove away using language only demons would understand.

In her rearview mirror, the pack brayed in laughter.

⊹

With only minutes to spare Riley hustled up the road as fast as she could, clutching her father's trapping manual to her side. It had been under the spare tire, but so far she'd had no time to dig into it.

Rod, the volunteer, issued a welcoming smile as she approached.

"I'd stay and talk, but it's league night."

"League?" she asked.

He slipped off his coat far enough for her to see he was wearing a red bowling shirt. "Six Feet Under" was embroidered on the back.

The Six Feet Under Pub & Fish House sat across the street from the cemetery. On rare occasions her dad would take her there as a special treat when they had a few extra dollars left at the end of the month. The trappers held their parties and their wakes there. Yet another tradition.

"Need any help?" Rod asked. When she shook her head, he hurried off.

Riley set the circle with only a brief twinge of anxiety, then dialed Peter.

The moment he answered, she started in. "You won't believe what happened at school!"

Her friend wisely listened without interrupting.

"Wow, they sound like complete dogs," Peter commiserated. "Sorry I wasn't there."

Riley sighed. "It's the usual crap, Peter. They have to pick on some-one, and I'm it. I'm always it."

"Not always. Sometimes I am. We're different, and that bugs them."

"I have no clue how I'm going to get the lipstick off my windshield," she grumbled.

"Hold on." She heard the clicking keys in the background. "Am-monia will take the stuff off."

"Thanks!" Not that she had any in the apartment, but leave it to Peter to find the answer.

"So what's it like being Lucifer's whore?" he joked.

"Peter!"

"Just kidding," he said, then laughed. "As for your other problem," he continued, "if you didn't trap demons those skanks would find some-thing else to hate about you. Like your hair or your nose or something."

"What's wrong with my nose?"

"Don't get me started," he replied.

"Peter," she cautioned, "you don't want to go there."

He laughed again. "Don't let them get you down."

"I won't, but it's always this way. When I was a kid—" She halted, aware she was about to reveal one of her deepest secrets.

"Go on," he prodded.

This was Peter. He wouldn't laugh at her. At least not for long.

"You remember how in junior high I never fit in? I had this thing I did every summer. I tried to be someone new, someone different, so that when I went back to school all the kids would say, 'Wow, Riley's cool.' Of course it didn't work. No matter what I did, all they saw was the old me."

"So that's why you were so weird the first couple weeks of school. I could never figure it out."

"Yeah, I probably acted pretty strange."

"I like the old Riley," Peter admitted. "She's cool, even if she's Lucifer's biatch."

"Enough with that."

"Oh, we're grumpy. At least you ended up at a Starbucks. I got sent to a day-care center. It's still open during the day."

"So what's that like?"

"It smells of kiddy poop and baby powder."

She smirked. "Do you get to sit on a tiny chair?"

"No, but we have to lie down on these little mats and take a nap after our juice and crackers."

She let the laughter roll free. "I miss you a lot, Peter. I wish you were in class with me."

There was a moment's hesitation. "Could you repeat that?"

"Why?"

"So I can record it. That way I can replay it when you start calling me a butthead again."

"No way. You missed your chance."

"So you know, I'm trying to get transferred to your school."

"Really? Think it'll work?" she asked, her hope surging. Then everything would be fine again.

"Don't know. The warden didn't have a thing to do with the new school, so it was just random bad luck. I figure I might be able to affect that randomness in some way."

"How?"

"Not the kind of thing we want to discuss on the phone."

Which meant he was trying to hack the education department's computer system and generate a transfer.

"Be careful," she said. The more creative the endeavor, the less the educational types would like it.

In the distance she saw Simon approaching. "Gotta go. It's one of the trappers checking on me." *The one who just happens to be my new boyfriend.*

"Be careful out there," Peter warned. "Oh, and I'll have a printout of all this stuff from your dad's disk ready tomorrow morning. Ring me and we'll set up a time to meet, okay?"

"Sure. Night, Peter."

"Later, Riley."

Simon called out his greeting, and after she'd invited him in, he joined her in the circle. The candles barely flickered.

"Thought I'd see how you were doing," he said, shielding something behind him.

"I'm tired. Class ran late. I almost didn't make it on time," she replied. *Whine much?* "Sorry, I'm a little cranky."

"Well, this should help. I got you a present."

He brought his arm around, showing her the object he'd been hiding. It was a brand-new blue tarp still in its clear plastic wrapper.

Other girls get flowers, I get a tarp. And she didn't mind a bit.

"You're awesome, Simon," she said, meaning every word.

"Aren't I?" he replied, waggling his eyebrows.

Riley quickly tidied the ground. Pinecones and rocks were evil and became more so as the night progressed.

"Here, let me help," Simon offered. Together they laid out the tarp, then the sleeping bags, her blanket, and other necessities. "Is there anything left in your apartment?" he asked, waving a hand at all her stuff.

"Yes!" she said, shooting him a mock glower. "Pop-Tart?"

"Sure! Got strawberry?" She dug inside the box and found one. Treats in hand, they settled on the makeshift campsite, sharing a blanket.

"So what happened to your windshield?" he asked, around munches of the tart. "It's got something red on it."

Riley gave him the quick-and-dirty version. To her surprise, his face colored when she told him what the lipstick had said.

"You're nothing of the kind!" he said, frowning.

"Thanks." It felt nice to have him stick up for her. "I haven't decided how to get even yet."

"That's a waste of time. It screws you up more than it does them."

She cocked her head. "You don't lose your cool when Harper's being an asshat; you're polite all the time, even to the demons. How do you do it?"

He tapped his cross. "It helps me find my center."

"Mom used to talk about that sort of thing." Treasured memories arose. "I liked going to church with her. She took me to a Latin mass once. It was all spooky and mysterious," Riley said.

Simon gave her a sidelong look. "I didn't realize your mom was Catholic. What about you?"

"I'm not sure. I think God's up there somewhere watching over us, but if He is, He must hate me."

Her boyfriend slipped his arm around her, pulling her closer. It made her feel good deep inside.

"He doesn't hate any of us," Simon explained. "He just tests us. Unfortunately, your tests have been really hard."

"What about you?"

"Haven't really had any tests yet. Nothing major, that is."

He leaned closer and then placed a gentle kiss on her lips.

Though surprised, she didn't push him away. He was a good kisser. Not that she'd had tons of practice, but she knew she'd be happy if he kissed her again. And he did. This time the kiss lasted longer and tasted of strawberries. He finally pulled himself away, a faint blush on his cheeks.

"You are such a temptation," he muttered, shaking his head.

He makes that sound like a bad thing.

To her disappointment he suddenly rose, like he didn't trust himself alone with her. "I've got to go. I promised my mom I'd be home in time for dinner."

"Must be nice," she said wistfully. With a family as big as his, it'd be chaos, but you'd never be lonely.

He pondered for a second. "You should come over sometime. Mom makes incredible fried chicken."

Did he just invite me to his house?

"I'd . . . like that," she stammered.

"Good. My parents want to meet you. I've told them all about you."

Me?

She stood and delivered a quick peck on his cheek. Another kiss ensued, and this time there was no hurry.

"Definitely a test," he murmured. "You call me if you need anything."

"I will. Night, Simon."

"Good night, Riley."

As he walked away, she replayed the last few minutes.

He kissed me. He invited me to dinner and his parents want to meet me.

This was moving way faster than she'd expected.

TWENTY-FOUR

Riley reluctantly looked up from her father's manual, clicking off the flashlight to save the battery. She was deep in the section on how to trap Threes, the part she really should have read before going it alone. Her visitor was Mortimer. He was still in the fedora and the long trench coat.

Riley yawned a greeting.

"Good evening. How are you, Miss Blackthorne?" the necro asked in a husky voice. It sounded like he was coming down with a cold.

"It's been better," she said. Then she held up her hand before he could make his usual offer. "If anyone asks, you did your thing and I shot you down like every other night. That way we're not wasting our time. Besides, I'm too tired for it."

Mortimer smiled. "You're not like the others. They usually curse at me. I appreciate that." He paused and then asked, "Do you really enjoy trapping demons?"

"A week ago I would have said yes because I could trap with my dad. Now? Not so sure. I've got a new master, and he's a real asshat."

"Ah, I know how that works. We have a similar system to the trappers'. New summoners are required to work up through the ranks. I was assigned the task of maintaining the reanimates when I first started. They require some care or, well, things get pretty bad after a while." He held his nose for effect.

"Can't hang an air freshener on them and call it good?" she joked, exhaustion making her punchy.

Mortimer chuckled. "No, but if you treat them carefully they look and smell better than when they were first inhumed. It's an art, you see."

She rose and stretched. For once her thigh didn't bitch about the move.

"How long have you been a necro?"

"We prefer being called summoners."

"For you, summoner. All the rest of them are necros in my book."

He gave her a genuine smile. "I've been reanimating the dead for over five years. It's a living. Before that I worked at a mortuary."

"So the dead have always been your thing, then?"

"Pretty much." He looked up the path. When he turned around there was a frown on his face. "Time to go. It's been good talking to you. You have a good night, and do be careful."

"You too, Mortimer."

"Mort. That's what my friends call me." He tipped his fedora and headed up the walk. As he made the turn toward the entrance, she saw another figure approaching. To her surprise, Mort veered off among the graves rather than pass the newcomer on the road.

"I got ya some food," Beck called out, holding up a bulging paper bag as he strode toward her.

Maybe you're not so bad after all.

He paused at the edge of the circle. "Ah, damn, my boot's untied. Here, take this," he said offering the bag. Riley started to reach across the circle, then paused. Something didn't feel right. She looked down at his boots. Beck always double-knotted his. She remembered him saying how he didn't want to fall over his laces and get eaten by some dumbass demon.

She stepped back and checked him out with a more critical eye.

No duffel bag. Beck always had it with him, even at her dad's funeral. And Mort had gone out of his way to avoid this guy.

"Nice one." If she'd reached across the candles to claim the bag, she'd have broken the line of protection and her dad would be someone else's property.

It didn't surprise her when "Beck" evaporated into a swirl of leaves, revealing the creepy necro. None of the others attempted such sophisticated magic.

"You are smarter than most," he observed. "I'm rather enjoying the challenge."

"Yeah, yeah," she said, making talking motions with her hand. "It's not happening."

"So you say," he replied. With a whoosh, the circle flared into the night like he'd touched it, then it subsided. The summoner was gone, a whirl of leaves shooting up the path like a malevolent tornado.

Riley heaved a sigh of relief. She needed to ask Mort about this guy, because it looked like Mr. Black Magic Necro wasn't going to quit until he'd scared the living crap out of her.

⁂

Morning brought a light frost and a black plastic bag tied to her car door handle. After much fumbling with cold fingers, Riley untied the bag and dumped its contents on the frost-painted hood. A thick manila envelope slid out, along with a wad of paper towels and a plastic bottle of ammonia.

There was a note attached.

Warm car first, then clean windshield or you'll be sorry.

"Peter strikes again."

While the car warmed, she dialed her friend.

"Got the delivery?" he asked without bothering to say hello.

"I did. Thanks," she said, watching the heat make small circles on the windshield. The bag's contents sat on the seat beside her. "How'd you get out here?" Peter didn't have a car, and she doubted the warden would let him take off so early in the morning on his own.

"David dropped it by for me as he was headed to work. He thought it kinda weird I was having him make a delivery to a cemetery."

David. His next oldest brother who wanted to be a pilot but was working at a bakery instead. "Man, there's a lot of a paper here. What is all this?" she asked, hefting the nearly inch-thick envelope.

"Everything that was on your dad's disk. It's all about Holy Water, or at least as much as I got to read. The warden kept checking in on me last night, so I gave up."

"I'll go through it," she said, "but I have no idea why my dad was going to all this work. He never said anything about this."

"Definitely a mystery," Peter replied and then crunched on something through the mouthpiece. Cereal no doubt.

Rivulets of water ran down her windshield in response to the blast of heated air. Time to break out the ammonia and destroy Brandy's work of art.

"Thanks, Peter, I owe you."

"Definitely." He hung up.

Riley leaned back in the car, savoring the warmth. She really wanted a nap, but she had barely enough time to clean the windshield, grab a breakfast sandwich, and get to Harper's. If she was late the master would find another way to torment her. With her luck it would involve more demon poop.

She reluctantly stashed the manila envelope in the glove compartment for later.

⁘

The Three was gone; apparently her master had sold the thing to a demon trafficker. She tidied up underneath its cage before Harper told her to, which seemed to aggravate him. By the time she'd finished, Simon was packing his car for a run. He'd barely said two words to her over the last couple of days, at least when Harper was around. All her daydreams about how cool it would be to train with him hadn't materialized.

"We're going trapping," he explained. She started to ask whether she could come along but stopped at the warning look in his eyes.

Harper lumbered up, clad in a thick coat with a duffel bag in hand.

"I decide who goes and who doesn't go on a run."

Riley took that to mean she wasn't invited. That changed the moment the two men were in the car.

"So get your ass in here, Brat," Harper ordered. "We don't have all damned day."

No way I can win.

Riley eased into the backseat and slammed the door. Part of her was stoked. She was out of that smelly building and doing what she should be doing—trapping demons. Well, not her, exactly. This was Simon's show, and from the conversation in the front seat they were after a Grade Four Hypno-Fiend, or Mezmer, as the trappers called them.

Harper supplied the directions.

"What are we getting into?" Simon asked, turning off Memorial Drive and heading north toward downtown. His voice held a hint of nervousness.

The master shoved some paperwork over the seat back to Riley.

"Earn your keep."

Pushing a strand of hair out of her eyes, she skimmed the report. As with all trapping requisitions, the paperwork stated the complainant's name, address, and type of suspected demonic activity.

"A Mr. Ford says this boy is hanging around his daughter, Carol, and getting her do things she shouldn't be doing. He thinks the boy is a demon because every time he tries to run him off, he finds himself agreeing with whatever the kid says."

"Sounds like a Mezmer," Harper said.

"He might just be a creep," Riley said.

The master trapper gave her a strange look over the seat. "Been there, have you?"

Sure have.

Riley had met Allan right after Beck had tossed her to the curb. She'd been vulnerable, and Allan had taken advantage of that. It hadn't mattered that her father had disliked her new boyfriend from the moment they'd met. In her mind, Allan was the only thing in her life that mattered and she'd do anything for him to keep him interested in her. And she had. It'd started with the small stuff—lying, sneaking around, stealing cigarettes from the grocery store, though neither of them smoked. It ended the day she'd been one step away from stuffing a two-thousand-dollar mini laptop under her jacket. He'd told her it would prove that she loved him.

The instant her hand had touched the computer a shock ran through her entire body. The future unfolded like a bad movie: It wouldn't be him at the police station getting yelled at by the cops; he wouldn't be fingerprinted, thrown in a cell, or have to face the judge; he wouldn't have to endure her father's horrified disappointment.

Freaked, she'd hurried out of the store minus the computer. As Riley passed the security guard he'd given her a nod. He'd known what she was going to do.

"Smart move, kid," he'd said.

Allan hadn't seen it that way. When she'd admitted she couldn't do what he wanted, he'd shouted her down in front of everyone in the parking lot, calling her a stupid bitch. Then he'd hit her.

Riley touched her cheek, remembering the sting of the blow, the taste of blood in her mouth, his furious face only inches from hers as he'd called her nasty names.

She'd found the courage to leave him swearing in that parking lot. It'd taken three bus rides to get home. When her father saw her and the growing bruise, his face went crimson in anger. She'd collapsed in his arms and told him all of it. When she'd finally stopped crying, he'd asked her only one question.

"Do you believe you deserved to be hit?"

"No!" she'd said. "He had no right!"

Her father's expression had melted into relief.

"Always remember that, Pumpkin. *No one* has the right to hurt you."

Then he'd hugged her and taken her out for ice cream to celebrate her lucky escape from The Worst Boyfriend Ever. A few months later she'd heard Allan had broken his new girlfriend's arm during an argument.

I got off so lucky.

"Hey!" Harper called out, snapping his fingers and causing Riley to jump. "Pay attention, will you? If you think you know all this, you're wrong."

"Sorry," Riley said. "What were you saying?"

"I was saying that Grade Four demons are devious mothers. They sing a sweet song in your ear, and next thing you know your soul's got a brand on it courtesy of Lucifer. Sometimes they do it fast, sometimes slow. Doesn't matter which, because your soul is what they want, before or after they fuck you over."

Simon twitched at the obscenity.

Harper kept going. "Once they claim your soul they have two choices—harvest it right then and there, in which case you are dead meat, or sell you to a higher-level demon to curry favor."

"What does the higher-level demon do with a person's soul?" Simon asked, frowning.

"Since you're still alive, they own you. You're their bitch for eternity." He turned to Simon. "Tell us the difference between an incubus and a succubus."

Her fellow apprentice sighed, not pleased at having to discuss such matters in front of Riley. "A succubus seduces males and takes energy from them during the sex act. An incubus does the same with women."

Harper nodded. "They're evil. No other way to say it."

"So how do you stop them?" Riley asked.

"A Babel sphere does the trick," the master replied.

She wasn't that far in the manual. Maybe she should have read ahead. "How does it work?"

Harper huffed like she was ignorant. "Tell her, Saint."

The so-called Saint, who'd been doing some heavenly kissing the night before, studied her via the rearview mirror. "The Babel sphere translates what the demon is really saying, rather than what it wants you to hear. It reveals the fiend underneath the illusion."

"Once we're sure this is a demon, we'll bust open a Babel and then bag the damned thing," Harper said. "Piece of cake."

Riley caught a glimpse of Simon's face in the mirror.

That wasn't what either of them was thinking.

TWENTY-FIVE

The Armageddon Lounge wasn't busy, but the folks inside eyed the three of them like refugees would a free Sunday buffet.

This is where Beck plays pool. It fit him—a seedy End Times–themed bar with eight pool tables and a big-screen television running some college football game. The green felt on the tables was worn, and the painted concrete floor needed mopping. It smelled of cigarette smoke, which meant the owner had paid the city extra for that option.

Harper nodded toward a young couple at one of the tables.

"Probably them," he said. The boy was almost Simon's height, five nine or so, with black scruffy hair and a collection of metal in his eyebrows, nose, and tongue. Riley wondered how he could afford all that bling. The boy wore stonewashed blue jeans and a black T-shirt that said "I'm Perfect! Deal!"

No ego there.

As Riley moved closer she examined the girl. The paperwork said she was fifteen, but Carol Ford looked older. Her hair was blunt cut and blond, her face remarkably plain. Riley couldn't help but notice the dark circles under her eyes. Either Carol was ill, a druggie, or her boyfriend really was an incubus sucking the life out of her. No matter what the cause, no amount of concealer was going to fix that.

Simon unzipped his trapping bag and set it on the floor next to him. Next to it went a bright blue lunch tote.

"Excuse me, are you Carol Ford?" he said. She turned toward him and blinked repeatedly like he'd shown a bright flashlight in her eyes.

"Yes?"

"I'm Simon Adler. I'm a demon trapper. You might have a problem I can help you with."

Riley envied him: He sounded so in control, except with Simon it came from his faith, not years of experience.

"You don't need to talk to them," the boy said in a commanding voice, turning his full attention their way. "Your 'rents sent them."

"Parents?" she asked, like she'd forgotten she had any.

"There's been a misunderstanding," the boy continued. He put his arm around Carol, who shivered at his touch, and not in a good way. "Her 'rents don't like me, but we're meant for each other. It's not fair that people keep getting in our way. You should leave us alone."

He sounded reasonable, but so had Allan when he was on his game.

"It's not like we don't care for each other," the boy continued. "You love me, don't you, Carol?"

Carol nodded like a puppet.

"I won't let anyone hurt her," the boy continued, then let his eyes roam to Riley.

The moment their eyes met, Riley felt the weight of his attention like they were the only ones in the bar. She could hear him talking to her, but it didn't seem that anyone else heard him. He was telling her how she was so pretty, how he was sorry she was all alone now, that he'd make it right. How he'd never leave her like everyone else had.

You trust me, don't you? he asked.

There was a loud snap and both apprentices jumped. Harper had busted a pool cue over one of the tables.

"For God's sake, get on with it, Saint!" he ordered.

Simon jerked to attention and clutched his wooden cross, his lips moving in silent prayer. A moment later a sphere impacted the floor and exploded in tiny glass fragments. Carol gave a gasp of surprise as the air immediately filled with the smell of cinnamon and a mosaic of flickering lights. The lights rose with the scent, then veered directly toward her boyfriend, encompassing him.

"What is that?" she asked nervously.

"Evil . . ." the boy hissed. "How dare you!" He flailed at the magic as his honeyed voice took on a reedy quality. Higher and higher it went as his face shifted from handsome to hideous in a reverse makeover. His clothes vanished revealing a body that looked like it'd been dipped in mud. The brown layer was cracked in places, revealing sallow skin underneath. His bloodred eyes bore into Riley, glowing in the bar's muted light. He had no horns, but a long barbed tail flicked behind him like an angry cat as his taloned hands clawed the air.

With the clothes gone, Riley caught a glimpse of what no mortal should see.

Oh, great. Now that's seared into my brain forever.

Once it dawned on the bar's patrons that they had a naked demon in their midst, there was a stampede for the front door. When Carol saw her boyfriend's real form, then looked farther south, she shrieked and backpedaled.

"Her soul I nearly had," the demon shouted. "Evil you are!"

Simon ignored him, donning a pair of heavy latex gloves.

"Boon I grant all of you!" the demon offered.

"Get screwed," Harper replied.

The fiend began to shrink like a child's balloon with a slow leak. As he diminished in size, the demon yowled and swore and flailed his hands, but it didn't stop the magical process.

That is so cool. I wonder how it works.

Finally he was only a foot tall, stuck inside a circle of bright twinkling lights that resembled a miniature force field. Simon scooped up the snarling fiend, dumped it in the oversized lunch tote, zipped the container closed and padlocked it. The magical charms tied to the handle rattled as he picked it up. Apparently they were supposed to keep the fiend from clawing his way out.

Riley clapped, pleased at Simon's success. "Trapper scores." He gave her a modest smile, but she could tell something was bothering him.

Harper didn't share her joy. In fact, he glared at the pair of them. "What the hell were you two doing?" he demanded. "I told you he'd mess with your head, and you stood there like a couple of dummies!"

Riley didn't bother to argue. If the fiend could get into Simon's mind, it could get into anyone's. She turned her attention to Carol. The girl seemed paralyzed, staring at the container that held her ex-boyfriend. Copious tears rolled out of her eyes.

"He's . . . he's a . . ." she stammered.

"Demon. They happen," Riley said, trying to sound supportive.

The girl wailed and flung herself into Riley's arms.

"Let's get out of here," Harper ordered, casting a wary eye around the bar. A crowd of curious locals had formed at the door. "Don't want to waste my time explaining this to the cops."

As Simon toted the demon outside, the bartender got in Harper's way, bitching about the broken pool cue and all the glass on the floor.

"You want us to turn him loose?" Harper demanded. The guy paled and shook his head. "Figured so."

Once they were outside, Riley pointed Carol toward the police station.

"Go over there and call your parents," she advised. "Tell them you screwed up."

"I thought he was . . ." the girl said, sniffling. She blew her nose. "He was so . . ."

"Wrong for you."

"But they'll ground me," Carol cried, totally focused on her ruined love life and not the what-might-have-been if the Four had won this round.

Getting grounded or spending forever with a demon?

"Small price to pay," Riley said, patting the girl's arm in sympathy. "Trust me on that."

✣

Simon remained dead silent on the drive to Harper's place.

You caught the demon. That's all that matters. Did he really think the thing wasn't going to try to con him? That he was immune somehow?

Harper was quiet, too, so Riley spent time trying not to stare at the lunch tote on the seat next her. She could hear the demon in her mind offering her a boon if she'd set him free.

"No way that's happening, so just shut up," she muttered.

Harper gave her a stern look over the seat. "Is it talking to you?" She nodded. "Tempted?"

"No."

"Why not?"

"Because I'm a Blackthorne," Riley replied, before she could stop herself.

He smirked. "Like that makes a goddamn bit of difference."

The demon kept bugging her so she took a mental vacation to the night before and the kissing. Its voice faded away to nothing.

The instant they reached Harper's building, the master was on her case. "There're some Ones in the office. Take them downtown to Roscoe Clement on Peachtree Street and sell them. You'll get seventy-five a piece for them. Get the paperwork signed, got it?"

"Sir, I don't think that's a good idea," Simon chimed in, troubled by the order. "Roscoe is—"

Harper delivered a blistering look at the older apprentice. "Not your call, Saint." He jabbed a finger at Riley. "Be back by the time we are."

And that will be? She didn't dare ask, not with his black mood. Harper barked orders at Simon, and then they were gone, the old Dodge belching smoke. Going somewhere to sell the Four.

But not to Roscoe. Now why is that?

Her dad had spoken of this Roscoe dude, that he sold adult videos, barely legal sex toys, and bought demons on the side. How he'd received

Church approval to be a trafficker, no one knew. Her dad had warned her to stay away from the sleaze unless he was with her. Now Harper was sending her to Roscoe on her own. It was like throwing a chunk of bunny entrails in front of a Three.

"Bet you didn't do that to Simon," she groused.

Riley found the four fiends sitting in their individual sippy cups on Harper's desk. They were all Biblios.

One was sleeping, but the others got in the finger before she stowed them in her messenger bag. The paperwork went in next. It was in quadruplicate—a copy each for the trapper, the trafficker, the city, and another page for when the demon trafficker delivered the fiends to the Church. Every demon sale was tracked from the time the fiend was captured to the time the Church took control of them.

According to the Trappers Manual the paperwork went all the way to Rome. She could imagine the accountants in the Vatican pouring over the reports, tallying them into some huge ledger that dated back to the Middle Ages. Maybe the pope got to see the ledger with his coffee every morning. Which meant maybe someday he'd see Riley's name and all the demons she'd caught.

How cool is that?

TWENTY-SIX

Fewer cars should equal more parking. That hadn't been Riley's experience. The city's predatory search for revenue, including converting the empty parking spaces on Peachtree Street to makeshift shops that had to pay a monthly fee, made it difficult to find a place for her car. As she waited for a blue van to finish unloading so she could scoop up the parking place, Riley tugged out the manila envelope and leafed through the pages. Peter had separated the contents into specific stacks with sturdy binder clips. She studied the first batch, flipping up her eyes every now and then to see how the unloading progressed.

"The History of Holy Water"

Her father never approached a subject by half, and he hadn't changed his approach when it came to the sacred liquid. In her hands was a detailed account of Holy Water's legends and folklore in minute detail. He had a list of miracles attributed to the sacred liquid, old wives' tales regarding its use, even a chart that showed how Holy Water was manufactured and distributed in the Atlanta area.

Riley checked the van—still unloading—then returned to the page. The local manufacturer, Celestial Supplies, created the Holy Water in a plant in Doraville. From there it was sent to a licensed distributor who supplied various stores in the city. Every single pint, quart, and gallon of the holy liquid was tagged with a sales tax seal and cataloged by batch number.

"And we care about this why?" she said, frowning. Maybe her dad was going to write an academic paper or something. "But who would read it?" She'd admit that some of the folklore was kind of cool, but the rest was a snooze.

Farther on she found page after page of numbers, an inventory from Celestial Supplies that represented every single batch of Holy Water produced in the last six months.

"Whee!" she said, rolling his eyes. This wasn't getting her anywhere. She looked up to see a stocky guy close the van's rear door and lock it. He jumped in and pulled out of the parking spot.

"Mine," she said, grinning.

Riley trudged past the Westin, one of the few hotels still open downtown. Smokers huddled together outside the front door, puffing away. One of them had a Deader standing near him, holding his briefcase. The live guy in the expensive suit was talking rapid-fire over his cell phone, pacing back and forth, leaving a long tail of cigarette smoke behind him.

Riley's eyes met those of the reanimate, a petite Hispanic woman in a black pantsuit and white shirt. The combination did nothing for her gray skin. Her hair was held back by a clip, and she looked so sad. Maybe she'd been this guy's secretary before she died and he didn't want to replace her. No matter what, she was his slave now.

That has to suck.

Riley gave the woman a sympathetic nod. The Deader returned the nod. That surprised her. They usually stared at the world through empty eyes. The woman's owner gestured and she came closer, opening up the briefcase and offering its contents for his inspection. He chose a sheaf of papers and returned to his marching, ignoring everyone around him.

Sorry, Riley mouthed. She didn't get a response.

The intersection of Baker and Peachtree lacked a traffic light. Constant bike and moped traffic zipped past her, and one rider nearly clipped her toes. At least horses weren't allowed in downtown anymore since no one really wanted to wade through the manure.

A few doors down from Max Lager's, a popular brewpub, sat Roscoe's Emporium. You'd have to be blind not to find the place. It was dripping in neon.

In the front window a sign announced "Don't Dick with America!" Right below was a giant condom. Just to make the point that Roscoe was a deeply patriotic sleaze, it enlarged to ridiculous proportions and then changed colors, rotating through red, white, then blue while "America the Beautiful" played through a pair of ancient speakers.

The strap on her messenger bag slipped and Riley adjusted it. Tiny voices rose, barely audible. She tapped the side of the bag.

"Knock it off." Silence fell. It was safe to assume that middle fingers were hoisted in her direction.

Riley stood outside for at least a full minute hoping God or whoever was in charge of the universe would step in and she wouldn't have to do this. When there was a disappointing lack of divine intervention, she shuddered and pushed open the door.

As her eyes adjusted to the dim light, she saw the huge video screen on the far wall. From a set of audio speakers came the low moans and the "Oh, baby," murmurs of the siliconized porn star hooking up with a hunky Latino. A knot of customers were clustered in front of the screen, fixated, mouths agape.

My dad is spinning in his grave.

Roscoe spied her immediately, like he'd been expecting her. He stood behind a lengthy glass counter showing a potential customer something Riley didn't recognize. Whatever it was, it certainly didn't look comfortable no matter where you might put it.

"Be with you in a sec," he called out, drawing all eyes to her.

Thanks, perv.

While she waited, Riley rooted herself by the front door, refusing to wander through the shop. Not that she was a prude or anything, but a few of the customers looked scary and they watched her every move.

Eventually Roscoe huffed his way over, his big belly arriving ahead of the rest of him. His rusty brown hair was too curly to be natural. He had tattoos on both arms that proved mermaids were *really* into sailors.

Even before she had a chance to say a word, he licked his lips and grinned. "This way, girlie. We'll do the deal in the office."

Girlie. She shook her head. Apparently Harper had called ahead so this should go fast. *Anything to get me out of this place.*

It was hard to tell where the store ended and Roscoe's office began. Rows of rainbow-colored vibrators sat on uneven shelves behind a rusty metal desk. Nude calendars adorned the other walls, while a small television featured a truly disgusting video involving cheerleaders. There was even a framed photo of Roscoe on the wall. The newspaper clipping below it said that the "adult entertainment czar"—Riley smirked at that—had paid over fifty thousand dollars in state licensing fees and sin taxes in the past five years. Which was why the city tolerated his smut. As her dad would say, they got their cut.

Roscoe crunched down into a worn leather chair. The move made his vast stomach roll over the top of his jeans, fighting a battle against the tight T-shirt. It wasn't an attractive sight. Especially when the T-shirt had a line drawn across the nipples and lettering that said "Must Be This Tall to Take This Ride."

Uck.

Roscoe kept staring at Riley's chest like he'd never seen breasts before. Then his eyes went cunning. "I can get you work. Three hundred a film. Might as well use those assets of yours for something worthwhile."

"What?" Riley asked, confused.

"Once you know the ropes you can bring in some serious cash. Maybe even a grand a pop," Roscoe explained.

He wasn't talking demons.

A thousand dollars to star in a porn flick? That made trapping wages look anemic.

"If you want to make some money on the side, well, you could charge a lot being so young. I got contacts, you know? Get you right to work. Course I take a cut, but we can trade it out if you want."

Trade it out . . . Acid rose, burning her throat.

Riley made sure the office door was open behind her.

With a dry chuckle, Roscoe ran his eyes up and down her body, assessing her as if she were a piece of prime beef. "So let's see the goods."

The urge to run slammed head-on against her assignment. Harper would be furious if she didn't sell the Biblios, and she knew revealing Roscoe's plans for her cinematic future wouldn't make a bit of difference.

How would Simon handle this? She discarded that thought immediately. He was too polite. Beck? That's who she should be channeling right now.

Riley glared at the porn king. "Okay. Goods it is." He leered until she removed the Biblios from her messenger bag, lining them up on his desk, though she didn't like getting *that* close to him. One of the fiends was working on his lid, feet braced on the sides of the sippy cup in a vain effort to unscrew it. She tightened the lid just in case.

"I'm here for Master Harper," she announced. "Nothing else."

Roscoe looked crestfallen. "You sure?" She nodded defiantly. "Damn. Passing up some good money. You've got a fine body. It'd look good under the lights."

"Not happening. Now can we get on with the deal *for the demons?*"

Roscoe leaned forward, the grease on his nose shining like a beacon. The expression on his face almost made Riley vomit. "Ninety a head," he offered, scratching his belly thoughtfully.

Ninety?

He interpreted her silence as a stall for more money. "Alright. A C-note for each. At that price I'll take all of them you can find."

"As many as we can trap?" she asked, hedging. Harper had said to expect seventy-five. What was she missing here?

"You heard me. A hundred apiece. That's my deal."

Harper said to sell them and it would be righteous to see his face when she returned with that much extra money. Maybe the Church had authorized higher payments and Harper hadn't gotten the word yet. Riley pulled out the paperwork and laid it near the cups. "You'll need to sign for these."

Roscoe's forehead bloomed in sweat. "Don't need the Church's paperwork. I've got a new buyer. They pay more, and that's why I'm giving you more."

"Who's buying them?" Riley asked.

"Not your concern, Baby Doll."

Baby Doll? Double uck.

"I can't sell demons without the paperwork," she said. It was the law.

"Okay, make it one-fifteen a head," Roscoe replied. "That's as high as I can go. Tell that old bastard you got seventy-five each and you lost the paperwork, then you pocket the difference."

Her cut would be $160, enough to buy groceries for a month. If this was a setup, Harper was making it real tempting.

It isn't right.

Riley reluctantly shook her head. "Unless you sign the paperwork, no deal."

"Don't get a bug up your ass, girlie. I'm doing this as a community service. As far as I'm concerned you could flush them down the toilet."

Riley began to repack the demons into her messenger bag, her stomach sour at the way this had played out. *Harper is going to lose his mind.*

"Hey, what are you doing?" Roscoe asked, lurching out of his chair.

"Doing what I'm supposed to," she said, packing faster now, eager to get away from this weirdo.

"One-twenty," Roscoe said. "That's more than you'll make anywhere else."

The sleaze bled desperation; she could taste it in the air. Something was going on with this guy, but it wasn't her problem. As she tucked away the last demon his sweaty hand grabbed her arm.

"You can't do that. You have to sell them to me," he barked.

She jerked her arm away, sickened by his touch.

"You're being stupid," he growled.

"Not the first time."

Riley pushed her way through customers and employees. The moment she reached the street, the demons erupted into a chorus of raucous cheers.

Even Hell has standards.

✛

Fireman Jack had been fairly easy to find since there weren't that many vintage firehouses left in the city. Riley squared her shoulders and poked at the doorbell located next to the overhead door. No answer. She pushed again and the service door began to open.

"Hello?" A hand waved her in. It was attached to a young guy, probably in his twenties. He was clad in blue overalls and wore high-top black-and-white-checked tennis shoes. His hair was a nest of spikes. Simi would love this dude.

"Yes?" he asked, eying her critically.

"I need to do business with Fireman Jack," I said. "I'm Riley Blackthorne."

"Blackthorne?" An eyebrow raised. "Right this way."

As she followed him inside, Riley realized a fire station was a good choice for a trafficker. The trappers could pull their vehicles inside the building, close the overhead door and offload the larger fiends. No chance for the things to get loose and maul a passerby.

Her nose caught the brimstone stench of demons before she heard the growls. There were a half dozen Threes lined up along a back wall in their individual steel cages. They all slobbered and flashed their claws,

fur rippling in waves. The floor beneath them was spotless. She wondered if the guy in the high-tops got stuck with cleanup duty.

"Blackthorne's daughter," one of demons howled. The others picked
up the chant and magnified it.

She kept the shiver to herself as she passed by the last cage.

Two flights of stairs got her to Jack's office, though it took some
time to get there since her thigh didn't like the hike. The office was
big and airy with light streaming through four skylights, illuminating
the old red brick walls. She liked this place. It felt good. Maybe if she
got rich someday she'd buy a fire station. A quick look around proved it
wasn't just Jack's place of work. A queen bed sat in one corner along
with a tidy kitchenette, and on the other wall a flat screen streamed
stock quotes.

The owner of the place sat behind a large wooden desk. It wasn't a
fancy piece of furniture, but it'd seen years of use. Jack looked near her
father's age. Mid-forties. Old but not ancient like Harper. Jack had
dark brown hair with silver streaks at his temples and wore blue jeans, a
red shirt, and those barber-pole suspenders. Not hard to spot him in a
crowd. A baseball cap sat on his desk. He was a Yankee fan.

The man was on the phone. He raised a hand to give him a second,
then went back to the call. He was questioning someone about regula-
tions regarding demon disposal.

While she waited, Riley checked out the long wall to her left, which
was blanketed in pictures and paintings. There was a common theme—
famous fires. London, 1666. Chicago, 1871. Atlanta, 1864 and 1917.
Even the Lenox Plaza fire just last year. That had been started by a
couple of horny Pyro-Fiends. Luckily that didn't happen too often, but
when it did the results were way incendiary.

Jack hung up the phone and pointed toward a wooden high-backed
chair.

"Riley! Have a seat. How are you doing?"

"Okay, I guess. I'm with Harper now."

Jack made a gagging motion with his finger, and it set her to laughing.

She could see why her dad liked this guy.

"Actually, that's not fair," Jack said. "He may be a platinum-class dick, but he's a good trapper. You'll learn a lot, providing you don't kill him first."

"So far I've become an expert at cleaning up demon crap." She raised her chapped hands for proof.

"Gotta start at the bottom," he said, smirking. The smirk faded as he opened a drawer and dropped a file folder on top of the desk. It was full of legal-size papers. "I had a look at the contract the debt collectors sent over."

"And?" she asked, unable to read the news on his face.

"They have a solid claim against your dad's body."

She banged the back of her skull against the wooden chair, the discomfort short-circuiting the anger and tears. "No way we can stop them?"

"I've filed a motion asking the court to rule on some specifics of the claim. The best we can do is stall long enough that it doesn't matter."

"I'd pay the money if I had it," she said. "I really would."

"Since you are a minor, you don't owe them anything. The reason they are going after the body is that's the only money they can hope to receive. Sorry I don't have better news." He put away the folder. They studied each other for a few seconds. "Anything else I can help you with?"

"I'm here to sell you some Ones."

Jack pulled a face. "Why me and not one of the other traffickers?"

"Harper sent me to Roscoe. We couldn't come to a deal."

Jack leaned over the desk. "He sent you to Roscoe? Good God. Does Beck know?"

"No."

"Make sure he doesn't find out. He'll go ballistic."

"I know. The sleaze offered me a job making porn flicks." It was her turn to make a gagging motion. "Then he offered me one hundred and twenty dollars for each demon."

Jack gaped. "One-twenty? He can't be selling to the Church at that price. We only get eight-five apiece for them."

"Could Harper be setting me up?"

"Maybe. You never know with him." Jack thought for a moment. "I don't usually buy anything below a Grade Three."

"I figured, well, you and Dad were buds and . . ." she said, turning on the charm.

The trafficker laughed. "Playing me already? Well, you got the face for it. How many?" he said.

"Four. All Biblios."

Jack leaned back in his chair, slipping his thumbs under those garish suspenders. "If you turn out half as good as Paul, you've got a future in this business. I'm not stupid. I don't want to piss off the next generation of trappers."

She cocked her head and waited. It felt like there was more.

"Okay, I admit it," Jack said. "I love it when an underdog wins, so I'm pulling for you. You'll get a lot of grief because you're female. Give it right back to them, okay?"

He didn't call me girlie, Baby Doll, or Princess. Jack moved up to the top of her Good People list.

"Let's see the little guys."

She set them out, one by one. The Biblios were swearing again.

"What does the Church do with them?" she asked.

"The official answer is that they put them in special containers, ship them off to monasteries in Europe, and the monks pray over them. It puts them to sleep. Eventually they disappear. The Church thinks their souls are saved. I think they return to Hell and are recycled."

"How long does that take?" she quizzed.

"I don't know. I honestly think they disappear so they don't have to listen to the endless chanting." He studied her intently. "You sure you want to sell them to me?"

"Yeah, why not?"

Jack hesitated for a second then tightened the cup lids, even though she'd just done the same thing.

"Okay, it's on your head then. Seventy-five apiece."

She nodded, though it was considerably less than what Roscoe had offered. While Jack counted out the money, she thought things through. "Did my dad say anything to you about Holy Water?"

"No. Why?" he asked, looking up from the vintage green safe behind his desk.

"I found some notes of his. He was researching it, but I don't know why."

"Ask Beck. He'd know if anyone does." Jack swung the safe door closed and handed her an envelope. "Don't put this in your bag. Someone might try to take it. The locals know folks coming out of here have cash on them."

She tucked the envelope in the waistband of her jeans. They signed the paperwork and the deal was done. He rose and offered his hand, and they shook firmly.

"Remember me when you get your journeyman's license. I'll be interested to see what you catch. I'll buy whatever you bring me."

Now that rocks. At least someone is on my side.

TWENTY-SEVEN

Riley laid the cash on the master's desk in a neat stack right next to his box of cigars.

"You sold them?" Harper asked. There wasn't a whiskey bottle in sight, and his eyes were predatory, like he was waiting to pounce. It gave her the creeps, and she wished Simon were here, not out buying trapping supplies.

Riley dumped the paperwork in front of him. A frown appeared as he flipped the pages. She'd sold the demons for the amount he'd said and brought him the cash and forms. Why was he upset?

"You sold them to the fag!" he bellowed.

Uh-oh. That's what Jack had meant when he said it was on her head.

"Why the hell didn't you go to Roscoe like I told you?" Harper demanded, his voice echoing off the open rafters. "Can't you do one damned thing right?"

"I went to the perv. He wouldn't sign the papers."

"Why the hell not?"

"He said he'd give me one-twenty apiece for the demons as long as I did the deal under the table." She took a gulp of air. "He said to tell you I got seventy-five and lost the paperwork, then I could keep the rest."

Harper's eyes turned flinty black. Faster that she thought he could move, his hand shot across the desk and grabbed her forearm. The fingers dug in like iron. "You're lying."

She tried to twist out of his grasp, but he only tightened his hold. "I'm not lying! Stop it. That hurts."

The master suddenly released her and she staggered a few steps away, fear coursing through her. Harper was too volatile. The next time he might hit her.

He produced a full bottle of whiskey from a drawer. The amber liquid sloshed into a cracked glass. "I don't sell to fags. Never have, never will."

"I didn't know," she retorted.

"You just did it to make me look bad. You're as twisted as your old man," he spat.

You leave my dad out of this!

"Get the hell out here," he shouted, "or I swear you'll be bleeding."

Riley barely reached the front door when glass shattered in the office.

"Goddamn Blackthornes!" Harper cursed.

Simon looked up as she fled into the parking lot. When he saw her face, he dropped a box back into the trunk of his car and hurried up to her.

"Are you okay?" he asked.

"Don't go in there," she said, shivering. "He's crazy. He's throwing stuff."

Simon studied her for a moment, then after a quick look at the building he put his hands on her shoulders and gave them a gentle squeeze.

"What happened in there?" he asked.

If she told him, what could he do? Argue with Harper? Get tossed out of the Guild? That wouldn't help either of them.

Riley shook her head, pulled away from him and hurried toward her car.

It's not your fight.

✢

The shakes finally subsided by the time Riley slumped on her couch. She pulled up her sweatshirt sleeve and studied her arm. Five dark finger-sized bruises stood out against her skin. She tugged the sleeve down. The bruises would eventually fade. Her fear wouldn't.

"He's going to keep doing this. He's going to keep hurting me until I quit."

Her eyes filled with tears.

I don't know if I can do this anymore, Dad. I'm so scared.

Her phone rang and she jumped at the sound. Reluctantly she dug it out of her bag. It was Simon.

"Riley, where are you?" he asked. Behind him she could hear street noise.

"I'm at home."

"Please tell me what happened. I don't want to walk in on him without knowing."

"I sold the Ones to Jack. Harper didn't like it." *And then he hurt me.*

"Did he . . . hit you?"

She sat up on the couch. Apparently she wasn't Harper's only target.

"I'm okay, Simon."

"I'm so sorry. I was hoping he'd be better with you."

Not a chance.

She flipped the phone closed. Her fear sheeted off her like a thin layer of ice in the full sun. "Harper, you miserable . . ." He'd dissed her dad. He'd hurt her and Simon.

Her father's voice asked the question as clearly as if he were sitting next to her.

Do you believe you deserve to be hit?

"No." And though Harper scared the hell out of her, she wasn't giving up. She'd just stay out of his reach from now on. He'd had his one shot at her, and there would be no others.

There was a tentative knock at her door.

She opened it, leaving the chain in place, still on edge. It was Beck, who wasn't known for knocking so softly.

"What?" she grumbled.

She could tell by the way he held himself that he was upset.

"Simon called. He was worried. He thought Harper had hurt ya."

"I'll handle it," she said evenly.

"Riley, he's a vicious SOB. That's why I wanted ya with Stewart."

"I'll handle it," she repeated. How she'd do that she had no idea, but if Beck got involved he'd end up in jail for assault and lose his trapping license.

"What set him off?" She told him. "Oh, God, I thought ya knew Harper didn't like Jack."

"How would I know that?" she complained. "I'm an apprentice. I'm not supposed to know stuff, but everybody thinks I do because my dad was a master."

Beck absorbed her tirade without a twitch.

It wasn't fair chewing on him. He wasn't the problem.

"Sorry." She unlatched the chain and waved him in.

He didn't budge. "I thought we might go for a ride. Talk it out."

"I'm not in the mood for—"

"I'm trappin' this afternoon and I need backup."

"What are you after?" she asked, still dubious.

"A Firebug."

A Pyro-Fiend. He knew what kind of bait to use.

"Well?" he asked, hands jammed in his jeans pockets. It made him look his age for a change.

"Will Harper be pissed if I trap with you?"

"Count on it, if he finds out. Does that bother ya?" he asked.

"After this morning? No way."

Riley barely climbed into Beck's truck before it was in gear and rolling out of the parking lot. She hastily attached her seat belt. She knew if she let him steer the conversation they'd keep talking about Harper, so she headed it in another direction.

"Simon trapped a Four at your pool hall this morning. It was really slick how it got into my head."

"Hard to ignore 'em, especially if they're comin' on to ya." Beck gave a dry chuckle. "There was this succubus who worked the convention circuit downtown. Damn, she was a hottie. I really hated trappin' her, but I had no choice."

"She didn't get to you?" Riley asked, curious. "I mean, in your head and all."

He smirked. "She got to me every way she could, and then some. The things she was sayin' to me . . ." He whistled. "It'd make any man fall on his knees and beg to be her slave."

Riley gave him a long look. "Then how'd you tune her out?"

"Carrie Underwood. Hummed one of her songs. Did the trick just perfect."

Beck dodged a streetcar and continued north along Peachtree Street.

"So where is this Firebug?" she asked.

"At the law library."

Riley swung her head toward him, panicking. "I can't go there! Not after what happened the other day." He cracked a wicked grin. "You lie!" She landed a light punch on his shoulder because he so deserved it. "So where *are* we going?"

"It's in a parkin' garage at Atlantic Station." He eyed her. "Have ya found yer daddy's manual yet?" She nodded. "How far are ya into it?"

"Grade Threes. Pretty disgusting reading. They even eat fiber-optic cable. How sick is that?"

"Well, that's about as far as yer gonna get."

"What do you mean?"

"I took out the back section, the parts that covered Fours and up. Don't want ya tryin' to trap an Archfiend or nothin'. Ya made the rest of us look bad enough takin' out a Three, ya bein' an apprentice and all."

It took a while register what he'd done.

"You removed the rest of the manual," she said flatly. No wonder the thing hadn't been as thick as she'd expected.

He shot her a broad grin. "Just keepin' ya safe, Riley girl. Ya'll thank me one day."

Not in this lifetime.

✛

It took the better part of an hour of skulking around the parking garage to finally locate the fiend in question. As they hiked through the multi-story concrete structure, Beck remained on guard the entire time. It felt weird trapping with him, but she had to admit she wasn't afraid.

He can handle anything. Her dad had taught him well.

"Not quite what ya thought trappin' would be?" Beck asked. It sounded like Harper's question, except there was no malice in it.

"I figured it'd be more exciting. Less hiking, for one." She'd managed to keep up with Beck, but it had been a struggle with her sore thigh. "I've never seen a Pyro."

"Evil critters. They love fire. It fascinates 'em."

"Like Fireman Jack."

"Yeah, 'cept he doesn't go around settin' 'em." Beck did a quick one-eighty, surveying the area around them. "It won't be out in the open on the top deck, so this floor has to be it."

"Glad to hear it. All this incline stuff isn't feeling good on the leg."

He shook his head like he'd been stupid. "I'm sorry, girl, I didn't think of that. Ya wanna wait in the truck?"

Did he just apologize? That had to be a first.

"I'm good," she said, ignoring the jittery muscles and the cramping as best she could.

Beck scrutinized the area with wary anticipation. "Ya need to stay behind me. If this goes wrong, book it," he ordered.

"Wrong how?"

"Like if this thing gets a couple cars burnin'."

Exploding gas tanks. Not good.

"Hold this, will ya?" He handed over his duffel bag. It was so heavy she nearly dropped it. "Careful! There's spheres in there."

"You could have warned me it weighs more than I do," she groused.

"Ya need to build yerself up, girl. Only way to handle a full trapper's bag."

Muscles. Right. Just what I need. "Why don't you pack lighter?" she asked.

"Ya need all the gear with ya."

"Why? You know this is a Two."

"Higher-level demons can act like the lesser grades. Ya think yer trappin' a Three and it turns out to be a Four, and if ya don't have the right equipment, that's an LLM."

"Huh?"

"Life. Limiting. Mistake." He stripped off his leather jacket and tossed it on a nearby car. He was wearing a "Take No Prisoners" camo T-shirt underneath. It was looser than most guys would wear. He wasn't looking to show off his muscles but making sure he had plenty of room to move. Picking up a white sphere, Beck began his search. Luckily there weren't as many cars as on the floors below. A sparking noise came from underneath an old SUV. It was one of the big monsters, the kind that no one would buy anymore, what with gas running ten or more a gallon. It was originally black, but now it was covered in a fine layer of dust like it'd been abandoned here.

Something red, like a giant rubber band, snaked out of the tailpipe.

As it reached the concrete floor, it took shape. It looked a lot like an eight-inch-tall red rubber doll with horns and a forked tail. It grinned a mouthful of sharp teeth, then snapped its fingers. Brilliant red-gold fire shot out of its palms.

"Trapper," it hissed.

"Howdy, demon. Nice flames," Beck replied.

A second later a bolt of fire went streaking toward him like it had come from a military flamethrower. He deftly stepped aside, and the bolt exploded on the concrete next to him. It'd happened so fast Riley hadn't had time to react. If Beck was frightened, he certainly wasn't showing it.

"Roast you, trapper!" the fiend hissed, snapping its fingers again. Then it caught sight of Riley.

Before her companion could shout a warning, a bolt came straight at her. She shrieked and cowered as the flames raced over the top of her. There was a sizzling sound as they struck a concrete support. The scorch mark was four feet wide.

Holy crap. Now she *was* scared.

The next fireball went straight at Beck. He weaved, lost his footing on a patch of oil, and fell to one knee. The sphere in his right hand shattered and magically charged water burst forth in a rolling wave across the floor. In a few seconds ice crystals sheeted across the concrete like frost on a windowpane in deep winter. Beck struggled to his feet and quickly backed off to avoid being trapped in the rapidly freezing pond.

"I need another one!" he called out.

With a high-pitched cackle, the fiend hopped onto a nearby Honda and began to fire incendiaries at the unarmed trapper.

"Throw a sphere!" Beck shouted, dodging and ducking to avoid the flames.

Riley pulled one out without looking, about to dash it to the ground.

"Not that one!" Beck cried out as an arc of flame caught him. "Get a white one!"

White. She put the duffel bag on the ground and frantically rummaged through the contents. Beck cried out as another gout of flame got too close. The cackling fiend was playing with him.

"White!" she shouted. "Got it." She hauled back to dash it on the floor of the garage.

"Up! Throw the thing up!" Beck called out, and then rolled between two cars to avoid another burst of flame.

"Up?" She took a huge breath and underhanded the glass ball straight up toward the concrete above them.

The demon turned toward her, igniting a massive fireball on its palm.

"Oh, God."

The sphere struck the garage ceiling an instant before the demon set the fireball loose. Beck yelled something, but by then it was too late.

Pure white light slammed into her eyes, blinding her. Stumbling backward, she crashed into a support and landed hard.

Beck shouted again. The demon shrieked.

Then it began to snow.

TWENTY-EIGHT

Riley pulled herself up against the concrete pier. Nothing was broken as best as she could tell, but she knew she'd have more bruises by morning.

It was snowing in the parking garage. Serious snowage, like somehow they'd moved this battle to Chicago in January. There was already three inches on the concrete, and it wasn't melting.

She hunted through the falling white until she found the demon. His fire was out, thin tendrils of gray smoke curling upward from his hands. He stormed and shouted and cursed but couldn't generate a flicker.

"Beck?" she called out.

He hauled himself out from behind a car. "Ya okay?"

Ouch. My butt hurts. "I'm good."

Carefully he worked himself across the frozen pond and tagged the Pyro. It didn't try to run, its movements slowed by the cold.

"Kiss my ass, demon!" Beck whooped, and shot a fist in the air.

He slid his way over to her, nearly falling. "Hold this," he said, and dropped the Pyro into her hands.

It was uncomfortably warm, like a hot rubber ball, and it glared at her malevolently.

"Blackthorne's daughter. We know thee. Boon we grant . . ."

She ignored it. What she couldn't ignore was the weird look on Beck's face.

"What?" she asked.

"It said yer name."

"They all do," she said, shrugging. "Always have. I told you that."

"They don't do that to me."

"That's cuz I'm special," she said, winking. Adrenaline flowed out of her body by scoopfuls, and she felt really tired.

"Special, huh," Beck mumbled. He pulled a lunch tote from his trapping bag. It was large for a tote, bigger than the one Simon had used for the Four, and it had a logo on the side from some Gainesville bait shop. He unzipped it, revealing jagged chucks of dry ice.

The demon began to wail and curse, twisting in Riley's grip.

"Tough break, asshole," Beck said. He took the demon and dropped it headfirst into the dry ice. The ice hissed and went white. The cursing stopped as Beck zipped the container closed.

"Do those magical charms really work?" she asked, pointing at a nest of them attached to the handle. They seemed to be made of jade and wood.

"Supposed to, at least that's what the witches claim."

"Just checking here: I thought I was supposed to watch," Riley said, unable to resist pulling his chain.

"Ya were," Beck replied, suddenly serious. "If anyone asks, I threw both globes, okay? If not, there'll be hell to pay."

She nodded wearily. "Whatever."

It had stopped snowing, though there was at least five inches on the garage floor. The giant pond was covered with it.

"Should have brought our ice skates," Riley said.

Then another idea dropped into her head. How many times would she get a chance like this in Atlanta? Turning her back to her companion, she packed herself a snowball.

"Beck?" she called out, all innocence.

"Yes, kid?" he replied, turning toward her.

Kid? That did it. She threw the snowball and it struck center chest. He *oofed*, glared, and then stalked toward her, intent on his prey. "You called it, *Princess!*" She turned to escape, but a snowball hit her right on the butt. He'd planned a similar ambush.

"That wasn't hard to hit," he joked.

"Are you saying my butt's big?" she demanded.

His grin grew wider, egging her on.

"Die, Backwoods Boy!" Two more went his way and only one connected, splattering him just north of his belt buckle. She scurried to rearm herself, knowing the battle was heating up.

"Backwoods Boy?" he called out, frowning. "Ya got no respect, girl."

He slid on the ice, moving faster than she'd anticipated, and swooped in like a basketball star. A mushy snowball dropped down the front of her jacket. It melted into her bra and onto her skin, making her shriek and dance around until the remaining snow fell out of the bottom of her sweatshirt.

Laughing at her antics, Beck was already packing another missile. She ducked at the last minute, and it glanced off an expensive sports car.

"Step away from the car!" the auto's alarm voice commanded. "Step away from—"

"Let's get out of here before someone calls the cops," he advised.

The Corvette's alarm was still issuing orders when they reached his truck on the first level. He toted the demon and the duffel bag while she took control of his jacket.

"You okay?" she asked, noticing the back of his T-shirt had a sizable scorch mark.

"A little crisped but not bad. That's why I took off my coat. It's the third I've bought this year." He eyed her as he stowed the gear in the front seat. "Ya really don't know the spheres by color?"

"Dad wouldn't tell me about them."

Beck mumbled something under his breath. "He figured ya'd quit, get a real job." He thought for a moment and then nodded to himself. "Let's find some food and we'll work on that."

"Can we get barbecue?" she asked, suddenly hungry. "I haven't had barbecued chicken in forever."

A big grin appeared on her companion's face. "I know this great place on Edgewood. Mama Z's. It's a dive, but, damn, the food's good."

"What about that thing?" she asked, pointing at the bait container.

"We'll do a drive-by to Jack's. It'll stay quiet until the dry ice thaws, then it'll get nasty again. Best it's Jack's problem at that point."

"What's he do with them?"

"Throws them in a bigger canister of dry ice."

"Doesn't that kill them?"

"No way," he said, shaking his head.

As Beck drove out of the garage, he gave the parking attendants a big toothy smile and a wave. "There's some snow on the fifth level. Thought ya might like to know. Y'all have a nice day, now!" he called out.

No wonder Dad liked working with you.

✛

Beck did the drive-by to Jack's. She remained in the truck as he completed the transaction and collected the payment.

"Two hundred and fifty," he said, shutting the door. He promptly dropped half of it in her lap, mostly in twenties. "That's yer cut."

"But—"

He raised a callused hand. "I know, yer not supposed to be earnin' anything unless it's with Harper. So if anyone asks, ya didn't get a cent."

She looked down at the money. "Thanks."

He shrugged. "Saves me having to loan it to ya. Ya did help out back there."

"Help out? I totally saved you."

She expected argument, but it didn't come. "Sure did. Thanks... Riley."

An apology and a thank-you, all in one day? This has to be a dream.

They'd picked up the food and headed for her apartment. Along the way he'd shared some of his knowledge of Firebugs and how her dad had taught him the ropes. Riley didn't interrupt, hoping this would never end. It was nice not to argue with him. She actually liked the guy when he wasn't going all Big Brother on her. After all, they had a lot in common. They were both trappers and they both adored her father.

"I guess it was only right ya followin' in the business," he said, making the turn toward her place. "Ya got it in the blood, all the way back."

She gave him a puzzled look. "What do you mean? My grandfather was a banker."

"That was his day job. Yer granddaddy and his people were all trappers. It calls to ya no matter what."

"My grandfather was a trapper?" Her parents hadn't mentioned that, like it was some dark secret.

"Yer great-granddaddy too. Blackthornes have been trappin' since forever. Like the Stewarts."

"I didn't know that." No wonder she'd had this feeling she *had* to do this. In some ways, that was sorta disturbing, like she didn't have a choice. "Why didn't Dad tell me?" she asked, her anger stirring.

"Never wanted his daughter to be a trapper. Too dangerous."

That she couldn't argue with. If she worked at the coffee shop like Simi, she sure wouldn't have gotten clawed up by an espresso machine.

"What about your people?" she asked. "Where they trappers?"

He shook his head. "Didn't trap demons, only small varmints. Too busy runnin' bootleg whiskey and tryin' to stay out of jail. I'm the first one in the family."

"They must be proud of you."

"Not to hear them tell it."

‡

When Beck set the carryout bag on the kitchen table, he hesitated.

"Which chair can I sit in?" he asked.

"That one," she said, pointing at hers.

He reached for it and then changed his mind. "I better wash up first," he said. As he walked down the hall toward the bathroom, he stripped off his T-shirt. He wasn't just singed. There was a big red burn between his shoulder blades, intersected by newly healed claw marks.

"Beck?"

"Yeah?" he called out.

"We need to treat your back."

"Nah, it's okay."

She fished a bottle of Holy Water out of his duffel bag, checked the label to ensure it was fresh, and then wedged herself in the doorway of the bathroom so he couldn't escape.

He saw the look in her eyes. "That bad?"

"Not good."

He blew a stream of air out of his lips. "Sink or tub?"

"Tub."

She used the entire bottle on his back and shoulders as he bent over the bathtub to keep the Holy Water from going everywhere. Some got in his hair, but he didn't seem to mind. From her vantage point she could tell he definitely had muscles in all the right places. Simi would say he was hunkalicious, but this was Beck after all.

"Those claw marks," she said. "You got them the night Dad died, didn't you?"

He stood up, swiping damp hair off from his forehead. "Yeah," he said softly.

"You kept Dad from being . . ." *Eaten.*

"He'd have done the same for me."

"Thanks." He shrugged like it was no big deal. She couldn't push it much further or he'd get more uncomfortable, and that usually made him surly. She loaned him one of her dad's T-shirts and tossed his in the garbage.

Famished, Riley attacked the chicken, the sweet corn, and the mashed potatoes with a vengeance. It was as good as her companion had promised.

"This is great stuff," she said, wiping barbecue sauce off her face. "It's really hot. I like it that way."

"Best in Atlanta," he replied. "I'll take ya there when Mama's workin'. She really likes me."

"You charmed her on purpose, didn't you?"

"Never piss off the people who feed ya. I learned that in the Army."

It was an opening she'd not expected, a chance to learn more about him.

"What was it like over there?" she quizzed.

He didn't answer for some time, but his eyes went distant, like he was seeing things she couldn't hope to understand.

"I felt alive for the first time in my life. Kinda weird, if ya think about it, what with all that dyin' around me. Somehow I knew I was supposed to be there to help those guys. Get a few of them home in one piece, not in some body bag."

"Dad said it was hard on you, that you changed."

Beck rubbed his chin. "Ya see so much. I was young and I didn't know how to handle it."

"You're still young," she said. "You're not that much older than me."

"I don't feel like it," he admitted. "Never really had a chance to be a kid."

"Do you regret going over there?" she asked, wondering what sort of hell he'd endured.

"Some nights, when the dreams won't leave me be." Beck slowly pulled his eyes up to hers. "Other times, no. I don't fear dyin' now, not like some. I've seen it too many times."

"Why trap demons?" she quizzed.

A faint smile came to his face. "Because of yer daddy."

"Like me, then," she said.

"It's a good enough reason."

He rose and headed for the couch. Instead of stretching out like she thought he would, he began to dig inside his duffel bag, carefully laying out different colored magical spheres on the seat cushions.

"Come here," he said, beckoning. "I'll give ya the quick and dirty on these things. Just act surprised when Harper does all this, okay?"

"It'll be our secret," she promised.

The spheres ranged in size from a golf ball to a grapefruit on steroids. There was every color you could think of—white for the snow globes, clear for the Holy Water, blue for the grounding spheres, purple for Babel spheres, and so on. He explained each one in detail, then put them back in the duffel bag.

"That wasn't so hard," she said, sucking on the last of her iced tea. It was more syrup than tea, just the way she liked it.

"We're not done." Beck dropped his hand into the bag and pulled out a blue sphere. "Quick, what is it?"

"Ah . . . ah . . ." she struggled.

"Think! The demon is fixin' to nail ya, and yer not givin' me an answer."

"Babel sphere?" she guessed, then winced. *Wrong!*

"Babel spheres are purple." He handed it to her. "This is a groundin' sphere. It pulls a Geo-Fiend into the earth so it can't summon weather or make earthquakes."

"It didn't work for Dad."

"It did. The demon got lucky."

He pulled out another sphere.

This one she knew. "White. It's for Firebugs."

"That was too easy." Another appeared in his hand.

Red. "Ah . . . oh, Lord." This was hard.

"A shield sphere," he said.

And so it went until she could pretty much identity each sphere for its properties and use. Whites went up, the rest went down. Blues needed to contact metal. Purples needed to land at the demon's feet. Reds only lasted a short time.

"Did Dad ever say anything to you about the Holy Water?" she asked, holding up one of the spheres.

"Only that he was worried that it wasn't workin' as well as it used to on some of the demons."

"What kind of demons?"

"Threes. Why ya askin'?"

She waved him off. "Just wondering."

He returned the orbs to the bag and zipped it shut. "Ya still confused about the spheres?"

"Yeah. Were you at first?"

"Got it right off," he said. "No sweat."

"You lie!"

A boyish grin told her she was right. Then he set a small box on the couch between them.

Riley stared at it then up at him. "For me?"

When he issued a quick nod, her heart rate sped up. There was no writing on the box, so she had no clue what might be inside. It could be something really neat.

The moment the lid came off, she gasped. A long black demon claw sat inside. The top of it was captured with silver wire and it had a thick chain curled up behind it.

"Is this . . ." she asked with a slight shiver.

"Yeah, it's the one out of yer leg," he admitted. "I asked a friend of mine to make it so ya could wear it. I hope ya like it."

In some perverse way, she did. A lot. When she looked up at Beck, concern covered his face. This really did matter to him.

Riley looped it over her neck and then held it away from her body so she could see it. The claw looked scary close up, just like its former owner.

"It's awesome, Beck!"

His expression relaxed. He acted like he wanted to say something more but then shook his head. Standing, he put the strap of the duffel bag on his shoulder and scooped up his coat with his free hand.

"Take a trip to the market tonight. Introduce yourself to the witches who make these puppies," he said, tapping the side of the bag. "They'll tell ya how the spheres work."

"But what about Dad?" she asked, confused. She'd need to be at the graveyard in an hour.

"I'll watch him 'til ya get there."

As he reached the door she called out, "Beck?" He turned around, reminding her more of the young man who'd gone to war, not the old one who'd returned. "Thanks. For everything. I mean it."

A slow grin edged onto his face. "You're worth it . . . *Princess.*"

Her tennis shoe hit the door a second after it closed.

TWENTY-NINE

As Riley waited for Simon at the edge of Centennial Park, she tried to relax. Her back was sore from playing tag with the concrete support and she still felt scorched, though she'd washed her hair and changed clothes. No wonder trappers bought most of their threads secondhand: they had the shelf life of fresh oysters. Riley returned her attention to the nest of papers in her lap. If her father had one weakness, it was details. Riley only wanted to see the bigger picture, not the complete history of Holy Water since the dawn of time. She wanted to know why he was interested in the topic, but so far she'd not found anything that answered that question. One thing came through clearly in his notes—her dad was worried.

Frustrated at her lack of progress, she jammed the papers into her messenger bag. Her hand trailed up to the chain that secured the demon claw. She'd pulled it out a couple of times to look at it, marveling how really neat it was, but then hid it again. Metal was valuable and it wouldn't be smart to let anyone know she was wearing some. The silver in the chain and the wrapping was the good stuff, the kind her mom used to have before they had to sell it to help pay for her chemotherapy.

"I bet this was way expensive," she mused. She still couldn't believe he'd done it. *I guess I really don't know him that well.*

The whole afternoon felt different, like aliens had kidnapped Backwoods Boy and rewired him to be nice. He'd acted like he wanted to be with her, laughed at her jokes, didn't make her feel like she was being goofy at all. He'd even taught her how to trap a Firebug.

Hope it lasts. It'd be good to have him as a friend, maybe even a trapping partner once she made journeyman.

Simon, however, fell into a different category altogether. *Oh yeah.*

She looked up to see him approaching on the brick sidewalk, his eyes skimming the ground. He moved deliberately, as is he were thinking through some deep problem and was only vaguely aware of his surroundings. He'd sounded only half interested when she'd invited him to join her tonight. Initially she'd panicked, thinking he was growing tired of her, but that worry vanished when he'd agreed to see her.

As he grew closer, she called out, "Hi there!"

He shrugged. The Silent Order of Simons was back.

And they think girls are moody.

"Hey, no fair being so quiet," she nudged.

He looked embarrassed for a second. "Sorry."

Riley took his hand and squeezed it. When he didn't return the gesture, she dropped it. For a half second she wondered if she'd done something to tick him off, but she couldn't think of anything. This was just Simon. Sometimes he was fun, sometimes he was silent.

"What did Harper do to you?" he asked in a voice so quiet she almost didn't hear him.

"Yelled a lot."

"That's it?"

"Yes," she lied.

A relieved sigh. "Keep out of his reach. He'll beat you for no reason," Simon warned.

"You?"

"All his apprentices," he said, then fell silent again.

As they walked into Centennial Park she forced her mind to happier times as a counterweight to grim reality. When she was little, Riley's parents would tote her downtown to play in the five fountains, which were laid out in interconnecting rings like the Olympic logo. In the summer when it was blistering hot, the park was always crowded. Vendors sold kosher beef hot dogs, vegetable samosas, and root beer floats. This place was all about good memories.

Despite her companion's uncomfortable silence, she couldn't help but share that feeling. She gave him a playful hip-bump.

"My parents used to bring me here when I was a kid. I loved jumping around in the fountains."

To her relief, Simon roused from his melancholy. "Mine did, too. We'd run around for a couple of hours then pile in the car and fall asleep. Mom and Dad appreciated the quiet since there were so many of us."

Riley looked longingly at the water spraying high in the air toward the evening sky. The lights were on tonight, making the droplets sparkle like diamonds. As they walked by the nearest jet she pushed Simon closer to it. He yelped in surprise as the water hit him and then charged after her. She tried to run but her thigh wasn't cooperating.

"Got you!" he laughed and grabbed on to her. He lifted her up and spun her around. When her feet were on the ground, he wore a smile. It made her feel good again.

When they broke apart, Simon caught her hand and held it tight.

"Thanks," he said. "I take myself too seriously sometimes."

"Only sometimes?" she jested. "You'd make a great monk. You're good with the silent bit."

"I thought about the priesthood," he admitted, "but I decided I'd rather hunt demons. That way I can marry, have kids." He looked over at her, like he was judging her reaction.

"How many?" she asked.

"Three, maybe four. More than that is too many, unless you have a lot of bathrooms."

You'd make a good dad.

They paused at the edge of the Terminus Market. It was barely after dark and the market was growing more active, like a bear stirring out of hibernation. The lights made the multicolored tents glow like giant

Christmas bulbs. Her dad had claimed it wasn't like it used to be, as if that was a good excuse for not bringing her here.

She remembered mostly baked goods and craft items, but now there was a bit of everything in row upon row of tents, lean-tos, and camping trailers. People wandered from vendor to vendor, toting items they'd purchased—used tires, homemade bread, a basket of apples. There was a white nanny goat and its owner was milking it into a shiny pail. Riley gave Simon a puzzled look.

"He sells the milk," he said.

"Isn't that against the rules?"

"Yes, but the city ignores what goes on down here. As long as the stall fees are paid, they're happy."

As they passed a shop that sold jerky, Simon shuddered. "I don't trust that stuff," he confided in a lowered voice. "The guy says it's beef, but you never know."

"Well, it won't be rat," she said. "The Threes eat all of those."

"I'm thinking coyote," Simon replied.

A little farther on she spied a brawny man pounding something out on an anvil. A glowing red fire blazed behind him. A shower of sparks would fly into the night air when his young assistant worked a ragged set of bellows. The man was stripped to his waist, but even in the cold air he was perspiring from exertion, sweat defining the ropy muscles on his arms and chest.

"A smithy?" Riley said. "Guess it makes sense."

"Cheaper to fix what's broken than buy new," Simon explained.

Riley stopped in her tracks and did a slow one-eighty. "This is like something out a movie," she said. "Like an Arabian market or a medieval faire."

"With a Southern twist," Simon said, pointing toward a tent. The menu posted on a hand-lettered sign included grits, collards, fried chicken, and sweet potato pie. The pie sounded good, but she was still full from Beck's magnificent barbecue.

Simon paused in front of a tent stocked with different-sized bottles of Holy Water. Riley picked up a pint. It was manufactured by Celestial Supplies, the company her father had mentioned in his notes, and the date stamp said it had been consecrated two days earlier. She rotated the bottle in her hands and checked out the city's tax stamp, which shimmered in the dim light. Since Atlanta couldn't collect money from the Church, they taxed their by-product.

"Always check the date," Simon advised. "It has to be fresh if you're treating demon wounds. If you're warding your house, not so much."

Riley thought about the Holy Water she'd used on her claw wounds. Carmela had said it must have been old, but the guy she'd bought it from had assured her it was fresh. So which was it?

"You're frowning," Simon said.

"Just confused. I read in the manual that you have to reapply a Holy Water ward at regular intervals, but it didn't say why."

"It's thought that it absorbs evil and becomes less potent. That's why they sell a lot of it to prisons and jails."

"And nursing homes, hospitals, schools, government buildings— you name it," a hefty salesman explained. He was dressed in a blue suit like he sold life insurance. His hair was patchy at the top, and he clutched a sales pad in his hand. "It's the only way to keep your family safe from Hell's terrors," he added.

At that he shoved a multicolored brochure into her hand that ex-tolled the virtues of Holy Water and its protective properties.

"So how would I know if this is fresh or not?" she asked, thinking back to the demon-wound fiasco.

The salesman tapped a fingernail against the pint she was holding.

"Each bottle and every glass sphere has a batch number that in-cludes the date the Holy Water was consecrated. It's state law."

She already knew that. "But can some of it be less potent?"

"No," the salesman said curtly.

Well, that got me nowhere.

"How much is this?" Simon asked, holding up a pint bottle. "It doesn't have a price."

"Ten."

"Whoa, that's high," Simon protested, his eyebrows rising in astonishment.

"The city raised the tax rate again."

The salesman spotted another potential customer and took his sales pitch elsewhere.

"Ten for a pint? It used to be that much for a gallon," Simon muttered. "That's outrageous. No wonder the price of the spheres has gone up so much."

Riley tucked the brochure into her messenger bag, and her hands brushed against the papers inside. They reminded her of her father's research.

"Is there any way a demon could become immune to Holy Water?"

Simon immediately shook his head. "No way. All Hellspawn react negatively to the concentrated power of divinity." It sounded like he'd quoted that from some book.

Then why was my dad so fixated on this?

Simon took her by the elbow and gently steered her to the right. "The stall we want is this way."

As they rounded the corner, Riley gasped. The bright orange tent in front of them was full of dead people.

"They sell them here?" she asked, appalled.

"The necros always have a tent at the market."

Riley did a quick count: There were seven Deaders and one live guy. He was doing all the talking. The Deaders stared off into space, probably wondering what happened to them. At least the salesman wasn't hawking them like used cars or that would have really set her off.

"How much do they sell for?" she whispered.

"I've heard as high as five thousand," Simon replied. His voice hardened. "It makes me sick."

She frowned. "What happens to their souls?"

"I asked Father Harrison about that," Simon replied putting his arm around her waist. "He said the Church isn't really sure what happens, but they believe the soul isn't completely free if the body is walking around. Only the necros know for sure, and they aren't talking about it."

"What if the body goes rogue or something? Starts eating people."

Simon laughed softly. "That's only in the movies. These guys aren't good at thinking things through, and they're definitely not zombies. They don't eat at all."

"But they're not mindless," she said, thinking of the woman on the street with the briefcase.

"No, somewhere in between." He steered her elbow again. "Come on."

As they walked away, she noticed a man watching her from the tent where knives and other sharp pointy things were sold. He was holding a sword. Not holding it actually, but owning it, like he knew exactly what he was doing. His sleek black hair was pulled back in a ponytail and tied with a leather cord. A glossy black leather jacket covered his broad shoulders and muscled arms. With a bit of imagination Riley could picture him on the cover of a romance novel. He turned in her direction, then saluted with the blade like a cavalier might his queen.

It was an effort not to melt in her tracks.

"Riley?" her companion nudged.

"Ah, sorry," she said, but she really wasn't.

When she looked around again, the man was gone.

Who was that guy?

"Bell, Book and Broomstick," Simon announced, unaware her mind was elsewhere. The midnight-blue tent was sprinkled with gold and silver stars, and there was a long table in front of it laden with amulets, velvet bags, and other witchy stuff.

Riley knew Simon well enough not to use the *W* word. He was way touchy about anything supernatural and somehow had convinced himself that the spells inside the crystal spheres weren't really magic. No matter what he called it, it *was* magic and the trappers used it or they ended up dead.

And sometimes they died anyway.

Behind the counter was a tall woman in Renn Faire garb, her russet-brown hair an unruly mass of curls. A multicolored dragon tattoo started at her neck and descended deep inside her dark green peasant blouse. When she saw Simon, she leaned over the counter, displaying ample cleavage for his benefit.

"Hey, how's my favorite trapper?" the witch asked. From her tone, Riley could tell she loved playing with Simon's head.

Riley's boyfriend noted the cleavage but pulled his eyes away with amazingly little effort. "Just fine. Ayden, this is Riley," he said, gesturing. "She's an apprentice trapper."

"Paul's daughter?" Riley nodded. "Goddess..." the witch replied. She stepped from behind the table and enveloped Riley in a big hug. Her hair smelled of patchouli incense.

"We all miss him," the woman said, stepping back, her eyes clouded.

An awkward silence fell between them.

Riley cleared her throat. "Beck would like you to tell me about the spheres."

The witch brightened. "Ah. Sphere Lecture One-Oh-One. My pleasure."

"I'll wait here," Simon said, his hand in the pocket where he kept his rosary.

"I promise I won't turn you into anything that eats flies," Ayden teased.

Simon stiffened, but didn't move.

The witch waited until they were inside the tent and then leaned close to Riley. "I love messing with him. He's a real sweet guy, but he hasn't learned that his faith isn't in competition with anyone else's."

"Did you give him the sphere lecture, too?"

She nodded. "He wasn't that receptive."

As they walked deeper into the tent, the soothing scent of jasmine enveloped them. Lanterns hung from the tent poles and in one corner someone was having a Tarot card reading. Waving her forward, Ayden knelt in front of a large wooden chest adorned with arcane symbols. Some of them Riley recognized—an ankh, the Eye of Horus. The rest was anyone's guess. Celtic maybe.

"We keep them in the chest because they're easily broken," Ayden explained, opening the lid.

Tell me about it.

The witch dug out three spheres and placed them in Riley's hands. One red, one white, and one blue. It made her think of Roscoe's front window, which wasn't a good thing.

"So how do you make these?" Riley asked.

"We buy the glass spheres, blend the ingredients, and fill them using a funnel through that little port." Ayden pointed toward a small cork plug on the side of the sphere. "Once they're filled, we reseal them. Then we go into the forest on a full moon and charge them with magic," the witch said.

"Do you dance around a fire or something?"

"Depends on the magic. Sometimes we're skyclad, sometimes not."

"Sky . . . clad?" Riley asked.

"Nekkid, as they say in these parts," Ayden said, winking.

"The mosquitoes must be a bitch."

The witch issued a rich laugh. "You should come sometime."

Not if I have to be nude.

Riley slowly turned the sphere in her hand. "The Holy Water bottles have a tax stamp. Why don't these?"

Ayden groaned. "I hear that's on the legislature's agenda next year, but our lobbyist is trying to push that back. They want to tax all magical items."

"How much do you charge for these?" Riley asked, tickled to find someone who would give her straight answers for a change.

"We ask for a donation to cover our costs. It doesn't seem right to charge you guys for keeping evil at bay."

Riley's appreciation of the witches rose even further.

"Okay, I admit we have an ulterior motive, besides the good karma, that is. It makes it harder for some of the radical groups to claim we're in league with Hell when we're supplying the means to take them down."

That made sense.

"First thing I always say about the spheres: Think outside the box. The trappers like to believe that a certain sphere should only be used on its primary target. Like a Babel sphere for Fours or a snow globe for Pyro-Fiends. That's shortsighted."

"Why?"

"Because the magic can be used in a number of ways. Think about the properties of the spheres and match them to the effect that you want to create. You can combine the spheres so they enhance each other's properties. Every time I mention something like that to a trapper they get all weird on me."

"Even my dad?" Riley asked. He'd always been open to new ideas.

Ayden spread her hands. "Paul was beginning to come around, but old habits are hard to break."

Riley's cell phone chirped. She pulled it out and muted it. Probably Peter checking up on her. After Riley dumped the phone in her bag, Ayden held up a sphere. White particles swirled inside like a vintage snow globe. The only thing that was missing was an ice skater in the center.

"So let's start with a white and go from there," the witch said.

A half an hour later Riley was outside the tent, her head swimming in details. Whites were created using air and water magic. The grounding spheres were a combination of earth, air, and fire magic. It went on from there.

I'll never keep all this stuff straight.

She found Simon pacing outside the tent. "You done?" he asked, clearly eager to be somewhere else.

Riley nodded. "Want some hot chocolate?"

"No, thanks. I need to get home."

Oh. So much for making this a date.

Riley checked her cell phone. Three calls, all from Beck. He hadn't left a message.

I knew it was too good to last.

THIRTY

Quit stallin'.

Beck sorted out his trapping bag, which hadn't needed the attention, then did it all over again in a new configuration. If he'd had his gun-cleaning supplies he would have stripped his Sig and given it a thorough cleaning. None of his efforts helped him forget the Two's voice calling out Riley's name. Lower-level fiends didn't do that. To them all trappers were the same.

In his gut he knew it meant something. He needed advice, but who could he ask without screwing up Riley's future with the Guild?

"Harper?" he mused. "No way." The bastard would use the information to throw her to the wolves. "Stewart?" That was a better choice, but the master might feel inclined to let the Guild know Hell was taking a personal interest in Paul's daughter.

"Ah, damn." What could he do?

After much thought, Beck decided on a less-risky course of action. He waited until Mortimer had made his rounds and then fired up his cell phone, his nerves pushing him along. The call was to an old trapping buddy in New York City who he could trust with a secret.

"Patterson. What kind and where?" the gruff voice asked.

"Jeff? It's Beck."

"Hey, Den. What's up? Long time, no hear."

"Got a couple questions for ya. Ever seen demons workin' together? Like a Geo-Fiend and a Three?"

"Nope. That's the only thing that saves our asses. If they ever get smart, they'll nail us. Why?"

"It's happenin' here. That ain't all. Ya ever hear tell of lower-level demons callin' a trapper by name?"

"No, only Fours and above. It's not until they reach that level they have that sort of knowledge. And an Archfiend, hell, they can tell you the size of your dick and when you last cheated on your wife."

"Good reason not to get married."

Jeff laughed. "Why are you asking?"

"We got an apprentice who's bein' called out by every demon from a One on up."

"Damn. Has Lucifer got his hooks in the guy? That might explain why Hell knows him."

Could Riley have been rolled by a demon?

"No, the trapper's on the level."

"You sure? Sometimes you can't tell. It's not like they've got a big brand on their forehead or nothing."

"No. Both a Five and a Three have tried to kill her. Lucifer won't snuff one of his own."

"Her?"

Patterson he could trust. "If I tell ya who it is, ya can't spread it around."

"Doesn't go any further."

"It's Paul's daughter, Riley."

"What's she doing in the business?" Before Beck could answer, Jeff added, "Following her dad, I guess. Anything else weird about her?"

Beck told him about Riley trapping the Three, how she brought it down on her own. "It was the one that double-teamed us the night Paul died."

"Blackthorne's dead?" the man exclaimed.

Beck felt like a fool. He shook his head at his stupidity. "Ah, I'm sorry, man. I thought ya'd heard."

"No, I've been out of town fishing in Canada. You should do that sometime. Get your mind off the job for a few days." A pause. "How'd he die?"

Beck made it brief. There was a long silence, and then Jeff cleared his throat. "I've never heard of this kind of thing before."

"So what do ya think about all this?"

"I think I'm damned glad I'm up here."

Beck sighed.

"If Lucifer's fiends know her on sight and they've already gone after her, she needs a change of scenery," Patterson replied. "Out of Atlanta, for sure."

"Yeah, we're ass-deep in demons right now."

"We're not. You could send her up here. Course, that doesn't mean they won't track her down, but it might be a local thing, you know?"

Beck had a better idea. "She's got an aunt in Fargo."

"Put her on a bus. Those Dakotans are a testy bunch after the fiends caused those big floods a few years ago. Demons don't get too much of a chance up there anymore, if you know what I mean."

"Thanks. I owe ya, Jeff. I mean it."

"You're buying the first round next time we meet. Later, guy."

Beck closed his phone and dropped it on the blanket like it was a live grenade. His gut felt like he'd swallowed a mile of barbed wire.

"Too much weird shit goin' on," he muttered. Most of it seemed to be centered around Paul's daughter, but that didn't make any sense. Hell was taking too much of an interest in her. The Pyro-Fiend had been the final straw.

No matter how much he'd enjoyed teaching Riley the ropes like her daddy had taught him, he shouldn't have taken her trapping with him. She'd done fine, better than most apprentices, but he was just being selfish. It was hard to admit he liked being around her. She reminded him of Paul in a lot of ways, and when they were together the ache in his chest faded, at least for a little while.

There was only one way to handle this—cut her loose, make her hate him like she did when she was fifteen. He had to get her out of town until things settled down. This was a battle he had to win.

If not, Hell would have the last word.

⊹

For once Riley wasn't nervous about seeing Beck, despite his numerous phone calls. This afternoon had proved they could get along, have fun together. He'd even given her a present, one that no other girl in Atlanta could claim.

The moment she crossed the circle, he was on her.

"Why didn't ya answer yer phone?" he groused.

"Because I was busy learning about spheres," she said, puzzled at his attitude. *Like you told me to.*

"Who'd ya talk to?"

"Ayden. Simon introduced us. She gave me her card in case I had more questions."

"Simon?" he snapped.

"Yeah, we made a date of it."

Something passed over his face for a fraction of a second, but she couldn't decipher it.

"Why am I surprised?" he grumbled. "Here's the word: Ya need to call yer aunt, see about stayin' with her."

What? Where's that coming from? "I want to stay here."

"Ya need to be with family," he said.

"I don't need to be with family that can't stand me. You don't know her."

He shouldered his duffel bag. "Doesn't matter. Just make the call."

This was his "my way or the highway" tone again. He was worse than any parent. At least the 'rents made the effort to explain after they ordered you around.

"Everything was good with us this afternoon. What happened?"

He huffed but didn't answer, as if she weren't deserving of a reason.
"Is this because of Simon?"

His face went as tight as his fists, causing the candle flames to shoot
heavenward. "Don't fight me, girl. Ya can't hang 'round here anymore,
goin' on dates like this is some sorta picnic. Ya need to be out of this
city as soon as possible."

Omigod, you're jealous. Why hadn't she seen it before? No wonder he'd
given her a present, he was trying to compete with Simon. *Like you have a
chance, buddy.*

Riley clenched her own fists. "You hate it that I'm dating. That's
why you want me gone. You think we'll break up if I go to Fargo."

"It's not that," he said, shaking his head.

"Oh, yeah it is. You can't stand me being happy. You just want me
lonely and miserable like you."

"Girl—" he began in a warning tone.

"Admit it, Beck. Nobody cares about you because you act like a
butthead all the time."

He took a menacing step forward. "Cut the lip, girl. Yer outta here,
even if I have to throw ya in the back of my truck and drive yer butt to
Fargo."

"You wouldn't dare!" she snarled.

"Ya got three days. Make it happen or I will." He spun on a heel and
marched out of the circle. It ceased blazing the moment he crossed it.

"You miserable piece of . . ."

Riley bit her lip as he tromped out of sight. She'd been so stupid.
Why did she think he'd changed? He'd just tried to soften her up so he
could get his own way.

And I almost fell for it.

⁜

Even by the next afternoon the hurt still lodged in Riley's throat like a
chicken bone she couldn't cough up. She'd spent most of the day doing

odd jobs for Harper and keeping out of range of his explosive temper. She had succeeded because the master and Simon went to trap a Three near the casino in Demon Central. Once they'd left, she worked on her demonic curse words. It was amazing how many applied to Beck.

More than once she wanted to pull off the claw and throw it away, but she couldn't make herself do it. It was *her* claw, not his. She'd earned it. She'd just have to forget that he'd given it to her.

Yeah. Like that'll work.

All the while it was hanging there, reminding her of what it had been like when he'd been nice. Now that he wasn't anymore.

If that wasn't bad enough, she had the ho-bags to deal with at class this afternoon. If they had any sense they'd know not to get in her face. Her fuse was too short, and if she nailed one of them, she'd be out of school in a sec. No school equaled no driver's license. Mass transit so wasn't her thing.

This time Riley parked her car close to the coffee shop and in plain view of where she planned to sit. She needed to be outside before the bitches to reduce their options for vandalism.

Brandy and her band were waiting near the entrance. At least they weren't all wearing the same color tonight. That had been too weird. Riley ignored their giggles and pointing, retrieved her messenger bag, and then locked the doors.

"Hi," a voice said. She turned to find one of the boys standing nearby. "You're the demon trapper, right?"

"Yes." He was the scrawny kid who sat next to her in class. His clothes were at least a size too big for him and made him look like an emaciated scarecrow.

"So who are you?" she asked, not sure what was up.

"Tim." He shot a nervous glance toward the pack of girls. "I... well, I got this project I'm working on and I wondered if..."

"Geek alert," one of Brandy's droids called out and made claxon noises.

Tim stiffened.

"Ignore them." Riley said, turning her back on the pack.

Her move seemed to spook him, and he scooted backward. "Ah, ah ..." he stammered. "I've been doing some research into the types of demons, and I thought, well, you being a trapper and all and ..."

"Go on," she prodded. If this took much longer, she wouldn't be able to claim the seat she wanted.

"I'm confused as to the differences between Biblios, Kleptos, and Pyro-Fiends."

The kid had obviously done some research.

"Why do you want to know?" she asked.

"I want to be a trapper when I'm older."

You've got to be kidding. He was way too skinny. A Three wouldn't even consider him an appetizer.

"Don't bother. It's not that much fun."

"But—"

She walked around him like he didn't exist and headed for the front door.

"But—" he tried again, and then she heard the pack laughing. When she looked back Tim was still standing by her car, his face telling the world how devastated he felt.

"Just deal with it. I do," she grumbled.

When Mrs. Haggerty called them inside, Riley pointedly sat in the back of the room. Brandy kept shooting her looks, followed by a knowing smirk.

They've got something planned.

Math flew by, followed by a short state-mandated course in personal hygiene. That drew a lot of snickers since the info was pretty basic, though a couple of the guys in the back of the class definitely needed the refresher.

Then Mrs. Haggerty moved on to the Civil War.

"We're going to start with a discussion about the burning of Atlanta. Anyone got any thoughts?" she asked.

A boy on the other side of the room raised his hand. "It was just symbolic, nothing more. Other than Sherman tearing up the train tracks, it wasn't going to bring the war to an end any faster."

"Exactly," another kid chimed in. "It didn't matter either way. It was only a hit on the South's ego."

Riley fought the urge to raise her hand. Best to keep out of the spotlight.

"Riley?" the teacher prodded. All heads turned toward her.

That didn't work.

"Atlanta was a storage depot for the South's war supplies, so burning the city *was* a major strike against the Confederacy," she explained. At least all those years of listening to dad ramble on about the war were finally paying off.

"But you don't approve of Sherman's tactics, do you?" Mrs. Haggerty asked.

Riley was blindsided. *How did she know that?*

"Why don't you tell us *your* view of General Sherman. It's unique, to say the least."

Oh jeez. "I think he was a domestic terrorist."

One of the kids whooped in support of her theory. "Radical!"

"Why do you believe that?" Mrs. Haggerty pressed.

Riley had no choice but to give it up. "He didn't have to destroy the city. I think he liked playing God, and if he'd done the same thing today he'd be labeled a terrorist."

"Even in the time of war?" the first kid asked. She thought his name was Bill.

"Sure. The city had surrendered and been evacuated. Then the day he's leaving town, Sherman has it burned to the ground. That's just evil."

"But he didn't burn all of it," Bill argued. "He left the churches."

"Why did he do that?" Mrs. Haggerty probed.

Riley knew the answer but figured it was best not to be labeled a know-it-all.

Bill struggled. "He didn't want to?"

The teacher shook her head. "A priest pleaded with Sherman not to burn the churches and hospitals." She let that sink in. "For your homework assignment: I want you tell me if you think the general's actions were warranted or not."

There were groans and Riley's was one of them. She rose, stuffing her notebook into her messenger bag.

"Riley?" the teacher beckoned.

Not good. That would give the droids time to mess with her car.

"Yes, Mrs. Haggerty?" she said, walking to the desk. Hopefully this would be quick.

"When they sent over your file, your term paper was in it." She handed it over. "I might not agree with your views but at least you had the courage to say them."

Riley stared at the red letter at the top of the first page. She broke into a grin. "I aced it?"

"You did. Solid research, sound argument, even though it was preachy at times. Good work."

Riley's smile grew wider. "Thanks!" *Wait 'til I tell Peter!*

She jammed the paper into her bag and headed for the door. A kid was standing in front of it, blocking her way. It was the one who always sat away from the windows and didn't say much.

"You really a demon hunter?" he asked. His eyes looked weird, as if he were wearing some kind of special contacts.

"Demon *trapper*," she corrected, trying to dodge around him. He wouldn't move. "Look, I've got to go." What were the droids doing to her car? If they'd lipsticked her windshield again . . .

"You hunt us," he said with a faint lisp.

"Not unless you're a demon," she said.

"Some say we are." The pale kid smiled. His canines were pointed. Add in the pallid flesh, the inky black clothes, the frilly white shirt, and suddenly she got the picture.

A vampire wannabe. Give me a break.

"You will not harm us," he said solemnly, precise weight on each word.

What is it with the plural thing? It wasn't like he was the King of England. "Look—whatever your name is—I trap demons. Dee-mons. That's it. I don't go after vampires, werewolves, shape-shifters, none of those things." *Or crazy people who think they are one of the above.* "I've got too much to deal with as it is."

"That's not what we hear."

"*We* who?" she asked, frowning.

"The Nightkind."

"The night kind of what?"

The boy's face twisted in a grimace. "We rule the dark hours and fear no one. Not even a hunter."

"Trapper. Whatever." *I so don't need this.* "Now can you move?"

He swept backward and let her pass. "We won't forget this," he called out as she sailed through the door.

I will.

The car looked fine, at least at first glance, but the expressions on Brandy and her bitches told her that might be a false assumption. She checked the tires. All fine. No way they could get under the hood. They couldn't put anything in the gas tank because the gas cap was locked. Riley's worry faded. They were playing with her head, and they'd done a good job of it. She hopped in her ride and heaved a sigh of relief when it started. As she drove out of the parking lot she checked the rearview mirror. The pack was laughing hysterically.

What's with them?

THIRTY-ONE

The right rear tire was flat—as in Riley wasn't going anywhere. Now she knew why Brandy and her bunch were so merry.

I am going to kill them all. Slowly. Painfully. And in public.

Now what? Call Beck?

"No way." He'd take that as an opportunity to give her more grief.

Simon? That was a possibility, but time was running short. By her watch she had half an hour to get to the cemetery and recast the circle.

Putting her to-go hot chocolate on the top of the car, she unearthed the spare and jack out of the trunk. Her dad had taught her a lot of things, but changing a tire wasn't one of them. "This should be fun to watch," a voice taunted. Instantly furious, she turned to incinerate the fool. The words died on her lips—it was the romance cover dude from the market with a bemused smile on his tanned face.

Riley's fury went flat like the tire. "Oh! It's you," she said, feeling like an idiot. "You're the sword guy." His smile widened. "Did you buy it? The sword, I mean?"

"No. The . . . *heft* was all wrong."

Riley's throat went dry. She swallowed, twice.

"I'm Ori, by the way."

"Rrriley."

When he moved closer her skin started to tingle. "Need some help?" he asked.

She could only nod, trying hard not to drool.

He handed her the hot chocolate, saying he didn't want to spill it, then jacked up the car. The way his muscles moved made her wonder why he even bothered using the jack. Riley realized she might owe the skanks a big thank-you. This guy was soooo nice to watch in action. Despite the scenery, she gave her watch a quick glance. If he was quick about the tire changing, she'd still make it to the cemetery with a few minutes to spare. Dad came first, hunk or no hunk.

The lug nut things that held the wheel spun off. Spare tire on, lug nuts tightened, jack down. He tossed the flat tire in the trunk after giving it a once-over.

"Someone mad at you?" he asked.

"Why?"

He pointed at the valve stem. "This has been messed with. That's why you had a flat."

Riley let loose a stream of curse words.

"You're really fluent in Hellspeak."

She cocked her head. "How do you know I was swearing in demon?"

"Just well educated," he said. He slammed the trunk lid and then pulled out a handkerchief to clean his hands. It made him look strangely aristocratic.

Her watch beeped, reminding her the world was still in motion.

"I've gotta get out of here. Thanks for helping out."

"Not a problem. Maybe we'll see each other again sometime."

There were a million other questions she wanted to ask, but they'd have to wait. After climbing in the car and buckling her seat belt, she looked up to give her helper a wave good-bye. He was gone. She searched for him on the sidewalk. On the other side of the street. No Ori.

It was like the earth had swallowed him up.

How do you do that?

✛

The moment Riley had everything in order at the graveyard—setting the circle went off without a hitch—she dialed Ayden. The witch had to know some seriously spooky ways of settling the score with Brandy and the droids.

"So let me get this straight," the witch said, the noise of the market making her hard to hear. "You want to bring the wrath of Riley down on these girls, am I right?"

Wrath of Riley. Oh, yeah.

"That's it. Plague of frogs, the whole Biblical thing."

"Okay. I'll be there about eleven. What part of the cemetery are you in?"

Witches make house calls? Who would have guessed?

Riley gave her the information and Ayden hung up.

"You hags are so going to eat it," she said, grinning.

From that point on the evening played out like clockwork. She spent some quality time with her dad, telling him about her day like he could hear her, then there was Mort's usual visit. Lenny appeared wearing a new coat that seemed to glow in the dark. He seemed especially proud of it, but it didn't get him any leverage when it came to her dad's corpse.

"I hear some debt collectors got paperwork in the pipeline to have your dad exhumed," Lenny said, adjusting his tie. "Save yourself the grief, girl. Let me take care of him. I'll make sure you get the money."

"Nope," she said, slicing up a Fuji apple with a pocket knife from her dad's trapping bag. "They're not getting him. Neither are you."

"Stubborn. I have to respect that, even if it's stupid."

"Stubbornly stupid," she said. "That's what I'm good at."

"You'll change your mind."

"Nope. Besides, you're nowhere as scary as that creepy guy who does all the dark magic stuff." At Lenny's puzzled look she added, "You know, wears a cape and turns into a mass of swirling leaves."

Lenny's face went pale. "Oh man. I didn't know *he* was after your dad." The summoner took a step backward. "If he asks, I wasn't here. Ever."

"But—"

Lenny was already hustling away as if a pack of Hell hounds were on his tail.

"Whatever works," she said and popped a slice of apple in her mouth.

The witch arrived a few hours later, and after the invitation she waltzed through the candles like they didn't exist. She placed a small picnic basket on Riley's sleeping bag and sat down. After taking some time to arrange her voluminous purple skirts, Ayden popped open the basket.

"Wine?" she asked.

"I'm underage," Riley said. "I might get you in trouble."

"Not if I'm a witch."

"How does that make a difference?"

"You do magic, don't you?" Ayden asked, gesturing toward the lighted circle. "Then that makes you one of us. As long as the witch is at least sixteen, they're allowed to drink during magic ceremonies. You are over sixteen, right?" Riley nodded. "Good. I hereby declare this a ceremony, so therefore you can drink legally."

Riley frowned. "I've never heard of that law. You're making that up."

The witch raised her right hand. "I swear it's true. The bill snuck through the last legislature. I think the politicians were trying to throw a bone to the Pagans. We're getting to be a big voting block."

Riley filed all that away for future reference as Ayden poured them each a glass. The witch raised hers to the sky.

"Hail to the God and Goddess. Keep us safe this night and help Riley Blackthorne find wisdom."

That wasn't quite what Riley had in mind, but she took a long sip of the wine anyway. It was really good, a blend of cherry and grape and some other fruits she couldn't quite place. She noted the bottle didn't have a label.

Her head immediately began to buzz. *Definitely homemade.*

"So tell me what you want to happen," Ayden said, leaning back on an elbow. With her long skirt, curly hair, and well-rounded figure she looked like an oil painting you'd find in some musty old gallery.

Riley straightened up, her head still buzzing. "I want to tag those hags. You know—make their hair fall out or get their periods for a month. Something like that."

Ayden raised an eyebrow. "That would make you happy?"

"It would make them back off."

"But what would it do to you? Would it make you feel better?"

Riley groaned. "No," she admitted. "I'm so tired of people dissing me."

Ayden leaned over and put more wine in Riley's glass.

"Goddess, you sound like me at your age. Here's what I've learned: You can't make them like you. All you can do be is be stronger than they are."

"You mean I should screw with their cars?"

Ayden rolled her eyes. "No! You've got enough problems without inviting more backlash."

Riley wiggled on the blanket, uncomfortable at the witch's tone.

"Then what can I do?" she asked.

"What you do is build up your inner strength."

Riley groaned. She'd hoped for a righteous, butt-kicking spell and instead she was getting the Yoda treatment.

"You need an example?" Riley nodded. "Okay, we'll take some folks you know. Simon, for instance. His faith is his strength."

"I know that." This wasn't getting her anywhere.

"What about Beck? What's his strength?" Ayden quizzed.

"Backwoods Boy?" Riley smirked. "Chugging beer? Being a control freak? Playing God?"

"Whoa, things not going well between you two?"

"Just peachy as long as I do whatever he commands, but when I tell him to get screwed, things get nasty."

"Ohhkkkay." Ayden took a deep breath. "The question still remains: What is Beck's strength?"

"Being a hick."

"You're sure of that?"

"He was born near the Okefenokee Swamp. You don't get more hick than that."

"Beck plays the role for a reason. Sure, he's a South Georgia boy, but he's good at being what everyone else expects. If they don't expect much, he can get away with a lot."

Riley didn't buy that, but she wasn't going to argue. "I don't see what that has to do with me."

"Beck has found his strength and he uses it. So has Simon. You need to find yours. What is it that makes Riley special? What is it that you stand for? Do you really want to use magic against these silly girls? Are you willing to reap the consequences of bespelling them? Because trust me, there is always a cost to magical retribution."

Damn. "No," Riley admitted. "I just want them to treat me right."

"That may or may not happen. Sometimes they're going to hate you."

Now the witch sounded like Peter. "So what *can* I do?" Riley asked.

"Be yourself. You're an apprentice trapper. You're a girl. That's a cool combo. Don't hide that."

Riley shook her head. "That's not going to help with this crowd. They think I'm knocking boots with Lucifer."

Ayden snorted. "That's their problem. You've got enough of your own."

Riley fidgeted with the chain, then pulled out the demon claw. The witch's eyes clamped on it.

"Is that what I think it is?"

Riley nodded. "It came out of my leg. Beck had it made into a pendant for me." The expression on Ayden's face told her another lecture was coming. "Please don't tell me how he's looking out for me."

"Okay. Lie to yourself if it makes you feel better."

Riley shot the witch a glare. "Do you have anything that will help me with those hags, or are you just here to make me feel bad?"

The witch reached into the picnic basket and pulled out a light brown chamois bag about the size of a playing card. "Maybe this will help you. It'll boost your self-esteem."

Now we're getting somewhere. Riley took the bag and opened it. She looked to the bottom to find . . . nothing.

"Ah, it's empty."

"Of course," Ayden replied. "It's up to you to fill it. Find things that mean something to you, that represent times where you've overcome an obstacle, learned something important. Put those items in the bag and they'll help you find your strength."

"I'm not sure if that's going to help much." *Unless I put a brick in it and nail Brandy between the eyes.*

The witch suddenly tensed. She pulled an amulet bag from a pocket and clenched it in her hand, her eyes riveted on something outside the circle.

"What's wrong?" Riley asked, trying to see what had spooked her.

"Necromancer," the witch whispered.

"It's no biggie. They come and go all the time," Riley replied, and took another sip of wine. Maybe Ayden could come tomorrow night with more. It made all this sitting around totally bearable.

A tornado of leaves whirled down the path and stopped short of the lighted circle.

"Oh, it's just him," Riley said, shaking her head.

"I see we've added a witch to the mix," the necro said as his body appeared. He was dressed as always, cloaked with staff in hand.

How does he know Ayden's a witch?

Riley took another sip of wine, boosting her courage, then struggled to her feet. It took a lot of effort. "Look, I'm getting tired of this. Who are you?" she demanded. "And why all this Dark Lord crap?"

She heard her friend suck in a sharp breath, like she'd done something unbelievably stupid.

"The little witch understands that remark wasn't wise, but you're too ignorant to know who you're playing with."

"So tell me already."

The hood fell back. Riley half expected to see two burning red eyes in a bleached white skull. Instead, it was a pretty normal face, an older one with winter white hair that reached his collar. His eyes were deep black and an arcane symbol glowed gold on his forehead. It didn't look like one of those you bought and stuck on yourself. No, this one was embedded in the skin.

"I am Ozymandias," he said. "Does that help?"

"Nope," Riley said. "Not a bit."

"They don't teach you anything in school, do they?" He leaned on the oak staff like he was tired of explaining things to simple people. "'My name is Ozymandias, king of kings: Look on my works, ye mighty, and despair!'" At her blank expression he added, "Percy Bysshe Shelley?"

"I don't do dead poets." She plopped down on her blanket; the wine definitely getting to her.

"The dead ones are the only ones that count," the summoner replied. Their visitor shifted his attention to Ayden. "So little witch, why are you here?"

"Keeping the trapper company," Ayden replied coolly.

"It is best if *your kind* stay out of the matter. If not, there will be difficulties."

"Warning noted," she said evenly. "And returned."

So much for the warm-fuzzy approach.

"I am surprised you're bothering with a dead trapper," Ayden said.

"I have no need to explain myself to *your kind*." Ozymandias shifted those bottomless eyes to Riley. "You don't fear me. That is a mistake I shall rectify."

Riley waited for him to turn into something repulsive, slam himself against the circle, be infinitely creepy. Instead, the leaves swirled off into the night and then vanished in a brilliant flash of light.

That was far scarier than anything else he'd ever done.

"I'll get you my pretty . . ." she murmured, and then hiccupped.

The witch wasn't smiling.

"Man, has he got issues. So what's with him?" Riley asked. "Why does he want my dad?"

"I really don't know. He only summons the dead to gain knowledge. That's why he's the most powerful of the summoners."

"Master trappers know stuff the rest of us don't. Maybe that's why."

Ayden shrugged. "Ozymandias controls not only the dead, but the living. He works the dark magics, and it is said he knows the paths between the worlds and walks them without fear. He wields the—"

"Stop! In English, okay?"

After a steely glare, the witch dumped the rest of the wine into her glass then took it down in one long gulp.

"In English?" she asked, throwing the empty wineglass into the picnic basket.

Riley nodded.

"You're in serious shit."

THIRTY-TWO

Riley forcibly extricated herself from her car, wincing on a cellular level.

"This is so wrong," she mumbled, rubbing her temples. If anyone could brew wine that didn't give you a hangover, shouldn't it be a witch?

Apparently not. Morning had brought a thumping head, dry eyes, and a desperate desire to curl up and die.

The aspirin will kick in. Yeah. Any. Minute. Now.

She groaned and made herself take a gulp of bottled water. Maybe that would help. Shuffling inside, she found Simon hosing down the concrete under the cages.

When he saw her, he turned off the water and gave a low whistle.

"Ouch," he said. "Hurts to be you." She nodded. "Anything exciting happen last night?"

You mean other than pissing off the most seriously evil necro in the entire city?

"It was really quiet."

Simon eyed her long black skirt, the result of not doing laundry for over a week. "You've got ankles," he jested. "Who knew?"

"I'm not in the mood," she said. "Too much of Ayden's witchy wine."

"Could have warned you. I've heard the witches' brew is stronger than most."

"That's an affirmative. So what's up today?" she asked. "Please tell me it's a lot of sleeping and *no* shouting."

Simon coiled up the hose in a tight circle before he answered. "We've got a Three running wild in Piedmont Park. Apparently it tried to eat some lady's dachshund."

No way did Riley want to confront a dog-eating demon today.

As if he'd read her mind, Simon added, "You're not on the run."

"Thank God."

"Harper wants to you to clean out all the plastic recycling. I'll show you how to do that. It'll blow most of the day."

"Then tonight's the Guild meeting, and then I have a date with Dad." Before he could ask, she replied, "T minus three nights and counting."

"Almost there," he said, nodding his approval. "Oh, and Beck called to check in on you. He said to stop ignoring him, it isn't going to change his mind, whatever that means."

So much for that plan. She turned her phone on. Five voice messages, all from Backwoods Boy. She deleted them.

With a creak of the recliner springs their master appeared in the doorway to his office. "About damned time you got here," he said, glaring at Riley. Then he saw her skirt, huffed, and shook his head in disgust.

Not going to apologize.

"Come on, I'll show you what you need to do," Simon said.

The task wasn't exciting, just tedious. First she had to sort all the plastic Holy Water jugs and bottles by size then by batch number and enter that information on a form.

"At least it's better than scooping demon droppings," Simon remarked. He seriously failed to hide the relief that someone lower on the totem pole was taking over the scut work.

Riley gave the ginormous mound of plastic a dubious glower. "Why would the city care which bottles are going to the recycling plant?"

"They don't, but Harper does. If you're a recycling center, you have to keep records."

There was more to it than that. "He gets paid for these, doesn't he?"

"Fifty cents apiece."

I knew it. It always came down to cash.

"Let's get a move on!" their master called. After another withering glare in her direction, Harper stomped out of the building followed by his senior apprentice.

He must sleep on a bed of nails. There has to be a reason he's such an asshat.

The weather was chilly, but her head didn't pound as badly in the fresh air, so Riley lined up all the jugs and bottles like plastic soldiers in the fenced lot behind the building. She made sure to keep a respectful distance from Mount Demon Manure and all the dead roaches.

Eighty-seven gallons, seventy-three quarts, and forty-nine pints. That would be over a hundred bucks in Harper's booze fund.

"Yeah, this is what trapping demons is all about," she groused. "Lucifer's gotta be freaking in his boots."

Thumbing through the sheets on the clipboard she found that her boyfriend had last performed this operation three weeks ago, then roughly at the same interval over the last eight months. The pages before that were written by Jackson, now a journeyman. Someday another apprentice would be looking at her sheets and dreaming of the day they made journeyman.

And hating on Harper with every breath.

Clicking the pen, she filled in a new form line by line. It wasn't easy as some of the labels were hard to read. It was on the tenth gallon she hesitated. There were a number of bottles from the same batch, but they should always have the same consecration date. The one in her lap was a problem. It had a different date than another of the same batch.

Brain fog. She took a bathroom break, swigged more water, and then returned to the work. "Somebody made a mistake," she said. Slapped a label on the wrong bottle. It could happen, especially if they had a raging hangover like hers.

By the time Riley worked through all the plastic containers she'd found forty-two that had mismatched batch and date information. One pint said it'd been blessed a week ago, while another from the same batch was ten days old.

She flipped back to Simon's sheets. No problems there. Same with

Jackson's pages. Whatever had happened was during the last three weeks.

"Why me?" She knew who was going to be blamed for this, even when it wasn't her fault. "Would they split the batches, consecrate them separately?"

Her gut told her no, and she had a way to prove it. Dropping the clipboard, Riley hiked to the car to retrieve her father's papers, the sheets that listed all the batch numbers from the last six months' production. If Celestial Supplies had split the production run it'd be on those sheets.

Right before she slammed the trunk she saw the pint bottle of Holy Water she'd bought at the gun shop. She picked it up. The label was hard to read after being soaked in her father's duffel bag. This pint had been blessed on the twentieth, one day before she trapped her demon. The gun shop dude hadn't lied to her; the Holy Water should have burned like liquid fire.

"But it didn't."

Riley closed the trunk and leaned on the car, wondering if it was time for more aspirin. Leafing through the pages she finally found the batch number that matched the bottle in her hand.

"What the . . . ?" She retraced her finger across the page to ensure she'd read the right date. The company's records said this particular batch had been produced and consecrated in mid-September, *four months earlier.*

"No, no, no!" she said. "This can't be happening." Trappers always chose their Holy Water by the date it was blessed.

If this stuff is four months old . . . No wonder her thigh had gone septic. She swallowed, twice, to ease the pressure in her throat. It did no good. "What have I gotten into?"

Riley trudged back to the battalion of bottles and scowled at them as if they were personally responsible for this mess. She began a new sheet, this time listing the company's "blessed on" date and the ones she was finding on the recycled bottles. Most of them matched perfectly, but the forty-two suspect ones did not.

On a hunch, she took one of the proper pints to the bathroom and ran water on the label. No reaction, even when she purposely tried to smear it. Apparently the ink was sealed in some way. She repeated the experiment with three of the suspect bottles. The ink blurred on all of them.

Riley slumped up against the wall with the bimbo poster, trying to get a handle on this. Why hadn't anyone else figured this out? Was this one of Harper's sick jokes? Could he be tampering with these bottles?

Much as she'd love to believe that, he didn't have a thing to do with the Holy Water she'd bought for her trip to Demon Central. This was a bigger issue.

"Someone's screwing with this stuff," she said. "And they almost killed me doing it."

⊹

Riley paused in front of the Holy Water vendor's tent in the market. She needed evidence, bottles that hadn't been opened so no one would say she'd tampered with them. Maybe there was some way to test the stuff, find out if it was the real deal. She'd leave that up to the Guild. All she needed to do was let the trappers know they had a big problem.

Going on the assumption that easily damaged labels equaled bad Holy Water, she picked up a random pint and did the wet-finger test. It was kosher. A bit more hunting found two pints that didn't pass muster. Grumbling under her breath at the expense, she dropped money on the counter and stuck them in her messenger bag. It dug into her shoulder with the increased weight.

"That it?" the salesman asked. It was the same guy in the blue suit.

"Not quite." She removed a couple of Harper's recycled gems out of a paper bag at her feet. "Batch numbers should have the same consecration date, shouldn't they?"

The salesman cocked his head. "They always do."

She handed him the pints. "These don't."

The man twitched an eyebrow, but he didn't bother to look at the labels.

"Look kid, I know what you're up to," he said gruffly. "You think you're going to sue us or something. We've seen all the games. We've got lawyers to deal with your kind."

Get in this guy's face or back down? Retreat sounded good right now. She'd got what she'd come for.

"Sorry," she said contritely. "I didn't mean anything by it. I thought you might give me a free bottle or something." As she reached for the empty bottles he grabbed them up.

"I'll hang on to these. You're not pulling this scam with anyone else."

Fine. I have more in my trunk.

"Now get out of here, kid," he ordered. "Do your shopping somewhere else from now on."

Riley walked one tent away, then ducked behind a rack of fruit. From between two stacks of apples she spied on the salesman.

Come on, act guilty.

The guy mopped his brow, look around cautiously, then fired up his cell phone. He spoke too quietly for her to hear him over the market din.

When a customer came near he stalked outside the tent, closer to her location. Suddenly he barked, "I told you, we've got a problem."

Riley allowed herself a smug grin as she scooted out the other side of the fruit tent and into the heart of the market.

Her crazy discovery had just been validated.

"You guys are so busted."

⁜

Still glowing from her triumph, Riley made her way to the tent that sold secondhand clothes. A mound of denim called to her, and she began her search for a decent pair of jeans to replace her demon-nuked ones. Most of the nicer pairs were several jumbo pizzas away from her size.

"Not good," she muttered, tossing aside another pair that had held promise.

"How about these?" a smooth voice asked. A pair was offered. Without looking up, she checked the label and then gave them a look-over.

"Nice. Good condition. And the right size." Then she glanced upward.

It was Ori. He wore a long gray leather duster over black jeans and a turtleneck. Her heart did a little flutter kick, making her feel like she was twelve or something.

How can one guy look that good?

"Thanks," she said, her mouth refusing to go in gear enough to say anything witty.

"Thought I should help out. You seemed to be on a holy quest."

"A quest for jeans," she said, smiling. "I like that."

He smiled, and it made his eyes seem even deeper.

"You gonna take those?" the vendor asked, causing her to jump. She nodded, handed over the ten, and got her change.

"How's about some hot chocolate?" Ori asked. "We can get some at a tent down the way."

Ah," she began. This was the third time she'd run into this guy—twice in the market and once on the street near the coffee shop. That wasn't just coincidence. He didn't feel like a psycho stalker, but you never knew.

"I'll buy," he offered.

They'd be in a public place. What was the harm?

Riley checked her watch. "Okay, but I've only got half an hour and I have to leave for class."

"Plenty of time."

They'd taken their hot chocolate to go and wandered toward her car at a leisurely stroll. Riley couldn't help but notice her escort was attracting a lot of notice, especially from other girls. He had that eye-candy effect.

"You look good in a skirt," Ori said.

"Thanks," Riley replied. "I need to do some washing, you know?"

He laughed, making the dimple in his chin more noticeable. "Is that why you were questing for jeans?"

"Yeah. My last pair got holes in them when I was trapping."

"At the library?" At her puzzled expression he added, "I read about that in the newspaper."

"Oh." She felt an intense desire to change the subject. "Are you from Atlanta?"

"No. I'm here on business."

Which didn't tell her where he was from. Mysterious had to be this dude's middle name. His voice didn't give her a clue—no accent to speak of. His clothes pegged him for someone with money, but that wasn't much help either.

Definite need for more info here.

"What do you do?" she pushed. They weren't going to get anywhere if she couldn't get simple information out of him.

They'd reached her car at this point. He hesitated, looked around them as if worried someone might overhear their conversation, then leaned close to her. He smelled different than other guys. Not different in a bad way, just different. Like a crisp fall breeze.

"You have to promise not to tell anyone."

"Are you, like, a spy or something?" she asked. That'd be awesome.

"No. I'm a demon hunter," he replied.

He was one of the elite teams Rome sent around the world to destroy Hellspawn.

"From the Vatican?" she asked, incredulous. Maybe the television show wasn't too far off after all.

Ori shook his head. "Most certainly not Rome. I'm freelance."

"Oh. I didn't realize there were freelance hunters. Why not work for the Vatican? Get the benes?"

"I prefer to work on my own."

"What are you hunting?" she asked.

"The demon that killed Paul."

Riley started at the mention of her father's name. "You knew my dad?"

"We met a while back. He told me about his daughter, how proud he was of you."

She couldn't remember her dad mentioning this guy, but that wasn't unusual. He only told her what he felt she needed to know.

"He said your middle name is Anora. I've not heard that before. What does it mean?" Ori asked.

"Light," she replied. "Riley Anora means 'Valiant Light.' My parents seemed to think that was pretty cool."

"So do I."

His gaze weighed on her and she found it hard to think.

"When you find the Five," she said breathlessly, "I want to be there. I want to help you take it down."

Ori smiled at her, and for a second she thought he'd agree. "No. It's best you stay out of harm's way."

Riley's excitement deflated. "You sound like Beck."

"That's Denver Beck, isn't it? Paul mentioned him. What's he like?" Ori asked.

"Oh, where do I start? Beck's mouthy and he lives to tell me what to do." *In short, he's so not you.* "Why do you want to know?"

A glimmer appeared in Ori's dark eyes.

"Just scoping out the competition."

THIRTY-THREE

Riley didn't remember much about the ride to class, her brain was too busy replaying her conversation with Mr. Mysterious. He seemed to know a lot about her, but so far she'd only scored his first name and his profession. And the fact that he was after the demon who'd taken out her father.

Good luck with that. Of course, she'd be the first to cheer if he could pull it off, but Fives were hard to bring down, especially if you were working solo. *Maybe the hunters were better at that sort of thing.*

The bigger problem was how to convince the good ol' boys that the Holy Water wasn't reliable anymore. Harper would be in her face the moment she opened her mouth, but she had to tell them, one way or another.

Riley shoved that worry aside the moment she pulled into the parking lot. She could only stew on one problem at a time, and right now she had some groveling to do. Guilt had gnawed on her like a rabid rat since she'd taken her Beck-induced anger out on Tim, the boy oh-so interested in demons.

Get it over with.

She blew a stream of air out of pursed lips and marched up to him. He tensed as she approached, his eyes darting around like a hare looking for a place to run.

"Tim? That's your name, right?" He nodded cautiously. "Hey, I'm sorry," she said. "I was a hag the other day."

It took a few moments for him to process what she'd said. Then he frowned at her. "You were."

She shot a glance at Brandy and her pack. She'd been just as nasty as them, which made her feel bad. "The best way to tell the difference between a Biblio, a Klepto, and a Pyro is by what they do."

Tim scrambled to dig a notebook out of his pack. Then he hunted for a pen. "Go on!" he urged, his eyes alight.

Riley gave him a quick peek into the world of the smaller demons, but not so much as to get her in trouble. The Guild would be upset if she told an outsider too much as it was bound to end up on the Internet. As she explained things to Tim, she began to realize how much she really knew and how much of it her dad had taught her.

"That's about all I can tell you or I'd have to kill you," she jested.

For half a second Tim looked like he believed her.

"Joking!" she said.

"Oh. Okay. Thanks!" Then he grimaced. "I'm sorry about your tire. They . . ." he angled his head toward the gaggle of girls. "I was really mad at you, and then Brandy told me to make it go flat."

Somehow that didn't surprise her. "How'd you do it?" she asked for future reference.

"Put a BB under the valve cap. Gives you a slow leak."

"Neat. I'll have to remember that." *But why were you carrying BBs in the first place?*

"Oh. Thanks for all this," he said, tapping the notebook with a bony finger. Tim took off. The reason for his sudden vanishing act was Brandy, with the pack right behind her.

I still want all your hair to fall out.

"You really trap demons?" Brandy asked.

Riley nodded, thinking of Ayden's lecture. If being a trapper and a girl was so cool, why not see how far that got her?

She pulled the claw out from under her sweater.

One of the droids gasped. "Is that from a . . ."

"Demon, yes."

"No way," Brandy said, leaning closer to study it. "You bought that at the market."

"No, they dug it out of my leg."

Brandy's eyes twinkled. "Prove it."

Riley's bluff had been called. If she backed down they'd think she lied and the harassment would escalate.

"See, I told you she wasn't for real," Brandy said, smirking.

The other girls hooted in unison.

"Bathroom," Riley said, waving the annoying girl forward. When the others started to follow she put up her hand like a traffic cop. "Just me and her. This isn't a public event."

Once the bathroom door was locked, Brandy continued to smirk until Riley raised the skirt far enough for her to see the six healed claw marks.

"Omigod! Those are gross!"

"I prefer the word *dramatic*," Riley said, dropping the skirt and smoothing out the wrinkles.

"Did it like, hurt a lot?" Brandy asked, eyes wide.

"Yeah, big-time."

Apparently satisfied, her nemesis retreated to the mirror and fussed with her hair. "Do you have a brush? I forgot mine," she said. Without waiting for an answer, she asked, "How do you get your hair like that? Mine is all over the place."

Riley looked over at her enemy. They'd crossed a line somewhere along the way or they wouldn't be sharing styling tips. She dug out her brush and handed it over. "Just lucky, I guess."

Brandy bent over, then flung her hair back when she stood up. She started working on the stray pieces, blending them in. "Did you see that weird guy with the teeth?"

"The vamp wannabe?"

"Yeah. He's really into all that. The black clothes, the red soda, the whole thing."

"Then why is he going to school in the afternoon? A real vampire couldn't do that."

Brandy hitched a shoulder. "Do you like this shirt?" she asked, turning around so Riley could get the full three-sixty.

"Yeah. Pink's not my color, but it's nice." *For someone like you.*

"I like it a lot," Brandy said, handing her the brush.

And then she was gone, probably to report to her entourage that Riley had gross scars on her leg and wasn't a lesbian because she hadn't made a pass in the bathroom.

That was weird, but it worked. No bad karma either. *Maybe Ayden was right.*

Class was full of math, sociology about seminude pygmies in rain forests, English literature, and even more Civil War. When Riley tried to figure out how all that connected, her brain went flatline.

At least I aced my paper.

The kid who thought he was a vampire keep leering at her, revealing those ridiculously pointed canines.

Note to self: Bring wooden stake to class.

"Don't forget the field trip on Friday," Mrs. Haggerty called out. "We're going to Oakland Cemetery to visit the Confederate section."

A field trip to a cemetery. Now that's special.

Riley found Brandy and the girls leaning against her car. "I swear, if you've messed with my ride again I'm going to rip you apart."

Brandy shook her head. Which meant nothing. "You heard the news, didn't you?" she asked, breathless.

Which could mean anything. "What news?"

"*They're* coming to Atlanta."

"They who?" Riley said.

"*Demonland.* They're taping the show here!" Brandy said, her voice rising in anticipation.

Riley had heard Harper say something about that this morning, along with the words *pansy-assed actors.*

When Riley didn't respond, one of the other girls chimed in. "Their website said they're going to meet with the local Trappers Guild."

So that's it.

"Will you get to see them?" Brandy asked, breathlessly.

"If they come to a Guild meeting, I will."

Brandy squealed in delight. The sound was almost sonic level in intensity. Riley waggled a finger in an ear to ease the pain, wondering how many bats had been stunned senseless.

"Oh. My. Freaking. God!" Brandy shouted, causing heads to turn across the parking lot. "That would be *so* cool." Then she reined herself in. "Can you get Jess's autograph? He's totally hot!"

Jess Storm Something-or-Other. Riley thought she knew which one that was. He *was* hot, especially in those painted-on jeans.

"Jess is dog meat to Raphael. Swoon. He's totally the shit!" one of the other girls said.

"Stacy, you're trash-talking my babe," Brandy argued, hands on her hips now. Apparently this was a long-standing argument. "Jess has the most amazing eyes."

Stacy shook her head, her hair whipping around her. "No way. Raphael's the man. He's got gorgeous pecs."

"The show is dumb," Riley said. There was stunned silence as everyone of the girls gawked at her like she'd blasphemed God or something. "But the guys? They're gorgeous. They've got great butts," she said, before she could stop herself.

Brandy giggled. "Jess's is the best!"

"No way!" Stacy shot back.

It went downhill from there as each girl listed off her fav's stats. By the time Riley left she had their numbers so she could send them cell phone photos of the TV guys when they came to the meeting.

If she could get their autographs she could actually be their BFF.

Maybe there is something to this whole karma thing.

✛

With traffic in her favor for once, Riley arrived at the Tabernacle way early. As she walked into the auditorium she saw Simon carefully applying the Holy Water ward. It wouldn't do to interrupt him, so she headed toward the bathroom and changed into her new jeans. No way she was going to endure the abuse from the other trappers because of her fashion choices.

When she returned Simon was still at it, painstakingly ensuring there were no gaps in the ward. Riley set the messenger bag full of pint bottles on the floor next to a folding chair and tried not to freak about what she was about to do.

"I will not wimp out." No matter how many times she said it, she didn't feel good about this. What if she was wrong and the Holy Water was okay?

Her phone chirped and she mentally thanked the caller, even if it was Beck.

"Riley! How's it going?" Peter called out.

"Pretty good. I'm at the Tabernacle. We're having a Guild meeting pretty soon."

"So how goes the Great Holy Water Mystery?"

Riley gave him the rundown, keeping her voice low so Simon couldn't overhear.

"You really think someone is messing with that stuff?"

"Yeah, I do." *Learned that the hard way.*

"Whoa. That's way illegal."

"I figured I'd better tell the Guild and they can take it from there." The idea that the Holy Water might not be so holy was too scary to think about.

"Will they believe you?"

Leave it to Peter to find the one weak spot. "Not sure. Some of these guys are way dense."

"I hear you. How did class go?"

Riley gave him the report and had him laughing by the end of it.

"At least they're off your back for a while," he replied.

"I hope so. If I get the photos and autographs, they'll be making me class president."

There was a long pause. "How's it really going?"

He knew her too well. "I'm okay and then I'm not," she admitted. "I go along and then *bam!* I remember Dad's gone and it all falls apart." Riley choked up. Her eyes glazed in tears, and she fumbled for a tissue one-handed.

"I get real tired of the warden bitching at me, but I don't know what I'd do if she wasn't here. Or my dad either."

"Three more nights and I'm done sitting vigil," she said, wiping her nose. "Then he'll be safe."

"We'll celebrate," her friend replied, his voice lighting up in antici- pation. "Then we can hang together more often."

That might prove a problem now that Simon was in the picture.

As if on cue her boyfriend reappeared, empty Holy Water jugs in his hands. He set them just outside the circle. Then he smiled and beck- oned her to join him.

"Ah, got to go. The meeting's about to start," she fibbed.

"Give me call later, okay?" Peter asked.

"Sure."

When she joined Simon he dropped a kiss on her cheek.

"Tease," she said, feeling bubbly and warm inside. Ori was gorgeous and everything, but Simon hit all the right places. She felt whole when she was with him, and right now that meant so much when the rest of her life was an empty shell.

"Let's take a walk," he said. The glint in his eyes told her he had other things in mind.

As they walked by the empty jugs, she paused. "Hold on." Kneeling, she wetted her finger and tested the labels. The ink didn't run.

"What are you doing?" Simon asked.

"Just checking something." She wouldn't share the news, not with

Simon or Beck. If somehow she was wrong she didn't want Harper taking it out on them.

This is my deal. And my dad's. She'd just finish what he'd started.

Simon's hand touched hers as they walked around the side of the Tabernacle. Her worry about the meeting faded. Being with him helped her forget her troubles, made her feel so good.

Is this what it's like to fall in love?

"There's a quiet place back here," he suggested, heading toward the rear of the building. It *was* quiet, nestled away from street. He pulled her into the shadows.

"That's better." Before she could say a word, he kissed her, a tentative peck on her lips.

"More?" he asked, watching her reaction closely.

"More."

The next kiss went on longer. Riley felt the warmth in her chest, then even lower. He pulled her closer, sliding a hand under her coat, then her sweater, his palm pressing against the small of her back. It felt wonderful and she didn't want him to stop.

"If Harper catches us," he whispered in her ear.

"We'll both be shoveling demon crap for months," she replied.

The next kiss deepened, became more urgent, needy. There was no space between them, and she could feel he enjoyed their closeness. Riley heard him moan and they reluctantly broke apart.

Simon sighed. "Such a temptation."

"But I'm worth it, right?"

The sparkling blue in his eyes told her he thought so. They sat on the steps that led to the fire escape. Content, she nestled herself against his shoulder, and Simon placed his arm around her, drawing her close.

"I really like you, Riley," he said. "In case you haven't noticed."

"Good to hear it," she said. "Just part of my cunning plan."

"Whatever that plan is, it's working."

They fell silent for a few minutes, just being close. She could hear his heartbeat slow to normal. Other guys might have tried to push her into something she didn't want, move too fast, but Simon hadn't.

Which is why I like you so much.

When the quiet became unbearable, she asked, "Why do you want to be a trapper?"

"Because it's a holy crusade," he replied without hesitation. "Like being a priest. I'm fighting against the forces of evil."

The strength in his voice said he believed every word. That made sense: Simon's world was black and white, right and wrong.

"I've upset you, haven't I?" he asked, quieter now. "I do that when I go all religious on people."

"It's just that . . ." She hesitated. "The demons, for instance. There's a big difference between a Magpie and a Geo-Fiend."

Simon shook his head. "They're both Lucifer's minions. It doesn't matter if one's less of a danger than another. They should be destroyed."

"Even a Magpie? I mean, they're not evil." The demon flitting around her apartment was kinda cute, actually, in a larcenous sort of way.

"Doesn't matter. They belong to Lucifer and warrant destruction," he said resolutely.

Suddenly it all made sense. "You want to be a hunter and work for the Vatican, don't you?"

He pulled back, studying her as if to see whether she could be trusted with a great secret. "I do, but I'd appreciate it if you don't mention my plans to the others. Especially Harper."

"I won't." The rivalry between the trappers and the hunters went way back, centuries even. Trappers caught demons. Hunters killed them. But that wasn't all. Hunters had the legal right to arrest, charge, and execute anyone who made a pact with Lucifer. Sometimes that was a trapper, which didn't make for good relations. It didn't happen much anymore, but the hunters still held those powers and all the trappers knew it.

She eyed Simon solemnly, trying to sort out her feelings for him. He seemed so gentle, so thoughtful, but that's not what a demon hunter was all about.

"Could you kill someone if you thought they were working for Hell?"

To her relief she didn't get an "Oh sure, no problem, they deserve to die" answer. Instead, she could see him wrestling with the question.

"Possibly," he said, brows furrowed.

"Even if it was some young kid? Could you do it?" she asked, fearing the answer. Was there a heartless monster lurking inside of him?

Simon's face clouded. "I don't know." He pulled her close again. "Too many questions. You make me wonder if I really know what I want in life. Besides, you that is."

Riley's heart double-beat. They were definitely moving this relationship along at warp speed. As if sensing her bewildered emotions, he tugged her closer and they remained that way until it was time to go inside. For once, Riley wished the rest of the world didn't exist.

THIRTY-FOUR

By the time they returned to their seats there were forty-some trappers milling around the center of the hall, trading stories and proudly displaying their latest wounds. It was definitely a guy thing.

Beck gave her a curt nod, but Jackson waved, clearly pleased to see her.

"See, they're accepting you," Simon remarked.

"Some of them."

Riley had expected her personal nemesis to tromp over and annoy her right off, but Beck and his two beer bottles kept their distance. If anything, he was pointedly ignoring her.

You are so jealous.

It was Harper that worried her. If she was going to tell the Guild what she'd discovered, her master had to know about it first. That was the way things worked.

She took a deep breath and went to him. "Sir?"

"Yeah?" he said, his bloodshot eyes telling her it hadn't been a good day. "What do you want?"

"I've discovered something about the Holy Water. Not all the bottles are the real stuff. Some of it doesn't work like it should, and I'd like to tell the Guild what I found."

His intense gaze made her itch. "Why the hell didn't you tell me about this before?"

"I just figured it out this afternoon."

He thought for a moment.

What if he doesn't let me tell them? What would she do then?

"Ah, what the hell, go ahead. I can't wait to hear this," he said, leaning back in his chair. The sly grin told her he was looking forward to her public humiliation.

"Thank you, sir." Right before she moved away, he grabbed her arm, digging in those fingers, causing Riley to grit her teeth. Why had she let her guard down?

He leaned toward her and whispered, "You make me look bad and you'll pay for it, girl."

I already am.

When Collins called the meeting to order, she made a point of not sitting near her master, breaking with tradition. Simon weighed his options and sat next to her.

You might regret that.

After roll call, Collins started the meeting. "You heard about that TV show coming to town?"

Hoots of derision echoed through the big hall.

"Yeah, yeah, I know," Collins said. "The producers want to work with us. They say they want the show to be more *realistic.*"

"They can start by making the demons look like the real deal," Jackson said. "I've yet to meet one who wears an Armani suit and drives a Ferrari."

"Ah, hell, they all do," Morton replied. "At least in L.A."

Laughter broke out.

"They asked if a couple of us would show them around the city, let them see what we really do," Collins explained.

"Why aren't they working with the Vatican?" Jackson inquired.

"The Vatican's reps shot them down, so now they want to slum with us."

"Setting us up to make us look stupid," Harper said.

"That's a real possibility," Collins replied, "but if we blow them off we might regret it."

"What about those hotties? Are they coming?" a young trapper called out.

"A few are. And they're paying for our time. Do I have volunteers?"

Hands shot up, and Collins took note of the names. The promise of babes and cash tipped the scales. Riley was surprised to see Beck wasn't one of the volunteers.

The president pointed right at her. "And you too."

"Me?" Riley squeaked.

"They say they want a female's take on all this," he said. "You okay with that?"

She felt Simon stir next her. "Get Harper's permission first," he whispered.

Good idea.

"Only if Master Harper is okay with it," she said.

The old trapper's eyebrows arched upward, like he'd figured out her game. "As long as the work gets done," he said, nodding.

Don't worry, you'll get a cut of the money.

"Then I'll let them know we're good to go," Collins said, making a note on a piece of paper.

Riley couldn't believe how easy that'd been. Maybe not toasting Brandy and her bunch had been a good thing.

Collins consulted his notes. "Anything else?"

Her heart jumped when Harper rose to his feet.

What is he doing?

"Blackthorne's kid," Harper began. Riley winced. "She ran into some trouble the other day when I sent her over to Roscoe's to sell some Ones."

Beck's eyes rose from his brew. His reaction was instant: The muscles along his jaw tensed as the knuckles on his right hand tightened around the beer bottle.

Let it go. Don't piss him off. He'll just take it out on me.

"What was the trouble?" Collins asked.

"Roscoe offered her one-twenty a piece for the demons as long as she didn't do the paperwork."

Beck's eyes snapped to her. She saw condemnation in them.

You think I sold them under the table. You jerk!

"She told him to stuff it up his ass," Harper explained.

Beck sagged in relief. She glowered at him, and he shrugged in apology.

"No trafficker's ever tried to roll one of my apprentices." Harper's scar tightened along with his jaw. "It's not going to happen again, I can tell you."

"You'll handle it?" Collins asked.

"Damned straight." The master returned to his seat.

Riley let out the air she'd kept pent up.

"Anything else?" Collins asked.

Now or never. Riley pulled herself out of the seat, her heart thudding.

"Yes sir . . . I . . . have something."

Out of the corner of her eye she saw Harper's face; it resembled a vulture waiting for something to die so he could feast on its corpse. She ignored him, focusing on the podium so she didn't lose her nerve.

"I have a question about the Holy Water. Is it possible for it to be blessed in different batches?"

Master Stewart shook his head. "I've been ta the plant. They've got massive tanks, holdin' hundreds of gallons of water. The priest blesses one tank at a time. Then all they do is put it in the bott-els."

"So every batch number should have the same consecration date?" she asked, feeling excitement rising within her. That's what the brochure said, but she wanted to lay the foundation for her radical claim.

"Of course. Why ya askin', lass?"

"I found some of my dad's notes. He was trying to find out why the Holy Water didn't always work right. He was worried that the demons were building up a tolerance to it."

Collins and Stewart traded looks. "Go on," the Guild's president urged.

"This is a master list of all the production runs for the last six months," she said, displaying the pages. "These show the batch numbers, which include the date the Holy Water was blessed." She set them down and took a hasty swallow from her soda.

Now it gets harder.

"I was recycling the Holy Water bottles for Master Harper and I noticed that some shared batch numbers, but the consecration dates were different."

"You sure?" Collins asked.

Riley nodded and pulled out three of the recycled bottles, setting them in a row on the table in front of her. She put a hand on top of one of the pints. "This one was blessed ten days ago." She continued down the line. "This one seven days ago, and this one five. They're all from one batch. According to the manufacturer's master list, this batch was actually blessed and bottled four months ago."

"Let me see those," Jackson said, walking over. He compared each of the pints, then his eyes rose to hers. "I'll be damned. She's right, these do have different dates. But why would someone do that?"

"Money," Beck called out. "I've got a buddy who works at the plant where they bottle the stuff. He said they're runnin' three shifts and can't keep up. A pint is going for ten bucks now."

"Twelve," Riley corrected. "I bought some before the meeting. Also the labels are different. Some of them don't react to water; some of them smear really easily. The fake bottles have the smeary labels. I wanted you guys to know about this so you can figure out what's going on."

"This happened in Cleveland sometime back. Someone was refillin' the bott-els with tap water," Stewart said.

"So is it just bad labels, or is the Holy Water counterfeit or both?" Collins asked.

"Let's test it," Morton said. "Anybody got a demon in their pocket?

How about you, Beck?" he jested, but she could hear the tension in his voice.

"No," Beck replied flatly. "Wait a minute." He turned toward her and tapped his chest. When she didn't respond, he did it again.

The claw. They couldn't get a live demon across the ward, but the claw wasn't alive.

"I think we might have something that'll work," she announced, pulling the silver chain into view. The black talon hung in the air, twisting at the end of the chain.

"Damn, that's nice," exclaimed one of the trappers sitting near her. "Never seen a claw necklace before."

"Is it the real thing?" Jackson asked.

"Totally," Riley replied.

She picked up a pint of Holy Water. "I bought this at the market tonight." She handed it Jackson and he ripped off the seal. Riley dipped the claw inside. After several seconds there was no reaction.

"Maybe you need a live demon," someone said.

"It should work," Collins replied. "It was once part of a fiend so the Holy Water should recognize that."

Jackson opened another pint and she repeated the test. Nothing.

"So which one do you think is kosher?" he asked. At least he believed her.

Riley tapped on the next one. "Its label doesn't smear when it gets wet."

Jackson ripped off the lid and she dropped the claw in.

And nothing happened.

Ah, crap. If this didn't work, she was going to be in big trouble.

"Riley," Simon began in a worried voice.

The pint bottle erupted in a torrent of bubbling water that shot out of the top and flooded both her and Jackson. She yanked out the claw, fearing it would be destroyed. The talon was snow white. As it dried, it turned black like an overripe banana.

"Wow!" Jackson exclaimed, wiping his face with a sleeve.

Take that, Harper. As she mopped off her face, she caught a glimpse of him out of the corner of her eye. He was frowning but not at her.

"What about the Holy Water for the ward?" Morton asked, all trace of humor gone. "Is it okay?"

"It's good," Riley said. "I checked the labels."

"Well, that's a relief," Beck said. He popped the top of his second bottle of beer and drained half of it in one swig.

While trappers argued among themselves, Riley slumped into her chair, head buzzing. They'd actually listened to her. Her dad would be so proud.

Simon touched her arm. "Good job," he said. His praise was at odds with the frown. What was bothering him? "Why didn't you tell me?"

"If it went wrong, I didn't want you in the middle of it."

He nodded, but the frown remained.

It took the Guild president some time to call the room to order. Nearly every trapper was talking, gesturing at her then the bottles.

Collins leaned forward on the podium and rubbed his face wearily.

"Well, this sucks," he said. "It looks like not all the Holy Water is the real deal. Since some of us are having the same issues with the spheres, I have to assume a portion of those are bogus as well."

Harper rose. "This is getting out of hand! We got traffickers buying demons under the table and Holy Water that's as useless as spit."

"Is this happening anywhere else in the country?" Morton asked.

Collins shook his head. "There've been no bulletins from the national office."

"Maybe Hell is finally getting it together," Jackson suggested.

"That'd explain a lot," Harper said. "Bet there's an Archdemon behind this somewhere."

"But why here?" Beck asked. "Ya think it's all connected somehow?"

"That's what we have to find out." Collins looked over at Stewart. "Call the archbishop and the CEO of Celestial Supplies. Set up a meeting. This is priority one. If we don't this get straightened out, we're going to start losing trappers. We need to get a handle on this now before it gets worse."

Riley relaxed. These guys would deal with it.

At that, Collins glanced over at her, nodding his approval. "Well done. That's impressive work from an appren—"

Collins' eyes went wide and his mouth dropped open.

Someone touched her shoulder.

Riley figured it was Simon, but both his hands were on the table in front of him. Probably one of the trappers wanting to see the claw. She turned and gasped.

Paul Blackthorne's corpse stared back at her.

Someone had reanimated her father.

THIRTY-FIVE

"Dad?" Riley whimpered.

"Paul?" Beck called out as he rose, his chair toppling over. Others surged to their feet, transfixed by the spectacle.

"My God, it's Blackthorne!" one of them cried out.

Her dad was dressed in the suit and tie they'd buried him in, his skin a sallow gray. Immense sadness filled his brown eyes. He stood just inside the Holy Water ward.

"Run . . . Riley," he croaked. "Run. Too many."

"Too many what? How'd you get—"

Deep growls echoed through the building, causing heads to turn. Furry bodies lumbered out of the darkness.

"Demons!" someone shouted.

Trappers surged to their feet, all talking at once.

Riley watched in horror as the Threes headed toward them. There were at least a dozen, maybe more. They lined up around the circle, snarling and slobbering, claws flicking in the air.

"Hold your positions!" Harper shouted. "They can't get to us, not with the Holy Water."

"Why are there so many of them?" Simon asked. "This can't be happening."

What are they waiting for?

The answer came a split second later.

"Pyro-Fiends!"

Red rubbery bodies ran along the sides of the building, leaping and twisting like ballet dancers, leaving bright crimson ribbons of liquid fire in their wake.

A Three launched itself against the ward and then flew back, howling and shrieking. It rose to its feet and assaulted the holy line again. Others joined it as trappers scrambled for their gear.

Beck was next to her, his duffel bag on his shoulder, the steel pipe in his hand. "Where's Paul?"

She looked around but couldn't see him.

"Dad?" she called. No reply.

Beck shoved her out of the way a split second before a Three broke through the ward. It scrambled to its feet and dove at a trapper. The man screamed in agony as it pinned him to the wooden floor with its claws.

"The ward's down!" Beck shouted.

"Out! Everybody out! Move it!" Collins shouted. Stewart began to herd his apprentices toward the nearest exit.

"Where's your trapping bag, Adler?" Harper demanded.

"In the car," Simon called back.

"Damn lot of good it's doing there." The old trapper dumped his into the apprentice's hands. "Snow globe!" As Simon dug in the bag, Harper gave Riley a shove, causing her to stagger backward. "Go!"

Not without Dad. Riley looked around blindly, but she couldn't see him. A cheer went up as someone lobbed a sphere high in the air. It broke open and snow began to fall. Then more snow globes. A thick blizzard fell into the smoke that crawled across the floor like a gray snake. Shouts echoed around her.

As the snow landed on her it melted instantly, plastering her hair to her skull. Riley wiped her eyes. She could only see a few feet in front of her; the exit signs were completely obscured in the storm.

Bumped from behind, Riley sprawled to the floor, barking her shins.

Something grabbed her leg and she struggled to pull free. There was a cry of pain and then a vicious snarl. She scrambled to her feet, knowing if she stayed down she was dead.

A Three stood between her and Simon, claws clicking, unable to decide who to eat first.

"Go!" Simon shouted to her. "Get out of here!"

His cry sent the demon his way. She saw it leap on him, rending and snarling. They rolled over and over on the floor, crashing into chairs and upending the tables. Blinded with fury, Riley grabbed the nearest wooden chair, folded it, and swung hard at the demon's head.

"Get off my boyfriend, you bastard!"

There was a sound like a cracking egg, and the fiend crumpled. Its paws twitched pathetically, then it stopped moving. She'd actually killed the thing.

"Simon?" She dropped the chair in horror.

"Oh, God," he moaned. "Oh, God it hurts. . . ."

His eyes wide in terror, he clutched his chest and belly as blood gushed through his fingers. She saw Jackson and grabbed him.

"Help me get him out of here!" she shouted.

They levered Simon to his feet, his face as gray as her dead father's.

"I got him," Jackson said, taking the weight from Riley. "Get going!"

A Three swept by her, howling in triumph as it vaulted toward one of the men. The trapper cried out and then vanished under a mass of fur and slashing claws. The demon raised its face, gore dripping from its muzzle.

When she turned to make her escape, Simon and Jackson were gone, hidden in the snow. Around her, demons leapt through the smoke, picking off their confused or injured prey. One of the Pyros hung from the big chandelier, raining fireballs from above.

She finally found Harper; he was hemmed in by a pair of Threes. Crazed with the smell of blood, they tore at anything that came near, even each other. That gave Riley an idea.

She crept to where her messenger bag had fallen. After looping it over her shoulder, she reached inside and her fingers closed around the only ammunition she possessed—a sub sandwich she'd planned to eat at the graveyard.

Harper slammed a Holy Water sphere into one of the demons. It didn't even react.

"Goddammit," the master swore. The fiends moved closer, knowing they had him.

"Harper?" she called. "Get ready to run!"

"Get out of here, Brat!" he shouted.

She did a high overhand pitch that sent the plastic-bagged sandwich between the two fiends. It hit the floor and they fell on it like junkyard dogs, slashing and clawing at each other. One began to tear into the sandwich. Enraged, the other demon attacked it. A battle ensued, the fiends were too interested in gutting each other than human prey.

"Come on!" she shouted, scooping up Harper's heavy duffel, the wide strap digging deep into her shoulder. The master trapper cautiously backed away from the fray and joined her.

"What the hell was that?" he demanded, eyes still on the squabbling Threes.

"Demon psychology." *If it's thrown at them, it had to be food.*

Harper seemed to accept that. "Where's Saint?"

"Outside," she shouted back. Or at least she prayed that was the case.

Harper motioned for his trapper's bag. He dug inside and armed himself with a steel pipe. It made her think of Beck.

Squinting, she tried to see though the falling curtain of snow, but there was no way she could find him.

Beck will be okay. He has to be.

Following Harper's lead, they made their way toward the closest wall, hoping to find an exit. Riley began to see the bodies. Chunks were missing, ropy entrails gaping from wide holes. Her stomach roiled at the stench of fresh blood, and she fought the urge to vomit.

A Pyro-Fiend ran in front of them, cackling as it laid down a trail of fire. Harper stomped on the flames with his heavy boots as they continued to edge forward. Panicked shouts rose as one of the lights crashed to the floor, sending a spray of glass in all directions. Riley realized she could see farther now as the snow globes exhausted themselves. Smoke billowed from the stage curtains as greedy flames inched higher into the building's superstructure.

No matter how hard she tried, she couldn't see her dad or Beck.

"Girl!" Harper growled. "Get him up!"

Riley found Jackson hunched in agony, his left arm burned to the elbow. She helped him up, seeing the panic in his eyes.

"Collins. They got him," he moaned. Riley couldn't bear to look at his wounds, but the smell of burnt flesh attacked her nose with every breath. She nearly gagged.

"Where's Simon?"

"Outside," Jackson wheezed.

The flood of relief nearly took Riley to her knees.

"Keep moving. We're almost there," Harper said, more to the injured man than to her. "We stay in here and we're done for."

⚓

Beck heard the growl and found a Three in full stalk mode. He'd know it anywhere. It was one he'd tried to trap with Paul. The one Riley had captured. Its eyes blazed a strange yellow, but the rest of it was like he remembered.

Someone had set it free.

"Trappperrr . . ." it snarled. A sphere shattered against its back. It twitched for a moment, but kept coming. Beck struck it with his pipe and it fell to the ground, then trotted off in search of a less-aggressive meal.

Beck found Morton by his side.

"The Holy Water's not slowing them down," the man said, breathing heavily. "Riley was right."

"Shit," Beck spat. He wiped a line of sweat off his brow.

"Yeah, I hear you." Morton set off toward a demon that was slashing through a table to get to a trapper.

Beck heard a shout and turned toward one of the exits. Through the billowing smoke he saw Riley. Harper and Jackson were with her.

"Thank God," he said. "Get her out of here."

The old trapper pushed open the door, checked to ensure there was nothing lurking outside, then gestured for Riley to leave. She ignored the master, looking back into the building, searching for someone. Then her eyes found him.

Beck gave her a salute. "Go!" he shouted.

She shook her head, waving for him to come with them.

His eyes met Harper's. The old trapper gave him a nod and shoved the girl outside over her protests. No matter what he thought of the old man, he owed him.

As long as Riley's safe nothin' else matters.

His heart singing of war and payback, Beck waded into the battle.

⁘

Chaos had set up camp in the parking lot. Wounded trappers sprawled on the asphalt, moaning, bleeding, and dying. Riley kept hunting until she found Simon. Someone's coat was jammed behind his head, and Stewart was bending over him, using a sweatshirt to stanch the blood pouring from his abdomen. Her boyfriend was unnaturally pale, his hands quaking as lips barely moved in prayer.

Another trapper knelt to take over for Stewart. He'd stripped off his shirt and applied it as a compress. It was immediately saturated with blood.

In the distance she heard the high wail of sirens, lots of them.

"We need ta get the lad out of here," Stewart said. "First ambulance, ya hear?" The other trapper nodded.

More men gathered around them.

"We're too close to the fire," Harper said.

"Aye. Come on ya lot, we need ta move the wounded now. This buildin's comin' down, and we dunna want ta be near her when she does."

A cold laugh floated across the parking lot, audible even above the fire's roar. Riley had heard it before—in the library.

No.

"Five!" someone shouted, and there was the sound of running feet as trappers scattered.

Stewart gestured. "Move 'em, now!" Men struggled to pick up the wounded, helping those who could still hobble across the street toward the park.

Harper turned toward her, his face sweaty and scar pulled tight. "Go with them, Brat. If it breaks through, get to hallowed ground."

He didn't understand. The Five was after her. She felt it call to her, offering her the ultimate boon: If she gave herself up, no one else need die.

Riley knelt and kissed Simon's ashen cheek, though she knew Harper and the others saw her. It didn't matter now.

"You stay alive, no matter what," she whispered. Simon's eyes weren't focusing, and she wasn't even sure he'd heard her.

With one last look at the boy who meant so much to her, Riley turned and headed toward her father's killer.

THIRTY-SIX

Frantic, Beck tried to fight his way through the flames to reach Morton. Threes had cornered him and he was screaming, begging for help. Beck managed to reach one of the fiends and bust its skull, but the remaining demons gleefully tore his fellow trapper apart and fell on his body for the feast.

"Sweet Jesus," Beck shouted, but it was drowned out as a low rumble filled the hall. He broke more demon skulls, but there seemed no end of them. They began to hunt him like a pack of lions does a cornered gazelle.

The final flakes of snow turned black, sucked upward in the rush of air feeding the burning roof. Beck bolted for the closest exit, jumping over dismembered corpses and the tangle of furniture.

The door was padlocked.

"Oh hell!" he swore. No wonder none of the others had left this way. He jammed the steel pipe between the lock and hasp, and tried to pry them apart. Behind him he heard snarls as the Threes closed in. It was only a matter of time before one jumped him and he'd be dead.

Slamming his weight against the pipe, he heard the chain snap. As he flung open the door, a steady breeze blew against his face. He sucked in the clear air and ran for it.

✢

Riley found the Geo-Fiend hovering above the parking lot next to the remains of a dented Volvo. The demon was more than seven feet tall, its deep ebony skin pulled tight like a wetsuit across a massive chest that any weightlifter would envy. Thick, corded muscles twined around its bullish neck. The face was like the maw of a volcano, glittering ruby fire seething inside the mouth and the eyes. Its horns reminded her of a steer, jutting out of the side of its head and then tapering to sharp points above the crown.

Oh my God.

"Get away from it!" Harper commanded, coming up behind her. He grabbed her arm, shoving her behind him.

At odds with its bulk, the demon made a delicate motion with its hand. A second later a sharp gust of wind slammed against them, blowing Riley into a nearby car. The door handle bashed into her hip. She slid to the ground, whimpering through the pain. There was a sharp cry behind her. Harper lay on the ground clasping his chest. In his hand was a grounding sphere. Somehow he'd kept it from being smashed.

Riley pulled herself up. The demon laughed again, making her blood freeze. Its offer boomed through her mind again like a cannon— her life or it would kill all of them.

Riley knelt next to the man she hated as much as the demon.

"Ribs," he said through gritted teeth. "Help me up."

She took the sphere from Harper's trembling hand.

"What are you doing?" he grunted.

Riley turned and moved toward the demon. Harper shouted for her come back, but she ignored him.

"This is personal," she said, though she knew he could not hear her.

As she moved closer Beck's voice was in her mind, telling her how a grounding sphere worked. She let that voice guide her. Riley lobbed the sphere at the Volvo. It smashed, exploded in a brilliant blue flash, and leapt to a nearby car. Then it faltered, unable to find more metal to complete the circuit. The magic faded and died, along with Riley's only hope.

Amused at her childish bravado, the demon responded with a twisted laugh that struck her like a blow. Did her dad hear that same laugh right before he died?

"Yes," it hissed.

With a flick of its wrist the ground in front of the Five began to heave and roll toward her like an ocean wave as chunks of black asphalt flew into the air. Then the wave halted. The thing was toying with her.

She took a cautious step back, then another, her knees still knocking.

The fiend grinned, showing her pointed teeth that gleamed in the flames.

"What about the boon? Do we have a deal? My life for the others." The demon hissed. "Swear it. Swear it on Lucifer's name!"

At the mention of its master, the demon shrieked into the night, shattering windows and making Riley's ears roar. She cradled her head as she stumbled backward in panic. The demon wasn't going to keep its bargain.

The wind began to pick up stray bits of debris from the parking lot, and pieces of gravel and broken glass stung her cheeks. This was how it killed her dad. She blinked her eyes and stumbled backward a few more steps.

Another grounding sphere landed near her, but it failed as well.

"Get back here!" one of the trappers yelled. "We can't hold it!"

"Like father, like daughter," the demon cried.

There was a crack and then a thick pop as a hole blew out of the asphalt behind her, spewing debris like a geyser, isolating her from the others. Steam belched from the hole along with a choking stench of mold, brick dust, and tar. Something swirled toward her out of the night—a dust devil. Before she could move, it caught her like a bird in a gale and slung her into the abyss.

Riley screamed and flailed for anything to grab on to. Her hands caught on some broken rebar. When she found a foothold, she levered herself upward so that her chin rested on the asphalt. It dug into her skin, making her jaw ache. Her relief was short lived—another wave came toward her, throwing debris into the air like someone shaking crumbs out of a tablecloth. When the ripple hit she would be gone, tossed deep into the pit.

As the wave approached, Harper shouted for help. There was *pop-pop-pop* of exploding tarmac. Debris fell like rain.

Riley closed her eyes and prayed.

Something grabbed her arm, and she cried out in surprise as she was winched out of the crater. Landing hard on her butt, Riley stared upward, fearing it would be the demon come to claim her soul.

Ori?

"You lead an interesting life," the man said, casually lifting her up and tucking her close to him as if he did this sort of rescue every day. He had no weapon she could see. Still, she could feel the coiled power in his muscles.

A roar of fury erupted from the Geo-Fiend, shaking nearby windows and setting off car alarms.

Ori shook his head. "Not yours."

Despite his warning, the ground wave continued toward them. Riley winced, waiting for the impact, but suddenly it evaporated. The demon roared again, shaking its fists like an angry toddler. In the distance she heard a church bell chime.

"Later, demon. We *will* meet again." Ori tugged on her arm. "Time to leave."

"But—" She looked around for Harper. He was being carried toward the street by a couple of trappers. That only left Beck, but there was no sign of him. The building was fully engulfed in flames now. If he was still in there . . .

Ori urged her along despite her vehement protests. The Five continued to generate a maelstrom of debris, moving closer to the remaining trappers, followed by demons queuing up for a final attack.

"I have to stay!" she said, pulling against Ori's grip.

"You stay, you die. That's not happening tonight."

They'd just reached her car when Ori abruptly halted. Swiveling back toward the fire, he frowned. "Well, well, now there's a surprise."

It took time for Riley's brain to process the scene. The trappers were huddled in a bunch, those still able to fight forming a protective ring around the wounded. But just beyond their ring was another one. It shone pure white, but unlike the circle at the cemetery every pinpoint of brilliance was at least eight feet tall and held a flaming sword.

"Angels," she cried in amazement. "Omigod, they're angels!"

‡

"*I'll be damned,*" Beck said, shielding his sooty eyes from the powerful light. The ring of glowing figures stood wing tip to wing tip, forming an ethereal barrier between the demons and the survivors. When a Three got too close, it shrieked and burst into flames like a tiki torch.

With howls of frustration and rage, the demons began to fall back, then one by one they fled into the dark alleys around the burning building. Only the Five was left, and with an unearthly roar it vanished in a swirl of black dust and mist.

A few of the trappers let out throaty cheers. Others gaped at Heaven's guard dogs.

"Where the hell . . . were they . . . when this started?" Harper grumbled, his sweaty face contorted in pain. He was bent over, working for each breath.

"Doesn't matter," Beck said, kneeling next to the injured master. "They're here now, and that's what counts."

THIRTY-SEVEN

Riley found herself at the gateway to the cemetery. Her car keys were in her hand but she didn't remember the drive. Ori was gone. Had she come here alone?

Every few seconds another tremor would shake her from head to toe like she had the flu. Digging in the messenger bag she pulled out her bottled water and drained it. She frowned. Where had the bag come from? She didn't remember picking it up. A quick check proved Beck's gift was inside her sweater. *At least I didn't lose that.*

Her mind was still dazed. How had the demons gotten through the Holy Water?

I should have checked it with the claw. What if I was wrong and it was the counterfeit stuff?

A profound shiver flashed through her.

Where had Ori come from? *Doesn't matter. He saved my life.*

Which left the biggest mystery of all. Was her dad still in his grave? There was only one way to know the truth.

Riley took off at a run down the asphalt path toward the mausoleum, as the bag bumped against her side. She hadn't gone far before her thigh cramped, forcing her to limp. Her lungs burned with each breath. She coughed deeply and tasted soot in her mouth.

He's there. I know he's there.

When she drew close to the mausoleum, she saw the glow of the candles. Riley cried in relief. It was some necro's sick game.

The circle was different. Bigger. It no longer encompassed the graves, but the entire mausoleum. Martha was in her chair facing west like she wanted a ringside seat to the Tabernacle's destruction. As always, she was knitting.

When Riley hobbled up the old woman smiled at her, pushing a row of stitches to the end of a needle. "Ah, there you are. I'm sorry about your dad, dear, but sometimes these things happen."

"Dad?" Riley swung her eyes toward the dark corner that housed her parents' graves. The ground above her father's wasn't a smooth mound anymore.

The grave was wide open.

"No!" she shouted. "No . . ." The circle of light burst high into the air, reacting to her anger and grief. Riley averted her eyes from the painful brilliance.

"What happened?" she demanded. "How did they get to him? The circle's still in one piece."

Martha looked up, her needles moving at lightning speed. "This one is. The first circle was breached, so I recast it."

"Why bother?" Riley asked, dumbfounded.

Martha paused mid-stitch. "Rod came down with a cold, so they sent another volunteer. He's fairly new. Unfortunately, he has a phobia about dragons, and that's exactly what came after him. He said the thing was twenty feet tall, and it shot a wall of flames at him. It was too much for the poor dear. He dove for cover and accidently broke the circle." Martha finished the stitch and tucked the knitting into her bag. "He's quite upset," she added.

"Oh, I bet. Just devastated." Riley coughed and then glared at the old woman. "Who took my dad? Was it the debt collection people? Give me a name." *So I can tear him apart.*

"The volunteer never saw the summoner."

Riley hung her head in body-numbing despair. "Dammit! It wouldn't have happened if I'd been here."

This was as much her fault as the dragon-phobic guy.

"Why the circle?" Riley asked. "What's the point?"

"It's for you, dear."

"The demons can't come here."

"But the living can, and some of the necromancers are sore losers. Best you stay inside the circle tonight."

Something in Martha's voice made Riley pause. The moment the volunteer invited her inside she scurried across the candles.

"Good night, dear. Don't worry, everything will work out," Martha said in that overly cheery voice of hers. She gave a wave and trudged into the night.

"Oh, yeah, things are working out great," Riley muttered. She glowered up at heaven. "Thanks for nothing."

It took some time for her to go to the empty grave. There was no Dad to talk to now. He was wandering somewhere around the city, playing slave to some rich bastard.

She fell on her knees in the red clay, staring into the deep hole. The pine coffin's hinges were twisted and broken like her father had busted out of a prison cell.

Fury roared within her. She shoveled the dirt back into the hole where it thunked inside the open box, bulldozing until her arms ached, muscles jittered, and palms were raw.

"So which one was it? Mr. I'm Totally Harmless Mortimer? Lizard Lenny?" *Or His High Lord Ozymandias?* She'd have to find out.

"We almost made it, Dad. Almost."

Riley stumbled to her bag and rooted through it until she found the chamois pouch Ayden had given her. She pried open the strings and then returned to the grave. Taking a pinch of clay from the ground, she dropped it inside the bag pouch.

The witch had said to collect things that made her feel strong, that defined her as a person. The soil that had covered her dead father would remind Riley to never trust someone to do her job.

They always fail you.

"I'll find you, Dad. I'll get you back here as soon as I can, I promise."

Then Riley gave into the much needed tears, wailing like a lost soul. She didn't bother to wipe the tears away and they dried on her cheeks, cracking in the cold night air. Salty testimony to the endless ache in her heart.

Knowing there was little she could do for her father or the other trappers, Riley toted the tarp and the sleeping bag to the west side of the mausoleum and arranged them on the hard ground. It was difficult to think, so she found herself making trips for single items—one for the bottled water, the flashlight, another for the blanket.

Curling up inside the sleeping bag, she sat upright and watched the fire. In the glow she thought she saw faces. Dead men's faces. She'd seen trappers torn apart, sickened by how much blood had poured from their bodies. Those images would never leave her. *Never.*

Simon. Would he make it through the night? What about Beck? Would morning bring more bad news?

"Please, God. I'll do anything not to lose them."

There was a stir of wind in the bare trees.

Desperate for something to occupy her mind, to keep her from thinking about Simon dying, she pulled out her cell to call Peter to let him know she was safe. The phone didn't work, didn't even light up.

She removed the back and found the wiring inside was fused.

"Oh, damn," she said, tossing it in the messenger bag, no clue as to how it'd become damaged. Her friend was probably watching the news reports, frantically dialing her over and over. *He'll think I'm dead.* So would Simi and all the kids at school. Maybe even her crazy aunt in Fargo.

"I could have been." A few more seconds and she'd have been at the bottom of that pit. She owed Ori her life and couldn't remember if she'd thanked him.

Her eyes finally closed, and Riley slid into tortured slumber. She heard someone calling for her. Simon. He kept crying her name, begging her to save him. She ran through the smoke and flames, kicking Threes out of her way like they were made of straw. Then she saw the pit. Simon was lying at the bottom, covered in blood. His chest was ripped open, and she could see his beating heart. He kept calling out to her but she couldn't get to him. His body sank lower and lower, fires raging beneath him. There were demons down there, with pitchforks and pointed tails. They howled in laughter and then pulled him into the depths as he issued one final pleading scream.

"Riley!"

She jumped and grabbed the flashlight for a weapon.

It was Beck. He stood just outside the circle hunched in pain and blinked at her like he wasn't sure she was real.

"Riley?" he whispered.

Is it really him?

She cleared her throat and wiped away the crusty tears. "If you mean no harm, then pass within."

He made a few more steps inside the circle before he staggered and fell into her arms, his duffel bag hitting the ground with a thump.

"Thank God!" he murmured. "Thank God."

He sagged and collapsed in a heap at her feet. Dropping to her knees, she shined the flashlight on him. Burns on his face, his right hand. His thigh had taken the worst of it.

"A Three?" she asked, and he nodded numbly, his hands clasped around the torn denim and ripped flesh.

"I've got fresh Holy Water," she said, taking off at a sprint for the mausoleum. When she returned he was still clutching the leg, his eyes closed in agony.

Which was only going to get worse.

She broke the seal. "You ready?" He nodded. The moment the stuff hit the wound he bellowed, writhing back and forth, making it difficult to keep the fluid going where it needed. She kept pouring until he sagged against the ground, his breathing labored.

"I'm so sorry, Beck!" she said. She remembered what it felt like, how her bones had burned deep within. *At least this is the real stuff.*

"Had to be done," he said through clenched teeth. "Go on. Do the rest."

Riley gently took his hand and treated it, then dabbed the Holy Water on his face. He kept his eyes closed the whole time.

As she made them a bed in the mausoleum, zipping the two sleeping bags together for warmth, she could hear Beck moaning with each breath. By the time she was finished her preparations he was sitting up, staring at the open grave. His hands quivered like an old person.

"It *was* Paul," he said.

"Yeah. He came to warn me," Riley said. Beck gave her a strange look. "I know that sounds weird, but he told me to run, that *they* were coming."

"How did he know?"

She shrugged. Beck was shivering again.

I can't help Simon, but I can help you.

"Come with me. It's too cold to stay out here," she said. To her relief he tried to help as she pulled him to his feet. It was hard going—he weighed more than she did and his leg was too numb to be of use—but she managed to guide him inside the building. Beck let her strip off his leather coat and wrap him up in a couple of blankets. Riley lit a candle and placed it on a ledge at the rear of the mausoleum. The dim light fell across his blackened face in a dance of light and shadow. She closed the heavy doors and sat next to him, tucking them into the sleeping bag. When she offered him a bottle of water, he downed it without pausing for air. His fingers tightened around the plastic and it crackled.

"Did you see Dad after . . . ?"

Beck shook his head.

"Maybe he didn't get out," she said.

"No, he's out of there. Any necro worth his salt would have made sure of that."

"How many dead?" she asked.

"Not sure. Ten at least," he said in a smoke-roughened voice.

She had to know. "Who?"

"Morton, Collins, Ethan. All dead."

"Ethan?" she asked, not wanting to believe it. He was one of Stewart's apprentices and was getting married in a few months.

"He went quick," Beck said in a thick voice. "Not like some of the others."

"What about . . . Simon?"

Beck didn't meet her eyes. "I don't know if he made it. They were tryin' to get him to the hospital. I didn't see him after that." He turned completely toward her now. "I couldn't find ya. Someone said the Five was after ya and I thought—"

"I'm okay."

He pulled her into a tight embrace. There was the sting of tears on her cheeks, but they weren't hers. He kissed the top of her head and murmured something. She didn't hear what he'd said, but that didn't matter. He was alive.

Riley wanted to stay in his arms, but Peter would be frantic by now. She unwound herself. "Is your phone working?"

Beck shook his head. "Happens sometimes around the groundin' spheres."

Crap. Sorry Peter.

The wounded trapper folded himself into the sleeping bag as Riley covered him with every extra blanket she had. When she slipped in next to him, he pulled her close, his injured arm over her for protection.

"I'll go back in the mornin'," he said faintly. "I'll see about Simon and the others."

"Were those really angels?"

"Yeah. Now get some sleep. Yer safe. I won't let anythin' hurt ya."

And she knew he wouldn't.

⁜

While Riley slept, Beck fell back on what he knew best. He remembered what it was like right after a battle. Everybody had their own way of dealing with it. Some guys drank, others shot up. He'd always go somewhere quiet and think it through, remember the stench of war, the pleas of the dying. He was doing the same now in the solitude of the old stone building.

Come morning, the trappers would have to face a new reality. They'd have to find out who was messing with the Holy Water and how the demons had crossed the ward. Was Hell making its big move? Was this really the end? So many questions that had no answers.

He pushed them all aside. There'd be time to figure all that out down the line. Instead, he calmed himself by listening to Riley's measured breathing, her warm body tucked up next to his. He'd thanked God repeatedly she was alive, and with those thanks came the truth that he'd been trying to deny.

I care too much for ya, girl.

Every person had a breaking point. Losing both Paul and Riley would have been his. How he would have stopped the pain, he didn't know. Didn't want to know.

Riley stirred, crying out. He comforted her and waited until she went back to sleep, gently stroking her hair. Morning would bring her even more hell. He knew what a dying man looked like, he'd seen them often enough in the war. His gut told him Simon wasn't going to make it, and that was going to rip her apart.

I'll be there for ya, girl. No matter what.

Beck took a deep breath and released it slowly. He had to stay strong for her, make the tough decisions. It was best that Paul's daughter never know how he felt about her. There'd be less hurt that way, for both of them.

Just keep her safe, God. I can settle for that.

THIRTY-EIGHT

When Riley finally stirred, Beck was gone along with his duffel bag. Rising on stiff legs she stretched and opened the door. It was past dawn, and the sun was higher than she'd expected. She broke the circle, packed her gear, and headed for the car. As she drove the thin curl of black smoke rising from the city drew her like a magnet.

The Tabernacle's burned-out husk seemed alien in the thin daylight. Two of the brick walls had collapsed inward, and the stained glass windows were gone. Disoriented bats chittered in the air, their roost history.

The area around the Tabernacle was blocked with barricades and the occasional police car. Riley stumbled to a halt. There was a makeshift morgue on the sidewalk closest to the park. She tried not to count the body bags but couldn't help herself.

Thirteen. About forty trappers had been at the meeting last night. That meant only twenty-seven had made it out alive.

She crossed the street and immediately encountered a cop.

"Can't go in there, miss," he said sternly, his hands crossed over his chest. Not knowing what else to do, she pulled out her trapper's license.

"You were here last night?" he asked, eyes taking in the bruises on her face, the singed hair, and the apron of dried blood on her jeans.

Riley nodded. He waved her through the crime scene tape without another word. The parking lot looked like giant gophers had gone berserk.

There was a municipal gas crew working on a mass of pipes. Some of craters had steam rising out of them, like in one of those apocalyptic movies.

She found Beck in a small knot of trappers. He held himself stiffly, moving in slow motion. As she grew closer to the group, Riley realized the topic of conversation was her dead father.

"I know what I saw," one of the men said. He had a bandage on his arm and a deep scowl on his face. "It was Blackthorne, and he was helping those demons."

"That's bullshit," Beck growled.

"Then how the hell did they get in? Someone had to break the ward. It sure as hell wasn't one of us."

Another trapper jumped in. "It had to be him. It's too much of a coincidence. Blackthorne shows up and a few seconds later we're deep in demons. No other explanation."

Riley pushed her way forward through the group, furious. "He came to warn me. He told me to run." The moment after she spoke, she realized it was the wrong thing to say.

"How'd he know that?" one of the trappers demanded. His name was McGuire and he'd opposed Riley's apprenticeship from the start.

"He wouldn't have broken the ward," she protested.

"If Blackthorne didn't let them in, who did? You?"

"It be time ta step back, trapper." It was Stewart. He had a thick bandage on his forehead. His skin was as pale as his hair, and he leaned heavily on his cane. "We'll work it out later. Right now, we need ta take care of our own."

The irate trapper didn't back down. "I know what I saw."

"Did ya ever think that's what the beasties wanted ya ta see?"

Grumbling broke out around them, for and against the argument.

"We gotta know who we can trust," McGuire replied. "It's all connected—the Holy Water, the attack, the demons working together." He pointed at Riley. "It all went wrong when she joined the Guild. She's to blame!"

Stewart put himself between her and the angry men. "Go stock yer bags and get back ta work. The city hasta see we're still out there. If not, they'll be callin' in the hunters as fast as ya can fart a tune."

The group slowly dispersed.

Stewart pointed at Beck. "Take this one home, will ya, lass?"

"But I was going to the hospital," Riley began. "I want to see Simon. See if he's . . ." *Still alive.*

The master pulled her aside. "Yer worried about him. I am too. But Simon has family ta watch over him." He looked back at the injured trapper. "Ya hafta be there for Beck. He only has you."

Riley sighed. "I'll get the car."

⁜

Other than providing directions to his house in Cabbagetown, Beck didn't say a word. Finally he pointed to a driveway that led to a compact green house with white trim. The mailbox had his last name stenciled on it and a purple clematis vine wound its way up the wooden post. She wasn't sure exactly what she'd expected, but this wasn't it.

Beck climbed out of the car like it took every bit of energy he possessed, but he refused her help up the stairs. Instead of unlocking the door he sank on the top step.

"You okay?" she asked, concerned.

Beck stared into the middle distance. "It's all goin' wrong. I don't understand." He looked over at her. "Which necro took him?"

"No idea." Riley tugged on his arm. "Come on." He didn't budge. "I've never been inside your place," she urged. "I want to see if it's as messy as mine." *Anything to get you out of the cold.*

Beck seemed puzzled by that. "I'm sorry. I thought ya'd been here. Yer daddy was, off and on. He liked it." A melancholy smile creased his face. "He said he wanted to buy ya a house like this."

Riley didn't want to think about what might have been. Not ever.

He finally got the front door open and tapped away at the alarm panel. The beeping ceased, then he limped into the front room.

Riley was greeted by dark hardwood floors and a braided rug to clean your feet on. There were pegs to hang coats and tan walls with pictures of Okefenokee Swamp. He'd surprised her again. The house was way clean by guy standards. There were no moldy chunks of pizza on the counter or dirty underwear lurking on the floor. In fact, the place was as clean as her own.

She pointed him to a kitchen chair and asked, "Where's your Holy Water?"

"Hall closet. Get a bottle for yerself and carry it with ya from now on."

"Why?"

"If ya need a quick ward, pour a circle and get inside it. It's better than nothin'."

"You're thinking the demons aren't done with us."

"I'd say they're just warmin' up."

Other people's closets held stuff they never used like ice skates, Christmas ornaments, old pairs of shoes that were long past their prime. Beck's held his trapping supplies. Everything was methodically organized, shelf by shelf, and included several pints of Holy Water, steel bags, coiled rope, spheres—you name it. Even a spare length of steel pipe.

Riley found the freshest bottles, verified the labels with the wet finger test, and returned to the kitchen. She put one in her bag. Beck still stared at nothing about twelve inches in front of him.

"Time for some more pain," she said.

"Is it the good stuff?"

"Oh, yeah."

He slowly stripped off his jacket, then his shirt. He took the pint from her. "I'll do it."

Works for me.

After washing her hands, Riley rummaged around inside the refrigerator and found eggs and some sausage links. More hunting helped her locate a frying pan, which she set on the gas stove. A sharp yelp came from the bathroom, then a stream of swear words, most of them starting with *f*. Then another yelp. The shower began to run.

That's the good stuff. Riley turned the heat down under the links, suspecting it might be a while before he emerged. While Beck showered, she used his home phone to call Peter's cell.

"Hello?" a wary voice asked.

"Peter, it's Riley."

"Riley! Where have you been? Omigod, you scared me," he said, his voice thick with worry.

"I'm sorry I didn't call sooner. My phone got fried, and I spent the night in the cemetery."

"They had it on the TV all night. I thought I might see you in one of the pictures and then I'd know you were okay. When I never saw you . . ." His voice trailed off.

"I'm so sorry, Peter."

"You knew all these guys who died, didn't you?"

"Most of them."

"What about Beck? Is he okay?" She told him a few details but left out the worst stuff. Peter didn't need her nightmares.

"So that's it, isn't it? They'll have to close the Guild?" he asked.

He almost sounded hopeful. "No. They'll have trappers come in from other cities. We'll start over."

"Oh."

"Peter, I'm not giving up on this. I want to be a trapper. Even more now!"

"I know," he said softly. "It's like watching you play tag with ravenous wolves. One wrong step and they rip you apart, and I can't do a thing about it. I don't know if I can take that anymore."

Peter might not have known it, but he'd drawn a line in the sand. On one side was the way their lives used to be—chatting about school, complaining about their parents, all of that stuff. On the other side was Riley's new life. The one that could get her ripped apart.

"We can talk about this later, Peter." No way could she handle this on top of everything else.

Silence.

"Peter?"

"The point is we never do talk it out. That's not the way a friend-ship works. I can't take this anymore. I mean it."

Then he hung up on her.

Riley felt sick inside. When she dropped the phone back into its cradle, she found Beck watching her from the hallway.

"He hung up on me. He can't deal with me being a trapper."

"It's hard for them," he said, his voice rough. "They don't under-stand what we do, why we do it." He shook his head in regret. "It tears 'em apart worryin' about us."

"It doesn't have to be that way. My mom was okay with Dad's work," she protested.

Beck arched an eyebrow. "Sure about that?"

Riley wanted to argue, but she'd overheard her parent's hushed con-versations. Her mother had worried every moment her husband was out of her sight, afraid that one day Paul wouldn't be coming home.

Beck slumped in the doorway. "When I first started I thought I could have it all. Now all I see is a life on my own, at least until I get too old to trap or some demon makes a meal of me."

Riley shivered, running her hands up and down her arms. "God, that's so . . . brutal."

"It's the price we pay for takin' on Hell."

Her breath hitched at the thought.

To his credit Beck stayed out of the way as Riley cooked the rest of the meal. He ate what she put in front of him without bitching that the eggs were overcooked and the toast too brown. She found herself hun-grier than she'd expected and cleaned her plate, wondering how she could eat after what she'd seen the night before.

Does that make me a ghoul?

It wasn't until Beck finished a second helping of toast, lighter this time, that he started to talk. "Jackson's injured, but should be back pretty soon. Stewart's up and goin', though I don't think that's a good idea. Harper's ribs are banged up."

"Is he in the hospital?"

"No, he's at his place. He'll need help for a time."

"What comes next?" Riley asked, sipping on the coffee. It was too strong, but then she'd never been good at making the stuff.

"Funerals. Then we've got to do all that damned paperwork for the national office. They'll have to send us a master to start trainin' replacements." His voice trailed off. "It'll be a couple years before we're back to full strength, unless other trappers move here."

"Will they?" she asked, brushing the last of the crumbs off her sweater.

"I sure as hell wouldn't move here, not with that happened last night," he replied. "Be lucky if we can keep the ones we got."

He was probably right. "I'll keep an eye on Harper, help him if I can," she said.

That got her a long look. "Thought ya hated him."

"Doesn't keep me from looking after him." *As long as I keep out of range.*

"Well, that makes sense," he said, indicating the meal. "Ya did the same for me."

Why did he make everything so personal? "Beck, I don't hate you; it's just that . . ." She had no idea how to explain how much he rubbed her the wrong way, or how good it had been that day when they were trapping together. How much she wished it was always that way. "I want it to be okay between us, but I'm not giving up Simon just because you don't like him."

"He's okay." Beck stared down at his empty plate. "Truth is, yer right. I'm . . . sorta jealous of him. He's lucky ya like him so much. Any guy would be."

I like you too, but you don't see it.

Not knowing how to tell him that, Riley rose and shoved her chair under the table. She reached for the plates, but he stopped her.

"Please call yer aunt, let her know yer okay. I'll get ya a bus ticket to Fargo."

Back to that again. She shook her head, her fingers digging into the back of the chair. "I'm not leaving, not with Simon the way he is."

Beck rose, face set. "I know ya care for him, but he'd want ya safe. The demons shouldn't know yer name, but they keep callin' ya out. That Five was willin' to kill every last trapper to get to ya. That's real bad, Riley."

She heard fear in every word. Fear for her. "It doesn't matter what the demons are doing, I'm not leaving."

"Somethin's goin' down in this city, girl, and yer in the middle of it."

"Doesn't matter if I'm in Fargo or wherever. If the Five wants me, it'll find me. Game over." When he opened his mouth to argue, she waved him off. "You're wasting your time. I'm staying, and that's the end of this conversation."

"Yer one damned pigheaded fool," he growled.

"You would know what that's like."

With a snarl, Beck swiveled on his good leg and limped down the hall. A door slammed. Then there was a loud thump, like someone had struck a wall with his fist.

Buy all the bus tickets you want. There's no way I'm leaving.

THIRTY-NINE

The ICU nurse in the blue scrubs took one look at Riley and went wide-eyed. "Are you okay, miss?" he asked, rising from his chair.

Riley could only imagine what she looked like. She hadn't taken time to change her clothes, hadn't even thought of it. Then she caught her reflection in the waiting room window. Her jacket was dotted with scorch marks, and one sleeve had a long slit in it. Her hair hung limp, frizzled at the ends from the heat. Both her sweater and jeans were caked with a thick layer of dried blood.

"Ah, yeah, I'm okay," Riley said. "I'd like to see Simon Adler."

Don't tell me he's dead. Please, don't . . .

"Are you family?" the nurse asked skeptically.

"Ah . . ."

"She is," a voice called out. It belonged to a young woman standing in the waiting room door.

The nurse still appeared skeptical. "Okay, but five minutes only," he advised.

The young woman took Riley by the hand and led her farther down the hall. She was blond with blue eyes, about Riley's height. There was a slight thickness at her waist. A baby bump.

"You're Riley, aren't you?" she whispered. "I'm Amy, Simon's sister. He told me about you."

"You got married last summer," Riley said.

The girl nodded. She put a protective hand her stomach. "I'm going to have a baby," she said.

They walked in silence until Amy paused outside a room.

"How bad is . . . ?" Riley began, then lost the will to finish the question.

"They say he lost a lot of blood, that it hurt his brain. They say he's not there anymore. That we have to decide if we keep him on the machine or . . ." Amy's eyes brimmed.

Oh, God.

They hugged, sharing tears.

"He's the greatest brother ever," Amy said between sobs, her head buried in Riley's shoulder. "Why did this happen to him?"

The images of lacerated bodies, ferocious demons, and all that blood steamrolled through Riley's mind. She could hear the screams, the snarls, the crisp crackle of the flames as if she were inside that building once again.

"Are you okay? You're shaking," Amy said, pulling away.

"I'm okay," Riley said, but that was a lie.

Amy took her arm. "Bro told me how much he liked you. He said you were special. I thought you should know that."

"Thanks, I . . . he's special to me, too."

After she squeezed Riley's hand Amy made her way back to the waiting room.

He's not there anymore.

Riley gingerly pushed open the door to Simon's room. A nurse looked up, gave her a nod, and then finished hanging a new IV bag. It had blood in it. She left without offering a word of encouragement.

Which means there isn't any hope. Riley had learned that when her mother lay dying.

Simon was so pale he'd qualify as corpse, and the medical equipment seemed to dwarf him. A ventilator kept him breathing. Air in, air out. A long green line sprawled across a monitor, registering every heartbeat.

Tubes were everywhere. One snaked out from under the covers and into a bag to collect his urine.

Riley swallowed hard, moving slowly to the side of the bed. Just last night they'd been kissing, holding each other, talking about the future.

She slipped her hand between the cool metal rails. Simon's felt like lukewarm marble. He didn't twitch when she touched him, didn't squeeze back. She remembered the soft look in his eyes. How he'd treated her like she was the only girl in the world. Bending over, she pushed a piece of hair off his forehead and then kissed him.

"Hurry and get well," she whispered in his ear. "We're getting behind on the kissing."

No response, not even a flicker of an eyelid. The ventilator continued to push air into his lungs and the heart monitor beeped, but no one was home. Even Riley could tell that.

"You can't be like this," she said. "You can't leave me alone. I don't care what it takes, but you have to get better, Simon Adler. I'll do anything, you hear? Just don't die on me!"

Nothing. Her tender hope began to disintegrate into tiny wounded shards.

Simon had told her his faith had never really been tested.

Now he was serving as a test for those who loved him.

This one I'm not going to pass.

⁘

As she cried at the elevator, Riley saw the angel in the hallway. Nobody else seemed to notice it, despite the white robe and the feathery wings neatly tucked behind its shoulders. In fact, a nurse walked right by it, then ducked into a patient's room intent on her own business.

The ethereal messenger beckoned to Riley, then pointed toward the chapel down the hall. Riley hit the down button again, hard.

"You are a stubborn girl, aren't you?" the angel said. The voice sounded so familiar. So Martha.

The knitting-addicted cemetery volunteer was an angel?

"You're kidding me," Riley said. "Why didn't I see you like this before?"

"I didn't want you to," Martha replied. She pointed toward the chapel again.

"What do you want?" Riley replied, not willing to budge.

The angel puzzled on that, scratching a wing in thought. "Some fine alpaca hand-dyed yarn would be a good start. Oh, and I'd love to have a pair of rosewood needles."

Riley tried again, her frustration rising. "What do you want *with me?*"

"A chat, dear, before it all goes to Hell."

Feeling really dumb talking to something no else seemed to notice, Riley gave in and shuffled her way toward the chapel. Pushing open the door, she found Martha in the front pew, but now she was dressed like an old woman, orthopedic shoes and all.

"How do I know you're not one of *them?*" Riley asked.

Martha spread her hands. "We're on hallowed ground."

"Didn't help last night," Riley retorted. "We were behind a holy ward and inside a building that used to be a church."

That got her a pensive frown. "The bottle of Holy Water in your bag—pull it out." The angel cupped her hands. "Pour some for me."

How did you know I had that?

Riley's own hands were shaking as she did the honors. She waited for the screech, the sprouting of horns, the flick of a barbed tail. Instead, the liquid pooled in Martha's hands and started to glow greenish gold. Then it vaporized into a mist and spread throughout the room.

"Wow," Riley said, watching it float on invisible air currents.

"I love doing that," Martha admitted. "Now take a deep breath and tell me what it reminds you of."

Riley inhaled. "Summer, at the beach. I can smell the saltwater and fresh watermelon."

Martha sighed. "I can't smell a thing. You mortals are so lucky."

Riley screwed the cap on the Holy Water and dropped it back in her bag. This was God's representative. If she couldn't complain in person, the angel would do just fine.

She drew in a tight breath. "Who took my dad?"

A shake of the head. "Next question."

"How did the demons get inside the ward?"

"Evil neutralizes Holy Water. Too much evil and..." The angel spread her hands.

That only made Riley more upset. "Why did your boss let all those people die? We're on your side, or don't you guys get that?"

"Everything has a reason. You have to trust His divine will."

"Trust?" Riley shouted, her voice echoing in the small room. At this point she didn't care if she was turned into a pillar of salt or whatever. "That might work for you, but it's been an epic fail for me. I prayed for my mom. She died. I prayed that my dad wouldn't get hurt. He did anyway. Now Simon's ... Now he's ..." She sank into the pew, palm clamped over her mouth, tears bursting from her eyes. The shaking started again, making her muscles lock up.

"You really care for him, don't you?" Martha asked softly.

Riley nodded. She found a piece of tissue in her pocket and blew her nose. "He's ... I think I ..." *I think I'm falling love in with him.*

"So you are," Martha replied. "We'll ensure your young man recovers from his injuries, provided you agree to help us."

Riley blinked in confusion. "I'm already helping. Trapper, remember?" she said, pointing at her chest.

"We'll need more than that. When the time comes you must do something for us, no questions asked."

That didn't sound good.

"Why do I need to make a deal with you? Why don't you just help him? He's your kind of guy. He follows all the rules."

The angel didn't reply, which only gave Riley time to feel totally selfish. Why would it matter what they wanted as long as Simon was alive? But what if this was a trick and they didn't make him better?

Martha looked upward toward the ceiling and then gave a quick nod like she'd received further instructions from an unseen superior. She dropped something on the pew next to Riley.

It was a tract, one of those "THE END IS NEAR!" ones that you find under your windshield wiper at the shopping mall. After last night's horror the crude illustrations of collapsing buildings, earthquakes, and billowing flames hit too close to home for Riley's comfort.

With a snort of derision, she pushed it aside. "This is total crap. They've been saying that for years."

"Ever since the beginning," Martha replied gravely.

"So what does this have to do with me?" Riley demanded.

The angel stood, fussing with her cuffs. "Because if you accept our offer, you're the one who's going to stop it."

"Me?" Riley sputtered. "Are you kidding?"

"No."

"Hello? I'm seventeen. I haven't even gotten out of high school yet, and you think I'm going to stop the end of the world? What *are* you people smoking?"

The angel raised one silver eyebrow. "Joan of Arc was your age when she led the French into battle."

"Wait, don't tell me. I know how this story ends. Roasted martyr. Yeah, that's my dream job."

"It's your choice," Martha said. The angel vanished leaving Riley in a room that smelled like watermelons and with the fate of the world hanging over her head.

Let Simon die or owe Heaven big-time?

"That's no choice!" Riley called out.

There was no reply but the sound of the furnace kicking in. No chorus of angels or hisses of demons. Only hot air blowing in her face.

Riley started to laugh. It had a hysterical edge to it. "You're just messing with my head."

Any moment now Martha would return, admit that it'd been a big joke.

When that didn't happen, Riley retraced her steps to the elevator and stared at the buttons. Up or Down. Simon lives. Simon dies.

She remembered his calm presence at her dad's funeral, him kidding her about her ankles, them sharing their dreams. She'd fallen for him, and there was no way to deny that.

My choice.

"Okay, you got a deal," she said, not sure if anyone heard her. "Do whatever it is you do."

She waited, but nothing happened. Maybe it took a while. Maybe it was a test and they'd let him die anyway.

The elevator doors opened and she got on. Right before the doors closed, Amy joined her. They shared sad smiles.

"I need to get some sleep," the girl said. She patted her tummy. "Growing a baby makes me tired."

A child her brother might never see.

As they walked out of the hospital along the sidewalk toward the parking garage, music filled the air. Amy dug in her voluminous suede purse and retrieved a cell phone.

"This is Amy. What? What do you mean?"

And then she shrieked and took off at a run back toward the hospital.

Good news? Bad news? It could be either one. Amy's shriek hadn't been very specific.

"Hey! What happened?" Riley called out.

She didn't get a reply.

Simon's sister made it to the bank of elevators faster than Riley, pregnancy not hampering her speed as much as a demon-clawed leg. The doors closed before Riley reached them.

"Damn!" She bounced back and forth from foot to foot. "Come on," she grumbled as she kept punching the button. No elevator.

An older woman watched her and delivered a matronly shake of the head.

"You young kids are just so impatient nowadays."

Riley punched the button three more times to further demonstrate her youthful impatience. By the time the next elevator arrived she was about to brave the stairs, leg cramp or not.

Pushing through the double doors into the ICU, she found the area in front of Simon's room crowded with family. There was lots of crying and hugging going on.

When she drew closer, they cleared a way for her.

"That's his girlfriend," one of them whispered to another.

As she stepped inside the room, the first thing she heard was Amy's sobs. There was no mechanical whoosh. The ventilator was off.

Riley closed her eyes, feeling the shakes coming again. She'd given Heaven her word. Had they'd failed her? Like always?

"Riley, look!" Amy exclaimed. "He's awake! He's breathing on his own."

Riley whipped open her eyes, desperately wanting to believe it was true.

The breathing tube was gone, and the nurse was carefully positioning an oxygen cannula in his nose.

"Simon?" Riley said, putting all her prayers into the one word.

Her boyfriend's bloodshot blue eyes slowly opened, and a croak came from his lips. Then he saw her at the end of the bed. "Ri . . . ley," he whispered.

Joy burst through her like a lightning bolt. Simon was alive and had a working brain, or he wouldn't know who she was.

"They did it," she said. "Omigod, they did it!" She sucked in the pungent, unforgettable scent of watermelons. The Angel Martha had been here and pulled off a miracle.

As Riley shared a celebratory hug with Amy, the truth hit her.

Her boyfriend was going to live.

Heaven had kept their part of the bargain.

Which means I'm on the hook for the rest.

Turn the page for a sneak peek at the next thrilling
Demon Trappers novel coming in Fall 2011 from
St. Martin's Griffin!

ONE

❦ ✛ ❦

2018
Atlanta, Georgia

Inside the Grounds Zero Coffee Shop was the most amazing hot chocolate in Atlanta, maybe even the whole world. It appeared Riley Blackthorne would have to wade through Armageddon to get it.

"The End is near!" a man called out to the passersby. He stood near the entrance holding a homemade cardboard sign that proclaimed the same thing. Instead of having a scraggly beard and wearing a black robe like some Biblical prophet, he was wearing chinos and a red shirt.

"You've got to prepare, missy," he said, and shoved a pamphlet toward Riley with considerable zeal. The tract looked remarkably like the one she had in her pocket. Like the one the angel had given her right before she'd agreed to work for Heaven to save her boyfriend's life.

"The End is near!" the man shouted again.

"Is there still time for hot chocolate?" Riley asked.

The End Times guy blinked. "Ah, maybe, I don't know."

"Oh, good," she said. "I'd hate to take on Hell without fueling up."

That earned her a confused frown. Rather than explain, she jammed the pamphlet into her jacket pocket and pushed open the door to the coffee shop. The man went back to exhorting passersby to prepare for the worst.

The Grounds Zero didn't look any different from the last time she'd been here. The smell of roasted beans hung in the air like a heady perfume and the espresso machine growled low and deep. Customers tapped on laptops as they enjoyed expensive coffee and talked about whatever was important in their lives. Just like every day. Except . . .

Everything is weird now.

Even buying hot chocolate. That used to be easy: Place order, pay for order, receive hot beverage. No hassles. No worries about hordes of demons or the end of civilization.

That didn't appear to be the case now.

The barista kept staring at her, even as he was making the drink, which wasn't a good thing as he nearly scalded himself. Maybe it was the multiple burn holes in her denim jacket, or the ragged slice down one shoulder that revealed the T-shirt underneath. Or the fact that her long brown hair had a frizzled, been-too-close-to-a flame look, despite two shampoo sessions and a lot of conditioner. At least she'd changed her jeans, or the guy would be staring at all the dried blood. Blood that wasn't hers.

"I saw you on TV. You're one of them, aren't you?" he asked in a shaky voice, brown eyes so wide they seemed to take up most of his face.

On TV? Riley had no choice but to own up.

"Yeah, I'm a trapper." *One of the few lucky enough to survive last night's slaughter.*

The guy dropped the ceramic cup on the counter, sloshing some of the brown goodness over the side and onto the saucer.

"Whipped cream?" she asked, frowning now. Even if the world was ending, hot chocolate had to have that glorious white stuff on top, or what was the point? He reluctantly added some, keeping his eyes on her rather than the cup. Some of it actually went inside. "Chocolate shavings?" she nudged.

"Ah . . . we're out," he said, backing away like Riley had horns coming out of her skull.

Which I don't. She would have noticed them in the bathroom mirror after showering away all the smoke and blood.

It's just one creepo guy. No big.

But it wasn't just him. Other customers stared at Riley as she made her way to an empty booth. One by one they looked up at the television screen high on the wall, then back to her, comparing images.

Ah, crap.

There, courtesy of CNN, was last night's disaster in glorious color: flames pouring out of the roof of the Tabernacle as demons ran everywhere. And there she was, illuminated by the raging fire, kneeling on the pavement near her injured boyfriend. She was crying, holding Simon in her arms. It was the moment she knew that he was dying.

Oh, God. I can't handle this.

The saucer in Riley's hand began to quake, dislodging more of the hot chocolate. It'd been bad enough to live through that horror, but now it was all over the television in full and unflinching detail.

She paused near a booth as a picture of Simon appeared on the screen. It must have been his high-school graduation photo since his white-blond hair was shorter and his expression stone serious. He was usually that way, except when they were hanging together, then he'd let his guard down, especially when they were kissing.

Riley closed her eyes, recalling the time they'd spent together before the meeting. They'd talked of things close to their hearts and he'd admitted how much he cared for her. Then a demon had tried to kill him.

Riley sank into the booth and inhaled the rich scent of the hot chocolate, using it as a means to push the bad memories away. The effort failed, though it never had in the past. Instead, her mind dutifully conjured up the image of her boyfriend in his hospital bed, tubes everywhere, his face as white as the sheets.

Simon meant so much to her. He'd been a quiet, comforting presence after her father's death. Losing him so soon after her dad was unthinkable. And Heaven had known that. What else could she do but agree to their terms: Simon's life in trade for Riley owing Heaven a favor. A really *big* favor. Like stopping Armageddon in its tracks.

"Why me?" Riley muttered. "Why not someone else? Why not Simon?"

He was religious, followed all the rules. He'd be the perfect guy to keep the world from ending.

Instead they chose me.

A chime erupted from her messenger bag. The moment she'd sent a message to one of her classmates saying she was alive, it seemed like most of Atlanta had responded. Even technology called up bad memories. The cell phone was her dad's and it'd been with him the night he'd been killed by a Grade Five demon, a Geo-Fiend as the Trappers called them. Now the phone was hers. Every time she held it she thought of him.

Another chime. On some level it felt good to know people cared, but most of them were just trying to hear the inside story.

Not happening.

Riley typed a response to the last message:

I'M OKAY. PASS IT ON.

To her annoyance, the hot chocolate had cooled beyond what was acceptable drinking temperature, but she sipped it anyway. She kept her eyes riveted on the cup's contents, away from the television screen. Someone scraped a chair across the floor as they sat at a table and Riley jumped at the sound, half expecting a horde of demons to pour through the front door at any moment.

The cup trembled in her hands. ·

I have to find my dad. It was unlikely his body was buried under the rubble at the Tabernacle, not when a necro went to all the effort to summon him from his grave. By now that very necromancer would be lining up someone to buy Master Trapper Paul Blackthorne, if he hadn't been sold already. Once he was owned by someone it'd be nearly impossible to get him back. She could take his new owner to court to prove the summoning hadn't been legal, but rich people had expensive lawyers and she was barely making the rent. By the time the case reached a judge her father would be back in the ground, anyway. Deaders weren't good for much more than a year, even with the best of care.

What is it like to be dead and walking around like you're still alive? Besides the creep factor, it had to be truly weird. Did her dad remember dying? Did he remember the funeral and being buried? Did he even remember he had a daughter?

Spiky cold zipped down Riley's spine. She had to get her head in the game.

I'll find him. I'll get him back in the ground and that'll be the end of it.

A timid voice broke through her dark thoughts.

"Ah, ah . . . 'scuse me?" it said.

Riley looked up to find a freckled-faced boy watching her. He was about seven years old with big, brown eyes. *When he gets older, girls are going to love those.* A man stood right behind him, his hands on the boy's shoulders.

"Go on, son," he urged, smiling politely.

The boy gathered his courage. "Can I . . . can I have your aut'graph?"

You're kidding me.

"But I'm . . . I'm . . ." *Not important.*

"You fought all those demons," the boy said. "It was awesome!"

Awesome wasn't the word she'd have chosen. Hellish. Bloody. Brutal. Still, the kid was so sincere she couldn't blow him off.

"Sure." Riley scribbled her signature on a Grounds Zero napkin with the pen his father handed her. The boy beamed like he'd just met the president or a rock star.

"Thanks!" He took off like a shot, bearing his prize back to a woman who sat at a table near the front of the store. Probably his mother.

Riley handed back the pen. "I'm not anyone special," she said, feeling like a fraud. "I'm just an apprentice. The other guys, they're the real deal."

The boy's dad shook his head. "I think you're selling yourself short. We just want you to know we think y'all are real brave. We're praying for you."

"Thanks," she said, not knowing what else to say. *We're going to need it.* Mercifully, the guy retreated and no one else came up to her.

Her eyes wandered back to the television. A different reporter was doing a play-by-play of last night's horror. He had it mostly right—the local Trappers Guild had held a meeting at the Tabernacle in downtown Atlanta just like they always did. In the middle of the meeting, the demons had arrived. Then it got bad.

"Eyewitnesses say that at least two different kinds of Hellspawn were involved in the attack and that the trappers were quickly overwhelmed," the reporter said.

Three different kinds, but who's counting?

Riley frowned. The trappers hadn't been overwhelmed. Well, not completely. They'd even managed to kill a few of the things.

When she went to pick up the cup of hot chocolate her hands were still shaking. They'd been that way since last night and nothing she did made them stop. She downed the liquid in small sips, knowing people were watching her. Talking among themselves. Someone took a picture of her with their cell phone.

Ah, jeez.

In the background, she could still hear the reporter on CNN.

"A number of the trappers escaped the inferno and were immediately set upon by a higher level fiend."

The higher level fiend had been a Grade Five demon that'd opened up deep holes in the ground, spun off mini tornadoes, and caused the earth to shake. All in an effort to take out one trapper.

Me.

If it hadn't been for Ori, a freelance demon hunter, the Five would have killed her just like it had her dad.

"Eyewitnesses are saying they saw angels last night," the reporter continued. "We had Dr. Osbourne, a professor of religious studies at UC Santa Barbara, review the videos. He's with us here today via satellite." A gray-haired man appeared on the screen, solemn and stern. "What's your take on this amazing event, doctor?"

"I've watched the videos and all that is visible is a circle of incredibly bright light that surrounds the demon trappers. I have colleagues in Atlanta who've claimed to see angels in your city. They've appeared throughout the Bible to Abraham, to Jacob. Sodom and Gomorrah rated two of them. In this case, they were actively protecting the trappers from Hellspawn. Biblically, I'd say that's significant."

Last night all the rules of engagement had changed.

Riley dug in her messenger bag, retrieved a pen and began a list on a crisp white napkin.

Find Dad
Bust Holy Water Scam
Save the World
Do Laundry
Buy Groceries

As she saw it, if number three on the list didn't work out, the last two weren't going to be needed.

TWO

Feeling a tickle in his throat, Denver Beck coughed deeply in an attempt to purge the stale smoke from his lungs. It did little good. In the distance, firefighters moved across the Tabernacle's rubble, working on the hot spots and searching for charred bodies in the mounds of broken bricks and charred wood.

I should have died last night. In the past, it wouldn't have mattered. Now it did. It was fear for Riley that had driven him out of the smoke and flames.

To his right, Master Trapper Angus Stewart leaned heavily on his cane in the late afternoon sun. His usually ruddy face was nearly the color of his white hair, pale against the bloodstained bandage tucked into his hairline. They stood near one of the many holes in the Tabernacle's parking lot, the stench of burnt asphalt hanging heavy in the air. Beck bent over and stared into the hole's maw, which was laced with tangled wires and debris. A thin column of steam rose from the center of the crater.

"How does a demon do this kind of damage?" he said, shaking his head at the sight.

"The Geo-Fiend just waved its hands and this abyss appeared. They have some strange power over the earth and the weather," Stewart said in his rich Scottish accent. It was still noticeable, though blunted by a decade in Atlanta.

Beck straightened up, the demon wound on his thigh cramping in protest. The dressing was leaking and the drainage had soaked into his blue jeans. He needed more aspirin—his temperature was up, and every now and then his teeth would chatter. Like a mild case of the flu with claw marks as the bonus.

Everythin' has changed now. He knew angels were for real; he'd seen them around Atlanta. Most were the ministering kind, the most prolific of Heaven's folk who came and went doing whatever God wanted them to do. He hadn't seen any of the higher realm, the ones with the flaming swords. He had last night.

Beck shook his head, unable to deal with how eerie the things had been. At least seven feet tall, clothed in eye-blinding white with shimmering alabaster wings edged in gray, their fiery swords had roared like summer thunder and filled the night air with the crisp tang of ozone.

"I've never heard tell of Heaven steppin' in to protect trappers," Beck said in a lowered voice, mindful of a television news crew on the other side of the parking lot. They were all over the city now, trying to get a handle on one of the biggest stories to hit Atlanta since the Olympics. "Why're the demons workin' together now? It feels like a war's brewin'."

"So it does." Stewart cleared his throat. "Seein' the angels make ya a believer?"

Beck blinked at the question. *Had it?* He'd never really thought much about God, and he figured the feeling was mutual. "Maybe," he admitted.

Stewart huffed in agreement. "The city will be wantin' action."

"Master Harper will take care of that, won't he?" Harper was the most senior trapper in Atlanta and Riley's master. From what Beck could tell he was a serious piece of work, but a good trapper when he wasn't drinking.

"Nay, not with his ribs bein' the way they are," Stewart said. "I'll have to take the lead." He paused a moment, then added, "I'm pleased ta hear young Simon's gonna make it. That's good news for Riley."

"Yeah," Beck replied, unsure of where the old master was heading with that last comment.

"She and Simon have taken a fancy ta each other, did ya know? They were holdin' hands and kissin' before the meetin'. They didn't think I saw them."

"Kissin'?" Beck felt something heavy form in the middle of his chest, like a thick stone weighing on his heart. Had to be because of the demon wound, they always made a person feel weird. It wouldn't do him any good to think of Riley as more than just Paul's little girl.

"Ya didn't know?" the master asked, all innocence.

Beck shook his head. He'd known Riley and Simon were spending time together—they were apprenticing with Harper and saw each other every day. But he hadn't realized their relationship had gone that far. She was only seventeen, and now that both of her parents were dead he felt responsible for her. Sort of like a big brother. Maybe something more.

"Yer frownin', lad," Stewart observed.

Beck tensed, uncomfortable with the old trapper's scrutiny. "Simon's okay," he acknowledged. "But he's not what she should be thinkin' about right now. I'll have a talk with him once he's better. Warn him off." *Let him know if he goes too far with her I'll rip his damned head off.*

The master gave him a fatherly smile. "Let *them* sort it out, lad. Ya canna keep her in a bubble the rest of her life."

Wanna bet? It's what Paul would have wanted and, if he was honest, the only way Beck could sleep at night. As he stared at the broken landscape and the savaged building, his mind filled with images from the night before. Of demons and the trappers battling for survival. Of Riley in the middle of the flames. How close he'd come to losing her. Beck shuddered, ice shearing through his veins.

Stewart laid a heavy hand on his shoulder, startling him. "I know ya stayed inside that furnace until the very last. That takes stones, and I'm damned proud of ya. Paul would have been as well."

Beck couldn't meet the master's eyes, troubled by the praise.

The Scotsman's hand retreated. "Ya can't carry it all on yer shoulders, broad as they are."

He sounded just like Paul, but that made sense—Master Stewart had trained Riley's father, who in turn had apprenticed Beck. From what Paul had said, the Stewarts were some of the best demon trappers in the world.

This man thought he'd done all right last night. *He's just bein' nice.*

As if knowing a change of topic was needed, Stewart asked, "Any idea who pulled Paul from his grave?"

That was the other thing hanging over them. Though he'd been dead for two weeks, Riley's father had appeared at the trapper's meeting, summoned from his eternal rest by a necromancer. He was a reanimated corpse now, a Deader, money on the hoof providing he'd made it out of the Tabernacle in one piece.

"Riley did everythin' she could to keep him in the ground," Beck complained. "She sat vigil every damned night, made sure there was a consecrated circle around his grave. Then some bastard steals him when she isn't there. It just sucks."

"She have any notion who did it?" Stewart nudged.

"I didn't get a chance to ask her." Which wasn't quite the truth. Beck could have. They'd huddled together in her family's mausoleum in Oakland Cemetery until dawn, on hallowed ground in case the demons came after them. She'd been so upset about Simon and the others, she'd cried herself to sleep. At the time it didn't seem important to know who'd resurrected Paul, so he'd just held her close, kept her safe, thanking God she'd survived. Trying to work through his feelings for the girl. When he'd left her this morning she'd still been asleep, dried tears on her cheeks. He hadn't had the heart to wake her.

Stewart shifted position again, he was hurting more than he let on. "I canna help but believe there's a connection between the demons' attack and Paul's reanimation," the old trapper mused.

"How could there be?"

"Think it through. Wouldn't he have gone off with the necro who summoned him rather than droppin' in for a wee visit with his old mates?"

"I don't know," Beck said, swiping a hand through his blond hair in agitation. "I'll know soon enough. I'll find the summoner who did it and we'll come to an understandin'—Paul goes in the ground or the necro does."

Stewart stiffened. "Be careful on that account. The summoners have wicked magic and they'll not appreciate ya gettin' in their business."

Beck didn't respond. It didn't matter what happened to him; Paul Blackthorne was going back in his grave and that was that. He hadn't been able to keep him alive, but he could honor his friend's memory in other ways. He'd do it for Paul's daughter, if nothing more than to give her peace of mind.

"I hear that Five went after Riley, in particular," the master stated. "I wonder why."

Beck had no answer to that. Grade Five Geo-Fiends were the big boys of Hell who generated earthquakes and spawned mini storms as easily as he took a breath. A Five had killed Paul, and Beck was willing to bet it was the same one who'd gone after Paul's daughter during the battle.

Beck *was* sure of one thing—the demons were taking too much of an interest in Riley, calling her by her name. Hellspawn didn't do that as a rule. *Maybe I should tell Stewart. Maybe he would know what's going on.*

But if he did it'd only add to Riley's long list of troubles. Before Beck could make a decision, the master's phone began to buzz inside a coat pocket.

He pulled it out, frowned, and opened it up. "Stewart."

Beck turned his attention to the hole in front of him. One of the trappers told him that the Geo-Fiend had thrown Riley into this very pit. That same trapper hadn't known how she managed to escape, said there was too much smoke to see what had really happened.

Why didn't the Five kill ya, girl? There was one possibility, but he didn't want to think about that. No way Riley would have sold her soul to Hell to stay alive.

He'd thought Harper would keep her safe. He'd been wrong. *What if she'd fallen into that hole and never come out again?*

Before he could admit to himself what that loss would mean to him, Stewart limped back.

"That was Harper. The Guild's representatives are ta meet with the mayor in two hours. We need ta be there."

"We?" Beck said, caught off guard. "Me too?"

"Certainly. Ya gotta a problem with that?"

Beck heard the challenge and shook his head. "Can't the city at least wait 'til we bury our dead?"

Stewart huffed. "Of course not. Politicians wait for no man when they can lay the blame on some other poor bastard."